WHAT REVIEWERS ARE SAYING...

Ensnared by Innocence
2022 Maggie Award of Excellence Finalist

"Without a doubt, this author is going to the top of
my favorite historical novel author list. I really loved
this twist on the traditional historical romance novel."
5-Star Goodreads review

"I would give this a 10/10 rating. Beautifully written by
a very talented author... PLEASE read this brilliant
novel. I cannot wait for the next in series."
5-Star BookBub Review

"Witty, Enchanting and Roaring Hot!
I think I've found a new author to binge! I would
definitely recommend it as a good gateway book to
shape-shifters or to lovers of historical romance."
5-Star Goodreads Review

"Oh. My. Goodness!
This story caught my attention from page one. It is a
fresh take on the shifter genre. **This Regency novel
had every element a girl could want: several
mysteries to solve, smokin' hot heroes and sensible,
funny and courageous heroines."**
5-Star Goodreads review

"**Fantastic Story!!** I really enjoyed this book!"
5-Star Reviewer Emily P.

"I love the fact this is **shifter and regency** all rolled into
one...I was amazed by the storyline and couldn't help
how addictive I found this text...**I loved the originality
of this book** and thought it really stood out for many
reasons...
A true talent for writing." 5-Star Review

DECEIVED BY DESIRE

STEAMY REGENCY SHAPESHIFTER

ROARING ROGUES REGENCY SHIFTERS
BOOK TWO

LARISSA LYONS

Deceived by Desire, 2nd Edition Copyright © 2022 by Larissa Lyons
Published by Literary Madness.

ISBN
978-1-949426-26-7 E-book
978-1-949426-28-1 Print

Second Edition: October 2022

Proofread by Judy Zweifel at Judy's Proofreading.

Cover by Literary Madness.

CONTENTS

NOTE FROM LARISSA

During the early 1800s (and decades prior), some men in the *ton* paid particular homage to their attire: bright colors, flamboyant patterns, excessively high shirt collars—to the point that they were unable to turn their head without also turning their entire bodies. *Fops*, *dandies* and *coxcombs*, among others, were words used during the time to describe these gentlemen enamored with lace, ruffles, jewelry and any manner of affected ornamentation they could contrive—irrespective of perceived or actual sexual orientation.

The more I write, the more I diligently research, I realize how much I still don't know about the Regency—and *words* used during that time. So while I truly attempt to get things right, there will, no doubt, still be mistakes.

Hopefully not glaring enough to detract from the story. >^..^< Roar!

The action in *Deceived by Desire* begins where *Ensnared by Innocence* leaves off.

Both books are standalone entities, as far as the core love story and HEAs. However, one primary subplot thread runs through the entire Roaring Rogues series, and while there may be some overlap, new information is presented in each book.

If it's been a while since you read *Ensnared by Innocence*, or if you're jumping in with *Deceived*, the following character tidbits and story recaps will catch you up...

THE CURSE

The male offspring of the Hammond line are doomed to become beastly lions when the sun is in Leo, during mid to late summer, once they turn twenty-five. The only thing they know will mitigate the monstrous urges is nightly sex with a female. (I.e., fetching mettle with their own hand won't subdue the beast within.)

OUR LIONS (SO FAR)

- LORD BLAKELY, ERASMUS HAMMOND (BLAKE, E). The eldest of the London Hammonds and a marquis. He runs an infamous sex club which has the ulterior purpose of keeping an eye on the young bucks in town, ensuring none of them show tendencies toward succumbing to The Change.
- NASH HAMMOND, younger brother to Lord Blakely. If Blake is responsible and serious, committed to caring for family, then Nash is the ne'er-do-well scoundrel who cannot be bothered to look out for anyone other than himself. Envious over Blake's "Francy" and the love he's witnessed between them, Nash flees both his conscience and their sickening coos, determined to outrun the curse he cannot escape.
- PHINEAS, Nash and Blake's older cousin, has been missing since the night of his wedding ten years prior. The wedding that took place the summer he turned twenty-five.

OUR RELUCTANT TIME TRAVELER

- ADAM, from modern-day Texas. Lord Blakely's closest friend oversees operations at The Den. Trusted with the family secrets, Adam is one of the few people to know of The Change, after witnessing how his employer battles every summer against becoming a feline monster. Has his own quest to fulfill—when the time is right.

OUR LADIES

- LADY FRANCINE MONTFORT (FRANCY), a duke's daughter. Poised and serene yet determined to thwart the selfish aunt who would barter Francine against her excessive gambling debts. To avoid a forced marriage, she entices the disreputable Lord Blakely into a false betrothal that becomes all too real. When Blakely begins to avoid Francine, she defies her promise to never venture out at night as she and her cousin Tempest traverse London to confront Lord Blakely at his club.
- TEMPERANCE (TEMPEST) and PATIENCE, Lady Francine's cousins. Two very different sisters who also endure their trial of a gambling-addicted mother though in very different ways. Tempest has forged a relationship with her stepfather and with

Francine while Patience has forged an intimate relationship with the Art of Complaining. Francine has lived with their family since her parents perished several years ago. While Patience is as unpalatable as her mother (selfish, self-centered and scheming), Tempest is anything but; her exuberant support proving the boon Francine needs to confront her erstwhile fiancé—and proving she may be the one female whose charms might be sufficient to topple Adam's self-imposed rule of looking but not touching.

OTHER SUPPORTING CAST

- LORD HANSEN, engaged to Patience. But was it his choice? Did he "win" her hand across the green? Or is he perhaps more interested in her dowry?
- LORD TYNDALE, one of Lord Blakely's former "cubs"—young men Blakely takes under his wing to watch for signs of The Change the summer after the men turn twenty-five. Several years beyond that now, Lord Tyndale only visits The Den while entertaining out-of-town family, not because he wants to frisk or dally with the available wenches himself. So why is he the one stuck guarding Wylde's woman?

- LORD WYLDE, first introduced in *Ensnared by Innocence* and also featured in *Mistress in the Making* (set in 1815). The Paragon of Propriety (a name he disdains) is engaged to Tempest, but not for much longer. She's already informed him of her plans to offer a public jilt, thereby releasing him of any responsibility he might feel toward her. Something she decided upon learning that her own mother gambled her hand away and Lord Wylde stepped in to prevent some unsavory sort from snatching her up.

UNSAVORY SORTS

- Suspect(s) Unknown—A series of kidnappings and gruesome murders has taken place near Lord Blakely's club. Who is perpetuating this travesty?
- LORD PETERSON, LORD TATE, LORD CRANDALL—Several distasteful fellows mentioned or met in *Ensnared*.

PLACES

- THE DEN, the infamous gentleman's sex club Lord Blakely owns and runs with the assistance of his friend and club manager, Adam. Located just *this side* of respectable London, the small antechamber opens onto the street and is guarded by a doorkeeper,

BAYWICK, who ensures riffraff isn't allowed into the club environs.

SERIES TIMELINE

- Book 1, *Ensnared by Innocence*—takes place May through late August/early September 1812
- Book 2, *Deceived by Desire*—begins directly after the action in *Ensnared*, both continuing the London storyline as well as Nash's escape north
- Book 3, *Tamed by Temptation* (not yet released)—takes place spring through autumn 1812

For a peek at what Phineas is up to during 1811, read *A Snowlit Christmas Kiss*.

DECEIVED BY DESIRE

The happy tidings of his good escape. How fares my brother? Why is he so sad?

So looks the pent-up lion o'er the wretch that trembles under his devouring paws...

— SHAKESPEARE, *HENRY VI, PART III*

Family is indeed the sort of extraordinary advantage and blessing which few can boast.

— JANE AUSTEN, *PRIDE AND PREJUDICE*

1

THE WRETCHED HAT AND THE WRETCHED MAN

AUGUST 1812
ESCAPING LONDON

NASH ROUSED from his latest bout of self-pity long enough to crack his eyes open and watch the newest passengers climb aboard the already cramped, soggy stagecoach. The pair settled directly across from the corner he'd occupied for the past several hours.

He shifted and pressed his foot solidly against the floor of the coach.

Demmed inconvenient it was, having to share the dank spot he'd staked out as his own with the outwardly perfect couple. He kept his head lowered in the guise of dozing and refused to admit, even to himself, that he'd cared enough to peek.

People. Who needed 'em?

Certainly not Nash Hammond.

The stagecoach? Now *that* he needed, though if the blasted sky would just cooperate, not for much longer. He had enough money to buy his own horse—a splendidious one if he wanted. Hell, an entire stable full if he so desired—and actually had a stable. But then he'd have to care for it. Them. No demmed matter!

It was easier to put up with public transport.

Gave him something to think about other than his own contemptible problems.

"Pardon me, sir, but your foot snagged on my dress." The cultured voice cascaded over him like a heaven-sent waterfall, at odds with the jarring way its owner tried to wrench her long, surprisingly dry skirts from beneath his boot.

He refused to budge, kept his boot clamped down and continued to feign sleep as he'd been doing ever since the horses had splashed to a stop, the stagecoach rolling to a sodden halt behind them when the driver paused for a fresh team and additional passengers.

Folks left a slumbering man alone—Nash knew by now, reckoning he was drunk most likely—and refrained from asking him to scoot over. That was the pertinent motivation; if he was going to be trapped inside, then he'd make blame certain he had every bit of space he could muster. He always claimed an extra thumb's width between his body and the side of the coach, celebrating whenever he managed to secure more than the typical sixteen inches allotted to paying chaps like himself.

He'd begun his flight out of London as an outside passenger on the Royal Mail Coach—because it moved faster than lightning—but the incessant rains drove him inside and onto a public conveyance. Never could abide being exposed to the elements when it was pouring.

"Mister! My dress," the female hissed, trying in vain to arrange herself across from him. "It's caught under your boot!"

She pulled harder and he glanced at her through slitted lids, but the frothy contraption perched precariously atop her head hid her face.

Did she know that he'd stepped on her trailing hem on purpose?

Could she tell he was fighting back a gloat at her pathetic efforts to free her skirts? Did she have any idea of his pathetic existence?

Just as he tensed the muscles in his thigh to lift his foot, a ripping sound exploded from the floor and she plopped backward on the opposite bench, her skirts flying up to expose surprisingly inviting petticoats.

"Wretched man!" she muttered under her breath.

Acting no better than an unlicked cub, he was, amusing himself at her expense. He should apologize.

But he didn't move.

Or say a word.

He was too busy rumbling a fake snore and inspecting the luscious treat whose lacy hem remnants lay trapped beneath his sole and the fop who'd just climbed in after her, lurching more than a bit. The fop who she appeared to be wedded to, if the dandy's sour look toward Nash was anything to go by.

Figured.

Refined thing like that. Her in her fancy hat and white traveling dress—white! As if she shouldn't be covered from head to toe with a thick layer of mud and grime. How she managed to look so perfect and proper on a day like today, with her apricot-colored kid slippers, closed ruffle-edge parasol that matched her dress and immaculately gloved fingers was beyond him.

Her generous bosom looked anything but refined though, ready to spill from the not-quite-decent neckline with just the slightest encouragement.

Nash strangled on the sudden growl of desire that threatened to erupt, turning it instead into a garbled snore.

Criminal, the way his cock behaved. Rearing up as if it needed a warm quiver, as though he hadn't attacked his brother's woman just hours before. Blast him! His primed penis deserved to be ground beneath *her* heel.

"All set, m'dear?" the red-haired dandy asked on a hiccup, squishing close to the woman and plunking his arm across her shoulders in a proprietary move while he cast Nash a glower as if the man could read minds.

Nash's first-rate wattles caught the slight hitch in her breathing, his conk the hint of sour fear. "Indeed, Mr. Tate." She squirmed within her companion's restrictive embrace. "Thank you for asking."

Her cultured tones had turned puny. From vibrant waterfall to watered-down dribble.

Nash hunched lower, slightly lifting his lids to gaze at her from beneath the overlong fall of hair that blocked half his face. Some sort of netting hung from the brim of the ungodly confection perched atop her head, hiding her features. The curve of her cheek was visible—barely—but naught else.

Probably had the face of a sow, a pointy-nose, bulgy-eyed mama pig. God surely had to give such a one a curse to balance the bounty of figure He'd blessed her with.

The dandy patted his pocket and pulled out a snuffbox. He made a great show placing a pinch just inside his lower lip, which he ruined with another hiccup, then did everything in reverse, returning the snuff to his pocket. His actions were ludicrous, done with one hand as the other was still firmly ensconced atop the sow's shoulder.

Nash hadn't seen more flounces even at court. How the dandy's chin moved as his pursed lips blathered at her with so much starched linen and lace at his throat was beyond him. The clunch likely spent more time at Weston's than he did his own dinner table.

And shuddering fear, and green-eyed jealousy! his conscience taunted, compliments of Mister William Shakespeare.

Jealous? Jealous of the overdressed man and his feminine fortune? *Never. Never!* As if hearing the mental shouts, the man echoed...

"Never fear, m'dear," Dandy drawled, "only two days confined in this infernal conveyance—three at the most if this Scotch mist keeps up—and we shall arrive at our destination."

She left off gazing at the torn hem fraying in her fingers and glanced through that irritating netting at Dandy. "Will you please bring yourself to tell me where we are going?" she inquired so softly anyone without Nash's exceptional hearing would have missed it.

He *wished* he'd missed it, for the dulcet sounds of

her airy syllables would never let him think of her as a sow again. Pig-faced or not, she had the voice of a princess. "I am quite sure it will not ruin your surprise if you—"

"Nay! And leave off asking!" The dandy swatted her shoulder. "You will enjoy it," he added cajolingly. "I assure you."

At the threatening undercurrent in the man's voice, Nash lifted his head and uncrossed his arms. He remained slouched, giving the appearance of only casual interest. "You would not be taking the lady somewhere she prefers not to go, now, would you?"

The woman flinched. The sour scent of her fear now blasting off her in waves.

"Of course he isn't!" She trilled a practiced laugh. "Mr. Tate is forever treating me to new experiences and surprises."

"Mind your own bloody business!" the dandy bit out.

"Hear! Hear!" an older man in the opposite corner grumped. "Females present and all that. Mind *your* mouth!"

"Forgive me," the redhead reprobate said even as his knuckles whitened on her shoulder. To the others, he was all polish and shine. Slime.

Nash wanted to lose his breakfast on the man's gleaming Hessians. Instead, he tried to see past the netting, clueless where his sudden bout of chivalry had sprung from. "Ma'am? Are you well?"

He sensed her nervous smile, practically tasted the salty thickness of her looming tears. "I am wonderful. My life is...wonderful."

"See?" Dandy boasted, as if there had never been any doubt.

She was lying.

Nash cursed himself for caring. For even asking.

He didn't want the responsibility of sheltering a blame horse. What made him think he was up for the challenge of saving a bountiful-breasted, soft-voiced princess?

Sow, he told himself. A veiled sow. Oink.

Oink, oink! so cries a pig prepared to the spit. He intentionally butchered Shakespeare's original line, but couldn't stop from wondering...

Did lions eat pigs?

* * *

THREE DAYS, maybe two, if the stinking rain didn't sink this coach as it had the first one they'd climbed into.

Reginald curved his arm more securely around Eleanor's shoulder. He couldn't stay mad at her for more than a minute.

Damn but he was parched.

Thoughts of her always made his throat go dry. *So why can she not make your twanger go stiff?*

Ever since the Unfortunate Incident when his brother George John arrived unexpectedly at Reginald's townhouse and caught him with Neils, life hadn't been the same.

From the time they were in the nursery, Reginald knew he was different, knew with an inborn certainty that he should keep his sexual desires to himself. But even his sense of self-preservation couldn't stop him from finally expressing his inner yearning once he and Neils met. Lovers. They'd become lovers and Reginald had never been so happy.

Eleanor made the perfect foil—she attended all appropriate venues for a mistress and played her part well, keeping George John pacified and mollified.

Eh, eh. Reginald chuckled at his private jest.

Ironically, when it came to his older brother, no matter how much he positively loathed the man, Reginald secretly aspired to emulate him in every manner. George John was a true out-and-outer—the man boxed with Gentleman Jackson, rode with the prince, and was a top-notch gambler and womanizer to boot. With his wife tucked away in the country raising their three brats, two mistresses ensconced in London and reputations at more than one high-class brothel, George John was all the crack. And he had mistaken illusions that his younger brother was made of the same stamp.

When in fact, the only thing Reginald ever dreamed of cracking...was Neils.

Eleanor winced and he consciously relaxed his fingers, patting her shoulder. Leaning forward, he slid his tongue inside his bottom lip and gathered up the spit-soaked snuff. Hated the stuff. Only did it to look manly and because Eleanor had started clearing her throat and coughing every time he lit a cheroot these days—not that he blamed her on that score.

The fancy snuff tin had been the most recent gift from Neils and that alone made it worth using, though the constant reminder brought a pang each time Reginald pulled it out.

Determined to put his past love affair and liaison

behind him, Reginald spat the wad of tobacco on the lurching stagecoach floor. The brown blob slid toward the impertinent rogue in the corner.

Reginald straightened and smiled. He'd just shown the other man who was in charge. Easily discounting the way the stranger's eyes narrowed, he leaned into Eleanor, knowing he couldn't make his claim any clearer.

He really didn't need to. He owned her. Body and soul.

Owned her. The knowledge didn't bring the comfort it usually did. Because from the moment George John discovered Reginald in his own home, in his own bedchamber no less, and in an extreme state of dishabille *with another man*—and Eleanor nowhere in sight to mask his true actions—George John had made it his mission in life to "make Reginald into a real man" and "purge his soul of those detestable, perverted leanings".

Father would be appalled, Reginald had heard countless times. Usually followed by *A sodomite! In my goddamned family?* or *A Miss Molly—in the Tate family tree? Take care, Reg, the authorities don't get wind of this or you'll soon find yourself swinging from a branch.*

Yammering on and on, over and over, as if Reginald were to blame. If anyone was to blame, 'twas Eleanor.

At the thought, Reginald ground his teeth. If she'd been at home as she should have been, instead of flitting off to the sweet shop with her little teacher friend, then she would have been there to salvage his reputation.

But oh no. She'd been gone, George John had

found Neils *in* bed next to him and Reginald hadn't had a moment of solitude since.

"If that juicy flap under your roof cannot harden your cock, I will break it off myself," George John had threatened. "You take that bitch, prove to yourself—and to me—that you are capable of siring a babe. Damn you, Reg! You *know* how I have begun negotiations with Lord Volmering about his youngest chit. I expect you to do your duty and get her with child within a year of the nuptials."

Reginald had protested. But as always, it hadn't made a lick of difference. George John had his mind set on a connection with Lord Volmering—more decisively, a connection with Volmering's youngest's excessively large dowry entering into the Tate family coffers. Seatmates in the House of Lords ever since George John had unexpectedly inherited his title, they'd struck up a friendship three years and two babes late for George John himself to make the connection a reality.

So it was left to Reginald.

Left to Reginald to find a way to bed Eleanor and prove to both himself and his brother that he *could*.

Stupid everlasting stipulation in the marriage contract, if you asked him, requiring him to father a child *before* the dowry changed hands.

Nagging pressure made his loins twitch. The gin he'd downed earlier had gone right through him. He needed to piss.

Knowing they wouldn't stop for hours only made his bladder burgeon. Too bad his newest beaver couldn't double as a chamber pot. Deuced hot in here with all these muggy bodies clumped together like barnacles on a barge. Maybe he'd just sweat it out. But if that was going to be the case...

He removed his fine beaver and set it in his lap, not wanting to soil the hat band with perspiration.

He squeezed Eleanor's shoulder, thinking of how his brother promised—had damned well *guaranteed*—this trip would purge the "suck-pricking" urges—George John's term—right from Reginald's soul. Would cure him so that his cock would stiffen and spew each time he so much as *looked* at a woman.

Evidently, in addition to the mistresses and madams he consorted with in town, his brother had quite the collection of acquaintances with rather varied sexual tastes. At the thought of everything George John had hinted awaited him at the end of this journey, Reginald shuddered.

He just needed another drink. He'd get there. His blade would get there—be able to pierce the prize next to him and make his brother proud.

He had Eleanor. And his brother's friends to help him.

***

MERCIFUL HEAVENS.

The look on the stranger's face made all sorts of twittery discombobulations churn Laney's guts. Just like being with Reginald did, only in a not-quite-horrible way. Almost a good way, for even though her stomach had nigh lodged in her throat and her skin hummed at the fiery glint in his eyes, she couldn't look away.

Mayhap 'twas simply riding backward? Squished between the side of the carriage and the man who *owned* her—body, *not* soul—until her indenture expired. If she didn't expire first, that recent—*dire*—vision overriding her every waking thought and action the last few days. Until this gruff stranger demanded her attention and refused to let go.

Her stomach pitched again. Knowing the four horses and driver were just a meager distance away, barreling forward at a breakneck pace, didn't help. They travelled far too fast for the inclement weather. But then, Reginald had insisted they both change clothes after the morning's coaching debacle and he'd just tipped their new driver substantially to "Push on, man. Horses are strong, make 'em earn their hay."

Thanks to Reginald and his ill-timed impatience, she was now stuck enduring not only the stranger's avid inspection, but the coach jiggling her body so ferociously it was stewing up the Banbury cake she'd eaten to break her fast. Ugh. She knew better than to indulge in her love of sweet breads, especially when such an arduous, unknown journey awaited her.

And now she paid for such ill-thought-out—

Nay, it wasn't the public coach ride responsible for the locusts plaguing her belly. It was *him*. The surly stranger whose knees crowded her own, the heat from his expression warming her straight down to her previously wet toes.

The scowl on his face should damage his countenance, but on the contrary, his churlish expression combined with the daring lack of care he showed in his dress only piqued her interest. His jacket wasn't properly buttoned and his neckcloth was tied so haphaz-ardly the hollow beneath his throat where his collarbones didn't quite touch was visible. Absolutely scandalous!

Now if *he* owned her instead...

Laney groaned at her fanciful imaginings. Only one person owned her at the moment—for the next ten months, twenty-two days and some-odd hours—and that was Reginald Tate, the handsome...bastard next to her.

To distract herself, both from Reginald's smoth-ering arm across her shoulders and the stranger's piercing gaze, Laney chanced a look at Reginald, confirming his attention was elsewhere, and left off tearing the torn hem to shreds to bring her reticule to her lap and a comforting rustle to her ears. Mary Delilah's letter. She'd read it again this evening, after they stopped for the night, see whether she could make heads or tails of her friend's uncharacteristic wild rambling.

Reginald patted her shoulder and then removed his arm. Finally. Calling him *Reginald* in her mind was just one of a handful of defiant measures she'd undertaken lately to assert her independence, whether he knew it or not.

She took a shaky breath, but still smothered by his presence, it wasn't nearly deep enough. Why couldn't the knave have remained outside and ridden on top of the coach? The loud blast of thunder overhead mocked the question.

"I'll just enjoy another little nip, m'dear. I daresay it'll help the time pass." He scooted closer, branding her entire side, then pulled his ever-present flask from inside his coat pocket and tipped it back, pouring the contents down his gullet as if it were a race he had to win. At this rate, he'd be out before the next stop.

Would the stranger disembark there or remain on the coach? If that was his destination, would Reginald notice if she disembarked with him—and never got back on?

Oh, the fanciful ideas running through her mind. The tingly quivers running through her abdomen...

She found herself unraveling her torn hem again and trying not to acknowledge the increased flutters in her stomach at the thought of putting herself under the stranger's power. She should know better. She'd already put herself willingly under one man's control and that certainly hadn't improved her lot in life, now, had it?

Reginald Tate...

The man she once thought the answer to her prayers. The man she now concentrated heaven-bound prayers on nightly, requesting Divine escape.

She'd been barely sixteen when the dashing Reginald Tate had begun frequenting Mrs. Michaels Millinery and Fine Accoutrements where Laney had been indentured shortly after she turned thirteen. After three solid years making hats and waiting on "ladies" who looked down their fashionably pale noses more often than not—and pricking her fingers with milliners needles, hat pins and bracing wire just as regularly—the flattering attention the handsome Mr. Tate showered on Laney practically made her swoon.

His visits certainly brightened dreary days and long afternoons.

Two scant months after they met, he'd offered to buy her papers from Mrs. Michaels. Laney assumed he wanted her for his "Lady of the Night" and other than being woefully uneducated in the art of nighttime activities, she was otherwise agreeable. Since losing her grandmama and mother within a few months of each other and being passed from one relative to another until winding up on the doorstep of an aunt who was already burdened with her own gaggle of children and didn't want another, indenturing Laney at the first opportunity, she was nothing if not practical.

The allure of being pampered like a "lady"—even one bought and paid for—far surpassed the daily drudgery as the life of an unappreciated servant. At the time, her indenture to Mrs. Michaels was for another four years, which to the young Laney was a veritable lifetime. The position offered by Reginald seemed a godsend.

Instead, the rotten Mr. Tate had only wanted her to *pretend* to be his amour while he'd dallied in ways she'd often heard called sinful and sordid. She could hardly think of it without blushing, even now, half a year after Reginald had parted ways with his *male* paramour and renounced his *despicable, detestable acts*—Reginald's words, parroting his brother, she suspected—only to turn his immoral attention to her. Immoral because he didn't want her, but he kept trying to take her anyway.

His efforts and her fear only mounting until he'd brought her to this—stuffed like kippers on a plate among the other passengers. What if she'd declined Reginald's offer and remained with Mrs. Michaels? Would she have, perhaps, crossed paths with the gentleman sitting across from her?

And should he even be termed "gentleman"?

Most assuredly not. Not with the way he went without a hat when everyone knew the importance of fine head wear. "Choose your hat first," Mrs. Michaels had always told her customers, "and the rest of your ensemble will then magically follow."

And *not* with the way he brazenly persisted in staring at her so intently, his eyes glowing like orange embers. Why, her face felt *naked*, as if her veil hardly protected her at all.

"Stop staring." The words escaped before she could grab them back.

Reginald had gone slack. He leaned heavily against her, indicating his slumber, and Laney supposed she'd unknowingly relaxed her guard as well. Relaxed too much, given her awareness of the man across from her and her hastily spoken command.

Judging by the increased heat in his gaze, he hadn't stopped contemplating her either.

Did no one else notice his unusual eyes? The way they fairly shimmered with heat?

"Remove your hat."

The lace slipped from her fingers. "I beg your pardon?"

He leaned forward and caught the scrap before it drifted to the ground. Their knees collided. "Take off your hat. You appear to be the best view around, and I want to see the rest of it."

"Shhh!" she sputtered, never more grateful for the shielding netting than she was at this very moment. She tried to angle her legs from his, but between Reginald's sleeping body wedged along her side and the stranger's knees pressed intimately against hers, she couldn't move. "Please. You mustn't say such things."

He gave Reginald's sleeping form a disdainful glance and leaned even closer. "Why do you fear him?"

How did he know? "*What?*"

"You heard me." He made a show of returning the torn hem to her gloved hands, giving hers a gentle squeeze before releasing them. The unexpected gesture soared clear to her toes, which remained locked between his heavily booted feet.

"I asked why you fear him." His rumbling voice had gone all low and gruff.

"I'm quite sure you must be mistaken," Laney whispered, glancing at the other passengers, who all appeared intent upon passing the uncomfortable time as privately as possible, gazing out the windows or snoozing.

How was it no one took notice of anyone else? Least of all the intimate encounter between her and the stranger? Or how Reginald's head lolled about his neck with every jostling revolution of the coach's wheels? Laney couldn't miss how Reginald's jaw hung unhinged, his sour breath gusting over her shoulder. She had the sudden urge to upend the contents of his flask inside his mouth. Maybe he'd drown.

"You do not deny it." The firm statement, voiced with perfect elocution, drew her attention back to the ill-dressed man before her. The most unrigged gentleman to cross her path.

Gentleman? Gads! She had to stop thinking of him as such. No matter that his speech was as fine as she strived to make her own, he was nothing more than a shabbaroon. But one who so boldly demanded, "Remove your hat. I will not ask again and I want to see your face."

His tone made her think he'd be uncouth enough to rip it from her head if she refused. "You cannot! *I* cannot. Oh, do please sit back."

She couldn't think with his knees touching hers, with his finger idly nudging her leg. Was this desire, then? This awful achy, nervous, *splendiferous* feeling? The need to brush his hair back, to really see him? The need to be *his*?

For the thousandth time, Laney bemoaned her misspent youth and cursed her impatience. She hated Reginald and Mrs. Michaels all over again.

"How long have you been wed?"

His words startled. "Wed? I assure you we most certainly are not!"

"Related?"

"Heavens no."

And just like that, he was gone. No more teasing fingers. No more obscene nuzzling of her kneecaps. No more glowing eyes.

"Ah," he murmured once he'd straightened and returned fully to his own seat. His expression once again inscrutable, the playful, albeit intent, interest he'd shown seconds before wiped free.

"And what, pray tell, does that mean? *Ah?* You utter

that as if you pass judgment upon me. Are not negative judgments reserved for those of clerical persuasions?"

He fairly growled from his shadowy corner. If anything, he looked darker, more brooding. "You claim not to be bound to him, yet you choose to remain," he stated, disdain dripping from his scowling lips. "Keep the blasted hat on, then. I no longer care what you look like."

Unaccountably, she cared that he no longer cared. Stupid, stupid. She should be jumping from the stagecoach and running as far away from Reginald as she could instead of bantering with a moody stranger.

"You don't understand," Laney hissed, incensed with herself. Why in the world should it matter whether he understood or not?

Nash turned away from the shrouded feminine mystery, dismissing her and pulling the thin volume of Shakespeare from his pocket. One could only feign sleep for so long. "I no longer have the inclination to understand. Keep your protestations and your fear to yourself, madam. What you choose to do with your life is of no interest to me."

It was a blatant lie, but if he said it enough, mayhap it would become truth.

He had no business caring for anything, much less any*body*, at the moment.

Blast her and her infernal voice for tempting him to think otherwise.

For unlike his older brother who preferred hardened women—at least until Lady Francine came along

—Nash himself had always lusted after innocence and purity. *Virgins.* From the moment he became cursed and realized his body was no longer his own, he day dreamed about once-upon-a-times and happy-forever-afters, envying ordinary men with ordinary wives living ordinary lives.

He dreamed of one day having a pure wife. An innocent. As long as she composed herself as he imagined a lady would—caring for her family (which, to his way of thinking, meant her man—*him*) and caring for her home (the one he'd never had, not since his mother abandoned them shortly after his father did the same)—she didn't have to be a *lady* in truth or even very beautiful. A simple refined peasant or even a clean servant—he wasn't overly particular—would suit him fine. A woman who had saved herself just for him. *That* was what he truly desired.

But those were imaginings—the scant moments of fantasy he allowed himself in the lull before full wakefulness intruded and reality crashed down. He couldn't take a virgin. He couldn't have a wife.

Or children, or a family of his own. He wouldn't have peace.

Not as long as he was a monster.

Who'd practically raped his brother's woman.

Like a hive of angry bees the irate attention the veiled, behatted female still directed at him, buzzed and needled, made a mockery of his feigned disinterest. Dodging the annoying pests—both her and his reactions, he moved the curtain that was drawn against the rain.

Making a great show of gauging the location of the

sun—asinine, as it was blocked by storm clouds—he peered out the coach. "By my reckoning," he said to himself but intending that she should hear, "and barring a broken wheel or axle, or washed-out roadway, we should arrive at our overnight stop in six and a half hours." He sighed and sank back into his corner, letting the curtain drop. "Plenty of time to find myself a pretty wench for the evening, one who avoids wearing ugly hats. Or anything at all…"

"Wretched, wretched man!"

Good. He'd gotten to her. So why did he feel lower than the bottom of muddy pigs' feet?

And why couldn't he rid himself of the unwanted concern mired in his chest?

2

THE WAKEFUL WAKE, A TEMPEST BLASTS FROM THE FUTURE, & EGAD! ANSWERS?

Back in London...A Few Days Ago

Mum always said she was cursed; Grandmama insisted she was blessed.

Bah! Curses or blessings.

Didn't matter a whit as far as Laney was concerned. Either way, here she was again, hovering over countless mourners, sniffing food she couldn't eat and doing her best not to notice the rigid body on the floor. The dead body.

Laney hated the tradition of laying out the deceased. Whose grand idea was that?

Granted, the female gone to Kingdom Come appeared to be attired in her spruced-up Sunday best, but the skin of her ungloved hand was that eeric grey color, the shade that made Laney want to heave. She'd seen enough death.

How she detested these funeral visions. Although to be precise, this one was a wake, not a funeral, but a lifeless body was still...well, *dead.*

No matter how many times she thought the word or avoided looking directly at the corpse, the situation didn't change. There would be no reprieve until she learned what she needed to—even though she had absolutely no idea what that was.

The knowledge would come to her eventually. It always did.

Relax, Laney told herself, *allow whatever information the cosmos intends to reveal to reach your awareness. Then the ghastly experience will be over. At least until the next one.*

True. So drattedly true. Just as she'd recall the necessary details later.

When she woke up.

Being a "visionary"—her grandmama's term for it —was often the veriest of nuisances. Laney's mum had called a turnip a turnip, telling Laney from the time she was born until the time she died—Mum that is, not Laney—that Laney was *cursed* with the evil eye and only the devil's spawn could know the future.

Well now, the night Laney dreamt of her mum's passing two days before it happened had proven rather...*visionary,* had it not?

Enough piddling, Eleanor Catherine—Catherine because Mum had hoped she'd aspire to greatness —*Buckley!* her inner voice shouted, calling Laney back to the present...um, the *vision.*

Black-clothed mourners milled about the stuffy room, murmuring in hushed voices, all circling the pallid body laid out on an unhinged door in the middle of the floor.

Poor soul. Could they not have at least elevated the door by propping it on some chairs or blocks and raised the deceased off the dusty floor?

Laney drifted above the people gathered round, their muted conversations nothing but indecipherable mumblings until two of the mourners caught her attention, their words easily reaching her over all of the others.

"Pitiful, dying so young. Told her something of this sort would happen, I did," the whale of a woman wailed, bringing her handkerchief up to dab at her dry eyes.

"Should 'ave left 'im when she 'ad the chance," the tall female beside her confided with a confident nod, then ruined it with a tearful, watery sniff. "She whispered to me once that she almost 'ad, before they wed. 'Pon my word, 'tis tragic, so tragic!"

"Ain't that the truth? And her with child again, so soon after her first one died. Broke her heart, it did, that tiny babe dying before it was ever born. I suppose it somehow had an inkling things were far from ideal."

Their voices faded and again indistinct murmurings and mutterings came at Laney from all directions. Eventually she deciphered a new set of sentences, these heartfelt sympathies trading off with scandalous whispers. The comments were being bandied about between several women in the corner. Curiosity luring her over, she abandoned the grief-stricken duo and glided closer to the small group, her nose wrinkling at the unpalatable scents emanating from this section of the room.

"That's what did her in, I am convinced of it—the sorrow of losing her babe."

"Do tell! I thought it was the fall. Shattered her spine, my Simon told me."

"*Fall?*" a third woman broke in. One with the worst garlic breath imaginable—or even dreamable. Laney rose clear to the ceiling, hoping to distance herself, but she could still make out every harsh word, could still smell every stinking clove. "Well, I heard she *jumped.*"

"Jumped?"

One of them *hrrumped.*

"If that is the way of things, we undoubtedly won't be arranging a *proper* burial for her. The good folks populating *this* God-fearing community will not tolerate an evil one such as *her* residing in consecrated ground. I refuse to *stand* for it, I tell you."

The others agreed with haste. "Certainly not. If she took her own life, she doesn't deserve our pity. And to think, I brought our Sunday ham! What a waste."

"Jumped? She shall burn in hell for that, you know." Simon's wife had changed her tune. "Burn in hell."

"Likely already there," Garlic Breath said with conviction.

Gracious. Gossiping biddies, weren't they? And how long must she listen to their pointless blathering until learning the point of this vision?

Laney wanted to pinch her nose shut against the stench. Sweet breads tainted by decaying flesh. And garlic. Too many unwashed bodies—the live ones—crowded into the small room didn't help either.

Why was it she could see, hear and *smell* in her visions?

Didn't seem fair, did it?

Not when she couldn't eat too. The tables laid out along one wall burgeoned with a selection of treats unlike any she'd seen since...well, in forever. If she had been awake, her stomach would have growled loud enough to summon the dead.

Oh heavens. She really had to quit doing that! Jesting about the dearly departed. *She'd* be the one burning in hell if she kept that up.

With one last salivary glance at the aromatic baked goods—easily discounting the ham—and knowing it was useless to slaver over what she couldn't touch, much less taste, she went about the business of discovering why she was being shown this particular vision.

Grandmama had taught her they all had a purpose and that it was up to Laney to discover exactly what that was and what to do about it.

Like the time she'd seen the Schuberts' youngest two dying of typhus and had been able to tell their mother before the first symptoms ever appeared. Or when ol' Hank Roskin's horse had come up lame the very day his wife started having her birthing pains—and them seven miles from town! Laney never had been able to explain to Doc Colben how she'd known Mrs. Roskin was trying to birth a babe that was turned all backward weeks before the child was expected.

Stop stalling! her mind screamed. *You shall never come by any answers—or rest—if you do not muster the gumption to see which of the mourners you were brought here to recognize. And why.*

Laney acknowledged that she *did* have a propensity to jabber, even mentally, and procrastinate whenever a task discomfited her. But why wouldn't she be ill at ease? She doubted *other* young women had to deal with moaning mourners and crusty cadavers when they had gone to the land of nod.

Ponder tomorrow, she could almost hear her late grandmama advising, *gather the particulars when they're given. It's a blessing, dearie, a blessing.*

A bloomin', blighted blessing Laney was starting to wish she'd never been cursed, uh, *born* with.

Thoughts of her grandmother giving her strength, she bit the inside of her cheek and firmly tore her gaze from the platters of food—she'd abandoned her previous attempt the moment she noticed the honey cakes dripping in butter on one end of the table—and finally looked directly at the crowd. She focused on a face.

Nothing. No recognition, no sudden flash of insight.

She focused on the next one.

Again, nothing.

Face after face crystallized before her and not once did she recognize a single person or see anything that looked familiar.

Mayhap this vision wasn't meant for her? Perhaps some guardian angels had gotten their wings crossed or something. Wistful thinking on her part, but maybe —for once—she really wasn't meant to learn anything. If that was the case, then why was she not sleeping instead of—

A commotion at the door snagged her attention. Laney floated over to investigate and immediately wished she hadn't.

Because every bit of air in the room sucked out, leaving Laney gasping for breath. For standing right in front of her, well, *below* her actually, but still exceedingly too close for comfort, was Reginald.

Reginald Tate, her *owner*. Staggering drunk—as if that were a surprise—lurching through the door, bottle in hand.

Even looking haggard and two, maybe three, years older than he was now, visibly anguished about the poor creature who lay stiff as a board, dead as a doornail on the floor—oh, her wicked sense of humor would surely cause her to go up in flames—she still hated him.

Hated the sorry royster so much she wished she could wake up and cheer—that he was mourning someone, actually grieving. The bastard. Tricking her as he had, *pretending...*

Making *her* pretend.

He stumbled through the entryway and crashed to the floor, landing next to the grey body.

Laney flew as far away as she could and ended up suspended over the food-laden tables, refusing to acknowledge how her arm burned at the sight of him. How her heart shriveled at the thought of how much longer she must remain under his threatening control.

Reginald cried out and dropped the bottle which rolled away, amber liquid drizzling over the floor with every revolution. He scraped the tears off his cheeks and forced his arms under the stiff body that would soon be the diet of worms, tugging it upward.

The woman's head lolled to the side and snapped back, obviously broken, the bones in the neck useless. Shattering moans emanated from Reginald, long, low plaintive howls that shook the timbered ceiling above her. Astonishing. If she didn't know better, she would think he really cared. About a female, no less.

"Sorry! S-so sorreee!" He hiccupped. "Never meant for this..." His arms convulsed and he clutched the body tighter, cried louder.

And Laney thought she had died and really had gone to hell because staring at her, eyes wide open, clearly in pain, enshrouded in a death mask—sunken and *grey*...waxen and lifeless...

Was her own face.

Dead.

"Leave him while you're still able, Eleanor Catherine. You haven't much time," the corpse mouthed silently, then promptly vomited all over Reginald.

Laney screamed. And screamed. And screamed. Screamed so loud she finally woke up. Shaken. Shivering. Panicked.

But despite how many deep breaths she took, how many candles she lit, or how many times her eyes roved over the beautifully appointed bedroom, the travelling valise and trunk that had been brought out for their forthcoming trip, she couldn't stop trembling or rid her heart of the fear. Or her nose of the stench.

Gadzooks and zounds!

They'd been *married*? No...they *would be* married?

She and *Reginald*? And he'd get her with child? And a babe would die?

The terrified trembling redoubled.

Over her dead body!

Oh Lord.

If she couldn't fathom a way out of her current predicament, then the outcome was clear—*she'd* be the one feeding worms in unhallowed ground.

━━━━◦◦◦━━━━

STILL IN LONDON...
ABOUT SIXTEEN HOURS AGO

THE MOMENT the exterior door closed behind Mr. Adam and Francine, leaving Temperance ensconced in a world foreign to her sheltered existence, her lips started quivering like a leaf in a storm. "My," she breathed out quietly, trying to calm her racing heart and still her trembling limbs.

"My what?" Lord Tyndale, the only other occupant in this small windowless antechamber, turned the full focus of his irritated gaze upon her.

My, who knew Mr. Adam—Lord Blakely's assistant—would be so very intriguing? The brawny, sandy-haired American so different from the refined, staid English men she knew. *So big and gruff and masculine that—*

"My *what*?" Lord Tyndale repeated with a slight huff from where he lounged against the tall desk situated across from the street-side entrance, adjacent to the heavy door she couldn't stop glancing at.

"If I am to be relegated out here watching over

you," Lord Tyndale grated out—instead of on the *other* side of the solid door behind him, engaging in things she could only speculate over, he didn't say but his frustrated sigh made apparent—"the least you owe me is to finish what you start."

"My, I feel as though I have just skipped halfway across London. All..." Her hands waved in front of her chest. "Aflutter."

Temperance and her cousin Francine had braved the night to confront Francine's truant betrothed, Lord Blakely, the magnificent—if disreputable—suitor her cousin had garnered this summer. From attentive to absent, his mysterious behavior prompting her cousin to confront him—here, in his nefarious club.

Only to learn he wasn't present, as they'd surmised. But supposedly at home—where Mr. Adam had just aimed for with Francine, telling Temperance to stay silently put—"not a peep"—and he'd return posthaste to escort her home once he delivered Francine into Lord Blakely's safekeeping. But only after securing Lord Tyndale to "watch over" her while he was gone and ordering the regular guard, Baywick, into the inner environs of the club.

The environs she'd glimpsed moments ago, despite his efforts to the contrary. Temperance bit her lips against the smile that threatened, her body responding to the memory of Mr. Adam's strong hands, firm against her rib cage, when he'd picked her up and—

What might Mr. Adam's kiss feel like? The thought intruded, her mouth tingling anew. *His lips upon her own? Especially with that unfashionable mustache adorning his full upper lip?*

Her every sense flew backward a few minutes in time...

For after being held tight and long against his hard body—thanks to his inadvertent discovery of her cousin Francine changing from her men's garb into that of a lady, Mr. Adam had hauled Tempest to him, secured her face against his chest and held tight, preventing her from looking past his body—at the people upon the stage. Or at those watching.

It was a full thirty or forty heartbeats later that he muttered to himself, something that sounded like, "Damn me. Pulled her the wrong direction."

Whereupon, he unceremoniously opened the big door and shoved her right back through, with the terse instruction to "Knock twice the moment Lord Blakely's woman is decent."

"WRONG CHOICE," Adam murmured to himself, his normally unflappable thought process spinning a hundred different directions. "Wrong damn choice."

He'd just left two innocents *unattended* in the mouth of The Den? "God save me from this night." This week. This summer.

He'd thought a few years ago that his life couldn't get any weirder? That was before the murders started. Before E—Adam's name for Erasmus Hammond, Lord Blakely—started forsaking women, including his precious Francy, the past week and instead battling the beast within.

Before he'd realized just how much time would pass, how long he'd still be here—in 1812.

"For fuck's sake." Ignoring the boner that'd sprung up the moment he inhaled the soft beauty in his arms —and praying *she* hadn't noticed—Adam banged on the door twice, shielded his eyes and kicked it open. "Coming in."

Why was his voice so gruff? *Unreleased desire, you dumbfuck. You haven't gotten laid since you landed here and won't jack off in front of the cat and—*

"Shit! Not looking. But coming in." Making no attempt to subdue the Texan accent that he typically tried to shave off when around the Jane-Austen-era's uppercrust, he barreled in, feeling all sorts of cranky. "Cannot leave you two in here alone."

"Why ever not?" piped up the younger one. The one whose body had imprinted itself upon his in ways it had no business—absolutely *no* business—doing.

"Of a certainly, we are not going anywhere." That sweet, effervescent tone hit him in the solar plexus yet again. "Not now that we have found you and secured your agreement to assist with Francine's goal of locating Lord Blakely."

"God save me from English innocents." *Erotic-bodied ingénues who shouldn't be out at this time of night, in this part of town. In this club, by God.*

And wasn't that the truth? Not with the killings he and E had discovered this summer.

Had the murders been going on longer than that? Possibly somewhere else? Possibly discovered by someone else? Or had the monster hunting their streets only begun his villainous acts this year?

Keeping his gaze well averted from the shuffling noises coming from the middle of the room, Adam lowered his hand and angled his head past the edge of the door. He instructed Tyndale and Baywick to stay put until he called for them. Then, his palm-made blindfold in place once more, he yanked the door secure behind him. "Are you finished?"

"Just... About..." That was the serene, yet slightly breathless voice of E's intended. "There! I am ready."

"Oh, Francine, your hair." The other one. "'Tis positively atrocious."

"Ack!" an uncharacteristic squawk. "Quite right. Wait! Did you bring a brush?"

And the shuffling started off again, as one of them delved back into the duffle they'd brought.

"You can remove your fingers from your eyes now, Mr. Adam." The younger one nudged his elbow. "Francine is quite presentable, as you will see if you would but look."

Instead, he spared the spirited, if slightly flushed, English miss in front of him with what he hoped she would perceive as a glower.

He'd been here, in this time, for several years now. Had developed a bit of a distant crush on one of E's working girls, but he'd never been tempted to act on it. Not once.

Who wanted to dally with a working wench in this day and age? Who knew what manner of STDs a man might contract? And with no knowledge of medicine, biology or healthcare in the early 1800s, he had no wish to take that sort of chance with his pecker.

Dally? Working wench? Heaven help him, he was starting to think like them too.

No, by God, he kept it—his healthy pecker—stuffed

firmly in his single remaining pair of Levi's, bemoaning how the denim grew thinner every month and with every infrequent washing. Daily though, he took solace working the functioning copper buttons down the fly. The methodical, comfortingly familiar task keeping him firmly grounded.

He might have made his way deep into the past, but he hadn't forgotten where he came from—even if he wasn't sure he still wanted to return. Even if he did miss washing machines and helpful sisters who exchanged ironing for car repairs. That aside, not once had he responded so strongly to a female. Not since he'd been here. *How could you? You refuse to let one get close.*

Until this flushed, ebullient firebrand marched in here, demanding his assistance. Worming her unwelcome way into his arms—and his nostrils.

As he'd held her, the wisps of her upswept hair had tickled his nose. The whiff of her delicate floral fragrance put him in mind of the heady magnolia trees he'd climbed as a boy. Before everything had gone to shit back in Texas.

Nothing boyish about his response to this one.

Good heavens, she was young. Not even counting the two-hundred-plus-year difference in their ages. He couldn't imagine—

"All right, Mr. Adam. I am completely ready now," E's woman proclaimed. "Take me to Erasmus, if you would."

Great. Nothing like a midnight race through London, avoiding footpads, murderous SOBs and discovery to take his mind off the *dally*-worthy, fully off-limits *wench*.

The one he needed to deal with upon his return.

"AFLUTTER?"

The sound of Lord Tyndale's boot scraping against the floor drew Temperance's attention back to the man tasked as her unwilling guard—not that it had really left, even given her raving curiosity about Mr. Adam— and this club—the last few minutes.

"*Aflutter*?" Tyndale practically barked at her silence, mocking her choice of words.

They'd danced once, she and Lord Tyndale, early in the season. He'd trod upon her toes. Bosky as a foxed fellow could be.

She had not been impressed. Even though she recalled that he'd smelled pleasant, like the outdoors even on the fusty, crowded dance floor. Not impressed —despite how attractive he was, in a dark and dangerous way. Nothing like polite and polished Lord Wylde.

The man she was currently—temporarily— betrothed to. Someone she wished she could develop a *tendre* for. But after weeks of trying, Temperance had accepted she'd never feel *that* way toward him—the heaving, romantic, cannot-breathe-without-them sort of way she rather fancied feeling. It seemed Lord Wylde agreed, taking her proposed severing of their engagement remarkably well. The dear man also agreed they could postpone the public jilt until after her ill-tempered sister's nuptials—lest Tempest (his nickname for her, one she adored) be accused once again of attempting to overshadow Patience's life with her own.

"Feeling rather betwattled," Lord Tyndale said now, keeping her riotous thoughts mired on him. "Because you came this far, unescorted?" She couldn't tell by his tone if he were impressed by their intrepid rove or incredulous over the lack of decorum presented by two lone, unchaperoned females doing such a thing. "Or, mayhap you feel all *aflutter* because of..." His tone scoffed even as his attention returned to where her gaze kept veering: the door beyond his shoulder. "Curiosity?"

The door that led into the Inner Reaches of Lord Blakely's infamous club, The Den.

"Well, yes, certainly. Some," she admitted. Who wouldn't be curious?

Curious after glimpsing the elevated platform, well lit compared to the shadows surrounding it, with three partially dressed participants upon it—connected physically in ways her eyes had never before beheld.

Curious after experiencing her first kiss earlier this evening, the welcome-unwelcome one at the Stantons' rout. And that following the horrid confrontation with her sister, Patience (who was anything but).

In truth, her sister's ill-timed pout, and how Tempest had behaved a bit recklessly afterward whilst trying to put it from her mind, only made her thoughts return to that oddly pesky kiss. The one she hadn't really wanted—nor expected. But neither had she turned it away once firm lips pressed against hers.

What maiden would deny such an experience?

Especially when they longed to savor *all* of life's Grand Adventures?

Even if that particular adventure—her very first kiss—hadn't been what her girlhood dreams had cracked it up to be. Nor from a person she could truly be in alt over.

Mr. Adam, now? After being pressed so closely along his strong form? Her lips couldn't help but tremble. Couldn't help but wish it had been *his* that swept over hers, teased her mouth and tantalized her senses with her first adult kiss...

A whimper escaped.

Just as another sigh heaved from the man across the room. "Rowden's youngest?"

"His stepdaughter. Engaged to Lord Wylde." It seemed important she told him that. *That you remind yourself! You are still affianced; best not be acting all swoonish over Lord Blakely's Mr. Adam quite yet.*

True. Disappointing, but true.

"Where is he tonight, I wonder?" Lord Tyndale wanted to know.

She straightened. "He's been here?"

"Certainly. With a name such as 'wild', how could he not?"

The wretch let that settle uncomfortably between them. Then he added, "So. You are engaged. I never saw you courting."

"Oh?" She dragged one slippered, restless foot over the floor, hoping her skirts hid her agitation. "You see *everything,* do you?" *When you are not gin-fuzzed,* she barely refrained from saying.

"I did not make that claim."

She ignored him. Studied the door behind the desk. Did she imagine the slight scream coming from beyond?

Or was it more of a moan? Her belly swooped in response, fascination firing her imagination to complete more of the picture she'd barely glimpsed, of the two men with a woman between—

"You want to know what all goes on here?" She glanced back his way. A knowing, conceited smile crooked upon his lips. "Ask your betrothed. Why is the Paragon of Propriety not here with you now, I wonder."

"He's from town at the moment." Which was also why she and Francine had not sought his assistance tonight. And she *could* ask him what activities happened here, was tempted to boast such to the arrogant man in front of her. For she had every confidence Lord Wylde would tell her truthfully. "Not that 'tis any of your business."

Tyndale pointed over his shoulder without taking his mocking, heavy-lidded gaze from her. "The fun is that way. Whilst I remain in here"—he flipped his hand around to point at her—"with you. Seems to me that I deserve some sort of compensation for enduring such an onerous task."

"Of a certainty," she agreed with false gaiety. "Because watching over me is *so very* irksome. Like as not, the most challenging task you have attempted in a sennight."

He flashed her a grin, one that perked a few slumbering butterflies to life in her belly. Silly stomach. Could it not tell Tyndale was the dangerous sort? Not the type of fellow any sensible-minded miss should ever fall for. Mayhap 'twas simply her responding to tonight's earlier, somewhat mundane kiss still thrumming along her virgin lips. Or—most likely—meeting Mr. Adam that had those bothersome butterflies primed to respond?

Why, she'd gone well over twenty years without responding to any suitor, but tonight...tonight...

"Alas, I did not say that either." He gave an exaggerated sigh. "Onerous, irksome challenges aside, your presence still causes me to miss out on all manner of...fun."

"On the other side of that door?" Tonight, *she* wanted to experience some fun of her own. Wished fervently Mr. Adam would return. Mayhap she'd ask him about the trio meshed together— Nay, for he'd done all he could to shield them from her sight. So Lord Tyndale it was, it seemed. "Tell me what goes on here."

"I think not. You might tempt me to be the instrument of your ruin, but I know better. For I have no desire to meet Wylde on the dueling field nor to find myself unwillingly shackled with a wife."

"I have no interest in you either. So why do you not stop bothering me?"

"You are the one who keeps chattering."

"Hrmph. Your garret is to let if that is how you perceive things." Frustration and irritation battled back any surging butterflies—easily.

For *he* was the one prattling on when *she* was the one content to let her ears strive to hear what might be going on a few yards away. The one more than content to let her body relive the few moments in Mr. Adam's strong, enticing embrace, to let her mind conjure how her no-longer-virgin lips might respond to his masculine own...

———◦○○◦———

BACK TO THE PRESENT

A COLONY of sparrows whistled and chirped, darting to and fro, the tiny specks soaring against the blue canopy. Centered in a verdant field, amidst grass a vibrant green, stood an ornate gazebo. The birds chased each other through the immaculate woodwork, flying past the glossy paint as if pointing her attention to what was inside.

Through the slatted ceiling, she spied a mound of quilted blankets, piled up and covering the floor. Upon the quilts, a circle of flowers adorning her head, dress hiked to her waist, her stockings being rolled down by the most attractive gentleman, Laney saw...*herself!*

Her thighs quivered beneath his touch. A cacophony of flapping wings flittered about in her stomach, the muscles between her legs clenched, waiting, cream easing from her center.

"You're going too slow, darling," Laney said on a laugh, nudging the man's shoulder with one foot, her spirits soaring.

Somehow she knew, at that precise moment, in that particular meadow, her life was grand. Her being cheered down to her very soul. What a peculiar savvy to rise to her awareness.

Vision Laney kicked her foot higher, teased his

thick hair with her toes, delighted in the cool sensation of the strands, feeling the utter wanton and loving every moment. "Though I cannot believe I'm allowing you to do this here!"

"*'It is well done, and fitting for a princess.'*"

"Not that one again, you fiend. Did not the original speaker meet Old Mr. Grim after reciting that line?"

The gentleman tut-tutted, his broad fingers skimming over the exposed skin of her thighs, then down to her calves, until encircling her ankles. "Ah, but I have no intention of following in his footsteps. And what we are indulging in at the moment is exactly why I had this built, for where else would I undress the woman I love? There are far too many interruptions back at the manor."

Even as her loins shifted toward his questing fingers, Laney—the real Laney—gulped as her heart caught and tumbled.

He loved her? She tried to see him better, but the bright sun glinting overhead kept his face in shadows.

They lived in a *manor*?

"Interruptions?" she heard herself ask on a sigh. "You dare call our adorable children interruptions?"

"When they keep me from savoring your body, I do indeed."

Children?

He bent to nibble her thigh and Laney saw hair as dark as coal, overlong and falling against his cheeks. She raised her hand to brush it back but became distracted and instead grazed her fingertips over the well-maintained side-whiskers angling toward his jaw. The fine hair made her fingertips tingle.

"It's been ages since my tongue has tasted you," he spoke hotly against her thighs. "Entertained you."

The way he stared at her private flesh! Would that she could see his private parts too...

"Ages?" she heard herself protest. "Do you not recall yesterday when—"

"Lest you forget, I have slept since then," he growled over her skin, setting off all manner of riotous sensations in her legs—and increasing the ones in between.

Why was she not embarrassed? Mortified beyond reckoning, positioned as she was? Splayed open to his avid attentions, undressed as she was becoming?

How did she know that he was handsome? It wasn't as though she'd yet been granted a view of his face. But oh, the things he could make her feel! How was it he seemed to know her body so intimately, sliding his fingers to her slit and parting the heated flesh to edge the tips inside? Without so much as a *by your leave*?

The birds sang louder. The sun shone brighter.

Her body craved *deeper*. "Taste me now, my darlin' king. Please."

"Aye, Princess." And with an intoxicating wiggle of his fingers, he lowered his mouth to the apex of her thighs and inhaled. "You know I only wish to serve you."

"I know you only spout clankers when...you 'ave me...at your mercy..." Her words strangled on a gasp as his tongue replaced his fingers and he stared up at her, the intent look in his heated eyes stealing her breath.

Heated, magical eyes. Eyes that *glowed*.

LANEY JERKED UPRIGHT. Her gaze bounding back and forth in the cloud-dimmed coach. She'd nodded off? Had anyone noticed?

Her bits pulsed, rapid contractions that left her both vaguely satisfied and yet craving more—*intensely* craving more. She shifted, pressing her thighs together.

Her skin sizzled everywhere, inside and out as a fine quiver racked her frame. Her chest heaved as she sought to catch her breath. Of a certainty, though this vision had been immeasurably more pleasant than the one that tortured her sleeping hours the last few days, and the other dark ones in the weeks before, it proved no less disturbing.

The stage lumbered to a stop at a noisy inn. The birds in her mind quickly replaced with stomping horses, yelling coachmen and a multitude of people and chickens milling about. The rains had paused but thunder boomed in the distance.

The driver jumped down and called for new horses before opening the door to let the steps down. "Privy break, folks. Be quick about it. We ride out in seven minutes, rain or shine."

Her heart thumped madly. The clenching in her loins had deepened and slowed. Laney fought to remember. Had it been a mere dream? Or was it truly a vision? A message?

What had happened to her elocution? She prided herself on always sounding like a lady, ever since learning how, and she'd dropped an *h*!

He'd said he *loved* her. So it most certainly had to be a dream.

But if it *was* a vision... Perhaps the irritable stranger was the one to help her escape her current situation?

Reginald clambered down, the vast sums of gin dulling motions. "Eleanor! Get ou' here, woman," he barked, standing by the door. "You have m' beaver."

"And that will never do," she muttered, reluctantly following.

When she reached the steps, she glanced back. Seeking knowledge from the corner occupant...

Only to find those glowing, *knowing* eyes on her.

❧

THE ALLURING FRAGRANCE of her unmistakable desire assaulted Nash's nose.

What had she been dreaming of? And why the hell did he care?

Stupid woman. Staying with a dandified fop who scared her.

If she didn't have the gumption to leave a man she wasn't bound to, then it was beyond useless for Nash to give a tinker's damn.

He waited for everyone else to disembark, secured his book in his pocket, then climbed out as well. Ignoring the mist that blanketed everything, he stalked away from the main building and past the stables with long strides that quickly ate up the distance over the wet ground. If he didn't stretch his legs, he'd roar his brains out.

What he wouldn't give for a quick run through a field. He hated being cooped up.

By a conveyance. A house. Or by people.

Didn't matter. They were all intolerable. As was his fascination with—

"Sir! Please wait!" Fascination interrupted.

Nash looked over his shoulder but didn't slow his pace. "Where's your drunken keeper?"

Why did he sound so bitter? Her choices were her own. It was no fur off his back if she chose to tie herself to such a man.

The veiled princess was nothing to him. Nothing. Less than nothing.

The lion doth protest too much, methinks, his damnable conscience misquoted.

She literally ran to catch up with him, sliding over the mucky ground. He finally halted just outside a thick copse of trees. Out of pity. Not interest.

"He's refilling...his flask...inside. Please...ah..."

The infernal netting still hid her face, but regardless, he had to fight the urge to grab her hand and take off—the image of running through the forest and bringing her with him filling his mind.

Absurd.

"Ah, would..." It was taking her a moment to catch her breath, but more than that, he sensed her hesitation to speak as she took pains to carefully open the fancy parasol she'd boarded with.

To hell with it. "State your piece, madam. I wish a drink as well."

He didn't, but she didn't have to know that.

Overhead, she twirled that flimsy parasol in her

gloved hands, swallowed audibly and articulated quite plainly, "I know this is indelicate, but would you please consider purchasing me from Reginald?"

He coughed, positive now that the veiled princess had attics to let if she expected *him* to somehow save her. "*Buy* you?"

"I speak of my indenture. Mr. Tate owns me— Well, more precisely, he owns my services for the next ten and a half months."

"That's less than a year. Why can you not just wait—"

"That cannot be borne." She heaved a deep breath —one that caused her bosom to swell. "It's imperative I alter my situation before then."

"*Imperative?*" he stressed, indicating how little he credited her claim. "And you expect *me* to buy you from him?" Surely his misbegotten existence couldn't become any worse. Here she was, playing at bo-peep, expecting him to be her magical fairy...godfather or some other similar drivel?

He wanted to ask who owned her before Tate. What had she done to so displease her prior benefactor that would land her with one she now sought to escape? With *his* assistance? The very concept made the air around him seethe—with her expectation. His resentment.

Indenture business was all well and fine, when one learned a trade. But to sell this soft-voiced, bound-up package of sin? To *own* her? He couldn't repress a shudder.

"Aye. Please, sir. If you would."

She stood there, head cocked to the side, parasol atwirling, waiting.

A rush of wind and fresh rain pattered down around them. On top of them. And she didn't move. Nothing but that blasted spinning parasol.

Lord save him from frothy females. Who smelled of arousal.

He needed to fuck a wench and then get drunk. Or maybe get drunk and fuck a wench. Either way suited him. *Then* he'd stop thinking foolish thoughts about princesses and setting up his own stable.

"Nay."

The parasol lurched to a stop. "Nay?"

"Nay. No. I won't." *Never.* Nash spun on his heel.

"Wait! Please!" she called after him, but he turned a deaf ear on her pleas, even when they became more frantic. He quickened his pace, sloshing his way back to the tavern.

"But, sir!" the cry trailed off, then echoed again.

Hardening his heart to the sound of her disappointment, he loped through the yard, dodging the scurrying ostler and stable boys. Hurrying his escape, he barely missed kicking a chicken. Fowl creature. Matched his foul mood.

Maneuvering around several passengers already on their way out, heading back to the stage, he entered the tavern and shook off his person. Deuced rain.

Magnificent titties or not, the princess was obviously three horses shy of a team of four if she thought he was about to come to her aid with the first flick of her parasol.

Rescue her? When he knew not where he'd lay his head after the stagecoach reached its destination? Wasn't even sure where that might be, just that he'd ended up in France last year, Spain and Italy the two years before that and had decided to try Scotland for a change. So he was heading north. North into the unknown.

Rescue her? Not bloody likely.

Paying not a dram of attention to anything but his own regret—however impossible—Nash sauntered up to the bar and plunked down two coins.

Who said he needed to wait until tonight to start drinking? And since when did he develop a fascination for breasts? He'd always considered himself more of a bum and beard man, not one who salivated over diddeys he couldn't even see.

An arm suddenly went around his shoulders. "Bar-keep, a shot of your finesht for my fellow traveler 'ere!"

Tate had turned up surprisingly friendly, now, hadn't he?

How had he not noticed the dandy standing—more like listing—at the bar? *Distraction, thy name is Princess.*

He hissed and extracted himself from the one-armed embrace. "Least we haven't gotten bogged down like those other two coaches we saw," he said by way of a small spot of gabber. He *could* be polite when the occasion warranted it, just usually chose not to bother. "Dame Fortune must be on our side."

"Good fortune, eh?" Dandy replied, taking a healthy swig from the glass in front of him, then pouring the remainder into his flask with hands that shook, sloshing some over the side.

Fine waste of fine liquor, Nash thought, savoring

the first sip, surprised to find it wasn't watered. He took another.

"'Fraid I haven't noticed any fortune," Tate said louder than necessary. "Not today. 'Specially not with all my attention focused elshwhere..." The last was a lewd slur and Nash had to fight the urge to wipe the fop's repellent touch off his shoulder.

Repellent? If Nash were honest with himself, he'd admit a stab of jealousy over the flawless attire the other man wore. Simply because a certain female was apparently drawn to the man didn't give him cause to hate the fop on sight. But hate him he did.

"I see th' way you keep lookin' at her, you know."

Tate had something Nash inexplicably wanted. Therefore, he hated the man on principle. "Oh? Have you, now?"

"Yessh indeed," he affirmed in a sickening lilt. "Now take care you do not be doin' anything foolish, my good man. I would hate to be forced to challenge you to a duel."

Nash saluted the fuddled fribble with his glass, bared his teeth in a grimace that he hoped passed for a smile and offered, "I could take that as an insult or ask you to define 'foolish', just to make sure we understand each other. But as far as I can tell, there's no charge for looking and I'm not interested in anything else."

The fop nodded. "Jusht so's we understand."

"Just so."

Nash heard a stable hand tighten the harness on the fourth horse. They'd be pulling out in moments. Might not have another chance... "Why must she hide her face under that rum topping? Hideous, is she?"

Tate nodded. "As a cow."

Figured.

"Moo*oink!*" Nash muttered under his breath.

"Eh?"

"Said they all look the same in the dark. Good for us, eh?" Nash cuffed him on the shoulder in the guise of friendship. Jealous? Certainly not. He wasn't jealous. Didn't want the full-uddered pig for his own. Hell no. He wasn't that much of a jolterhead.

"All ready!" The call came from the door.

Nash irrigated his tongue with the remainder of his drink, then planted his glass on the bar. "Time to go."

"Oh, they'll wait for me. Don't doubt it for a shecond," Dandy slurred. "I tipped 'em too."

Conceited arse.

At least the humid stink of the place and the full-bodied liquor wiped his nose free of the fragrant desire Princess exuded.

He wished his cock would forget the sight of her dugs as quickly as his nose forgot the scent of her cream.

How much were indentures?

The thought formed before he could squelch it.

3

CURSED BLESSINGS CONJURE INVISIBLE VERMIN

A TRUE LADY *never allows others to stand in the way of her own happiness*, or so Laney's friend Mary Delilah had said on more than one occasion.

Granted, Laney had never sought to be a "true lady"—she'd had enough of their airs and looking up their haughty noses when she first arrived at Mrs. Michaels' shop. But happiness? Now that was worth seeking, even though she often despaired of ever remembering what it meant to experience true happiness.

You are in command of your own contentment, come what may from forces beyond yourself.

Recalling her friend's teachings always warmed Laney. A pity the stranger's refusal had chilled her to the bone.

Why should his abrupt dismissal cause her such

dismay? There were other men. Other routes to safety...

Ignoring the well of hopelessness that filled her at his rejection, Laney took the moment of solitude in the coach to loosen the strings of her reticule and retrieve the most recent letter she'd received from Mary Delilah Middleton.

Dear tolerant, wonderful Mary, the closest friend Laney had in the world, the one person who had made her time at Mrs. Michaels' bearable. Laney glanced at the date in the top right corner, admiring as she did so, her friend's penmanship, which was perfection as always.

June 1ˢᵗ, the Year of our Lord 1812

Mary was always so formal. Laney did a quick calculation. Seventy-seven days since Mary's last post. Just over two and a half months since she'd had word from her friend—and this one delivered into her hands one afternoon when Reginald was out. Laney suspected Reginald of intercepting her mail. Ever since his odious brother caught him *in flagrante delicto* and he'd severed ties with Neils, Reginald had become irrational.

Determined to put the unpalatable situation from her mind, Laney flicked the not-so-crisp sheet, wrinkled from being stuffed in her bag. Since the first unsettling vision a few weeks prior—compounded by the latest one of death and doom—she'd taken to keeping her friend's last letter with her at all times.

Small comfort, perhaps, but life had knocked her about sufficiently that she'd take comfort where she found it. She strove to give every appearance of reading the missive with her utmost attention, her efforts hampered as the coach dipped and swayed when not only Reginald, but the rest of the passengers and the dratted stranger climbed back inside.

How was she supposed to concentrate with a heavy lump lumped in next to her and an attractive scoundrel shuffling his booted foot directly alongside hers?

"Appalling!" Absolutely appalling, his lack of manners.

"What, dear?"

"Yours too!" she couldn't help but complain when Reginald turned his liquor-soused breath her direction.

"Eh?"

"Nothing," she apologized contritely, "I misspoke."

'Twas difficult not to flinch when the boot slid forward, practically caressing her instep.

Additional passengers clambered up top, creating such a ruckus the mêlée above her head just barely drowned out the one inside her chest.

"Wha's this?" Reginald attempted to grab the letter from her lap, and Laney used the abrupt shift of the coach lurching into motion to quickly fold and stuff it back inside her reticule.

She didn't trust him not to confiscate this one too. "Simply my list of traveling reminders, Mr. Tate. Nothing you need concern yourself with."

"Very well. Here." He dropped his hat into her lap and slouched until his head lolled against her shoulder. "Think I shall shnap a bit, m'dear."

Shnap? What she wouldn't give to be in a position to *shknock* some sense into the lout.

Tempted to allow his hat to fall to the floor and be

trampled underfoot—if not the stranger's, then hers—Laney nevertheless grabbed it and held on. It was either that or release her vexation once and for all and clout both men in their upper story with the spanking-new beaver.

As if the thoughts racing through her mind were on full display, the stranger kicked up one corner of his mouth, drawing her attention to two nicks across his lips.

What manner of activity might have resulted in such a scar? From a hat pin perhaps?

Knowing she had several on her person, Laney decided to spend the remainder of their journey contemplating how, if he persisted in his refusal to be swayed by her requests, perhaps a hat pin applied to his posterior might prove more convincing.

'Twould be satisfying in the extreme.

Although, with every tilt of his eyebrows, glint of his eyes and flex of his foot, it became more difficult to formulate a plan of escape *and* ignore the restless yearning growing between her legs. Gads, but this trip was proving to be disastrous indeed.

⎯⎯⎯⎯⎯◦⎯⎯⎯⎯⎯

He hated Eleanor.

Bloop. Bloop. Bloop. His head was swimming like a bedeviled finless fish!

He hated Eleanor.

Bloop. Bloop.

Hated Eleanor.

Nay. He really didn't. But Reginald most certainly hated how being around her made him feel.

All inferior and ineffective. Impotent.

Hated—

No he didn't, the one, small, still-sober part of him protested. How could he resent the most innocent ray of sunshine in his life? He couldn't...

But deep down, Reginald knew he did. Was slowly starting to detest her with every shred of his being. How had his life come to this? Where would it end?

With your cock driving into her hole and your seed erupting inside her puss, that's where, some inner demon prompted.

Reginald practically heard George John cheering. His brother had tutored him enough.

"Since our father met The Maker, I'm in charge of this family..." Repeated so often of late, the words echoed in his drowning brain. "And Tates don't breed mollies! Now I don't know the details and I don't want to know 'em, but you got a stunner situated under your roof and you better start plowing into her or by God—"

Fired up after one of George John's inspiring speeches, corned off his arse after breaking things off with Neils, Reginald had tried to do just that—tried to take Eleanor. To assert his claim. Validate his ownership.

His body had only embarrassed them both. She'd seemed willing enough, if not necessarily eager, but his pecker wouldn't poke. She was too...curvy. Just touching her made his hands feel ill, as though vermin crawled and shat over every finger.

So he drank some more and tried again.

He'd almost made it inside her that last attempt, before his pump-handle petered out. Along with his pride. How much was a man supposed to take?

And then she tried to escape. The damn paid whore tried to leave him! Abandon—*him*! Leave him alone with the sinister schoolings of his brother and the inescapable ache of his not-to-be-borne lonely heart. Unacceptable!

Reginald hadn't needed a speech from George John to know it was time to show Eleanor just who owned whom.

He'd never meant to mark her as he had. He hadn't meant to do it. Hadn't planned it, nor thought it through. Her resistance... Her rebellion... *She* just made him so nauseatingly mad, he couldn't stop himself.

Couldn't stop from sucking on the cheroot between his lips, drawing hard and causing the tip to flare... Couldn't stop from pulling her closer, shoving her sleeve up, her glove down and baring her arm.

Couldn't stop from applying the end of the cheroot to her skin and holding it there. Holding it there while her flesh sizzled and smoked, while she attempted—unsuccessfully—to jerk from his grasp as tears came into her eyes and finally fell free...

And then he did it a second time.

He hadn't been able to stop any of those actions. Nor had he been able to halt the erection that flared to life along his cock. For once, Reginald had felt like a *man*. In control of his destiny—and his woman.

But neither had he been able to staunch the guilt that dogged his steps for days afterward.

Eleanor had locked herself in her room. Reginald had locked himself away with another bottle, hoping to drown his guilt. Instead, smothering his common sense.

Bloop. Bloop.

Which was ultimately why he'd undertaken this deuced journey before he permanently scared—or scarred—Eleanor. Or completely lost whatever remnant of self-respect he still laid claim to.

For, according to George John, the end of this journey held the one thing Reginald needed above all others—the promise of sexual oblivion. His brother assured him the house party they were heading toward would drive Reginald to the edge of fear and pain that would harden his cock for a woman as nothing else. And keep it hard. Curing him once and for all.

It was his only hope.

That if he took her soon...discovered what truly fired his blood *for a woman*, he could finally make use of Eleanor. Then set her free.

After he proved to himself and George John that he *could* get a female pregnant.

⚬

WRETCHED MAN! Laney was still fuming hours later when they stopped for the night and the uncooperative, unhelpful and wholly *un*intriguing stranger stepped on her skirts with his other foot in his haste to exit the stagecoach.

Reginald was no help. Or no harm, either, practically swoon-addled as he was.

When had he started drinking strong spirits as if they were ale? The past few weeks had seen an increase in his imbibing, surely, but even so...had she ever known him at all?

When they'd met, she'd thought him the most dashing, most handsome, kindest man in the world, and he had been—until his elder brother unexpectedly came into a title and a wagonload of airs and then started pressuring Reginald to marry.

Laney wasn't sure whether it was subverting his true nature or another reason entirely, but ever since he'd severed ties with his friend Neils, Reginald had begun behaving differently toward her. He'd developed a malicious bent. One that now terrified her. Though not as much as his brother did. Every time George John was near, his eyes narrowed with a look that told Laney if she wasn't under Reginald's "protection", she'd have far more to fear.

The ostler poked his head in, past the coach's doorway. "Yous both gotta get down, miss. I needs t' wheel the coach into the stable an' un'itch the 'orses. Clean the mud and bracken what dried on the underside, cloggin' the life outta my coach. An' the patience outta my day." His jaw tightened. "'Ope the wheels ain't cracked."

"Certainly. I...um..." She nudged Reginald.

A half snore-snort was his response.

"Can you give us a few moments more?"

The man tipped his hat, a look of pity in his eyes. "Yessum. I can spare a coupla minutes, but I ain't got all night."

"I shall rouse him and we will step down in a trice."

"'Ow about I send a stable 'and out to 'elp?"

"Yes, please. If you would be so kind."

This was her chance. With Reginald stupefied, she could leave and be far away by the time he came to his senses. A surge of excitement gripped her.

She could really do this! Giddy over the prospect, Laney only halfheartedly paid attention when a young man from the inn came to help drag a soused Reginald from the coach.

"W' there yet?" Reginald asked, hanging on to the youth like the soggy drunk he'd become.

"Jus' about," the tall, gangly boy, just short of becoming a man, answered before turning to her. "Me name's Johnny, ma'am. Me family runs The Black Boar."

"W' there yet?" Reginald repeated.

Bore was right.

"We're at The Black Boar Inn," she told him, not caring when his prize beaver fell and landed in the yard. In a pile of wet horse manure. She certainly wouldn't be picking it up!

She moderated her tone to disguise any hint of her plans. "This pleasant young man will escort you to a room while I secure our lodgings and supper. I shall be up presently."

She looked at Johnny, eyebrows raised in query, forgetting for a moment he couldn't see her beyond the veil. Lifting her shoulders, she tacked on, "Assuming that is acceptable to you?"

"Sure 'tis, ma'am." The youth stumbled once, then hefted Reginald's dead weight against his side. "I'll git your gent fit as a fivepence an' take 'im straight up the stairs. You can talk to me mama about supper an' order up a bath if the tub ain't done been claimed."

"That would be most appreciated, thank you. Ah, just one thing..." She motioned for Johnny to stop and scoured Reginald's pockets for the coins he always kept on his person.

Weakly, he tried to bat her away. "Whadya doin'? Get your hands off me, woman!"

As if she wanted them there either, the fool. "I'm in need of funds, Mr. Tate, to pay the innkeeper."

That reached through his raddled brain and he shoved several coins at her.

While she followed the men inside, then veered off toward the main counter, her mind raced over a hundred and one things.

With the unexpected windfall Reginald had just handed her, her opportunities seemed vastly improved over what they had just seconds before. But she couldn't run off like a featherbrain. She still had the marks on her arm, testifying to his temper. Nay, if she was going to escape for real this time, she had to ponder and plan.

She needed to eat first, mayhap set aside a spot of food for later. No time for a bath. Who knew how long Reginald would remain in his drunken stupor?

All she had to do upstairs, once she confirmed he was fuddled for the night, was locate her indenture papers. He always kept them locked in his trunk. Granted, they might be registered with the magistrate or some other officious official back in London, but as Laney had no intention of ever returning to the capital city, it shouldn't matter a whit. As far as she was concerned, she'd be free!

<hr>

POSITIVELY AGES LATER, or at least that's how it seemed, though only a few minutes had passed, Laney was still waiting her turn to pay for the overnight lodgings. *Still.* Every other passenger had claimed a small portion of the common room or obtained the key to a private one upstairs. Everyone *except* the scoundrel with the glowing eyes.

Heavens, but the man was tall. And had excessively broad shoulders. She'd like to see him take his fives to Reginald—one clout and her "owner" would hit the ground like a discarded shovel. Probably not move for a week.

'Twas a pity that the stranger wouldn't help her, but she'd take care of things herself. Laney Catherine Buckley was no weak-willed female. No sirree. She had a plan, and as soon as she escaped—

A surge of dizziness slammed into her. She swayed forward and bumped into *his* broad back.

"Bloody hell! Watch it, you cupshot bloat," he called over his shoulder.

Dizzy. Nauseous, unable to make sense of the sudden assault, she tottered into him again, despite his efforts to shake her off.

"Dem bloat." He wrenched around and his eyes widened when he saw who dared crash into him wasn't exactly a drunk degenerate.

He steadied her upper arms. "Pardon me." His tone

had softened. For the first time in their acquaintance, he sounded concerned. "Do you need assistance? A drink? To sit down?"

So faint she could hardly stand, Laney nodded, stalling. "A restorative, please..."

Then it happened again—'twas as though her brain flipped itself upside down, upending her balance and her equilibrium. She staggered forward, straight into his chest.

Candles flared to life, one after another all around her, leaving her nude body bathed in their golden glow. Beyond the flickering light, it was black as pitch. A cloying, perfumed haze hung in the air.

Thin red streaks slashed across her exposed skin. Rivulets of blood dripped from several.

She bit her lips against the urge to cry out. Against the pain.

Her woman's mound throbbed in agony. She looked down and saw the torn flesh between her legs.

Bloodied. Raw.

She blinked. Distraught. Dismayed...totally dumbfounded as she sensed her very life slipping away.

Beyond the evil, ominous darkness that bound her, she heard the sounds of excitement, sensed the wildness...the primal atmosphere of a pack of feral animals closing in for the kill.

She shut her eyes against the pain. Against the surety of death.

For unlike the last gruesome vision she beheld, this wasn't the casual disinterest of a mourner attending the wake of a stranger. Nay, this was the panicked certainty that her minutes on earth were numbered and no matter how she might plead, her dying breath was imminent.

She was surrounded by too many participants eager for her death—wishing for it, praying for it. Expecting it.

A crack exploded next to her ear and her eyes flew open.

Naked, his own body speckled with blood, Reginald stepped into the circle of candles. The sinuous serpent of the leather whip he wielded came closer and closer as it alternatively snaked along the rough stone floor and glided through the midnight air.

His eyes were wild; his breathing heightened. He bore the look of a madman... Of one in a delirium.

What had they fed him? Made him swallow or smoke?

Between his legs, his cock shone. Hard for once. *Red.*

Covered in her blood.

The lash whispered past her ear, sliced into her neck and she flinched. Then again, lower, carving into the flesh of her breast. "Stop!"

Laney fought against the bonds that held her captive and cried out with all her might. "Nooooo!" She wasn't ready to die. She wasn't! "Stop it! Quit kill—"

"Woman! What in God's name is wrong with you?"

Dazed, Laney blinked. Her runaway pulse thundered in her ears. Her flesh burned from the sting of the whip. Terror clawed its way over every inch of her skin. "Noooo!"

"Stubble it! Reasonable people don't scream over nothing," the deep voice accused while he shook her harder. *He.* The man from the stagecoach.

The stagecoach. The inn. The Black Boar.

She repeated the litany, her breathing labored. "Black Boar... Black Boar..."

No one is trying to kill you. Not yet.

She stood in line at the tavern, owned by helpful Johnny's mama. They'd stopped when the rains bogged down the roadway, preventing their traveling at night. *Night.*

Darkness and whips and blood.

The vision persisted, encroaching across her furiously blinking eyelids, no matter that she tried to focus on the present—not the future.

Gads, she was going to die. A horrible, pain-filled death. *If* she didn't escape from Reginald straight away.

A shudder racked her frame and the man's fingers tightened on her arms. He muttered something about hats and swine, but his prattle was secondary to the feel of the whip striking her flesh, of warm blood dripping between her thighs. Down her legs.

Laney stomped her feet to blot out the unsettling sensations, then realized she'd somehow wound her fingers in his jacket, making it quite impossible for him to release her. Unconscionable—depending on such a surly brute. What *was* her body thinking?

Thrusting him away with more force than necessary, she let loose a frustrated cry and bent to slap at her legs. Fast, frantic swipes followed by several hops of her feet. "Bugs! Dashed bugs!" she shrieked, hoping to direct his attention away from how she'd leaned into him. Away from her inexplicable seconds of sheer madness—for that's how she must appear to the others; off her head, a ramping loon. "A spider—on my dress. Nothing more."

With faked confidence, she straightened, still gasping for breath, but firmly back in the now, more relieved than ever that she had the shielding veil to hide behind.

"Do forgive me." Her voice was composed as crystal, she was pleased to note. "I positively detest insects. Loathsome creatures."

"You are one totty-headed female," he said dismissively, turning back to the proprietress who was staring at Laney as if she'd just accused the place of selling bottled leeches. Too bad they weren't. She'd like to slap a few of the suckers on Reginald's soused form right about now.

"Please. Forgive me." Never had a vision come on so strong or been so intense. Never had she become *locked* within it and unable to separate her present from scenes of the future. Even now, the dank feel of the dark dungeon seemed to be sucking at her—no leeches necessary—luring her deeper into the pit of what would happen lest she make swift, significant alterations to her current plans.

But when the heavy, malodorous air tried to worm its way back inside and disorder her thoughts, she leaned forward and inhaled. The strong musky scent of the brooding stranger filled her nostrils, enticing her to breathe him in, which she did—gratefully. Deeply. The remembered strength of his arms told Laney more than anything that she was solidly in the present, her nightmare nothing but brain mist. Not real. Not unless it came true... *Until* it came true.

That settled it. After being shown the outcome if she left on her own, 'twould be foolhardy to proceed. "Definitely shan't be running away," she whispered under her breath, more determined than ever to flee Reginald, but totally clueless how to go about it. Why couldn't her bloomin' visions show her *what* to do, instead of simply the result of her actions?

"I don't 'ave no spiders in my establishment! The Boar's a banging place, it is." The woman behind the counter drummed her fingers over the rough wood and glared past the comfortable-smelling stranger at Laney as if she'd eject them both if her "husband" wasn't already upstairs—and insensible thanks to over imbibing. "Now, missus, are ye feelin' poorly or not? I cannot be bringin' no sickness inside. You'll 'ave to get your mister and get out if—"

"Nay. I'm not ailing. Not at all." Laney locked her legs to stop their trembling and gestured toward *him*. "Please conclude your business. I shall patiently await my turn."

"THE ROOM?" Nash prompted the proprietress, heartily annoyed at the caterwauling woman hovering behind him. "I haven't been stuffed in a damp stagecoach all day just to stand here and dawdle all night."

"With 'er mister already upstairs we only 'ave one room left. You can 'ave it but th' latch is busted. Had to board—"

"It will do." He didn't mean to bark, but hell, if he

was afraid of being robbed—which he wasn't—he could always shove a piece of furniture against the door. And after having his hands on *her*—though for very different reasons than he'd been fancying all demmed day, he was more than ready for the privacy of his own room. "The key?"

Was there even going to be a key? If the lock was broken... He rolled his shoulders, stiff from hours traveling—stiffer, down low, because of the blasted pig princess. "Do I need one?"

The innkeeper's puzzled expression didn't ease, in fact, it kept bobbing between him and the deranged princess. Her little bug-begone dance had him wanting to slap the dem hat from her head, dislodge the veil and see what all the hullabaloo was about. Lift up her skirts while he was at it—inspect her legs and anything else he might find. He doubted any insects had scurried beneath her dress. On the contrary, her inane screaming had most likely sent them all scurrying into the next shire.

God-dem, but the woman had a set of lungs on her beneath those disguised diddeys! And if he didn't find a pair to fondle and fuck soon, he'd be the one screaming.

Today was just one trying delay after another. If it weren't for the cursed rain, he'd be on the road in a trice, moon or no. As it was, he plunked the appropriate coinage on the counter and the proprietress gratefully swept up the money in exchange for a room key—finally. When she handed it over, he closed his fingers around the cool metal and hesitated.

"Do you have anyone you...ah..." Nash stumbled to

a halt and looked over his shoulder at the dull swift behind him. He scowled at the veiled mystery, then turned back to the proprietress and flipped another coin on the counter. Hell, his request for feminine company would have to wait. "Will you at least send up a bath?"

"I can do that, I can. I shall get me Johnny right on it. Your room is directly up th' stairs." She pointed the opposite direction from the main entrance. "Third door on your left."

Grabbing up the bag by his feet, he gave the spider-hating female one last dark look and then disappeared around the corner.

———⊃o⊂———

NASH PACED the confines of his room like a caged lion.

Only his cell contained a decent-sized bed—something to be thankful for—small table, shuttered window, closed to keep out the earlier rains, and an overhead lantern he kept having to duck beneath.

The door latch worked fine to his way of thinking, but that didn't make it any easier, being confined in the small space.

Staying with Blake the last few days in his topping townhouse had spoiled Nash to elegant accommodations and spacious surroundings. Which made the contrast of his current abode that much starker.

With every swath he cut across the meager floor space, the lantern cast his shadow over the room. His shadow—stalking to and fro. Hell, he fancied he could see the four-legged creature that haunted him in his place. And he didn't have to look very hard, either.

There was no reason he should feel this primal and primed to tup. Not now. Not yet. It wasn't as if *he'd* gone days without. Nay, just as he did every year when the sun passed through Leo, he abandoned his dreams and turned himself over to battling the beast the only way he knew—by prigging any willing wench around. Once a day sufficed.

At least it always had, until this blasted week—thanks to his brother's sudden fascination with love and monogamy. After last night's encounter, the one that finally left both him and Blake sated, with the curse slumbering at last, anticipated a full day of ease—twenty-three hours at least. So why in blazes had the need come upon him with such urgency *now*?

He still had a several-hour span to find today's wench, so why was his skin simmering with arousal? It couldn't be the way he'd responded to the wretched cries and shrieks of the annoying female who'd bedeviled him all day. Couldn't be his instinctive—and unfamiliar—urge to protect her from whatever demons crossed her path, even the unseen, eight-legged variety.

Nay, definitely not that.

Mayhap the curse was growing worse.

Mayhap he was becoming weaker.

Mayhap it was simply her dem magnificent teats.

Or the remembered intoxicating scent of her cream. But no...the sharp, sickening bite of terror she'd exuded downstairs had wiped away any hint of desire.

Hadn't it?

Beyond perplexing, how she'd become unhinged like that.

But not your problem!

Nay, his problem was the primed prick stirring the front of his pantaloons. Bloody hell. He'd allowed the two other passengers who wanted private rooms to go before him, intending to be the last one. Intending to ask that a wench be sent up to his room. But oh no, Miss Veiled Will-You-Not-Buy-My-Indenture-Please-Kind-Sir had to come along and spoil it. Batting her eyelashes, or so he'd expect, if her face wasn't in hiding.

A tap on the door heralded the arrival of his bath. "Mr. 'ammond? 'Tis Johnny. With your tub."

Nash swung the door open, gratified to see the huge vat of steaming water carried by a strapping lad, followed by two maids. The young man deposited the metal tub in the middle of the floor. It practically took up every bit of spare walking space, bringing his pacing to an end it seemed.

Though his body craved a relaxing soak, his mind perked up when the maids shuffled in with even more boiled water, judging by the careful way they carried the pots.

Neither wench had the body, or the veil, of his recent tormentor. Which was fine with him.

After a fast glance and quick blush, one of the maids avoided looking at him, but the other one boldly held his gaze as she walked backward from the room. Nash stopped Johnny just before he exited. "The wenches. Do they entertain upstairs?"

The lad smiled knowingly. "Fer a price, they do. Which one 'as your fancy?"

"I care not. Either will suit." Nash retrieved two coins from his pocket and pressed them into Johnny's palm. "The first is for you, for hauling the bathwater. The other is for the wench. Tell one of them to return in thirty minutes." Looming curse or no, he could delay relief that long, surely.

"But it's suppertime. Mama expects them ta serve—"

How much longer must he wait? Getting prigged hadn't been this difficult since... Well, since Francine unknowingly addled his brother. *God-dem her.* "Fine, then. *After* supper. And bring me a bottle of cognac."

"Cawn-yak?"

"There a problem?" If he had to wait, he might as well indulge. If anything, tipping a bottle should take his mind off his rousing need.

"I don't think Mama keeps cognac," the youth repeated the word as if he'd never heard it before. What? Did no other travelers through here appreciate the fine beverage to be found in western France and request it by name? Nash had developed an affinity for the rich brandy during last year's exodus. For about the eighty-seventh time this month, he wished he'd stayed abroad. Had never returned to England.

"What about ale? Or gin?" Johnny asked. "Ole Joncaey makes th' best ale in th' shire."

"Ale is for fops." And gin what the princess's owner had been swilling. And the longer Nash was forced to wait, the more he planned on drinking. "Do you have an unopened bottle of whiskey?"

Capped and corked meant not diluted. He hoped. He dug out another coin and held it up.

"Whiskey? I believe we do at that." The boy's face pinkened and he nodded hard enough to make himself dizzy, as if embarrassed he hadn't suggested that himself. But he wasn't too embarrassed, snatching the coin into his safekeeping. "Yessir. We should 'ave whiskey."

"Then why do you not bring that up?" Nash said through gritted teeth. Being in possession of his own horse was looking better and better. With that he could pick and choose his own blasted taverns. A snarl barreled up his throat; he swallowed it down and bit off, "*Now?*"

"Yessir." The boy, young man really, nodded, then left, pulling the door shut behind him.

The moment Nash was alone, he scraped the edge of his fingernails along his scalp, every individual strand of hair crackling like tiny knives shredding his skull. Dem again. His skin was sensitive.

His body crawled with need, each inch on edge. The demand for sex straining through him. Hurriedly, he slipped his clothes off and lowered his aching body into the hip tub.

"Ahhhhh," Nash sighed. Steam rose up around him. Warm, blessed steam, threatening to wipe away every care and thought.

Except that of his aching cock...and the perplexing pig princess below stairs.

4

A GRAND IDEA, A GRANDIOSE DOSE OF GUILT, & TIME WITH TYNDALE

"UM…JOHNNY, WAS IT NOT?"

Upon leaving the somewhat crank of a nob who thought The Black Boar was high and mighty enough to have his fancy French *cawn*-yak, Johnny glanced up from studying the coins in his hand to see the quiet, veiled lady from the coach standing just outside her assigned room.

He stopped and nodded, indicating the door behind her as he slid the coins in his pocket. "I did get the lantern lit an' your trunks brung up, ma'am, but your mister's daylights went dark 'fore I could get 'im undressed. I 'ope that's—"

"Of no consequence, thank you. Johnny…" Her covered head twisted from side to side, as if checking to make sure they weren't overheard. The hall was deserted. She pointed at the door he'd just closed. "I shall pay you to *not* send one of the girls to his room tonight."

Johnny tightened his fist around the money. The subject of female companionship wasn't exactly something to be *discussed* with, well, females, but she'd brought it up. "But, ma'am, 'e's expectin'—"

"I know full well what he expects." She leaned forward and pressed two gold coins into his other palm. "And he will receive it. Just not from one of your serving girls."

Two more! On top of the three he'd just been given?

So the poor woman wanted strummed, and with her husband out for the night, was hankering for her fellow traveler? Johnny was old enough to know it didn't matter where a body came from, how they dressed or talked made no difference. When it came to matters of the flesh—to hear Vicar Thompson proclaim—yearnings often overtook a body's common sense.

But he'd just been paid to do a job by the grumpy swell. Didn't want to find himself awash in trouble for not—

"*Please.*"

Johnny studied the two quid in his hand. Thought about the three more weighing his pocket. 'Twas well beyond what his mama paid him for months of doing her bidding.

"But the gent..." Hard to complain when he simply wanted to savor the coinage and add it to his growing stash in the stable. He had his own plans and they didn't include lugging luggage for his mama the rest of his days.

"I assure you that he shall never know. I will see to his needs, I promise," she whispered, curving her fingers around his, and even through her gloves, the heat reached his skin. "Just...I beg of you... Do not say anything—to anyone."

"You cannot go in wearin' the fancy 'at." He pointed to the area of her face. "Hiding your looks an' all. Nor talkin' all ladylike like you are. 'E will know for sure you ain't from 'ere."

"I... You are quite right. I will ensure I look—and act—as he will expect. Now please, not a word."

Moneyed folks were strange. But he was getting richer by the minute. "Nary a word, I swear. An' if you want, I can bring you a full bottle of whiskey." Johnny bit the inside of his cheek to keep from grinning when she handed him a *third* coin. He was having more fun this evening than he usually had in a fortnight. "Maybe if 'e swallows enough, 'e won't know it's you."

"Aye. Grand idea."

And mayhap, if he's satisfied, I'll get another coin tomorrow morn.

S-U-S-P-E-C-T-S.

Suspects for *what*?

The word itself brimmed with nefarious connotations. So not just simply club applicants that Blake was considering, but something more sinister perhaps?

Back in London the prior week, Nash had stumbled across the list labeled *Suspects*, but after a fast glance hadn't paid it much mind, not once finding the hastily scrawled marriage vows just beneath. Vows in his brother's hand.

Oh-ho! A lead fist had slammed into his gut causing Nash to stagger back from Blake's desk, mind reeling. If Blake had taken to scribbling vows, then his older brother was guzzling laudanum if he thought to convince Nash his engagement was nothing but a temporary sham.

It was real—or Blake's feelings were.

And that put them at risk more than ever before. Their family secrets. Their ability to remain as men—not transmute into monsters. Their very lives.

Everything was at stake now, because some juicy piece had gotten her claws into his brother.

That more than anything had sent him outside and into the stables, looking for those chains Blake had pleaded for...

The memories only made Nash shudder in his warm bath and grip the neck of the bottle, contemplating... Over half the amber liquid remained. No need to drink it all, right?

Where was his wench? She should be here by now, distracting him from his troublesome thoughts.

His teeth ached, nail beds grew heavy. Hair follicles stung.

The beast loomed.

Plan, man. What next?

Bed the wench. Pay her off. Secure his door, then drift off for the rest of the night, likely half of tomorrow, given how little sleep he'd had the last few days, how little rest his body had known thanks to how weak Blake had become and, by proximity, Nash as well.

That was it, *sleep*.

His plan: Slumber till Johnny or his mama came and rousted him from the room. Then catch the next, *later* stage, no matter where it was headed. He cared naught.

Oh no? Are you not curious about the pig princess and her dandy's destination?

No! Nay. He wasn't.

He wasn't!

He wasn't…

A RED HAZE covered his vision. Was he in hell?

Hell was supposed to be hot and horrible. Yet cool silk danced along his skin…

Nash jerked in the hip bath, startled awake.

Hell, he'd fallen asleep waiting for his wench? No wonder, really, the tumultuous thoughts spiraling in his upper story not giving him a moment's peace since last eve.

Your thoughts? I thought that was her dugs.

Dugs?

Those of the perplexing pig princess. Come now, man "you are a most notable coward…the owner of not one good quality…" Face the truth: The perplexing pig princess has you in her grasp.

Just like Francine ensnared Blake.

Nash snorted and splashed around in the tub for the fallen whiskey. His treasure found, he lifted it from the tepid water, dripping and tempting, to uncap the bottle for another gulp.

The soothing burn flowed past his sensitive teeth,

easing a fraction of the tension knotting his muscles. Two more swallows to calm his ire toward the unknown, absent wench and he screwed the cap back on. But kept a firm hold on the bottle's neck. Wasn't falling asleep again, not the way he felt now. Irritated. Cantankerous. Ready to prig.

Hazy images bombarded his brain, driving him to uncap the bottle once again.

Ripping Francine's shift.

Had he?

Growling at her when she dared breach Blake's home—their summer sanctuary where they hid from the curse. Practically from each other. Certainly from any finer feelings toward females.

Ever since their mother's betrayal, Nash knew better than to trust *any* woman.

He could remember arguing with Blake days earlier, attempting to convince his brother to summon Francine, to ease the extreme suffering Nash witnessed.

"She's too delicate," Blake had claimed.

"Too puny," Nash corrected, just to aggravate the other man, tired of hearing how this phantom woman who refused to show herself "couldn't handle the beast, couldn't be exposed to the monster that resided within...cannot be expected to handle... *Us both.*"

Aye, he and Blake had shared a time or plenty before this year. Never had it mattered. A wench was a wench.

But then Francine had to come along and change *everything*. Until Nash barely recognized his one and only brother. The *only* person he'd allowed himself to think of and care about—if in his own remote, careless fashion—since their mother's disappearance. Since Phineas.

Damn him. Nash had known not to let himself care after his mother deserted them, but Blake and Phineas, older than him by five and six years, were his rocks. His family. Cornerstones in his aimless life. Until Phineas too vanished. After his wedding and the attack, gone without a trace. And Nash determined to do the same.

Don't linger, don't care. Ergo, don't get hurt.

Then why did he persist in feeling guilt over not leaving his brother a note about the list he'd found on Blake's desk? He could have shared knowledge, albeit limited, on one of the men named—

"For my part," he muttered, determined to stop thinking responsibly, "noble lords and nasty lions, I care not." Once again, mangled Shakespeare to save his sanity.

He gripped the bottle, tighter. Needing something to hold on to, the sliver of soap he'd been granted long dissolved.

The low-burning candle reflected through the thick glass, shimmering behind the golden liquid—when he balanced the bottle's flat bottom on one kneecap poking up out of the water. He stared through the liquor, transfixed by the distorted glow, seeking answers.

Seeking remembrances, accurate ones. From last night. Hating how the beast within stole not only sense and softness—what little he could claim—but sound memory as well.

Shoving Francine—that he recalled, all too clearly. Snarling at her, spittle flying from his lips, teeth half-transformed into fangs, eliciting both her fear and her remarkable determination to push her way past him in order to "save" his brother.

He could recall escaping up the stairs of Blake's townhouse, padding swiftly more like—crumpled to all fours, as The Change threatened to take hold completely and he fought it back with everything he had, both hoping he'd scared her sufficiently to see her fleeing into the night, yet conversely, praying she might be the one to bring peace to Blake, and in turn, to Nash himself.

That he remembered.

Being a monster toward her.

Much of the rest remained a confounding blur. Until he woke deep in the night, on the edge of the large bed, to the awareness of the cooing couple cuddled on the opposite side, their sickeningly sweet murmurs of love and everlasting happiness needling him from Blake's "happy" abode and back out onto the streets, alone. Where he'd always felt the most comfortable.

Alone. Where no one was allowed close enough to harm, nor hurt.

Alone, exactly the way he liked it.

The lion doth protest too much, methinks.

THE PRIOR NIGHT...BACK IN LONDON

RESPONSIBILITY STRUCK Lord Tyndale's shoulders like a runaway carriage toppling off a cliff. Hard, heavy and with unexpected haste.

He barely managed to muffle a snort. Him? Look after this fresh-faced, exuberant female?

When he failed at looking after his own flesh and blood?

Gah. Lord save him from outspoken, blustery Americans who didn't know their place. Practically ordered in here by the hired help—this dark box of a boring room—only because he had the misfortune to not be otherwise occupied? Because he'd considerately, *responsibly*, allowed his younger cousins, twins, and their friend—an oddly quiet, ghostly chap they brought with them on their first jaunt to London since graduating—to have first crack at the available "ladies".

Don't be a bellyacher. You had no intention of taking a crack at anyone's crack tonight. Tyndale grimaced, when his younger self (by a few months) would have chuckled at his own wit.

You're still too busy torturing yourself over Thalia.

True. He'd been a jolterhead all season. Ever since "losing" his sister last Twelfth Night.

Losing? His booted foot stomped at the renewed frustration, grief and confusion that wound through him daily—if not hourly.

Either she ran off—and with *whom* he had not an inkling—or she was taken. Nabbed. *Kidnapped.*

Half sister, really. He wasn't supposed to know about her. He'd been a child when she was born, when she got shuffled off first to a distant tenant, eventually to some girls' school. Had no clue of her existence back then.

But he held the title now—and controlled the family coffers, which included all the Tyndale wealth and lands—and responsibilities to care for them. And when his father's solicitor retired last year, Tyndale hired his own, knowing it was time he stop frittering and start focusing...only to have the new man point out numerous discrepancies. Hence, Tyndale had taken the time to learn what all that wealth entailed, and perhaps more importantly, where it went. Both now and in the past.

And *years* of consistent payments to the head-mistress of the Young Ladies Improving Academy made things abundantly clear.

After being raised alone, if not lonely, he had a sibling, after all. Upon learning that truth, he had managed to identify her, having his trusted man of affairs track the funds, locate the school and discern just *who* the Tyndale monies were paying to educate and house. Only to lose her before they'd met.

Had highwaymen attacked the public stagecoach she'd chosen? Or had *she* taken off with the travel money he'd arranged? Pilfered it and gone her own way?

Nay. For that made no sense.

He was the one who had sought her out, intent on fostering a relationship with the only sibling he could claim. He had no reason to think that she'd lied to him in her letters. No reason to think she would abscond with the piddling, in comparison, traveling funds when he'd expressed a desire to see her cared for—and had the wherewithal to make that happen.

He couldn't search for her publicly, not without risking her parentage coming to light. If she had any chance at a respectable future, he needed to locate her now as quietly as he had the first time. Bring her back to London and find her a position as a governess or companion—or, God and Thalia willing—shower sufficient funds on her that a merchant or mushroom's son might take her as bride.

You must find her first.

By damn. How?

"Your garret is to let if that is how you perceive things," the Annoying Responsibility across from him accused after several minutes of half-hearted conversation betwixt them, the vast majority of his attention focused inward.

Missing relatives, peculiar friends and heaps of guilt aside, now he had *another* female dependent on him. If only for a short while. But still...

This evening, shepherding his cousins and their friend around London had at least proved a distraction to his troublesome thoughts. And then they'd landed here, at The Den. He might have been a frequent visitor in years past, but this wasn't the sort of establishment he frequented of late.

Can you deny the pleasure you felt—earlier this eve? Savoring the...view?

Nay, and he wouldn't try to. He'd enjoyed the swiving action upon the elevated stage. The one he'd been watching before being hauled in here and tasked with a duty.

The very scene still occurring behind him—not to mention the one he'd witnessed in *this* very room mere minutes ago—made his fingers itch. Not for a drink, but a pencil.

He hadn't sketched for an age and was feeling rather...

Inspired at the moment.

For how often did one feast their unexpected senses upon a fully nude, totally lovely duke's daughter?

He could not help but recognize Lord Blakely's woman. The two of them proving grist for the gossiping biddies since early summer, societal matrons either scandalized that the sinister Blakely was taking to wife such a nonpareil—the Heartsick Duke's innocent daughter—or envious down to their bunioned toes that their own offspring hadn't snared such an infamous catch. After all, not every marquis owned and actively managed a sex club.

The minx before him gave another huff. He thought he'd heard "cousin" bandied about. Made sense, because despite the difference in their height— and even considering this one had remained fully clothed—the two looked much alike.

Didn't want to think about the one before him in an unclothed state, but his mind couldn't help but veer that direction. He was a healthy, able-bodied male. One who had not indulged for quite some time. Penance, as it were, for losing the sole female currently under his care—or the one who *should* have been.

Now, 'twas his job to keep *this* female occupied, at the very least safe, until Blake's man returned. "If you stare any harder at that door behind me, you may just succeed in crumbling it to dust."

She blinked. Jerked her attention from the heavy wooden portal and met his gaze once again. With those piercing sky blues narrowed his direction he could practically *feel*—all the way across the twelve-foot expanse separating them—her illicit interest in the club activities taking place beyond this room.

What was her name again? Had they been introduced before? Some vague recollection of meeting her once, early in the season, niggled, but if he was a guilt-riddled lob now, he'd been a veritable wreck back then, still reeling over the knowledge that he was no more equipped to command the title now than he'd been when he'd inherited it years earlier.

"You are particularly bothersome," she stated, "standing there scowling at me without offering a single shred of usable information."

He laughed at that, the rusty sound startling his ears as much as his chest. As if he'd tell such an innocent details about the debauchery within.

"Really, Lord Tyndale. First you bruise my toes"— he had?—"and now you provide not one whit of scintillating conversation."

Good. Let her think him inane. Perhaps then she'd keep her distance. He had no interest in anything to do with females, not until he located the one who had disappeared on his watch.

And why are you in London and not still in the country —scouring it?

Because he had appearances to maintain, by damn. And had he not scoured, traipsed, questioned, yelled and nearly lost his mind—not to mention his horse when the poor beast went lame, after he pushed it too hard—searching for Thalia and clues to her disappearance along the route she was to have taken? He'd offered escort, had planned to retrieve her from where she'd gone after her days at the academy were over—some lowly servants job she remained close-tongued about. Only to receive her letter stating she had no hesitation traveling alone and—by the time he received it—was already on her way.

Guilt seized hold of his innards and *squeezed*. Threatened—

"Who are you here with tonight?" Annoyance persisted, finally pushing off the wall she'd been glued to and approaching him. "One of the people I saw on the stage?"

As if he'd answer that.

Stop flying bats in your belfry, hashing over the past. Concentrate on this *female.* This *responsibility.*

His fingers flexed, beyond restless. Not holding something stronger than port, as had been his wont the past few months. Not sketching. Not poring over reports sent from his man in the country—the one still searching. *Not caressing the pale, inviting skin or swept-back blonde hair of the delicate beauty before you? Or any of the others available behind The Door.*

He did snort then, at himself.

Seeking a distraction from his wayward, worrisome thoughts, he pulled out his timepiece. How long had Blakely's man been gone? Ten minutes? Fifteen? Seemed more like eighty. He repressed a sigh and pocketed the clock watch. Should not the American ruffian return soon? How long did it take to deposit one willing female to her destination of choice?

And what—besides the obvious—did Wylde see in this one? Tyndale tried to look at her with a critical eye. Although entirely too young to tempt any serious interest from his quarter, she really was a fetching thing.

Though way too interested in the lascivious goings-on behind him. She'd likely lead Wylde on a merry chase—not at all the sort of woman Tyndale planned to pursue as wife. Any female he chose would be much less given over to bravado and brazen impulses—unlike this one, braving this bastion of male entertainment without escort—and much more sedate and serious. Somber, even. No wild miss interested in earthly goings-on for him. No one he need worry over losing to curiosity or corruption.

What had befallen Thalia? Had either curiosity—or corruption, heaven forbid—tempted her along her journey? Land her so deep in suds she could not escape?

And why had he not unearthed a single hint of her trail?

"Have you already dallied?" the one before him asked, stunning him to further silence. When had she come so close? Without taking a step, he could reach out and nudge her back if he so chose. "Did you perform on stage already? Or just watch? Who did—"

The door at his back bumped open, propelling him straight into her and saving him the hassle of sputtering a reply.

Tyndale found his arms full of mettlesome, forthright female—and his backside thrust forward—until the mounds of her breasts meshed to his front made every manly part of him stand at attention despite his best intentions.

By damn, when would this night end?

5

THE DECEPTION BEGINS...

Grand idea, my shaking arse.

Not quite an hour later, Laney stood outside the stranger's door. Hesitating. Trembling in her bare feet. Not quite terrified—but nearly so—at how her latest visions had brought her to the point she'd dare such.

Her willing-wench disguise was in place, so why was it she felt more exposed than ever? Did she knock and go through with the outrageous scheme of securing a new owner? Or should she use the rare opportunity of Reginald being unconscious and *locked* in their room—she'd taken that precaution, lest he interrupt her desperate plan—and escape into the night?

Really, what was stopping her? Why did she not take Reginald's purse? Be gone in mere minutes.

The opportunity seemed too fortunate to let pass, so she turned, discounting the odd pang abandoning her plan with the intriguing stranger caused, ready to leave on her own. Depend on herself and no one—

Chills crept over her skin. A hundred hat pins poked her brain. A giant weight lodged in her stomach, one that had nothing to do with excitement and everything to do with fear. A shudder rolled through her, so strong she gripped the doorframe to remain upright.

"All right, perhaps not."

Shaking off the dread, she considered furthering her association with the stranger, hoping to entice him to help her, whatever means it took. At once, the nausea evaporated, the rioting hat pins settled and a sense of happy anticipation flooded her limbs, making her buoyant—in body and in spirit.

Heeding the intuition, she balled her fist and rapped her knuckles against the door.

If Mr. Surly Stranger wouldn't buy her outright, she'd become exactly what he needed in a female, for however long it took—until he *wanted* to own her. Until he couldn't wait to protect and keep her—at least until the vexing indenture expired.

It shouldn't be that hard to feign sexual experience, should it? Didn't men know what they wanted and simply...*take* it? Her free hand tightened around the neck of the liquor bottle Johnny had delivered. If Mr. Growling, Glowing Eyes drank enough to become boosey, mayhap he wouldn't notice she was a whore without any whoring credentials.

Bare toes tapping nervously on the floor, she knocked again.

Splashing sounded beyond the door.

He was still in the bath? *Still?* The skin between her

eyes pinched. The rat—when she'd made do with a bowl of tepid water and a quick scrub?

Shouldn't he be itching to go, excited and eager at having an agreeable female ready to satisfy his every need? Shouldn't he have opened the door at the first hint she'd arrived, swept her off her feet and onto the bed, and commenced to...fornicate with her?

The candle lighting this end of the hallway had been easy to snuff, so she stood in hazy darkness. But despite the constant low rumble of patrons from below, she knew she was very much alone.

A woman with limited resources had to make her own luck, gamble on the opportunities life tossed her way. One man wasn't any better or worse than any other as far as Laney was concerned. At least, that had been her thinking until being exposed to the real Reginald Tate, the one goaded by his brother. Now that she knew some men were worse than others, she needed to command her own destiny.

If anything, that erotic vision of having a man's head between her legs had given her *ideas*. Without allowing the time to worry herself sick, she knocked again—with more force, turning her knuckles so that the side of her hand pounded into the door.

The rough wood scraped skin usually gloved. 'Twas beyond odd, being out of her room and improperly dressed.

Improper? A fraught giggle-cackle nearly escaped. She was standing in a hallway, wearing her oldest shift and *nothing* else. Today's footwear becoming soggy and mud-clogged as the day went on and her extra slippers packed at the bottom of the trunk she didn't dare scavenge deeply for fear of waking Reginald. Though she had unearthed the latest perfume he'd given her—it had come to hand easily enough. Out of spite, she hadn't worn it yet, though tonight, however inane, she'd taken the time to dab it on.

Poised to either kick the blasted door down, bare feet or not, or retreat to her own room, she hit the door harder. Louder.

A single curse. Then a growled, "Come!"

"Calling me to heel like a dog," she muttered, unfurling her fist to turn the knob. Not even locked? She should have barged right in.

Night had fallen swiftly after the stormy day and blackness cloaked the room; more splashing came from the center. By feel, she shut the door, fumbled for a moment with the lock, then turned to rest her back against the stout wood.

"At yer service, m'lawd," she said, pitching her voice higher and using an exaggerated version of the speech she'd grown up with. If not for Mary Delilah, she wouldn't know any better. "Johnny said you was wantin' ta...spill yer seed betwixt me legs."

There. That sounded whorish enough. Didn't it?

He muttered, "God save me from stupid women," and she bit back a retort. More clearly, he added, "Candle must have burnt out. Fell asleep in the bath. I apologize. Long day."

"Mmm, a bath sounds 'eavenly." Laney didn't attempt to subdue the envy from her voice. "It surely does, m'lawd."

He sighed. "What's yet another hour?" he

murmured, then answered himself just as quickly. "More torture."

Abandoning the support of the door, she took a step into the room. "Will ye really let me soak? M'lawd?"

"You need not call me that. Light a candle and join me. The water's lost all heat, but there's room enough. You may wash me."

As if she should feel *honored* by the command.

For some strange reason, she did.

But would not giving a washing be commonplace, for a servant to do? Perhaps if she roused him till he was pitch-kettled, he wouldn't notice her maidenhead when he breached it.

"Well?" Now he sounded impatient. "We're not here for church work. Make haste, woman."

With the candle lit, he'd see all of her. But she'd see him too… How might *he* look undressed?

"Certainly, m'lawd, right 'way." Curiosity prompting her onward, she bustled about in the darkness, fumbling toward the bedside table, scrambling to light the taper once found. Fingers on the flint, she hesitated. Uncomfortable—or unwilling?—to reveal herself.

Her illusion of privacy was all she owned of herself these days.

Though in order to change her fate, she positively had to convince or charm—or coerce—*this* particular man to help her escape Reginald. And she would do it too, no matter what it took.

Despite this afternoon's cursed-blessed vision, she

couldn't fathom this brute ever loving anyone but himself. She certainly didn't expect to like him or admire anything about him, not with his coarse manners and commanding ways. In truth, she didn't care whether he liked her or not, so she certainly need not expose herself on every level the first time they were alone.

"Well?" he grumbled. "Hurry it up. Cold in here." Did he just upend a bottle? "Awake and all alone."

She heard him take another swallow, so aye, he had a bottle of his own. Had already been partaking of it sufficiently—if his falling asleep in the tub was any indication.

Brilliant. Just what she needed—to saddle herself with another drunk.

"Come now," he urged after another swig, "no need to act missish. Or coy. You'll not leave wearing anything but a smile."

"What do you mean by that?" The heat burning her cheeks made her think she knew, but she wanted to hear him state it plainly all the same. Had her visions conspired to land her a bed-braggart? Perhaps Fate hadn't chosen poorly for her first time after all...

"I don't take my fists to women. Not mean in bed," he explained with a slight growl, one that reminded her of all his brusque, high-handed ways. "But I *am* impatient—and growing more so. Light the candle and join me. Either get to it or leave. Send up the other."

That would never do. Best you please him posthaste.

"Close yer eyes. It'll be bright," she ordered, unable to resist the lure of seeing him naked. Holding the taper well away from her face, she lit it.

With a puff of flame and smoke, the wick flared to

life. She gasped. And just as quickly, doused the glow with her fingertips. "Gad*zooks*!"

Another splash. Followed by a thump. "What is it?"

"The, uh...candle burnt out," she lied, surprised by the sting assaulting her fingers—which was what she got for leaving them on the taper too long. Because in that brief flash, the picture became permanently etched in her mind.

The picture of his fierce mien subdued by recent slumber and no longer hidden by the wave of dark hair falling across his forehead...his smooth bare chest and shoulders sprinkled with droplets of water...his strong thighs extending beyond the tub, lightly furred with fine black hairs that grew thicker just before the water covered the view...

Mighty mercy. His was a formidable, provocative presence. One that reached out to her in ways she hadn't anticipated.

And she was playing a tavern doxy who had seen it all before.

Shaking off any lingering trepidation and swallowing the desire to relight the candle, Laney resolved to play the part she'd assigned herself. *You're his willing wench for the night; behave like it!*

Rocking her hips from side to side—forgetting for a moment he couldn't see her—she approached him. The whiskey delivered earlier swung heavily from her hand.

More splashing met her ears. "Well then, pull the curtain and open the shutters, would you? Dark as Hades in here and I can't find my drying cloth."

"Very well," she huffed. Abandoning her sensual

walk, she made her way around the tub, only touching his skin once—if the sizzle assaulting her fingertips was any indication—until she located the back wall. From there, 'twas an easy matter to shuffle along until encountering the curtain. And the surprising revelation behind it. "There isn't one."

Judging from the amount of sloshes and curses, he'd risen to his feet in the tub. "What do you mean there isn't one?"

Now she had to stifle a laugh. Had to bite her cheeks to keep from giggling. Wasn't it grand when life worked in one's favor? "It appears to be boarded up. The window, that is. M'lawd," she tacked on. Ugh, she had to remember to stay in character. "There's nothin' to open."

How much longer must he wait for a piece of puss?

Seemed the universe was punishing him for his treatment of his brother's woman. Nothing had gone his way since he'd escaped Blake's London townhouse.

At first, he'd thought that somehow the family curse had been avenged or submerged or something of the sort because after sharing Francine with Blake, Nash's body and spirit had never been so tranquil, not since turning twenty-five when the roiling curse business first made its appearance.

But in the moments following his release, peace quickly turned to remorse and then to penitence, and he'd bolted into the night rather than face either of them.

By now he knew: the curse had only been playing

with him. Taunting him with the brief respite. For tonight, his body felt anything but serene.

"When's the last time you bathed?" he asked the sweet-smelling wench. The pleasant fragrance had been absent earlier when they'd brought in his bath water; nor had it been present when the bold one delivered his whiskey, along with a wink, a few minutes later.

Alluring scent or not, he had an aversion to females who doused themselves in perfume to mask body stench. "You said you wanted a bath. Do you need one?"

At her indrawn breath, he swore at his inability to see as well as his brother. They both had senses more acute than any man outside of their family, but where his sense of smell outdistanced any bloodhound on the planet, Blake was the one who could see in the dark better than a hawk.

It didn't help that he'd been drinking the last hour, intentionally imbibing, hoping the liquor might dampen his desire and fog his brain. Apparently it deadened his olfactory and visionary capabilities as well—stifled his ability to sniff, blunted his ability to behold.

Because her outline greeted his acute eyesight, the pale shift swaying against the wall, and she smelled better than a wench should, but that was it. Naught else. Seemed, though, that he didn't need any more— the moment she'd edged past the tub, his liquor-and-slumber-relaxed cock had jumped to attention and protested further delay.

Hell, if he'd known his body was going to respond

so lustfully, he wouldn't have groggified his mind with drink.

"Well?" he demanded when she remained silent, still unwilling to fuck a filthy strumpet, no matter how aromatically alluring.

"I bathed this morning. Sponged off this eve."

He stepped from the tub. "Good. Then you can dry me."

Two steps later he swept her off her feet, ignored her cry of surprise and smiled when her arms curled around his neck. Finally!

He tumbled back onto the bed, ready for his fill of warm, willing wench.

Something hard hit him on the back of the head. "Damnation!"

Now he could see. Clearly.

Spots. Bright ones that flashed before his eyes as pain cut through his skull.

If he hadn't already imbibed enough to dull at least some of his senses, he would have howled at the unexpected blow. "By the blazes, what are you trying to do? Kill me before I come?"

WHEN HE GROWLED IN AGONY, the bottle fell from Laney's fingers. It hit the floor with a thump and rolled under the bed.

"I'm so sorry!" She scrambled over him, tugging her shift out of the way when it caught beneath her knees.

Straddling his chest, she leaned forward and combed her fingers through his hair, searching for blood or a bump.

"Ow!"

She'd found it, just behind his left ear. A tender area that would likely knot bigger than a duck's egg by morning.

As she stroked over the spot, he gave another groan, but this one wasn't caused by a crack on the head. Nay, it appeared to be from another pain indeed as her fingers caressed his scalp, played with the shell of his ear and greeted what must be the softest hair in all of England. Soft, silky, and sapping any sane thought as she not only forgot about the part of prostitute she was playing, she forgot to breathe.

His hands found their way to her thighs. He pushed her shift up and anchored his palms above her knees—where no man had ventured before.

Laney wasn't even sure *she'd* touched herself there... she knew she hadn't when he groaned again and moved those long, searching fingers inward, toward her center. Her feminine muscles clenched, her pelvis rocked forward and—*mercy me*—she was riding his bare chest... His lightly furred, soft yet strong chest.

Wait. She hadn't noticed any hair there before.

Maybe she just hadn't been close enough. But she was close enough now.

Close enough to inhale his outdoorsy, hint-of-the-wild scent, close enough to feel every single strand of hair that whispered beneath her naked hands, close enough to hear the low growl of satisfaction he made just when his fingers encountered *her* curls.

Her breath returned in a whoosh and his hair slipped free.

"Come here," he practically purred.

What did he mean? Oh! Her vision. So he *did* like to put his face between her legs. She practically dripped at the thought, at the remembered sensations he'd created when he touched her there in the gazebo. "Mmm."

Her body creamed in readiness. She tried to scoot forward but only ended up dragging her damp flesh across his chest hairs. "*Ahhh.*"

She wound her fingers in his long hair again and moved against him, using her knees for leverage. Once more, she rubbed along his chest, encouraging her inner lips to separate, allowing the most intimate part of her body to glide sleekly over the hard muscle of his.

Her toes tingled. Her bits quivered. She pulled harder on his hair, afraid to speak, unsure what else to do. Shouldn't he be taking command by now?

She thrummed in readiness, ached at his slowness.

Wasn't he supposed to yank her legs apart and force his cock between as Reginald had tried? Why did the notion *not* fill her with dread? But only longing instead?

His fingers tightened on the skin of her inner thighs, then he removed one hand and pushed at her chest, angling her away. She released his hair on a moan and used both arms to brace herself as she leaned backward and stared up at the ceiling, blinking in the blackness, in alt and practically panting with the surety of what came next.

But he thwarted her. Did nothing other than level the intense gaze she swore sizzled her innards, but naught else.

The perplexing fiend's slow progress only frustrated her body; enraged the anxious worry that had hounded her for hours.

How could she convince him to help her if he didn't *take* her?

His lackadaisical pace most assuredly did *not* fit with her plans of seduction—hers—leading to salvation—also hers.

She hadn't expected to want his touch, to ache for it, by heavens. Nay, he was supposed to slake his lust, fall asleep satisfied, then wake ready to help her. Eager, if not downright pleased, to come to her aid.

In contrast to the pressing need that increased every second, his gossamer strokes barely whispered across her flesh as he gave a low growl.

"Touch me more," she ordered on a light gasp. "Harder." *Please.*

"Not yet." His low rumble tumbled straight past her heart and into her belly. Bounced around until she couldn't decide if 'twas arousal or anticipation or anxiety that held her in such thrall.

"Ah yes, my finely fragranced wench, just like that," he whispered gruffly when she lunged toward his mouth. Then he swiped several fingers down the seam of her muff.

She flinched, then shifted, trying to venture closer.

He touched her again. Lightly. Then again. Still not enough. Her patience snapped and years of ladylike training fled. "You dallyin' cur, 'tis time for you ta join our giblets!"

The darkness filled with his deep laughter. "Time for a taste, I do believe."

"You soddin' beard splitter. Get on with it—touch

me harder." Just when she brought one hand to her cleft, he yanked her the rest of the way up his body.

She landed on her back—his warm erection snugged firmly beneath her.

But she didn't have time to think about how hot and inviting *he* was, how he'd gotten her shift damp everywhere they'd touched, how his muscled thighs flexed beneath her... She didn't have time to think about any of those things because he was working his way up her crease, plying fingers and tongue over folds and flesh... and making her *burn*.

"Hail Mary," she whispered. Mary, her friend—not the Mother Mary—because the one topic Mary Delilah never taught Laney about was sex. Despite how many times she'd asked. Full of nimble-tongued eloquence on every other subject under the sun, Mary Delilah was reticent about sex.

But based on the way the stranger licked up and down her slit, thrust his tongue deep and swallowed loudly, growled his satisfaction, brought his hands between her legs and spread her open even more, this wasn't something she needed to learn over tea and crumpets.

This was something one only learned by *doing*. Or better yet, *enjoying*.

She stopped thinking about her past, forgot about her future and settled in for the most delightful ride between the body and tongue of her irascible stranger.

NASH EDGED his fingers over her warm affair, gathering the thick dew trickling from her like a mountain spring.

He brought one hand to his lips and licked, startled at the abrasiveness. Dash it, no reason for his tongue to be rough. Not yet. Hell. If The Change brimmed that close, better come soon. Else his cells would alter to the point he couldn't contain his feral lust. Wouldn't be responsible for his actions. *Should* be, but impossible to care about what one couldn't control, fought to remember...

A quick fuck. A swift grind. That was all he'd wanted. All he'd needed tonight. A fast release. Prigging a wench to erase the compulsion to Change, to succumb to the beast.

To obliterate impossible interest in veiled creatures.

Aye, that too, damn his itching hide.

For ceaseless hours, despite his efforts to deny it, his mind had been plagued with the idea of the pig princess scratching his itch.

So why was it the intoxicating scent of the tavern wench's desire went to his head more than the whiskey? Why did it seem as if he'd caught her scent before...savored her flavor on his lips?

He'd never been to this inn. Hadn't crossed this way.

How could someone with such an unremarkable, bordering on annoying, voice taste—*smell*—like ambrosia?

Nash thrust upward, forcing his cock along her spine, up between her shoulder blades.

He groaned.

His teeth and nails tingled. By the blazes. He'd sworn he wouldn't let it go this far again. Not after

Francine had driven his brother to the point of lunacy —or lionhood—when he'd avoided taking her once The Change had come upon them, causing Nash to lose his own self-mastery more than ever before.

But Lucifer's balls, just the taste of the female at his lips was enough to make him long for patience, pray for control. He released her thighs and bracketed her waist, pulling her sweet treasure flush against his mouth.

His tongue dove inside and he swallowed, drinking down what poured easily from her.

Had he ever tasted nectar this pure?

Her squeal penetrated his passion-soaked brain as she bucked against his mouth. He dug his fingers in, held her still, and angled his tongue high, searching out the tiny pearl hidden in her folds.

One flick, two—and she recoiled, dragging that cunny burrow of hers over his whiskered jaw and keening her pleasure to the heavens.

"God-dem, doll. That was quick." Nash licked his lips, wiped his chin, then licked his hand clean, one delicious finger at a time. "You're a fast one, aren't you?"

That squeal of hers echoed around them both, invading his blood, his cells, and causing his cock to harden further.

Almost sorry it was over so soon, but knowing he'd dallied longer than was prudent, he didn't try to stem the growl rumbling low in his throat. He was past ready, and since he'd done the gentlemanly thing for once—see? he wasn't *always* a selfish bastard—and given her pleasure first, it was time for his own demmed orgasm.

That or he refused to be held responsible for the consequences. Ah hell. And that only made him think of Phineas.

"That's...it?" the warm bundle on his chest asked.

"Not bloody likely," he snarled, suddenly mad at himself, at her. At his misbegotten life. "You'll not be earning your coins that easily."

"What?"

"*Shhht!*" Irritated now, Nash pushed her off, but kept her from leaving the bed by shackling one hand around her wrist. He climbed to his knees and forced her facedown beneath him.

"What are you doin'?" she shrieked into the mattress.

He smiled grimly. She'd find out soon enough.

The wench tried to rise but he contained her efforts with a hand to her upper back. "Stay put."

"But I—"

"You had yours, now it's my turn." With an impatient grunt, Nash searched in the dark until both hands had a firm hold on her shift. Matching actions to the ferocious beating of his heart, he pierced the thin material with his nails and easily ripped it apart.

"What're ya doin', you stupid whoreson?"

"Quit screeching. There'll be another coin in it for you."

Like a bloody trained mule, his hand returned to her back—now *bare*—and used the excuse of holding her down to fam her up.

Nash gripped his erection with his opposite hand. Holy hell, he was hard. He'd waited too prigging long.

The Change loomed closer, racing along his veins,

approaching the surface. He clamped down on his eager rod.

He hadn't watched the time. Had let too many hours pass...but still, he shouldn't be bordering the edge *now*... It made no sense, but then nothing had since learning that his brother—his independent, didn't-need-anybody and wouldn't-let-anyone-close brother—had *fallen in love*.

And with a true, genteel lady at that.

The kind of female Nash secretly longed for despite her being well beyond his reach. At least Blake had the title, the distinction of being a marquis, to go along with the curse.

What did Nash have?

A stinkin' plot of land somewhere in the north, gifted to him by Blake, that he hadn't cared enough to visit, much less inspect or oversee.

A habit of never sleeping in the same bed twice, never staying put or allowing himself to become close to anyone, because what bloody good would it do him?

And a rigid cock that wanted nothing more than to split the slit of the wench beneath him and take its pleasure *inside her body*.

But he couldn't even do that, now, could he? Nash gripped his pipe so hard he almost squeezed the semen right out. Of course he couldn't, not with the very real possibility of siring a helpless bastard, one condemned to endure the curse just as Nash and Blake did. Just as Phineas and the other afflicted kinsmen he didn't bother to consider because for him, it always came down to one...

Poor, lost Phineas.

The familiar thoughts of self-pity should have dimmed his desire to take his pleasure whilst seated inside her. They always had before. Instead, thinking how hopeless things remained only made him want to savor this particular female more.

Things are never hopeless, some unforeseen angel prompted.

Or maybe 'twas the devil.

Blake found someone, did he not? You can too. Go on, why don't you take your bliss inside her body? Claim her as your own? Thoroughly. In her hot, tight little cu—

He stomped out that direction of temptation. But it kept returning, taunting him...

Pretend you're her first...that she's your very own "lady".

Why don't you? Why don't you just—

"Because I damn well don't deserve it!" Nash squeezed his shaft harder. If he closed his fist around it tight enough, might it explode? Or shatter?

Silence the devil's impossible chatter?

God help him. It'd been an interminable, utterly exhausting week: traveling to London to find Blake in such a ramshackle state. Doing all he could to salvage his brother's sanity whilst fighting the beast himself.

Battling his past as well.

The physical turmoil made a thousand times worse by the emotional: the anniversary of losing Phineas. The reminders of his father's death.

His mother's abandonment.

His own worthless carcass...contributing to Phin's loss.

And Nash not being enough to keep his mother from leaving—

The familiar agony of that clamored for dominance but the fine-smelling, foul-sounding wench beneath him struggled to bring him back. Struggled against him.

Nash stroked his length, fast, furious actions meant to tame but ones that only inflamed. He couldn't come. Had to wait. But, oh God, her skin was soft...

"Don't deserve what?" she questioned, writhing beneath his restraining hand, attempting to roll over. He refused to let her.

So close. His orgasm was so close to the surface. Just a little more and...and... His hand moved faster.

Dem him! He had to calm down, couldn't spill his seed without the touch of a woman. It'd be useless. The compulsion to change wouldn't abate. He'd need to tup her again in order to stop it. As it was, he didn't have the god-dem restraint to go through this again. Not tonight.

He willed his hand to slow, willed his cock to relax.

'Twas like commanding the sun to stop shining.

"Deserve what? Should you not be—" the bit of prime protested again.

Didn't she know any better? He gripped the back of her neck and cinched his fingers, hoping to shut her up. Couldn't she tell he was struggling?

She reared up beneath him. "I thought you—"

"Shut the hell up, bi—*wench*," he barely stopped himself from calling her a bitch. "Don't want to hurt you."

He ignored her whimper and released his throbbing cock, groping in the darkness until he pulled the torn sides of her shift away from her arse.

When she kept fighting to sit up and twist around, he wound his fingers in her hair, tugging hard enough to let her know who was in charge. "Lady, I'm paying for the privilege. I took care of you, so quit—"

"But you didn't—"

"*Complaining!*" he roared.

Thank God she heeded him and finally shut her box. Stilled her struggles. Moaned her compliance.

Troublesome wench. Just because she was clean, her scent divine and her sweet little tuft tasted better than fine cognac was no reason for her to go and act all uppish.

She was just a paid whore after all.

It wasn't as if *she* were a lady. As though he had any cause to feel guilty for being so harsh with her. He still shouldered enough guilt from the debacle with Francine. Didn't need any more from a nameless, faceless wench in the dark.

Hers was just a body. Nothing more. Anyone's would have done.

But he had hers right where he wanted it. Lying prone between his knees. Under his power. Bought and paid for. His for the moment. Or as long as he chose to keep her. Maybe for the night.

His hand tracked across her arse, dipping in between her legs where he smeared her cream along her crack.

Dash it. How her scent beckoned. Her sweet, soft skin... Nash shuddered. His entire body quaked. She'd reduced him to this?

Impossible.

Wasn't her. Couldn't be. It was The Change.

Exhausted from holding back, he positioned himself over her, covered her spine with his chest, her arse with his groin. Nudged his thighs along hers...and sank down, wedging his cock between the glorious globes of her buttocks. Wished he could see the sight—his hard body atop her pliant, curved one—but at the moment, *feeling* was just as good.

He couldn't stop his sigh of relief at the friction of her plump bottom against his flesh...the heat rubbing against her brought roaring along his cock. Moist heat. Her sex juices surrounding him. Slicking his straining erection.

His mouth watered. Tongue probed behind his teeth. He wanted another taste.

Her murmured, "Mmmm...?" was a distraction. Why did her voice develop such an enticing lilt when she wasn't speaking words?

"That's it, doll," he returned, sliding along her arse.

Finally, *finally*, she allowed herself to relax and sink into the straw mattress. Her moan vibrated through them both when she arched her backside into his groin, eliciting a grunt as pure satisfaction wound through him.

He'd made it in time. The beast wouldn't win. Not tonight.

So he could make the next few seconds even better.

Stretching out, he aligned his legs over hers, tucking his feet around her dainty ones, blanketing her entire form. He rocked his hips in earnest, wedging his cock deeper along the crevice of her arse. Driving forward. Again and again.

He wound his left arm along hers and grasped her

hand, threaded their fingers. But instead of doing the same with his right, he wrapped it around her torso, scooted his palm between her sweat-dampened body and the mattress and slid his hand low until his fingers dove through the curls between her legs, parting the flesh below and sliding inside just enough to gather the thick honey waiting there. For him.

Pumping his hips faster, he curved his fingers inward, harvesting her essence. Then he pulled them free and swiftly brought his hand to his mouth.

Thrust. Lick.

Pump. Lick.

Thrust. *Thrust. Thrust! Lick and swipe and suck...*

And release...

"Uhhh."

His cock lurched along her butt and up part of her back as his mouth sucked his longest finger deep and he savored every bit of her he could salvage and poured out his climax...

Nash grunted like an animal while he came.

And for once, he didn't give a damn.

THE STRANGER'S feral shout caressed Laney's ears just as his release erupted along the skin of her back.

With every ripple of his body along hers, his warm seed spread over her skin. When he stilled, he tightened his arms around her and shifted, rolling to his side and bringing her and the remnants of her shift with him. The pseudo night rail was still on her arms, covering her entire front, but it was ruined now. Useless to wear under her dresses if it wouldn't fasten.

She waited, expecting him to toss her a coin and toss her off the bed.

So that's all there was? A disappointed hitch lodged somewhere in the vicinity of her heart—and sank lower. Just this vague unfulfilled yearning between her thighs? Why, *why* hadn't he finished inside her...*there*? That had been the entire purpose, had it not?

She clenched her thighs, the fingers he'd wound within his, unaccountably frustrated. Her woman's mound ached and rejoiced at the same time. His lips— his tongue!—had kissed between her legs and her body responded deep inside...a strange, rising pinnacle, one that told her she was about to experience what made the sex act enjoyable instead of simply endured. But then he'd stopped. *Stopped.* Completely withdrawn his tongue and touch.

Should she not have yelled out?

Maybe paid whores were supposed to remain silent? But how could she control her cry of delight when his tongue started bathing the weeping flesh between her legs? When embarrassment evolved into enjoyment and then amazement...

How his mouth felt so...so...miraculous.

Like her visions. They were miracles, Grandmama had told her, a gift from God.

And look what kind of trouble she'd landed herself into this time, paying attention to those so-called miracles! With a slumbering-snoring Reginald in the next room; with her naked, alone with the intense stranger, her body aching and yearning and... *Aching*, dash him!

Her clenched teeth nearly squeaked. He still had not relaxed his arms, given her leave to...*leave*. How much longer must she wait for him to dismiss her? Or perhaps, to push her to her back and plow inside her? To rut with her like a dog in heat—for that's what she'd expected from one with such coarse manners.

His breath sighed across her cheek. A faint exhalation of utter satisfaction, or so it sounded.

Certainly, for he'd *finished*, now, hadn't he?

Still peeved, it took her a moment to realize that he'd loosened his top arm from around her waist and slid his spread palm up her stomach—which contracted—past her breasts—which protested—over her throat—which tingled—stopping only when he reached her chin.

Still as a stone undergoing silent seduction, she waited once more.

One long finger separated itself from the pack and began to trace the contours of her jaw. His touch feathered over her cheekbone and across the arch of first one eyebrow and then the next, the caress so unexpectedly delicate, how was it she now tingled clear to her toes?

She barely breathed, willing him to continue.

"Tell me why you're here." The words rasped across her ear and an involuntarily spasm shook her soul. "Right here. Now."

Did he know? Was he about to explode and take her in anger? Was the gentle, soothing touch now cascading down her temple only a prelude to something vicious?

But how could it be when the sensual journey of his finger continued...tracing down her nose, the little divot above her lips...

"Tell me."

"'Ere? With you, you mean?" She stumbled over her reply, barely recalling in time to mask her voice as the pressure of his stroking finger remained as light as down, skimming over her quivering mouth. "Why, m'lawd, you tol' Johnny that you wanted—"

"Shhh." His touch settled more firmly upon her, stilling her response. "Not that," he continued, and his fingers began to move again, this time tracing the width of her lips, pausing at the corners, making her mouth dry up and her loins sweat. "Not that. *Here*. In this town, this inn. How did you come to be here at The Black Boar?"

I took the same stage as you, you dolt, she almost told the dull swift, but speech required too much effort. Easier to stay silent, enjoying the shivers careening from her stomach to her thighs, shivers created by his unanticipated exploration of her face...her neck.

She swallowed. Gracious, her throat had gone tight.

He tensed and the muscles of his chest rippled along her bare back. "Answer me. What brings a woman to a place like this? How long have you been here? *Why* do you stay?"

Clueless how to respond to such questions, she made a noncommittal murmur.

The arm around her waist tightened. "Circumstances? Desire? Do you choose to be here? I want to know, truly."

Need to know, she sensed.

"You're a most perplexin' man," she finally gave voice to her turbulent thoughts, gulping when his searching finger trailed down her neck, skidded past her collarbone and began that same slow, torturous journey over and around her covered breasts. Wispy tracks of his fingers that left streaks of fire in their wake and made her aware of the gaping hole in her heart.

Who knew men could touch like this? Who would have thought *he* would?

Why hadn't she let him rip her shift off when he'd tried? Why hadn't he just bought her dratted indenture when she'd asked?

Frustrated with herself, frustrated with him for leaving her *wanting*, she contemplated how to respond. Under the cover of night, in his warm embrace, 'twas easy to move past the customary veil that protected her every day from the outside, unknown world. "I believe I am here, in this place, at this time, simply because of fate, I suppose. Circumstance, I would say. My family..." How much of the truth did she want to reveal? "My family is gone, the ones who cared about me, certainly, and ..."

She'd forgotten her accent. Egad! She had to remember to play the role he'd expect. How hard could it be when she'd grown up not knowing any better? Tavern wenches wouldn't discuss their families with paying partners.

"I have come to realize *learnt*, I mean—that..." She trailed off, doubtful he was really listening. Knowing her answers didn't matter.

"Go on," he encouraged, and those amazing tingle-provoking fingers worked their way to her beaded nipple to dance around it. His nails snagged against the fine fabric, dragging it across her breast. Her inner workings clenched tight. How she wished he was dancing around down *there* again, between her legs.

Who knew thighs that felt so *wet*, could also blaze so fiery hot?

"Mmmm. Well...I 'ave been on my own fer a time, m'lawd, and that state suits me fine." There. She sounded prosaic enough, didn't she? Did tavern wenches even do prosaic? "I'm just muddlin' my way through to the end, best I know how."

Her abdomen arched forward as if seeking his touch, the slickness between her thighs encouraging her to brave asking for—

"And what do you think will meet us there?" he queried, and she never would have known by the seriousness of his tone that his fingers had just isolated her nipple right through the fabric, were pinching and plucking at the knot, encouraging it to tighten and harden. As if the nub needed any further encouragement.

"What awaits us at the end, do you think?" he continued—both his question and his nipple torture. "Heaven? Hell? *Nothing*? What do you believe in?" He released her aching nipple—without having fully satisfied her there either, drat him—and brushed his broad palm down her side, stopping only when he reached the bunched edges of her shift. He settled his hand firmly at her waist. But went no further.

She whimpered at the loss, struggling to form a coherent reply. The curiosity in his whispered question was unmistakable. As was the pain.

What manner of secrets burdened the irascible

stranger to such a point that he'd pose such weighty questions to a one-time bedmate?

Or did he challenge every wench who warmed his bed with such ponderous things?

"I don't know if I believe in 'eaven or in 'ell," she told him honestly, her mind whirling. How could she be having such a discussion with anyone? Especially with the scoundrel who'd stepped on her hem mere hours ago... "Maybe I'm in heaven right now," she mused, stretching her legs and tangling them with his, loving the slight hair-roughened texture of his masculine form against hers. "Maybe this is all there truly is—stolen moments in life that bring pleasure and happiness to one's soul...and flesh."

He grunted and tightened his fingers against her waist, and she held her breath. *Now. Now he'll flip me over and take me. Ease this throbbing, this ache created by his wicked, welcome touch—*

But nay...

He grunted again, lighter this time, longer. His hand went slack. Warm breath breezed past her cheek, tinted with spirits.

Her heart sank straight to hell.

Bothersome bloomin' buffoon! Her cunny cursed its empty state and she had to bite both lips to keep from upewing complaints like a fishwife.

The blasted fiend had fallen asleep!

6

THE PIG AND THE PRINCESS

———◆———

"Aye, folks, I do believe the rain 'as moved off durin' the night," the coachman chimed out as Nash climbed inside the cramped interior early the next morning, the words belied by the grey clouds hovering overhead.

Head aching from too much liquor, too little sleep and the knot the blame wench had cracked into his cannister, he had to restrain the impulse to clout the loudmouthed driver in his chops. Hell, even roosters weren't up this demmed early.

And why are you? Why are you still traveling on this stage? If you care not where you end up, then should it not matter how you get there?

Ignoring the uncomfortable prodding, he slouched in his corner after clearing his throat once to vacate the goose-carrying youth who dared to sit there. The kid scrambled to the middle of the cramped bench, honking goose and all.

Because despite his plans of the evening before—before the bath, before the wench—of lazing about and embarking later, here he was, claiming his spot on this particular stage once again, unwilling to relinquish his erstwhile traveling companions just yet...

"I'm told that just a 'air north, the roads are dry as week-old biskits," the coachman continued. "I 'spect we'll be makin' good time. Keepin' our stops to bare bones."

Bare. Like her supple skin. Skin he'd traced in the dark as a blind man might.

Bones. Like those delicate protrusions he'd mapped along her spine, on the front of her hips, beneath her breasts.

His head ached anew at the reminders.

Never fuck facing forward.

That was his motto. Creed to live by. Kept him from becoming too close, too tempted by any female.

The reminder made him wince. Sharing a wench with Blake was one thing; with three—or more—bodies involved, Nash could relax and partake of whatever felt good or struck his fancy. Certainly no chance of becoming overly attached to any one woman in *that* sort of scenario.

But with a lone female?

"Rules," he muttered, miffed at himself all over again. "Mind the rules. *My life shall all be done by the rule.*"

Look at how minding rules turned out for Anthony.

Bah.

Never fuck face-to-face.

He was an animal and he deserved to fornicate like one.

So why couldn't he shake the memory, however vague, of licking last night's wench from the front? Of nuzzling his nose in the downy curls above her slit?

And why, as God as his witness—a God who should just strike him down and be done with it—couldn't Nash shake the desire to bring the veiled jade now sitting so stiffly across the stagecoach, over the narrow aisle and into his arms? Why couldn't he stop imagining how he'd toss her ugly hat out the window, toss her skirts over her head and prig her senseless until neither one of them could stand?

Doomed.

He was doomed.

Doomed to stare at her, glower at the man with her. Doomed to contemplate what brought three such dissimilar individuals into such close proximity and how soon could he increase the distance.

"No one's gettin' down till we stop fer the midday meal," the driver hollered through the door as he put up the steps and secured it. Behind him, lightning forked across the sky.

"But, sir!" the goose-holding youth cried. "Me mam's waitin' at th' bend near—"

"Stifle it," Nash told the kid with a slash of his arm. "He's gone. Already up in his seat."

"But me mam—"

"Will have to wait. Why aren't you riding up top?" *Instead of letting your Christmas goose—in August—peck my pantaloons?*

"Mam said I'd be safer inside."

"If you keep your comments and your goose to yourself, you just might." It was a strain to keep the snarl to a minimum.

Enforced captivity.

Nash smothered a growl.

Ever since *she* sat down, the princess had been squirming. Demmed if he didn't smell her desire. Made his nostrils flare and his temper burn. How could her bits be inflamed by the jackanapes next to her? 'Twas beyond him.

A whip cracked overhead. The goose honked in his ear. The horses jolted forward.

They were off. Finally. What he wouldn't give to be loping alongside the steeds. Giving his legs and his lungs the freedom they craved.

Giving his brain and his honked-in ear a rest. Giving his nose a breather.

Away from the stench of her arousal.

Though anything was better than the fear he'd caught radiating off her yesterday.

This morning, fear was gone.

Replaced by desire so acute Nash half wished he'd foregone his own relief last night, changed into a furry beast and broke down the door to her room.

He would have seen her without the veil. Seen just how Molly Boy took her. Lodged his fangs around her nape and dragged her off. So *he* could play king of the jungle to her princess.

The family curse had finally done it—pushed him over the edge.

He'd turned into his demmed grandfather after all, a man without thought or care for anyone but himself. The bastard was to blame for the intolerable situation he'd condemned every one of his male descendents to endure. Pity, was it not, that one of those African lions hadn't sunk their teeth into his grandfather's neck and ripped it out? Left the old man bleeding to death on the savanna. Oh… yes. They had. Pity Grandfather had been rescued and healed. The old man should have been left to rot.

Since when are you so bloodthirsty?

Since Blake found true love? Or perhaps since a demmed pig and her dandy took the coach?

Her personal fragrance kept wafting past his nose. The alluring scent making flashes of last night's wench come to mind. The parts he remembered. Some of it was a blur. It happened like that whenever The Change got too close—made reality and the memory of his actions recede.

Self-preservation possibly?

The whiskey likely didn't help either.

So where was his foggy brain this morning when, with every swish of her shoulders, every flick of her gloved hand, something about her kept niggling the back of his brainbox?

She smoothed out her skirts, rearranged her dainty feet.

Her scent slammed into him so strongly his upper body staggered back. He *had* to be imagining things. That or completely losing his mind.

Because for one brief second, he entertained the idea that *she* was the wench who had come to his room, sweetly scented and eager—

Then she gave a sniff of disapproval, aimed his

direction—or so he perceived. Next she patted the arm of the redheaded fop as she took care to place his pompous hat firmly on her lap—a different one today, but no less expensive-looking. The entire time she kept her veiled face averted from Nash's. As if simply looking at him through that bloody netting would corrupt her person.

Love not a gaping pig.

Shakespeare's Shylock had that right and Nash better remember it. *Love not...*

His nails twitched. Just once, 'twould be such a relief to allow himself the luxury of Changing. Teeth to fangs. Skin to fur. Nails to claws.

He'd claw that horrid hat right off her head. Claw the honking goose right out the window.

Demmed female!

'Twas going to be an interminably long day. All because of her and her hoity-toity ways. Her dandified drunk of a man who *owned* what Nash inexplicably had started to crave—her touch. Her attention.

You are cracked.

Aye, he was.

And you're going to allow a few clouds to keep you cooped up in here? Next to goose flesh that should be warming your belly and across from downy flesh that's more than addled your senses?

Climb up top, mun. Clear the air and your nose before you succumb. Love not a gaping pig.

And then, bloody hell—as if the heavens punished him for existing—it started to rain again.

His cock insisted it was going to be a hard day as well. Excruciatingly hard.

She made a little mew of a cough, one that caused the veil to quiver in front of her face. Then those gloved fingers began tapping the brim of the beaver just as her slippered feet began tapping against the coach floor.

Without thought, he scooted his leg forward and trapped one of her bobbing feet between the side of the coach and his booted foot.

She tried to yank it free and he only pressed harder. Rain pummeled the coach.

She huffed, attempted again to free her foot, then finally gave up with a sigh that shimmered the veil, relaxing her struggles and remaining pliantly, silently, trapped by his efforts.

The growl he'd been trying to subdue for minutes turned into a purr of satisfaction. He crossed his arms, wedged deeper into *his* corner and feigned sleep.

Then he set his mind to the task of conjuring as many words as possible from the letters P-I-G-P-R-I-N-C-E-S-S.

A QUANDARY. That's what Mary Delilah would term Laney's current predicament. A *vexatious quandary*.

A refined vocabulary and polished manners, however, were far from sufficient to see her out of *this* predicament.

Ever since being passed off from one unreceptive relative to another, until finally landing in the lap of the aunt who sold her, Laney had realized that acceding with others' wishes proved easier than voicing what she truly wanted.

When a person didn't complain, didn't speak opposing thoughts—no matter how much they might think them—other people tended to overlook them, not take much notice.

Being overlooked—meekness, one might call it— proved a beneficial trait to cultivate, she'd learned, especially since reaching the point in her life where she no longer *wanted* people to notice her.

Men specifically. Ones like George John, who leered when they looked, pinched when they passed.

Much as *he* was doing now from across the coach. The leering, not the pinching. Only the heated lust she fancied gleamed from her stranger's eyes didn't make her want to duck and cower. On the contrary, after last night, she wanted to preen and crow.

Crow?

For what? His *cock*?

She stifled a smile at that admission. True though it might be, "ladies" weren't supposed to think such words.

Ah, but she was playing a *mistress*. Ergo, she could think them all she wanted.

Behind the safety of her veil, she allowed a grin to bloom across her face.

Allowed her inquisitive nature free rein...

What might his cock look like?

Only having Mr. Tate's limp member to compare, she was at a loss. Oh, but she was curious. Vastly so.

She'd seen erect stallions, mating dogs and sheep, but

not a *man's* solid erection before he mated with a woman. Not the way nature intended them (aged muzzy-headed souse pots lolling in mews didn't count). And though she'd certainly felt one last night, she still hadn't *seen* it…

As if aware of her secret thoughts, the particular man across from her flattened his lips, furrowed his brow and scowled.

Curiosity, once roused, was difficult to contain. Because regardless of how often he disavowed any interest in her or her indenture, she couldn't stop imagining how wondrous it would be for her vision to come true—to have his *love*.

Neither could she stop imagining how *his* penis might appear when aroused.

Penis, pecker, prick. Hair-splitter, bum-tickler. Sugar stick. She'd heard them all by the time she was thirteen. Heard them, but hadn't seen them. Nary a one. Until Mr. Tate's.

And that thought cured her curiosity faster than the rain dripped in through the crack in the door.

Until the next time she caught the stranger contemplating her hat.

And once again her rebellious mind was off, contemplating his cock.

Nip. Pips. Sire. Gin.

Gin. Now that was a good one.

Rip. Sip. Ring. Sing. Ping. Pipe. Sin.

Sin? Nash barely avoided wincing.

Was his brain trying to tell him something?

If he didn't *nip* this little fascination in the bud, he was sure to *sip* some *gin*, commit a *sin*, and *sire* a babe. That would surely put a *ring* in his nose.

Maybe one on her finger.

Damnation!

Might as well hit his topper with a *pipe*. Make his noggin *ping*.

Ping! *Ping!*

Bloody hell. What was he doing?

THIRTY-THREE MINUTES ELAPSED...

PIE. Pies. Sir. Sirs.

Too easy. Time for some more complicated pondering. Of the multiple-letter sort.

Rig. Rigs.

Just getting started.

Rein. Reins. Reign.

Hmm. Nash rolled his shoulders, stretching both body and brain.

If he could *reign* over The Change, maybe buy a *rig*, some horses to *rein*...

Peg. Pine. Pier. Pen. Pin. Pigpen. Piss. Pisser. Pier.

Pier? Wait. Already done. *Concentrate, man.* More letters...

Pierce. Piercing. Price. Prince. *Penis.*

Well, bat him straight to hell because now all he could think of was playing *prince* to her princess, *piercing* her *pisser* with his *penis* and wallowing in a fiery *pigpen* in lieu of the pits of hell. Someone should peg his *penis* to a *pier*. With a *pine pin*.

Is that the *price* he paid for his continued mental meanderings? Pointless pontifications?

What was *the price for indentures?*

Eighty-seven minutes after that...

Prise. Ripe. Inspire.

Spice. Spine. Siren.

He'd wager half the gold in his boot her *ripe* breasts were worthy of any *siren's. Spicy* (he allowed himself this small modification) to the lips.

More *inspiring* (this one too... He was beyond desperate; couldn't set his mind on anything else. Perhaps this is what came of having one's penis pinned to a pier with a pine peg?) than the *prise*-worthy *spine* of last night's wench.

He cringed, searching for salvation. His poor, beleaguered brain mired in the unceasing swamp of syllables and seduction...

Vowels! He hadn't yet exhausted vowels.

Ice. Ire. Iris. Epic.

Mayhap, if there were a God, the goose would lean over and peck out his eye. Eat his *iris*.

His besieged brain tracked backward. Cringed.

Cringe. And yet another one for the ever-growing *epic* list...

"Nipper!"

. . .

THE STRANGER SNAPPED his fingers and muttered under his breath. All morning, Laney had suffered through his unintelligible prattle.

Epic cringes being the most recent utterances.

They'd just stopped for their third team and now jangled forth on the soggy roads at an alarming pace. Alarming not only for how fast the horses clipped along, but also for how much sooner a journey of this speed would reach its end. How much sooner *she* might reach her *end*.

Dire consequences indeed.

But the events—or rather, the *non*-event—of last night overshadowed all else.

How could it not? When the stranger across from her kept peering from beneath dusky, thick hair that perpetually fell into his face. He wouldn't even flick it away, acting as if the strands right in front of his eyes didn't bother him in the least. But they bothered Laney. She continually had to stifle the compelling need to reach across the seat and brush his hair back so she could see him clearly, and if that wasn't the height of insanity, she didn't know what was.

Nothing had changed since yesterday. Well, nothing, save different passengers—that and a new set of rain clouds flirting with them the entire day.

Reginald still tipped his flask at regular intervals, oblivious to the missing hours from last night.

She still harbored an acute fascination for the man who had touched her intimately just hours before. A fascination that had more to do with his own confusing contradictions—from tender to intense, from caring to churl—than her own mind-defying visions.

Intimate encounters and arousing visions aside, she had no choice but to trust her intuition. Something about this man...he *had* to help her.

He would help her.

She simply could not accept anything else.

No matter how off-putting his manner in the light of day, she refused to give up until he agreed to buy her, even if she had to deceive him again to do it.

Should she not feel the slightest bit guilty for how excited that prospect made her?

Excited. Wicked. Wanton. Excited again...

"Press. Pressing. Resign." The last was groaned and he finally did flick his head, only to knock the back of it into the coach and wince.

She opened her mouth to apologize and swiftly covered her lips. Merciful heavens. She couldn't admit to knowing he carried a bruise of her doing on his stubborn, rotten skull, now, could she?

"Resign. Resign. Resign." Each hissed word was accompanied by an increase in the heat of his eyes, the searing attention he directed across the coach *and right at her*. An increase with the ferocity with which he smacked his cranium into the coach. Mayhap he really was cracked?

If so, then she was equally cracked for caring about what troubled him so.

But then, hadn't Mama always accused Laney of being a crack-brain?

"'Ere! Stop! Right 'ere!" The boy scrambled to exit the moving coach while maintaining his hold on the startled goose. "Stop!"

Flapping its wings, the honking nuisance had certainly claimed the stranger's attention away from her, allowing Laney the first full breath she'd had since climbing inside the coach.

"There's me mam!" the child screeched, waving furiously out the window. "Stop th' coach! Stop! *Please.*"

Feathers flew. Followed by a flurry of colorful curses.

"Mummy!"

Reginald roused and spilt what remained in his flask—which wasn't much—in his lap. Laney held back a laugh.

"Stop th' coach! Pleeeeeeese!"

"Stop the god-demmed coach!"

The stranger's voice must have reached the driver. Either that or the horses' ears, because they jerked to a halt so fast all of the passengers riding forward were thrown into the opposite seat.

Which meant that Reginald had a lapful of liquor, yelling child and squawking goose.

Laney had a lapful of stranger.

The stranger had a handful of breast.

And Laney wasn't laughing anymore.

━━━━◖●◗━━━━

Reginald used the unexpected delay to empty his bladder at the base of a nearby tree. A bird on a branch above used the disturbance below to empty his bowels.

Most of the passengers, those inside and riding up top, took the unplanned halt as a fortuitous occasion to stretch their legs.

The child used the stop to greet his crying mother.

The driver to complain to anyone who would listen.

The goose to peck a few ankles.

Laney saw the empty coach—save two—the most opportune opportunity to plead her case.

As for Nash? After suffering his own word-centered wanderings, he decided this was a prime chance to make *her* suffer.

"Please," she entreated the moment they were alone, "you must help me."

"Who says I must do anything of the sort?"

"Your honor!"

"That assumes I have any."

"You must, buried somewhere within that ill-kept sleeping-your-life-away façade."

"Tut. Tut. Accusing me of sleeping my life away? *'Why, then, should the sleeping man stir?'*" he misquoted quite appropriately, he thought. "Do you not know any better than to insult the hand you have begged to buy you? Though, I confess to curiosity on one point..."

She leaned forward eagerly, as if expecting a white knight to come charging forth from his pocket. Nash shifted, causing the corner of Shakespeare to dig into his ribs. He only ground the book in deeper. He deserved it for piquing her interest but still couldn't stop himself from inquiring, "Would he really defend your honor in a duel?"

"A duel? Reginald? Whatever makes you think—"

"He as much as challenged me yesterday. For my

own honor," Nash pondered out loud, fingering his jaw, "I really shouldn't have backed down. Should have accepted. Blasted a hole through his fancy-dressed gullet."

"You would do that?" she breathed on a happy-sounding squeak. "For me?"

"Hell no." He hardened himself against her flinch. "That would equate to me expending effort on another's behalf, and why would I bother to do that?"

"But you— I have seen you..."

It was difficult to feign continued disinterest. But he was determined. He relaxed his shoulders, plucked a feather off his thigh and flicked it in her direction. "Aye? Just what have you seen? Me coming to your aid? I think not."

"Your eyes—they glow!"

She was grasping. He could tell. Grasping at that flying feather in front of her face just as she was grasping at a convincing argument, one he'd accept. Too bad he was fresh out of goodwill, if not coins.

"What of it? Glowing eyes do not equal Good Samaritanship in my book. Or perhaps you are reading a different volume?"

"You should help me on principle!"

"*Principle?* P-r-i-n-c-i-p— Blast. No L."

"You are *the* most infuriating man."

"Thank you. I suppose we must deduce that you inspire me to greatness. *Inspire?* Did I—"

"Yes," she huffed, billowing out that veil he longed to rip from her stupid hat. "You said that word over an hour ago, along with a hundred others that made absolutely no sense whatsoever."

"A hundred?" He sighed in satisfaction, hearing the sheer displeasance in her lovely voice, seeing that bound-up-tighter-than-a-virgin's-morals bosom of hers heave with fiery indignation. "Hmm. I only counted ninety-seven. Must have lost track—"

"Oh, you odious man! You...you..."

"Aye?"

"You *swine!*"

Given the direction of his thoughts in the last twenty-four hours, 'twas no surprise he laughed outright. "Tut, tut, Princess. Name calling really doesn't become you. By your own admission, you belong to that fine figure of a man." He waved toward the open door of the coach where Molly Boy could be seen frantically scrubbing at a spot on his hat. "You will need to devise a plan to save yourself from his nefarious clutches. Trust me, I am *not* your man."

Then why did he suddenly want to be?

Insane! She was still hiding behind her vexing veiled hat. A different one today, but just as obnoxious. Couldn't even tell what color her hair was, much less her *irises*. All he had to go on was that cultured voice—now strident with irritation—her astonishing persistence and those glorious titties.

※

SINGER. Singers. Singe. Singes. Sipper. Sippers. Sipping. Spring. Springs.

Two hours later, he was still in the Land of Letter Lunacy. They'd stopped for a horribly delayed lunch—

thank you stinking rain—this time at a nondescript tavern and coaching station along the route.

Nash chewed and swallowed, chewed and swallowed. Tried to enjoy the meal. But the words wouldn't stop forming.

Icing. Icier. Irises. What color were hers?

Come *spring*, might he be *singing* for his *sipper*, having his brain cells *singed*?

Sipper? Hell, he meant *supper*—which hadn't even made the bloody list.

He ran an exhausted hand over his face. Exhausted because he'd kept it clenched all morning to keep from wringing the neck of first the goose, and then after it was gone, the dissipated dandy across the coach every time he spoke sharply to her or made a threatening move that caused her to cower.

When Nash wasn't wrestling with words and lamenting over lacking letters, he watched the pair. Studied every interaction, analyzed her every *reaction*...

Even now, after it had become apparent the man wasn't truly interested in her, not as a female, Nash just wanted to pound the cove into the ground for daring to treat her like sludge on the bottom of his shoe.

During the interminable morning, the man's utter disinterest in his "property" as anything other than that— simply something he owned—had finally reached Nash's princess-bedeviled brain. Tate certainly didn't want her for himself, not the way Nash had begun to crave.

What's here? the portrait of a blinking idiot.

Aye. Thanks, Shakes... That would be Nash, a Blinking Idiot. Allowing envy and jealousy envy over the man's spotless, impressive exterior and jealousy over the "lady" snugged to his side—to blind him to the man's true predilections...

If she truly wasn't his mistress, did that mean her wild claims of danger had merit?

It wasn't the dandy's sexual penchant for men that stung Nash into instant disfavor for he'd had friends at school who preferred to chase, rather than women, each other. As long as they kept their private— personal, bagpiping interactions—well, *private* 'twas all well and fine.

Nay, this man irritated on an entirely different level.

With his liquor-addled manner. His overly officious dress—who wore an expensive, top-lofty beaver in such close confines? And who treated their "mistress", pretend or otherwise, no better than a pair of ratty old discarded drawers?

Rum women—hell, *all* women—should be treasured. Cherished.

Not treated like a three-penny upright by men such as Mr. Ill-mannered Tate over there.

Nor even Nash himself. Which is why he, at least, aimed to only associate with experienced women he could amply reward—monetarily—when he behaved such a brute. But the silk-voiced female across from him?

The refined woman at the dandy's side wasn't a slattern to be used and abused.

And every time Tate shoved, prodded or pushed, verbally or worse, Nash had to fight the urge to plant the man a facer that would plant his sorry arse in the ground.

The couple sat directly across from him on the other side of the plank table—why couldn't he get away from her?—digging into their own meals, knowing that time was limited even though the food was plentiful.

Nash swallowed the last of his buttery roll and turned his plate a quarter turn to the right, ready to consume the remaining serving. He always did that—ate clockwise around his plate. Some chuckleheaded notion that just about the only thing in his life he could control and have any say over were his meals. Well, that, and how he took his women.

Plowing his fork through the chunky stew, he opened for a hearty bite when hell froze. So did his actions.

"Halt. Avoid that," she whispered quietly, for his ears alone.

Startled more by the heat generated by her gloved fingers perched atop the back of his hand than by the spoken command, his fork clattered to his plate. He looked up, surprised to find Fribble staring at his own plate, hand on his stomach, a slight green cast to his face.

Not a second later the man tripped over the bench in his rush to escape outside. In a blink, he was gone. Gone, along with most of the other passengers.

"What?" Nash questioned the lone female across from him. "Did I miss the call to move out?"

"Nay, but I assure you, you do not want to eat that."

When she spoke, the puffs from her words ruffled the veil. She removed her hand and pointed toward the stew. "Not even a bite."

"I don't?"

"Trust me. You do not."

And if that didn't make him a noddy after participating in the queerest interaction on record, Nash didn't know what would, because for some strange reason, he did trust her—at least on this, seeing that the entire serving of stew was still plopped, congealing, on her own plate while Fribble had apparently eaten all of his. A quick glance down the table confirmed that every plate sans stew was missing its passenger.

"Why do you wear a veil?" The words were out before he could remind himself he didn't care. "The rest of you isn't shrouded in black, so you aren't in mourning."

Her shoulders lifted in a noncommittal shrug, but her hand shook when she reached for her roll, the last item on her plate. Other than the stew.

Needing to know, he couldn't stop himself from asking again, "The veil? *Why?*"

She balled her hand and jerked it away from the bread. The monstrosity atop her head tilted back an inch, as if she were staring at him. "*Where* are you traveling?"

So she wanted to play tit for tat? "Very well. Away from London, as far and fast as I can go," he shared. "The veil?"

Her hesitation was just short enough to make him think she wasn't concocting a lie. "It's one of the few independent choices I make that Mr. Tate still allows. Why *away?*"

"Because..." His hesitation was probably long enough to cause her to question whether he was going to respond at all. "I did something in London I would rather not face. Not this decade, if I can avoid it. Why do you stay with him?"

"I told you…" She lowered her voice when the last remaining passenger stumbled for the door with his hand over his mouth. "I am indentured to him."

"You don't look like any servant I ever saw."

"And you may not pose another question until answering one of mine. Something illegal?"

"Morally, if not legally. How long has he owned you?"

"Thirty-six months and eight days. Are you saying that you do not have any particular destination in mind? You will go wherever the stagecoach takes you?"

"Where are you *two* heading?" Her precise numerical response left him almost speechless. But not quite. "I shall be sure to disembark before we get there."

He hadn't meant to be so hurtful. It just came out. The beast in him, only no excuse this time, not after satisfying himself sexually as he had the night before. Just because he wasn't in a position to save her, *not* that he wanted to, didn't give him leave to behave like an arse.

He opened his mouth to apologize but she beat him to it, saying, "Odious man!" yet without any true heat.

"Pardon me. I regret that. Sincerely. Cynical reflex, I suppose. There is something I intensely dislike about talking to a wavering veil instead of a breathing, blinking woman. Or maybe I simply take umbrage at being lumped on the head."

"That was an accident!" she claimed, then, "What are you running from?"

"Not what. Who." Nash barely kept the satisfaction

from showing on his expression, even though it was technically his turn to ask. At least he thought so. He was having a devil of a time just keeping up with their exchange. He hadn't felt so exhilarated since...ever.

"Who?" she persisted. "If you are not in trouble with a magistrate or a runner, then why leave?"

As if he'd tell this impertinent, veiled *servant* he was running from *himself*.

Nash grunted, thinking hard. Unknowingly—he'd stake his life on the "unknowing" part—she'd given him a very large piece to a very strange puzzle. A piece he was still pondering. "How much is your indenture?"

She squeaked. She actually squeaked and her gloved hands joined each other atop the table, tapping out a celebratory tune. "You shall buy me?"

"Now, I did *not* say that. Only asked how much. As much as a horse?"

"You would have to take that up with Mr. Tate. I have no idea the terms he negotiated with Mrs. Michaels or how much he's in a position to demand now." Her words tripped over themselves in her haste to answer. "I didn't care when I was younger and he wouldn't tell me now if I asked—trust me, I have."

Mrs. Michaels. So now he had his answer. Her prior "owner" hadn't been another single benefactor, but a bawdy house madam. An abbess who brokered flesh. What manner of parent would have sold her there to begin with?

Children as young as nine could be apprenticed, traded so parents have one less mouth to feed, a tidy pocket of coin in exchange. He swallowed the sour bile that rose.

"You're better off with Tate." At least he was only one man.

But one who doesn't want her...

"I am not. I swear it. Now please, will you not tell me *who* you are trying to escape from?" She wouldn't let it alone, would she? "Why are you running? Please tell me."

What, did she think that gave them something in common? "What does it matter?"

"It doesn't, not really. I just thought it prudent to confirm that you aren't wanted for murder or anything dastardly like that, seeing as how I am putting myself completely under your command."

And now he'd gone and given her false hope. False because he had no intention of buying her blasted indenture.

"Murder doesn't sit on my branch of the family tree, at least not directly. But don't go getting your hopes up—"

"Why not? You are truly my only hope."

Annoyed with her, with himself, with the entire bloody situation, he reached across the table and snatched the uneaten roll off her plate. He tore it in half before attempting to dissuade her misguided trust. "My *past*, Princess. My past. I'm trying to outrun my past, though I don't anticipate my future being significantly better, so you best not pin your hopes on a wanderer, one who keeps searching the continent for oblivion or forgiveness. Finding neither."

She unclasped her hands and slid them across the table, stopping just shy of touching him again. "That sounds like a very sad existence."

And why hadn't he shoved the entire roll in his mouth and shut himself up? He crammed in half and spoke around it, purposefully eating like an animal; there had to be more than one way to discourage her. "At least it is one," he choked out, "more than I can say for my cousin."

"Would you talk to Mr. Tate?" He heard the sound of a million dreams, all centered on him. So his glaring lack of manners hadn't dimmed her optimism?

Pitiful Princess. Did she not have anyone better to hang her hopes on? He swallowed. "How did you know about the food?"

She scooted back and turned her head as if glancing at the door. Amid the renewed patter of rain, groans and the unappetizing chorus of puking filtered in. No specialized feline eardrums needed either.

"The food?" he prompted when she remained silent.

"You wouldn't believe me if I told you."

"You'd be surprised at just what all I will believe."

But it didn't really matter. None of it did...

Whether she'd laced everyone's plate but his, which he doubted.

Whether she had a crystal ball and saw the future —when pigs wore tiaras!

Whether she had the face of a pockmarked gargoyle...

None of that counted worth beans. Because that earlier touch on the back of his hand, the one halting him from eating his stew, it had told him more than a year's worth of furtive remarks ever could.

With that innocent touch, combined with her

body's not so innocent response to their exchange and her earlier slip, Nash had puzzled together what had turned out to be very intriguing indeed. He leaned back, dusted off his palms and stared at her hidden face, unblinking. "I smell your desire."

That monstrous hat tilted to the side. "What?"

She'd returned to squeaking.

"I said, I smell your desire. And if I'm not mistaken—and I'm not—I tasted it last night."

***

BACK IN LONDON

WHUMP!

Tempest found herself squashed against Lord Tyndale.

The door behind him had flown open and launched him at her. Laughing and loud, three men came bursting through.

Struggling to free herself from the unintended embrace, she nevertheless couldn't help but gawk. Two of them were a matched set, nearly as tall as Lord Tyndale, though several years younger, and every bit as swarthy and swoon-inducing—if one were so inclined, which she wasn't—as he.

Their companion, equal to Lord Tyndale in height and age, proved just as captivating. Ghost-white hair atop a refined countenance that included a short beard—not something men their age sported in her circles—and pale, almost feral eyes that seemed to see straight through her, even as his companions had yet to pay her any mind.

"Tyn!" one of the dark ones exclaimed, speaking to Lord Tyndale. "This is where you escaped to? Whatever for—" Finally noticing her, he broke off. "Ho!"

"Ho!" his twin said at the same exact moment. "Who have we here?"

Their white-haired, bearded companion, the last one through the open door that had yet to fully shut it, giving Tempest the chance to angle her head around her keeper. *Drat.* No one was on stage. But if she ducked—

"Eyes down, Wylde's woman," Tyndale said in a stern voice, all hint of the frivolous roister gone. "You should not be looking in there."

"Who is *she*?"

"Where did she come from?"

"Never mind," said Tyndale, moving to stand in front of her—trying to shield her identity? That surprised her. She wouldn't have thought he had a chivalrous or gentlemanly bone in his body. "Jeffrey. Jasper. Leave off—"

"Does she belong to you?"

"Or The Den?"

"We're off to Farnsworth's."

"Are you coming with?"

"Heard Farnsy has some soirée—"

"Or something going on tonight and—"

"We managed an invite."

As though she watched a shuttlecock being bandied about, her eyes veered to and fro between the twins who managed to speak in tandem, practically over each other, and yet still make sense.

"You still haven't told us who she is," they both said at once and Tempest had to bite her lips against the smile that threatened. She'd never seen them before, so they hadn't been around during the season.

"You two have yet to give him a chance," the tall stranger, quiet until now, said in an indulgent manner somewhat negated by the deep rasp in his voice as he fully came into the room.

Tyndale nodded a thanks to him and pulled her further behind him with one arm while thumping the door shut with the other. "You need not know who she is, and nay, I'm not joining you at Farnsworth's. I have been tasked with a mission, you see."

Up close, she once again smelled the outdoors on him.

"You wouldn't happen to be—"

"Holding out on us—"

"Now, would you?"

One of them stepped close and eyed her entire form. "She's a prime piece, cuz."

The other one came up on her other side, despite Lord Tyndale's efforts to keep shoving her behind his back and away from the pair.

"Looks fresh and juicy."

"Just right for the plucking." One of them cupped her cheek before Tyndale elbowed him away.

Juicy plucking indeed. She tugged on his arm. "Are you going to let them talk to me like that?"

He grunted. "They are welcome here. Invited, even. You were not."

True. Once again, she was hard-pressed not to smile. Had she ever experienced so much focused male attention? Not since she was a child and her late father was complaining about her being underfoot when he was trying to concentrate, sending her either upstairs, back to the nursery, or outside, to entertain herself feeding chickens or corralling goats.

Her stepfather, Lord Rowden, had become a friend of sorts. Indulgent, mayhap too much, to the females under his roof—until her mother's excessive gambling came to light. Then his booted foot came down hard and fast, curtailing her evening activities, spending— and even her criticizing of Cousin Francine. Life had never been so grand as it had the last few weeks.

And now? Now that she could incorporate tonight's Grand Adventure—that still progressed and was not yet at an end—why, Tempest couldn't remember ever being quite so enthralled.

What other excited delights might tonight hold? For she still had Mr. Adam's escort to anticipate!

7

THE VERY NECESSARY NECESSARY, SOME IM-PATIENCE, AND THE ILLUMINATING LACK OF CANDLES

"I BEG YOUR PARDON?"

Laney must have misunderstood. The handsome stranger was on the verge of buying her indenture from Reginald, she knew it. But—but...*what* had he said?

He couldn't have said what she thought she heard. Impossible. Improbable. Totally implausible.

Incredible. That he was sitting across from her polishing off her roll—the one she'd been saving for "dessert"—and that he was considering saving her from a fate worse than death. Well, actually, the fate *of death.*

"I have misheard," she said aloud, every one of her senses keenly primed and ready to *pop.* "What did you say?"

Eyeing her as if he could see all of her secrets through the black netting, he made a great show of picking up the remaining half of her roll. Then he plunked it into his mouth and chewed thoroughly, s-l-o-w-l-y, masticating every doughy morsel to a pulp before swallowing—taunting her without words. Making her wait, the bastard. "Well?"

He took his time swallowing again. And again. She watched the contortions of his mouth caused by his tongue searching out every last speck of bread over first his top teeth and then the bottom, as he gyrated his jaw and cheeks, all while staring at her through her protective veil as if it were invisible. As if she were anything but.

Blatantly on display. That's how he made her feel. That and as if she were poised to topple over a cliff.

"*Well?*" Laney fought the urge to stomp her foot. Or kick it into his shin.

He lifted his ale, took a gulp, swished it around, and finished with a hearty swallow and an open-mouthed, "Ahhhh."

Just as she was cranking her foot back to let it fly, he grinned. "I had my head between your legs last night, licking your juicy quaint, did I not? M'law-dee?"

Laney sputtered. She gasped. Her foot plonked back to the floor with a thump.

"Had my tongue pushed far up your treasure, was swallowing down your sweet honey while you rode my face and screamed. Screamed 'm'lawd!' and poured yourself out over my mouth."

The dastard hadn't spoken to her this way in her vision.

But his wicked words painted a more vivid picture than she could fathom on her own. One in full color, despite the dark night in her memories. One that had her heart pounding and her mouth panting...the flesh between her thighs pulsing.

"And judging by the scent of your renewed desire, your sex is just as juicy now, mayhap more so, and you want me again. Right *there*." His voice hardened. "Don't you, wench?"

Laney squeezed her legs together.

"Ye damn whoreson!" she cried, abandoning every elocution lesson Mary Delilah had taught. "An' so what if I do? It ain't fitten table conversation, or did you leave yer manners in my muff along with yer tongue?"

The sound of her voice rang loud in the empty room. Echoed around the hollows of empty benches. Echoed within the empty hollow of Laney herself.

A true lady always moderates her vocabulary and speaks in a most becoming way. One of Mary Delilah's earliest teachings. One she'd just discarded like a sack of stones someone dumped in the Thames.

Gads, he'd never want her now. Who could blame him? Illiterate street urchins and uncouth street whores were a groat a dozen. Her countenance and her comportment—one thanks to God, the other thanks to Mary Delilah—were all that Laney could claim that set her apart.

Now she didn't have either of those. "Now look what you gone and done, you uncouth cove of a crois-sant stealer! You made me go an' ruin it all."

Laney pushed to her feet. "Now I'm goin' ta die 'cause of you. You an' your devil tongue! Crude and coarse, that's all ye are, steppin' on lady's dresses, stealin' their desserts. Wish to God I'd never...never..."

Eyes blinking furiously, lips mashed to keep from

spewing anything else, she stumbled over the bench and lunged for the door. Had to escape before she sobbed in front of him.

He jumped up and caught her when she rounded the table.

Intense, that was all she could think, grinding to a halt in his hard grip.

He was so intense. He clasped her wrists and pushed her back against the table's edge, hovering over her.

"*Die?*" The word slammed through her veil like a bullet. "Come now, Princess, save the dramatics for the stage. For that's what you are, is it not? An actress."

She tried to wrench free. He only tightened his grip, transferring both her wrists to one of his hands. He brought the other to the bottom edge of her veil. And stopped.

She held her breath.

"You an actress?"

Her lips unlocked for a whispered, "I am not."

The finger ran along the veil's lacy edge. "But your accent..." Directly in front of her face, his long, blunt-tipped finger creeped to the other side.

Trapped. For the first time since she'd donned the mask as protection, Laney felt trapped behind it. Again and again, his finger streaked across the edge, then slowed to a crawl. Tormenting her. As did his proximity, his words... "The way you smell... The way you sit, walk, *talk*..."

She gulped and her breath let out in a whoosh. "Until she moved away recently, my longtime friend Mary Delilah was employed at the Young Ladies

Improving Academy. On her half Sundays, she taught me to speak properly, to write. To compose and comport myself as a lady." Her gaze tracked that finger. What was he waiting for?

"Your *friend*?" The rough edge to his voice made clear his skepticism. "What did she gain in return for her unselfish, philanthropic endeavors?"

Laney yanked on her wrists. He held firm.

Firm. But not hurtful. She took solace in that—a measure of comfort that had been lacking in her interactions with men henceforth. Had Reginald or George John caught her in such a deception, she shuddered to think the outcome. "You make true friendship sound sordid. It was never like that. We may have made an odd pairing at first—the ill-educated shopgirl and the learned teacher—but our ages are not so very dissimilar. To show my thanks for her lessons, I made over her hats, created fancier ones than a prim teacher might wear, but ones she adored nevertheless."

"Fancy *hats*." He made them sound like a plague of serpents. "Is that what you call it?"

"'Tis a boon, being able to use one of my talents to benefit others."

"One of your talents?" He stroked beneath the veil, caressed jaw, then heated cheek. "You think to intrigue me regarding your other talents, do you not? Attempt to convince me how *I* might benefit?"

Face thrumming from his touch, heart pattering near to bursting, she all but panted. "Would you care for a hat? I could—"

"Hats. Whores. Not much difference than a few letters, eh?"

"I don't know what you mean," she whispered, both thrilled and terrified, and praying for his help all the more. "A whore is nothing at all like a hat."

"I should rip this one right from your head, expose everything you insist on hiding—"

"*Please.* Do not..."

"But I shall indulge your delusion of privacy. For now."

He dropped his hand. *To her bosom.*

"You lied to me," he growled, and his eyes started glowing again.

"Not—"

"You did. By action if not by word." He curved his palm over one breast and she jolted back, the uneven tabletop grinding into her buttocks. "Why?"

"I..." On its own, her traitorous breast pushed forward—into his hand. "I—I *need* you to buy me. 'Tis not safe for me to remain with Reginald. He's becomin' dangerous. When you..."

The jingle of horses passing by the open door snagged her attention. Anyone could walk in, but judging by the moans and shouts, not to mention the faint smells that had her nose wrinkling, today's meal still occupied everyone elsewhere.

He stepped closer, brought his legs right up to hers, bent at the knees and leaned in, twisting his body until his erection wedged between her clenched thighs. Then he slowly straightened, dragging his stiffened cock until it snuggled into her stomach. Her every muscle strained toward him in response.

"Go on," he said, moving his palm in a slow caress over her entire breast.

"When...when you said no, I thought..."

His hand tightened painfully. But it felt soooo good.

"Thought what? To trick me? To deceive me into buying you?"

Laney moaned. Couldn't stop herself from practically melting into him.

"Is that what you meant to do?" he asked again with a hard edge to his voice that corresponded to the hard way his fingers massaged her breast.

"Nay." Laney moaned louder.

"Nay?" He released her breast only to close his hand around the other one.

"No." He shifted closer, rubbed more firmly, and her bits ached anew. "No. Oh God. Yes! I thought if I satisfied you as good as a whore—one you would have to secure and pay nightly—then mayhap I could convince you to buy me from Reginald. Then you could have me any time you wanted."

"Any time?"

She jerked a nod. "At least until—"

And just like that, he was gone. Stepped away, released her, but left her limp and panting. Collapsing backward onto the table for support.

"Until when?"

"Until my indenture expires or possibly beyond, because I saw..."

"Saw what?" he demanded when she faltered. "That's the second time you mention seeing something. What are you, a professional eavesdropper? A 'lady' lurker? A humbugger, intent on cheat—"

"It's not like that!"

"Oh no?"

How much should she confess? It wasn't as though she trusted him, not yet. He might be listening, but he hadn't agreed to anything. He hadn't agreed to assist her—and he hadn't assuaged the ache he'd created and then left her with—twice now, dash him.

While she was trying to decide, while she stood there, her body yearning for his, her mind a jumble, the coachman stuck his head in just long enough to holler, "We're movin' out! Can't waste any more time 'ere!"

As if the interruption erased his own interest, without another word—or touch—her stranger whipped around and stalked to the door.

"Wait!" She rushed forward, her entire body a throbbing mass of *want*. "Please don't leave me here with—"

He spun back and snared her in place with those heated ember eyes. "Convince me again. Tonight. If you're going to play the whore, I want another performance." He stepped close and breathed the next words directly into her veil. "But know this, Princess—this time there shall be no fake accents between us, no clothes between us, plenty of light and no god-dem hat!"

* * *

"Uhhhh. Uhh. *Aaaaaaa*." Shit glided from Reginald's ass, burning on the way out just as it had on the way in.

Damn. He should never have eaten the venison stew, not after realizing Eleanor wasn't touching hers. But the stuff had a spicy jolt that fired away the concerns mucking his mind. So he kept at it, bite after bite, and by the time he'd seen her warn the stranger, it was already too late. Reginald was on his second helping.

Remembering how Eleanor touched the other man, knowing she was likely gazing at him even now with that moonstruck expression she'd worn around *him* when Reginald had first met her only made the skittering turds burn hotter.

Yow! His chapped arse screamed. He hadn't hurt this much since the first time he'd—

"Uhh." He bit down on the grunt, shuddering as the next person waiting for the boghouse began hideous heaving just outside the door.

Where was privacy for making a deuced diarrhea deposit when it was needed?

How he hated hearing people vomit. The sound alone was enough to make him sick. Before he knew it, *he'd* be the one shitting through his teeth.

How he hated using public privies. But it did beat squatting. In the rain.

If he had the strength, he'd skewer George John for making him undertake this deuced journey. Nay, skewering was too good for his domineering, sanctimonious brother. A bloody wound wouldn't make him suffer sufficiently.

The fiercest cramp yet seized Reginald's stomach and he bent double, groaning. Sweat coated his brow, beaded above his mouth, saturated his fly togs, and he fancied the sickening stew wafted from every pitiful pore.

Hell and the devil, he had half a mind to simply

marry Eleanor and be done with it. Nay, he didn't—have half a mind, that is. He'd just crapped out one lung, along with his brain.

"Kill me now. Just put me out of my god-damned misery," he prayed, looking at the dirty patch of earth between his mud-splattered—shit-splattered?—boots.

Marry Eleanor? Hmm...

That would certainly give his brother a bitter pill to swallow, but not nearly as bitter as the muscle spasms squeezing Reginald's middle. A fresh spurt of gassy shit burst forth, making his eyes water as much as his arse.

He wanted to die.

Men like him—they weren't made for roughing it outside of town, for haring off to house parties with only vague directions and assurances of even vaguer pleasures.

Men like him, Reginald thought despite the latest cramp to attack his stomach and the unmistakable taste of pre-vomit gathering just below his throat—he swallowed it down and *pushed*, worked the muscles in his rectum as he hadn't in months—men like him, they weren't meant to deal with women like Eleanor.

Frothy, feminine bits of frippery—who had flam-doodley foresight of the future. Such as when she accurately assured him it would hail by nightfall and there wasn't a cloud in all of London, or the time she told him the butcher had double charged his steward and Reginald hadn't yet received the bill. Devilish queer—her and her weird ways. Neither was she the biddable, docile creature he'd first thought when he'd begun "courting" her.

But she *was* the only female in his possession and

that made her precious indeed, worth more than any other. Certainly worth overlooking her little idiosyncrasies, or so he'd convinced himself once things began to turn sourly.

And she was so very beautiful—according to George John at least, who ought to know, considering his vast experience with women.

Ever since Reginald snatched her away from the milliner, after he'd cleaned her up and dressed her in expensive finery, every man who came within ear or eyeshot fell under Eleanor's spell. He supposed that's why she'd taken to wearing the veil whenever they went out in public the past few months. Didn't favor all the attention she garnered.

On one hand, it angered him that he couldn't show her off more, on the other, a compliant female was better than a contrarian, and giving in on this point had been worth it—she'd finally unlocked her door after the Cheroot Incident and began conversing with him again.

Plus that hood over her face kept him from suffering the look in her eyes—the one that made guilt churn fierce in his belly. But not anywhere as severely as this cursed stew.

Over the years she'd matured and filled out to the point that it hurt just to look at her. Kind of how his gut hurt now.

Just as he knew that he'd be puking his brains out in mere seconds—if he could stop shitting long enough to pull up his pantaloons—he knew he *should* find her appealing, so why did his cock not give a damn?

Perhaps that was the problem—she was too much *woman.*

If she had a leaner figure, wasn't so ghastly curvy...

But she was *his* woman, bought and paid for. And he wasn't giving her up.

But lunch was coming up.

Reginald kicked open the outhouse door and lurched sideways into the drizzle, holding up his pantaloons with one hand, holding his arse with the other while his stomach proceeded to regurgitate lunch, breakfast and however many pints he'd downed since sunup.

Could his beat-up body—or his burnt-out brain—feel any more wretched?

His brow needed to be wiped. His arse needed to be cleaned.

God. He missed Neils.

❦

Back in London

ALL PATIENCE WANTED WAS to be bound. For life. To a man. Was that too much to ask?

A man not her father (God rot his festering soul). Nor her stepfather, no matter that he—"Uncle Rowden"—at least gave the females in his abode leave to do... Well, tolerably near anything. Discounting how he'd brought the ax—practically the guillotine—down once he'd learned of Mother's excessive gambling.

Thank goodness for Lord Hansen, who came up to scratch, offering for Patience earlier this year. Without his warranted attentions, life would be positively unbearable!

Their wedding could not arrive with enough haste for her. Especially given how her younger sister —"Tempest" as the flighty little twit insisted calling herself these days—managed to secure a notable match in Lord Wylde her very first season. Postponed because Patience had, well, taken longer to *take*. Her particular brand of acerbic wit not entangling—er, *engaging*—the right sort of man until her fourth season.

Worst of all, was how Franny—their unpalatable, sun-worshiping, dirt-encrusted cousin—had snared herself a marquis. A marquis! And after declining every other fool who dared offer for the conceited chit the last few years.

A marquis! Patience's jaw ached from clenching it to keep from crying out at the unjustice—or was in injustice? Ugh! It mattered not! What mattered was *how* in high, hellacious heavens Francine sunk her grasping hooks in Lord Blakely—when Patience had to settle for a viscount? Why, 'twas unfathomable.

The very thought flared Patience's nostrils and gritted her teeth until the squeak made her flinch.

Every muscle tensed. She looked with narrowed eyes at her prey...nay, they hadn't heard. They remained oblivious to her presence. In the midst of savoring thoughts about herself, Patience had caught sight of the pair huddled in the dark, heard furtive murmurs, even if the content remained elusive.

And the two of them thought they could slip out— in the middle of the night—to go who knew where and do what could only be guessed at? And they thought they could do so without repercussions?

Ha.

A tight smile fought against her tightened jaw. Well now, she would just see about that.

———◦———

HIS PRINCESS WAS LATE. Excessively late.

Late enough to leave Nash pacing his second-floor room at The White Knight Inn & Tavern—a significant improvement over their last stop. Pacing and battling with his cumbersome thoughts. Ones that, uncharacteristically, had to do with things *outside* himself.

He knew one of the men on Blake's *Suspect* list sufficiently to offer input as to the man's character.

So why hadn't he left his brother a note? A simple two-word scribble, at the very least?

Too busy hieing off, eh? Afraid to stay, to risk caring...

Hadn't loving his parents taught him that?

His father may have been murdered—that was his and Blake's suspicion, despite their mother's last letter and assertion otherwise.

But their mother, now? She'd abandoned them *by choice*. Deserted Nash, who at a rebellious sixteen, still needed at least one parent. Especially after burying his father a mere two years prior.

But nay, his brother barely out of the school room himself had to not only assume the title and the estates, his seat in Parliament and all the sundry responsibilities, had to not only shoulder the burden of the curse, of Phineas's disappearance and uncertain fate, but he also had to deal with an unruly, irresponsible younger brother in Nash.

Was it any wonder Nash considered forming attachments—emotional or otherwise—the beginning of the end? His likely downfall...? Something to be avoided at all costs? Better to be alone and lonely than disappoint another as his parents had disappointed him...

As you have disappointed Blake, by not sharing what you know?

"Bother it." He stomped across the room, uncaring if he bothered those on the floor below. "Where the hell is she?"

As you keep disappointing yourself?

Seventeen minutes later, Nash refused to acknowledge the relief that swept over him at her tentative knock.

He opened the door and she swept inside. "You're late." At his first glimpse, his lip curled. "And you're wearing that....blame...hat."

"Nay, I am not." She twitched her skirts and walked past him.

He avoided slamming the door only by sheer will, but it gave him great pleasure to turn the lock and hear the echoing clink. He swung to face her. "Then, pray tell, what exactly is nesting on your head?"

By Zeus, he was glad to see her—even though he still couldn't, due to the latest monstrosity she wore. Forest green, with midnight netting and hordes of lacy gauze jumbled on top, a wide brim made a nest for the tiny bird perched over her idea pot.

As the evening had progressed without hint of her arrival, he'd begun thinking perhaps he had over-stated his hand that afternoon and wasn't going to have the pleasure of her company—he meant *body* —tonight.

What was it with this woman and hats?

Fortunately, he'd been wrong. Unfortunately, her taste in hat wear hadn't improved a lick. "There's a beak hanging over your forehead, bobbing at me."

"This style is all the rage, I'll have you know. I unpacked it earlier while searching Reginald's trunk for his linen sheets. I just finished putting him down for the night. He's feeling absolutely horrible, you know."

"Good." Nash took a step forward. Once another cloudy night had set in, he'd lit every candle the room boasted, then asked for more. He was getting a good look at her tonight. All night.

His window was open, but he'd drawn the curtains, keeping the draft to a minimum. The light to a maximum.

And wasn't it fortuitous, how the midday meal continued to occupy every passenger who had partaken? All but himself and the hat-wearing creature before him.

"His stomach still heaves every hour or so." She began fidgeting with her gloves, pinching the end of each fingertip and pulling sharply, straightening the wrinkles along each finger, methodically working her way across her hand.

So the other man was still in pain? Nash took another step toward her. "I shall say it again: *good*."

"And that is why I couldn't get away sooner." She swished past him when he came within arm's reach—only because he *let* her—and walked around the bed, past the window and over to the nightstand. "I see you have plenty of candles this evening."

"I do. Take off the hat, madam."

She fluttered nervously. The bird atop her head flittered as if it wanted to fly off—to freedom.

Did *she*? Was that why she came veiled despite his specific order to the contrary?

Was that why, even now, though her desire once again greeted his sensually satisfied sniffer, she seemed prepared, primed, *perched* to fly away?

He didn't want her leaving. But more than that, he didn't want her to *want* to leave.

So he halted his advance. Gentled his approach.

She intrigued him, this baggage of opposite impulses... *Buy my indenture, please, sir.* But nay, he wasn't permitted to look at her. *I'm 'ere to service yer every need, m'lawd.* But no, he couldn't see her...

But he could taste her. Remembered flavor tainted his tongue, tempting him all over again, as he swiped it over his lips, gratified at the smooth sensation. Had it been rough, had his savage urges been prompting him onward, he might have assumed his interest was more one of convenience than true attraction.

As it were, while the urges simmered tonight, they wouldn't be riding him hard for several hours, which gave him the clarity to question his powerful interest in her even while doubting his sanity.

If he kept her close, the beast wouldn't win this month. This year.

What do you mean keep her close? Any female will do.

Mayhap. But at the moment, actually ever since he'd first spied her, she was the only one he thought about. The only one he craved. Any female *wouldn't* do. Not this time.

Truth was, he wanted her body with a fire that raged in his loins over and above that of taming the beast within. He wanted *her*. And he was confused as hell about it. "Tell me your name," he demanded. "The fop calls you 'Eleanor'. What's the rest?"

The startled, glass-eyed gaze of the bird jerked to his. He imagined hers did as well. "*Well?*"

"Eleanor Catherine Buckley, my lord," she said promptly, responding to the authority in his tone. She left off fiddling with the candles and performed a curtsy fit for crazy King George.

Ah, so patience brought reward.

"Eleanor..." he sighed the syllables. A strong, almost regal name. It didn't fit the mercurial minx before him. Not one bit.

"My grandmama, and now Mary Delilah, call me Laney."

"Mary Delilah?" Could he be blamed for the hard edge that entered his voice? He hated being lied to.

"My friend. I told you of her earlier." Mary *Delilah*? He was supposed to believe that her "teacher" friend was just that? An instructor of manners? Ha. More likely one of Mrs. Michaels's older drabs, a temptress in every sense who'd taken a young Laney under her wing.

What of it if she lies? You have other uses for her mouth. Her body...

That he did. So he pushed away any bothersome, niggling feelings of hurt. He only cared what she could do for him. Tonight. Mayhap beyond.

Dost thou profess thyself, a knave or a fool?

"Grandmama?" he inquired lightly, determined to ignore the words of Lafeu, even as his laughing conscience cackled back, *I will subscribe for thee, thou art* both *knave and fool.*

"Died when I was eleven, my lord."

He walked forward, pretended not to notice when she stiffened as he drew near. He paused, one stride closer than her comfort permitted, and sat on the edge of the bed. He could touch her if he straightened his arm. Which he didn't. Not yet.

She was cornered. Cornered in the corner of *his* room. And she knew it.

And he was between her and the door. The locked door.

A flare of possession ran through him. So she wanted him to buy her? To *own* her?

A woman or a horse...

Responsibility was looking better by the second.

"There's no need to 'my lord' me, Laney," he said, intentionally testing this name on his tongue. It felt almost as succulent as her slit. "I'm a regular mister—at least away from London."

If a man who annually battled the physical urge to contort into a lion could be termed "regular".

And because going by his courtesy title *Lord* Nash

Hammond made no sense to his vagabond lifestyle. So he eschewed it every chance he got.

"Mr. Nash Hammond 'is your servant's name, fair princess'." After managing to impart that line without much mangling, he performed a mock bow from his sitting position. "Possibly at your service, depending on how the night progresses."

He chose not to inform her his brother was the Marquis of Blakely. Didn't know her well enough for confessions.

She remained silent. And unmoving.

The six candles he'd lit earlier showed her overly dressed form to perfection. She was a vision. In a pale sage dress that draped lightly to the floor, hiding those pretty peach slippers apart from when she walked. Absurdly—because they were inside—and *wearing* clothes was not the evening's focus, she also wore a matching spencer, fancier than the typical style worn outside of high society—done up to her chin, done down to her wrists. Buttoned-up, proper perfection. Just perfect for a princess.

Except for that hat and that god-blasted bobbing bird—the one that hadn't stopped twitching.

"Why are you all a twitter tonight?" *Why do you wear the veil?*

Why me? Why am I the one you chose to rescue you?

"Why am I nervous? Um... Let me douse the candles and I'll tell you."

Before he could respond, she leaned over and blew out the two on the nightstand. Smoke drifted past the hat, giving him the impression that his dreams were soon to follow.

Dreams? Since when did he dream of soft-spoken, elegant wenches dressed in demure finery locked in his bedroom—willingly?

Since forever...

Keeping her back to the wall, she edged past him. Rather than stop her, he cleared his throat. "One more. Leave the other three burning."

She squeaked her displeasure but didn't complain, doing as bade. Another flame extinguished. Leaving three. And a host of uncertainty.

At the far side of the room, she swiveled to face him. Gloved hands clenched. Bird unmoving for once.

Silence reigned.

"I'm waiting," he reminded her. "Why me?"

"I saw something earlier today that was rather perplexing. *Completely* betwattling, truth be told. I... It has given me pause, I'm afraid."

He had let her blow out three candles for that? "Are you? Afraid of me?"

A shake of her head said no; her silence told him perhaps. Which was never his aim. *Start slow, let the undeniable attraction simmering between you flare naturally.* "Take off your gloves."

At the note of quiet command in his voice, she moved to obey, then hesitated.

Three, he reminded himself. *Three chances to gain information. Use them wisely.* "Remove your gloves. Blow out *one* more candle and then tell me what you saw."

See? He could sound calm. Even with the compelling need to tear off her gown—with his teeth—running rampant through him.

Each of her gloves came off in quick, jerky motions.

She dropped them beside her, straight to the floor, the unstructured action making his heart catch.

With a puff of air, the candle was snuffed and she responded, subtly making her way to the remaining two tapers—but not so subtly that he didn't notice. "I was in a meadow, a beautiful flower-filled meadow shaded by a giant tree. A couple reclined there, beneath the tree...in a rather indelicate position."

"Indelicate?"

"Um...sexual."

Ah. Perhaps at one of their many unplanned "relieving" stops, she'd caught someone indulging in an afternoon session of jigging buttocks. But why that should unnerve one with her experience he couldn't fathom. "Were they from the stage?"

And what had they to do with her single-minded pursuit of him?

"Aye. I believe so. One of them at least. What has me perplexed is not so much *what* they were doing..." Her voice had gone all low and sultry, like a thick waterfall of desire that cascaded through his veins. "But what... What..."

"Go on."

"Another candle? Please?"

Two left. But he only needed the light from one to see her clear as day. He stood, glanced at the pile of unlit tapers next to the bed and smiled. He began unfastening his shirtsleeves. "Certainly. Not yet," he added swiftly when she leaned over, halting her actions. "I need for you to remove your dress first and finish your tale while you're at it."

The smooth column of her neck worked when she

swallowed. Worked again when he tugged his shirt free of his pantaloons.

The bird whooshed a circle when she turned her back to him. "You will need to do my buttons."

"Certainly," he said again, thinking how he planned on *doing* a lot more than just her buttons before their night was over.

Following her example, he shrugged out of his shirt and dropped it to the floor. He walked the short distance to her and inspected the tiny row of buttons that began at her nape and were quickly covered by more fabric. "Your spencer." He cleared his throat. "'Tis in the way."

"Oh. Heavens...," All breathy abandon with that starched-up unnecessary piece, she quickly unbuttoned it from the front and sleeves, tugging them just enough from her shoulders to allow the garment to gape at her back, until he could delve beneath.

Her breath hitched at his first touch.

"Like a raven." Nash couldn't stop the whispered comment.

"What?" She glanced at him over her shoulder. She'd braced her palms against the wall. The flame in front of her illuminated her profile through the veil.

He fought the urge to yank the offending hat off her dainty head and toss it beneath his heel. Grind it to a pulp with his boot.

But he'd made too much progress to change tactics now.

He caressed the sliver of skin on the nape of her neck exposed below the damnable headgear. "Your hair. There's a strand trapped around the first button.

Appears to be iridescent black like a raven's wing. Since dear dandified Reginald's is redder than his chafed arse must be at the moment, I assume this particular strand is yours."

"'Tis," she breathed, and faced the wall, her head swiveling on her neck as if it were floating. The bird almost took flight.

He began slipping the tiny buttons free, one after the other.

"What you observed?" he prompted. He wanted to lean in, press his cock to her flesh, but then he wouldn't have been able to savor the smooth, pale skin on either side of her spine he'd exposed above her shift—and 'twas assuredly worth savoring.

For a while at least.

"Either remove your hat wear or start talking, Princess."

She tensed. "What has me nerv—I mean, confused, is the, um, large cat that arrived."

Confused his furry arse.

This previously bold and vexatious sauce box now acts amiss? Demure? *Not* how he wanted her.

Was she so very reluctant to show her face? That she'd invented a Banbury tale to stall? Hell, she could have hideous gargoylian features and he'd still be hard for her—with that voice and figure. With her ability to enrapt and entice whether she behaved as a street doxy —with coarse language and utter abandon to match— or a refined lady, as her little brothel friend had taught her, and which had first enchanted him.

Best hasten her tale along, for he had more than buttons to uncover. Along with her skin, he wanted to learn more of her secrets... Why *this* wench? Why now? What was it about her, in particular, that drew him into her orbit—and made him reluctant to leave?

"So a cat arrived to join the couple in the meadow? Why would seeing a little kitty make you anxious about coming here tonight?" *If only she knew...*

Before he could tell what she was about, Laney stood on her toes and blew out the candle, engulfing their little corner into shadows.

Shadows from the one remaining—lit—taper.

"Laney."

At his annoyed tone, she undid the buttons from her neck to her chest, and then tugged on the wrists of her bosom-enhancing spencer, the one with so much starch and sleeves, 'twould be a simple matter to discount it as almost matronly—but not when the tight-fitting garment outlined her majestic shape. It fell away and she slid the dress from her shoulders. A couple of little hip shakes later and it too was on the floor, a billowing puddle of pale green around her stockinged feet. She toed off her slippers and her arousal saturated the air between them.

Anxious or not, she wanted him. Her body vibrated with it and his responded.

His ability to calmly barter and bargain was rapidly evaporating, replaced with the need to lift her up, sheath his cock between her legs and strum her until they both heard the heavenly chorus screaming hallelujah right along with them.

For the moment, he did none of those things. Hands flexing at his sides to keep from ripping her shift

—hadn't he already done that once?—he huffed an impatient breath. "The hat, Princess. Take. It. Off."

"The last candle?" she asked over her shoulder, from the safety of that blasted veil. Her not quite nude shoulder calling to his lips.

"Not until you're naked." *And I'm riding your arse.*

His hands went to his pantaloons. Fortunately for her, hers finally went to the ribbon on her shift. The ribbon that was tied snugly over those glorious dugs. He couldn't wait to taste them.

She loosened it and whipped the pale garment from her body the same instant he stepped out of one snug leg of his pantaloons. Then she sped by him before he could stop her—hat, blasted bird and all— and raced to the last candle.

"Don't you dare blow—" Nash took a step after her, tripped over his blame pantaloons and floundered just as she plunged the room into darkness.

Play with fire. You're going to get burned.

Laney knew it, but couldn't seem to stop herself.

Scrambling across the bed, she blindly reached for the extra candles she'd seen on the nightstand, intent on—

"Woman!" Nash Hammond grabbed her foot and held on to her scrambling form, coming down on top of her.

"Ompf!" *Mmmm.* Mad he might be, but hard he definitely was, his body so warm and firm and inciting, she didn't know why she'd been so nervous.

What of it if she'd had another vision of the two of

them? If he'd been making her a circlet of daisies and required more? What of it if he'd run off to pick some and hadn't come back?

What of it if who—*what*—had returned to her moments later had been the biggest, strangest "cat" she'd ever seen. If one could call it that—a mere cat.

It didn't look like any feline she'd ever petted. And though she'd expressed an interest, she'd never attended a travelling menagerie or even once visited the circus. Evidently exorbitant outings such as those were reserved for real ladies—or at least real mistresses, according to Reginald.

The color of sunset, with a full ruff around its head, its body shorn of fur but sporting a small tuft at the end of its tail... The creature put her in mind of one she'd seen in a picture book at the lending library while poring over various volumes with Mary Delilah just before she moved away to take up her new post. *Lion*, Laney thought. Animals that lived in the swampy jungles of Africa. Or was it the deserts of Egypt? The mountains of India?

Merciful madness! She couldn't recall, didn't know that she cared to, just knew that when the animal appeared through the trees, long and muscular, a posy of flowers—of all things!—bunched in its huge mouth...stalking forward as if it were there to claim her, consume her, instead of fleeing in absolute fright, Laney had only felt pride bursting through her chest, lifting her cheeks.

What of it if its eyes had *glowed*?

As the carriage had lurched to a halt for one of their many privy stops, she'd returned to her senses and been very frightened indeed. What did it mean? Did the bamboozling mystery bode more for her salvation or her ruination?

She pushed away the apprehension that had cloaked her all afternoon—ever since seeing the vision after setting the boldly inappropriate assignation with her hoped-for, soon-to-be owner.

She'd been afraid he'd see fear in her eyes, suspect she still wasn't telling him everything—which she wasn't—so she'd hidden. Hidden behind the stupid hat that even now he was grappling to take off her head—just as much as she was fighting to reach the candles.

Instinct more than anything.

Self-preservation.

What if he saw her face and didn't like it? Laney had always heard she was a pretty child. Had been told she'd grown into a lovely young woman. But her experience with men was limited to Reginald and his experience with women couldn't be much better.

What if Mr. Nash Hammond found her wanting? And her countenance was the least of her worries, for he was considering buying the indenture of an experienced whore, not an unintentional virgin.

"There!" He tugged and the hat came free. Along with several strands of hair.

"Ow!" She lunged forward and coiled her hand around the pile of tapers.

She angled her upper body toward the window the same second he did. Candles—and hat—went flying out into the night.

"You didn't!" he accused, as if he couldn't believe she'd actually thrown away his precious candles.

Hands no longer fighting with her hat, he fixed them on her shoulders, kept her stomach and breasts pressed into the mattress. "*Did not* just chuck the rest of my candles outside."

"You *did!*" She tried to roll over, to push him off her and face him, but the weight of his body atop hers felt too divine for her to make more than a token effort. "You threw my hat and my little tit to the ground. From a two-story window!"

"Your *what*?"

"My *bird*, you rotten...tit killer!"

He dove his fingers inside the twisted coil of her hair. Willy-nilly, hairpins flew free. Free. That's how she felt—practically naked, in his bed, in his arms.

Free. For the first time in memory, no one owned her or her happiness. But Laney owned both.

"And good riddance," he grunted, fisting his hand in a wad of hair and tugging sharply.

Her head snapped back. His furred chest rubbed over her back. Wait—hadn't it looked smooth earlier? A trick of the candlelight perhaps?

Mr. Hammond growled low in his throat and pulled on her hair again, rousing her entire scalp.

"You're the gruntingest man I have ever known."

Teeth at her shoulder, he answered, "And you're the most mysterious wench I ever crossed paths with," then bit down.

"Oh!"

He licked the spot, his tongue rasping over the hurt, the sensual touch rougher, dryer than she would have expected.

"Mmmm, how do you do that?" Her bum arched

upward, seeking the now-familiar press of his shaft, just as her bare breasts rubbed over the counterpane, abrading themselves on the homespun cotton, but still she *ached*... Everywhere, needing his intentional touch in places he was deliberately avoiding.

"Do what?" His textured tongue licked a trail of fire down the center of her spine.

"Make your tongue so rough? Oh. Mr. Hammond, please—touch me!"

He growled a humor-free laugh. "Just Nash. A *mister* doesn't have any place in bed."

He paused and licked over her bottom—long, slow swipes of that amazing, abrasive tongue, blanketing each cheek with extensive forays until every crumb of skin was on fire and craving more. She thrummed from the outside in.

"Touch you where?" he asked, releasing his hold on her scalp with a gentle draw down the length of her hair until he reached the ends. "Want to give me leave to figure it out for myself?"

She moaned her acquiescence, louder when his surprisingly sharp nails skidded over her sides and then disappeared.

She arched upward again, sensed him moving to the spot between her legs—the heated, pulsing spot with *his* name on it. His breath puffed across her arse, teased her bits... Clothing rustled as he kicked his pantaloons free...

But still he didn't touch her.

"My breasts, you beast!" she yelled, eagerly rising on all fours and presenting her most private places to him.

His. She wanted to be his. She wanted *him* to own her.

Own more than her indenture. Her body...her heart.

She wanted that tender lover from the gazebo, the one who cherished her with loving words, who treated her like a queen.

But she wanted this man too—the one who growled into her crease just before he began stroking it with his oddly rough tongue. The one who scraped his sharp nails over her thighs, dug them into her bum and caused little lightning streaks of pleasure-pain to thunder across her flesh.

The one who didn't demure when she thrust herself backward onto his face, encouraging, "Give me more... Of you. Mr. Nash Hammond, *you!* I need you now. Please..." but who instead bit at her article, kissed the quivering flesh one last time and pulled away only to return a second later, hooking an arm in front of her thighs, lifting them off the bed at the same time he pushed her head down against the mattress.

Aligning his staff at her swollen, hungry cleft.

Plying his hard flesh along her pliant entrance. Strong fingers joined in, reaching around to part her folds, to open her for the nudge of his erection.

Whimpering at his slow pace, she clutched at her breasts, dragged her nails over the sensitive flesh, arousing the puckered peaks, and caught her breath when he finally settled into place—eased past the entrance to her treasure and paused.

"Please. Don't halt," she cried, ramming herself backward onto the wide head, down the thick shaft.

Past the fragile barrier. She bit her tongue to keep from crying out, but couldn't stop her moan of satisfaction.

Gone now, allowing the most intimate parts of her body to surround the most intimate part of his. A snap of pain, one she embraced, just as her woman's flesh embraced the powerful man who'd breached her defenses. Physically and emotionally. For the first time ever…

It was gone, the last shred of her past.

The one that separated women from girls. Whores from ladies.

Laney from Nash.

And she couldn't be happier.

"GOD-DEM IT!" Nash roared, jerking out of her so fast he almost tumbled to the floor.

Might as well have—she'd knocked him senseless.

"Virgin? You're a bloody virgin?"

Nay, he was the bloody one, his nose wincing at the acrid odor of fresh blood wafting from his cock. His throbbing, pulsing, eager-for-her-cunny-like-it-was-heaven cock.

"A virgin," he repeated, unable to stop himself, as the feline urges mired his thoughts as though they were mud. V-I-R-G-I-N? He couldn't wrap his spinning mind around it. "A paid whore—who's a virgin?"

It wasn't possible. But then, neither was turning into a lion.

Twice now, he'd harmed an innocent, drawn blood. Twice now, he'd damned his soul.

He shook, shuddered, the primal urge to change

driving through him. Stinging his cells. Firing his rage along with his arousal.

Clamping a hand over his cock to keep it off her—*out* of her—he struggled for dominion over The Change. He struggled to keep his shape—and will—human.

He struggled for understanding.

Last night's deceit? Manageable. He hadn't known anything about her then.

But tonight's deception? His reaction to it?

Now that he'd learned of her grandmama, her teacher friend, her fear... Now that she'd made him care, 'twas the exact opposite. Control vanished.

"Why?" he roared, vibrating from the need to pound into her. "*Kwa nini hukuniambia?*" *Why didn't you tell me?* Remorse rode him hard. But not regret, for he craved her still. Dem her! A virgin? *I would have taken more care! "Ningekuwa makini zaidi na wewe!"*

Without his restraining presence, she rolled over. An illusion of luscious femininity staring up at him in the night.

That's all he could discern—her outline. Her shadow. Her *betrayal.*

That and the glint of unshed tears in her eyes each time she blinked, reflected in the sliver of moonlight allowed through a passing haze of a thin cloud, then just like that, *gone.*

Leaving him in total darkness.

Again.

8

THE VIRGIN WHORE AND THE GUILTY CONSCIENCE

LANEY SCRAMBLED TO SIT, every particle of her being so blazingly alive—so excited. "'Tis of no consequence, truly."

As he gurgled out several odd-sounding words, she reached for him. He stumbled off the bed. "It matters not, I tell you. Please do not assume guilt over something for which I hold no one responsible. Least of all, you."

"Responsible?" Sounded as though he choked on the word. Drat—why'd she go and douse *every* light?

"Can you not tell?" she implored, just needing him back. His glorious weight back upon her, his body back inside hers. "I *wanted*—"

"Responsible? For *you*?" Like an attacking viper, the accusation hissed at her, the sounds a grating mockery of his usual unhurried tone. "Never! *Kamwe!*"

The window lit naught but his outline, his posture stiff. Unyielding.

When all she craved was to *yield* him. Her body. Her heart.

Why had he backed away? Why did he behave as though her being a virgin was such a horrid thing?

"*Kwa nini hukuniambia?*" he cried out again. "*Ningekuwa makini zaidi na wewe!*"

She didn't understand the strange things he fired at her.

Didn't understand his confusing shifts of manner—from playful to abrupt, smooth to rough, gentleman to shatter-wit...

Though his contradictions perplexed, they also *excited*.

None of those trifling concerns held a candle to what she *did* feel—deep inside. That lonely spot no one had touched since Grandmama died, leaving Laney alone. Alone with her visions and no one to share them with—she'd never told Mary Delilah, not wanting to seem peculiar and risk losing her one true friend. Reginald didn't count. Laney only told him things to keep him a little in awe of her; 'twas the only influence she'd ever had over him. The only way she'd found to keep him from approaching her again...

But with Nash Hammond? Beautiful, haunted—hunted?—Mr. Hammond... He called to her as nothing else.

What was he running from? What would it take to soothe his soul? *Something she possessed?* Something within her that she was meant to share?

Surely her visions were telling her to try. As if

perhaps she could rescue him from his past just as she needed him to rescue her from her future.

At least the one without him in it.

Because perplexing visions or not—perplexing *man* or not—when he looked at her as he did now...with his eyes deep, glowing coals that lit the space around him, she could *feel* the echo of the love he'd expressed in her vision, knew it was only a matter of time before the emotion rang true and loud.

But right now she didn't want to wait for love. She wanted him. Wanted him as a lov*er*, soothing the persistent ache, the plaguing loneliness...

"Get back down 'ere and finish what you started, Nash whatever-your-middle-name-is 'ammond! You will not leave me 'anging a second time!"

He didn't budge, but, "*Second. Time?*"

Her lower body arched toward him. Why was he staying away? "Aye!" she hissed, pinching her nipples, wishing her fingers were his teeth. "Last night you stopped, left me aching. Just as you have now."

He convulsed forward, then again—as though his body wrenched itself in opposite directions. She rolled to her knees, hand outstretched. "Come back to bed, Mr. Nash 'ammond. Let me take care of you."

"*Ulidhani kunitunza?* Take care of *me*? *That* is what you think, you deceitful bitch?"

She gasped, more at the brutal tone than what he said. She'd been called worse.

His lips twisted in a cruel laugh.

"Why are you being this way? What are you saying? I cannot understand you."

"Course you don't, *jike*. Speakin' in *ulimi*

uliolaaniwa," he said with an unexpected roar tacked on to the end.

She jumped at his ferocity. Collywobbles assailed her stomach, somersaults her heart.

But she didn't think he'd hurt her. Didn't think he could, not the way he was avoiding her. If he wanted to attack, he'd be advancing, not retreating.

Mustering courage, she leaned forward and stretched her arm out farther.

"*Ulimi...uliolaaniwa?*" She repeated the strange sounds with caution, hoping to somehow calm him. "Is that—"

"Cursed *lugha.* Cursed bitch!" Snarling, he lurched forward in the shadows and batted away her hand. "That's right, *jike,* you heard me. Bitch. *Jike.*" A sobbed snarl rumbled from his chest. "*Binti mfalme. Princess.* Princess? God!" He swayed. "Thinkin' you can set your hideous cap for me, *binti mfalme,* you with your lady-like ways and packaged mystery, and get me to *care?*"

Trembling, she rose off the bed and stepped toward his shadow. "Mr. Hammond. Nash. Please—"

"Get back," he roared, shoving her away. A strange *pffft* sound came from his throat and he spun from her, falling to his knees. "Back! Back," he cried, the odd *tap-drag* of his nails scraping against the wooden floor. "Bringin' it all back, you are. The guilt, the hope...the bloody curse."

His hair flew as he shook his head. "Cannot care. Cannot. *Jike.* 'Tis all you can be to me. Nothing more than a breeding whore." He backed up again, everything shaking as he slammed one tight, misshapen fist to the wall.

His bent form wavered in the glow emanating from his eyes. His shadowed form rocked back and forth as he mumbled, more to the wall than to her. "Breeding?" His dark laughter possessed a maniacal tilt. "Cannot breed. Cannot have children. Cannot have *you*. *Nguruwe* Princess. Cannot... Cannot... Cursed...alone. *Haiwezi! Kamwe. Kulaaniwa.* Never! Cursed!" Another convulsion jolted through him. "Not bitch. Never *jike*. Princess. *Binti mfalme. Nguruwe*...oink...oink..."

More muttering. More shuddering.

The more addled his nattering grew, the more determined her conviction to help him.

"What curse, Mr. Hammond?" Heart strangling her throat, Laney tugged the quilt around her shoulders and tiptoed toward him. "Tell me of yours? For I live with one too."

He growled when she neared. Sniffed and snarled, but that was all. She shuffled forward in the near dark and placed a shaking hand to his taut shoulder.

He flinched. Low guttural growls filled the room, but he made no move to attack, despite his threatening words. His brutish behavior.

She knelt behind him, let her fingers sink into the short, impossible pelt of fur covering his back. Let full awareness sink into her mind.

Her visions weren't the only otherworldly happenings at work here.

He *pfffttd* again, rumbled more of those strange-sounding syllables, interspersed with words she did understand—*Swine... Princess... Curse... Horses... Hats...* And *Francine.*

Refusing to acknowledge how that last one tore at

her insides, Laney guided his bent form until he haltingly gained his feet and directed a stumbling, grumbling—previously sober, now somehow soused—man back to bed.

The bunched muscles beneath her fingertips flexed and strained. He kept sniffing the air, rumbling low in his throat and wincing every time she touched a different part of his body.

After long, agonizing moments that should have taken a mere second or two, he toppled upon the mattress with a moan, caved into a tight ball and stared up at her with glittering, pain-filled eyes. She ignored his warning growl and brushed her hand over his forehead, smoothing away the hair that was perpetually hanging in his face, oddly not surprised to feel that it had grown, become thicker. Just in the time since she'd doused the lights—what a mistake that had been!

She traced the fur-roughened skin of his cheek and jaw, unable to miss how his entire body shook as though in the throes of a life-sapping fever. Teeth clattered louder than hooves streaking across cobbles. Laney pulled her hand back, relieved he hadn't snapped it off.

Why wasn't she more afraid?

Because you heard him say he loves you...that you have children *together...*

"I shall retrieve some more candles, shall I?" She spoke calmly, hoping to sooth him. "And also ask the innkeeper to fetch the physician." Where had she abandoned her dress? Straining to see in the darkness, she continued, "I'll return before—"

"Nay!" He lunged upward and latched on to her

wrist, jerked her down before him. "You," he rumbled. "Stay."

"Ordering me about like your dog again, sir?"

Behind her, his entire form shivered, a clashing battle between his will and whatever demons held him in their grasp. He crossed his arms in front of her, held her tight to his chest, breathed in panting puffs over her hair and spoke haltingly as if pronouncing every syllable of the king's English took extreme effort.

"Don't. Go. Do. Not. De-serve. Rot. Hell. Stay. Princess. *Stay.*"

She placed her arms over his and hugged him back. "I'll remain, fear not. But do you not need…"

Scouring her mind for options, she recalled how he'd behaved last night with her, how he'd growled more, become rougher—but then turned tame after releasing himself over her bum. "Why do you not use me?" she suggested into the tense silence. "Can you simply spend your seed once again so you—"

"Nay!" His arms tightened, crushing her lungs. She didn't care, not when he forced out the rest of his tortured statement. "Choice. Curse. Pun. Ish."

He sniffed her hair, nuzzled below her ear, still quaking with the tremors that rocked his frame. "Stay."

She didn't understand any of it—not beyond the brief glimpses she'd been granted. Didn't understand the details of his curse, what was happening to his body, why he was rejecting the option she presented—rejecting her…

Why had the universe directed their paths to cross? Her visions practically force her to pursue him as her only recourse?

Because her visions gave her insight into him—the cursed man beyond what another would be granted? Why did he hold on to her now yet not take what she offered—herself—to ease his suffering?

She untethered one hand from the grip of his fingers and angled her arm till she could find his sweating brow, stroke lightly over his face, his...fur. *Merciful miracles. The man really is part wild cat.*

"Mr. Hammond," she whispered. "You are beyond fevered. Are you quite certain—"

"Not sick. *Cursed.* Apologies. Not bitch. Not *jike.*" His harsh, guttural voice strained with his efforts to mellow the words. "*Malkia wangu. Kaa. Tafadhali kaa,*" flowed from his tongue with ease. He licked his trembling lips, shuddered again. "My...princess. *Kaa.* Stay."

Stay.

For one who'd been pushed and prodded to *begone* and *be off with your troublesome self* much of her life, being asked to stay was quite the balm. Warming over and above his alarming body heat. His rumbled request giving her the comfort and very presence to stay.

For the moment, she was content with that. But come morning, she was demanding satisfaction. Satisfaction in the form of answers. And his body.

And if he didn't satisfy her with both, she'd bloody well challenge him to a duel!

⎯⎯⎯⎯⎯⎯◦⎯⎯⎯⎯⎯⎯

BACK IN LONDON

IN THE CRISP night air of the quality part of town, after struggling with his conscience and allowing the determined, serene Lady Francine to get the better of him, Adam swung off Magnum and assisted her down. "Are you sure now?"

She lightly knocked the valise she held into his thigh. "Aye, I am. As I have told you at least thrice before." She stomped feeling back into legs that must be giving her all sorts of pins and needles, given how it had been her first time astride. "Now which one is his?"

Heaving a sigh of guilt or regret or possibly hope, that this woman might just be the salvation his friend needed above all else, Adam indicated the stately home across the street and down three. "That one. Dark entry."

He'd paused Magnum beneath a tree at the corner, keeping watch in every direction and hoping to avoid detection from anyone else, in case the lady changed her mind. Because he knew Erasmus cared for her, he would do all he could to protect her reputation, whatever she decided.

And even though, to their knowledge, none of the missing or murdered women had hailed from quality neighborhoods such as this, he wasn't about to relax his guard for one second.

Before he could reiterate his plan to stay and watch, ensure she got safely inside and chose to stay, she was off, skipping lightly across the road and quickly ducking into the unlit entry, with doorknocker removed, indicating the inhabitants were not at home to callers.

He imagined he could hear the pounding she

lashed at the door. But in reality, he couldn't. The pounding of his heart was too loud.

He stood there gripping Magnum's black mane, patting the chest and petting the long jaw of his favored beast. Only swung up on the horse's back once the door opened and she slipped inside.

Now for his promised countdown. Wait and make sure she chose to stay. After being confronted with the truth of her fiancé.

The cool breeze blew past Adam's cheek. Didn't reach his lip. He brushed fingers over the thick mustache E always wanted him to shave, to fit in more. As far as everyone here knew, he was a rangy American from Texas—which he was. So what if he looked the part more like 1870s or 1970s? Shouldn't matter.

The same light wind chilled his neck and chest, now that he was no longer cradling Lady Francine atop his saddle on the swift ride here. *Minutes with her in your arms, pressed indecently close to every decent part of your anatomy and you don't even react?*

A light chuckle puffed through his tightly held lips.

It'd been surprisingly easy to erase the image of E's Lady Francine in the altogether.

Shamefully easy. And you call yourself a red-blooded American male? Faced with a lithe, nude body—and you don't even lust after it?

Hell no. That's my closest friend's fiancée. Lusting's off-limits.

And even if it hadn't been, there was the bro code to consider.

Does it apply to fiancée's cousins?

Adam shook his head, hoping the errant thoughts would fly out his ears.

No time for lusting, not when he had a club to manage. Elise to locate.

A cat to deflea.

See? Full life, he tried to convince himself, *no lusting needed.*

Bull-fucking-shit, boyo. You might have been able to ignore your body's responses to E's doxies, but come within five inches of that English miss waiting for you and you—

Five inches? Hell, more like five feet.

Barely an hour ago, he'd wished for a bottle of Bud.

Now he just craved the whole keg. He'd dunk his head in and stay down.

❦

STILL BACK IN LONDON

THE LITTLE BLONDE, ebullient one?

Or the older, reserved one? Perhaps the stout strutter?

Or...the hedge-born blonde—like one of his firsts?

Choices. So many beautiful, god-damn choices. It lifted in his heart, it did, the notion—nay, the *fact*—that he could choose any one of them he wished...

And...

Simply...

Take.

'Twas for research, after all. Scientific edification.

He wasn't particularly enamored with the blood involved—but was that not why he hired help?

Though the choices were his—*always*.

The pesky thrumming increased. The one that had started earlier, and without warning.

The one that vibrated from his toes to his nose, from the outer reaches of his fingertips all the way down to his soul. The fine trembling that took hold of his limbs, controlled his actions...

The Knowing.

He would choose one of them *tonight*.

One of the many blondes to unexpectedly cross his shadowed path this eve.

For had he not—unsuccessfully—tried a brunette last?

———

Dreams.

Interesting concept, that: *Dreams*.

There were daydreams, when one, with full awareness, conjures something they would very much like to experience or mentally creates a pleasant, ideal situation to see them past a difficult time.

There were *dreams*—lifelong ambitions, often kept hidden, secreted inside one's soul either because they seem too implausible to ever come true or because they could never be admitted to oneself in the light of day.

Best way to avoid disappointment—or complete and utter devastation—is not to admit what one wants. Pretend it doesn't exist. Then, living in complete denial, a person might *pretend* happiness.

Even if their existence didn't come close to their

secret desire—the one that would equate to true happiness.

But then...then there were D-R-E-A-M-S.

The sort one's mind often creates while the body is slumbering. Nonsensical, viewed in shades of grey, brief flashes of events and people that come together in confusing, complicating ways to entertain the conscious self during the wee hours.

However, on occasion, when the stars align just so, one picks the winning horse and has a vivid, slow-moving dream in all its colorful splendor, the kind of dream that leaves one in alt, in paradise, in desperate need to never, ever, *ever* awake. For then it might end.

Nash was in the thralls of one of *those* types of dreams.

The kind that tantalizes the body and soothes the spirit. The kind that makes a man *want* to sleep his life away.

Ahhhh. Utter perfection.

Sunlight streamed in through the window.

He recognized it, though his eyes—and mind—were shut tight against the break of day. But the warm rays heated his tired flesh, made him feel new, refreshed. *Relaxed.*

Oh hell, that was an absolute clanker.

Nash's bowstring-taut body was anything but relaxed. When the angelic vision in one's sinful dream has bathed one's brow, one's body—one's ballocks!—with languid strokes of cloth and water, when her firm touch has touched everywhere, soul deep... When her lips are even now caressing the length of the proud erection straining high toward heaven, how, *how* can a man be relaxed?

"Puh." A snort of disbelief puffed through Nash's lips. He tried to roll over, sink back into the blissful oblivion that had claimed him deep in the nighttime hours, but something stopped him from moving.

Could it be...the lips caressing his shaft?

HE CAME AWAKE WITH A JOLT. Jarred from the hazy peace that had so recently cushioned him from reality, the abrupt departure into wakefulness came as a shock.

Such a shock that it was a full thirty-four seconds before he mastered the ability, much less the will, to move. And in that measly half a minute, a host of astonishing realizations made themselves known.

He was naked and in bed.

He'd spent the better part of the night battling The Change. He knew because he remembered.

Remembered fighting the inborn instinct to turn into an animal. An abomination.

Remembered crushing down the primitive urges, just as he'd witnessed his brother doing not a week before. Fought to bury them so as not to harm the precious bundle of contradictory femininity in his arms.

Nash remembered Laney. Spirited, argumentative, *deceitful* Laney.

He remembered falling asleep just before dawn, exhausted from tamping down feral desires to mate, to *own*. Triumphant in his quest to remain human only because he had other desires vying for dominance. Those of caring, of concern. Of...hope.

But there was one glaringly obvious, monstrously gigantic thing Nash most certainly did *not* remember: Giving the black-haired wench leave to entertain her mouth with his wand!

His hips thrust upward, sliding his rod past lips he couldn't see, hidden as they were by her long fall of hair. But lips that were hot and plump and snug against his pipe.

Lips complemented by a tongue that alternated between tentative forays around his crown with ballocks-blowing suction...

A mouth that Nash wanted to see, to claim. *To kiss.*

He commanded his muscles to sit up. They disobeyed.

He commanded his lips and tongue to tell her to stop. They laughed in his face.

He told his heart to stop stuttering, stop *hoping...*

That insolent organ defied him.

He told his hands to release her hair, told his hips to still. Told his prick to stop dancing.

Nothing listened.

Then she started humming and his cock vibrated within her mouth.

"Bloody hell." And now he was dancing to *her* tune.

In. Out. Up. Down.

Fast. S l o w. Fast. S...l...o...w.

Suck. Lick. Hummmmmmmmmm.

Fast. Fast. Fast.

Take advantage of him while he was asleep, would she?

Declare he hadn't satisfied her? Not once, but *twice*?

Try to trick him by pretending to be a whore?

Well, he'd show her. Show her how a whore deserved to be treated. Show her how a man who walked on the wild edge of society minute by minute, ran from responsibilities day by day, and cursed his existence week in and week out took a whore.

Fast. Fast. Fast. Fast.

"No more!" Nash bolted to a sitting position. He used his grip on her hair to wrench her mouth away from his straining erection. Not giving her time to protest—not giving his cock time to either—he pushed her facedown across his lap.

His hand slid over skin like satin. She was nude.

Nude except for the pale silk stockings caressing her legs. One stopped mid-thigh. The other had fallen below her knee.

His eyes tracked back to the top of her thigh, then a hand's width above. A small brown mole smack on her right buttock, just to the left of center. Surrounded by pale, soft flesh...made more noticeable by the creamy stocking just below. The incongruity of that mole did something to him. It made him desperate to know more about her. What else had she been hiding? But more pressing, at least for the moment...

The sight of those *stockings* did something to him.

Whores don't wear silk.

The reminder sent his restraint flying. His palm followed.

"Aggghhhh!" Nash brought his splayed hand down on her right cheek, just inches above that wicked stocking.

She squeaked and flinched.

His erect cock responded, lurching along her stomach, the action made easier due to the glide afforded by her recent open-mouthed kisses.

How he needed to fuck her.

Her!

Laney of the silk stockings and prim reproofs. His hand came down again.

This time her squeak was a sigh. The flinch a quiver.

Laney of the monumental brass—asking him to buy her—and the monumental mounds, of which the undersides even now rubbed against his leg.

His hand came down again. Harder.

Not a squeak or a sigh, but a moan. The quiver, a squirm, inviting more.

Damn her.

Laney of the fancy dress and fancier manners—when she wasn't deceiving him and pretending...

But maybe 'twas *all* an act? Take in the country gentleman, get him to *care*, then rob him blind? Pocketbook, prick and passion. Wallet, wand and will.

His hand came down again. Much harder. Leaving the right side of her arse burning red, fiery hot.

His cock was rocking to the beat of her moans, still dancing to her blasted tune.

She hadn't tried to get up. Wasn't, in fact, protesting at all, and he stopped holding her down with his left hand and instead applied that one to the task *at hand*.

The task of punishing her.

For what, Nash no longer knew. He only knew she had to pay. Someone had to pay.

His left hand slapped her arse. His right moved to her thigh.

He slapped skin. *Pop!*

Heard her moan.

Slapped again. *Pop! Pop!*

Heard her groan.

Spanked her through the stocking. *Smack!*

"Oh...Nash..."

She wasn't supposed to *like* it...

She's perfect for you, is she not?

Driven by the demons that rode his soul, he pushed her limp form off his lap, rose to his knees and crawled over her.

"Up!" he growled. "Did you not learn to please your swells at Mrs. Michaels' Academy?"

"Academy?" she murmured on a sigh. "Mrs. Michaels is a mill—"

He overrode whatever protest she dared make. "*Up, I say.*"

She didn't move fast enough, so he shoved a pillow beneath her thighs, lifting her, positioning her arse in the air where he wanted it—at his disposal.

With both hands, he spanked the rosy flesh, over and over, stopping only when he realized she was leaning *into* the blows.

Then he saw his fingers and snorted. God-dem fur was growing on the back of his hands. His knuckles had contracted. Nails sharpened.

His sleep-sluggish brain noted what those pointed, not-quite claws had done. More importantly, what they'd *revealed.*

Centered between his "hands", surrounded by the

pinkened fleshy lobes of her buttocks, was her delectable anus. Shining like a beacon, calling him home.

Like a man starved, he dove in, his tongue licking along the shadowed crevice, going lower, circling the puckered bud...*tasting*.

Breathing in the scent of his lady.

His very own whore-turned-lady.

The lady he didn't deserve.

Attempting to banish the refrain, he licked lower, finding her swollen center. Finding it ready and weeping for him. Her honey flowed past his lips and over his tongue. Swallowing her nectar, boosey on her scent, her pleading refrain finally penetrated his brain.

"Mr. Hammond, please. Please! Nash. *Don't stop.*"

Don't stop *what*?

Wanting her with every fiber of his feral being? Don't stop licking her as if he'd never tasted anything so sweet? (He hadn't.)

Don't stop dreaming hopeless, stupid dreams?

Don't stop showing her what an animal you really are! Don't stop punishing her...

For making you care!

Nash straightened and curved his palm over his cock.

Now *he* was the one wincing. Devil take it, he was sensitive. A primitive growl erupted when he fisted his erection and brought it to her crack. Up and down he slid his cock head, from her pouting core to her twitching anus.

Teasing sensitive flesh. Taunting himself.

When you should be punishing her.

He brought his other hand to his mouth and sucked his thumb inside. It was the bluntest of his nails, the others already resembling claws. *Blast me!*

Ignoring the frustrated guilt that loomed, once he had it moistened, he placed the tip at her nock and pushed against the eager hole. Past the impossibly tight ring of muscles... He forced his thumb in as far as it would go.

Her arse started humping his hand, her bun seeking his stick.

Punish her, he would. She wouldn't be satisfied this time either! He wouldn't give her the demmed satisfaction.

Couldn't. Not and command any respect, not after her *betrayal.*

He slid his rod between her legs, coating it with her fragrant juices.

"So you want to act like a whore? Trick and deceive?"

More of those whimpered squeaks escaped the lady —no, the *whore*—on the bed.

Nash twitched a deaf ear, ignored her moaned pleas to *stop the aching* and yanked his thumb free, replacing it with his cock.

"Bitch," he cried, easing his wide head past the narrow opening.

"Whore," he confirmed loudly when her tight passage sucked him the rest of the way in—as though he belonged there.

"Lady!" he contradicted himself, realizing how wondrous it felt, riding her untamed, unplowed, *virgin* arse, plunging deep inside that tiny dark hole, expecting oblivion but instead finding infinite light.

"Laney!" His voice cracked when he shouted her name. Made it sound something like a benediction. "Oh God, sweet Laney."

Despite the confusion, he savored every rhythmic wave of her body's contractions along his shaft, found that his hand was positioned between her legs, massaging her slick flesh, fingering her nub as a fresh wash of arousal poured over him...around him. Cleansed him...

Washed away the hate, the despair, the guilt. Washed away his past just as she'd washed him. With her hands. Her mouth.

And again he was fighting his body, his urges. Fighting to hold on to the anger and the drive to punish, fighting to find the beast, but finding it all gone.

Gone.

Dissolved in the onslaught of orgasm. The purity of her passion.

The hand at her entrance parted her silky flesh in frenzied motions. His cock lunged inside her arse at a frantic pace. His heartbeat pounded furiously and still he fought to hold on...too soon. Too god-demmed soon.

His ballocks tensed. His butt clenched. His cock strained. His teeth ground against each other to keep from biting her shoulder and he erupted, his seed expelling harmlessly inside her arse. Hope gushing from him just as fast.

"Laney!"

And just like that. It was over.

Nay. 'Twas the beginning.

Instead of his sanity, he fought to catch his breath.

"Laney," he repeated, enrapt by how each undulating ripple of her body milked his cock. By how it took every drop of semen he'd released and drank it down. Consumed him. As he had her—

Until finding out she was a virgin.

A virgin whore.

Guilt assailed him all over again, mocking the beauty of the most profound release in memory. Cheapening it.

The viselike grip of her anus tempted him to stay forever, but he forced his cock to ease from inside heaven and he crumpled to the side. Spent, emotionally and physically. His heart rate refusing to slow, he stared at the pale wonder of her delicate spine, the gentle flare of her hips, reddened from his greedy grasp, knowing he should apologize but unable to speak past the emotion clogging his throat.

Emotion? Or guilt?

Nothing but a deceitful whore, part of him reminded, the part that didn't think he deserved anything more.

Do not call her that, another part insisted. *Mother would be appalled.*

Mother? What of it? She left, lest you forgot. Didn't care then and you shouldn't care now... Whore, that familiar, bedevilling part insisted.

Nash shuddered as guilt threatened to swamp him whole. His virgin princess wasn't a whore. She wasn't!

Oh no? How many times has she tricked you? Lied to you?

Stop it, he demanded.

Do not risk caring.

Too late. Too dem late.

But she—

Why, what an ass am I! That I, the son of a dear father murder'd... In an ironic twist, Hamlet's words spoke sense when his own thoughts could not. *Must (like a whore) unpack my heart with words...*

That's what he needed to do: *Talk* to her. Explain. Or try to, the—

Even now, the familiar guilt and taunting recriminations tried to take over, *the lying, deceitful bitch refuses to look at you, is keeping her head turned.*

This time he ignored the refrain. Sought to move beyond the guilt.

Why would she not look at him?

Afraid to look, mayhap?

Afraid because of what *he'd* see or because of what she would?

Afraid because her countenance wasn't all that a female's should be?

Given the glorious body she'd been blessed with, the melodious voice, the saucy, determined package concealed within, it didn't matter what her visage. Not to him.

But if she was afraid of what *she'd* see when she looked at him after last night, after he'd treated her like a prigging savage just now, then... Then there really wasn't any hope. He couldn't alter who or what he was. Lord knows he'd tried.

"God-dem it, Laney," he howled, so frustrated with

her—with himself—with *life*, he wanted to bolt out the window. Take off running.

Running away as he always did to keep others from becoming close. To protect his heart from falling, protect himself from being hurt again.

But for once, 'twas too late.

He'd already fallen and, damn his soul, he'd also caused her pain. That alone injured him beyond memory. Beyond recourse?

Oh, he could claim the beast ruled him—and it nearly had, but not completely. She'd seen to that. Her gentle touch and engaging presence. And what had he done in return?

Beat her arse and become the beast after all.

Renewed remorse threatened to drown him as the refuge of the open window beckoned. But nay. He was stronger than the monster within. More gallant than the guilt.

He would fight his urges to flee, and remain. Remain and convince her he wasn't an utter and complete savage. Not always. Not every time...

He curved his palm over her abused buttocks and squeezed the heated flesh with care. "Laney, Laney. What the hell are we going to do?"

Because he couldn't run. Not this time. Not until he figured out what he was supposed to do with a virgin princess.

Who wasn't.

9

TIME FOR A CHANGE

LANEY CLENCHED HER SORE, tingling bum. Zoodikers, but that had been *marvelous*. Unexpected, unanticipated, unpredicted and absolutely marvelous.

Who knew that one's bum could be used for such a thing?

Or that something so seemingly childish as a spanking would stimulate every particle of her being until she quite didn't care what Mr. Nash Hammond did with her body as long as *he* was the one doing it?

Now it seemed her turn to do something, did it not?

Yes, yes, yes... The tiny tremors contracting deep within every second prodded her on... *You can do it,* they seemed to say. Over and over, her body urged her mind, *Yes, you can.*

Slower now, but no less breathtaking... *Yes... Yes... Yes... Y e s...*

From puffy, numb lips to throbbing loins and lungs, she was a bastion of sexual repletion.

Yes... Yes... Yessssssssss.

Aye, she *could* do this, by heavens. The time for avoidance was at an end.

Gathering every bit of gumption she'd squandered over the years, allowing others to decide instead of making her own way, Laney rolled over and lifted her eyes to Nash.

He stared at her through the thick veil of her hair, the sloppy fall of his. Glittering eyes trying to penetrate past the strands that fell between them.

When had she become so very adept at hiding?

"No more," she said resolutely, propping herself up on one arm. With a swing of the other, she tossed back her shield of hair and faced him squarely.

There were so many things she needed to ask him, to tell him. Her visions, his eyes. Her indenture, his *fur*.

Their future. If there was one.

Though he appeared completely human at present —that perpetual scowl was back. Gracious, they both had so much to answer for. Addressing him after what they'd just shared was awkward indeed.

"Mr. Hammond, um..." Her mouth dried up. She wet her lips and tried again. "Nash, I—"

Raging thunder boomed into their door from the hallway. Her head wrenched toward the window, breezy sunlight streamed through even as another bolt slammed into their door. A second later, the top hinge came loose and the door crashed open.

She tugged the sheet around her as Reginald staggered inside brandishing a dueling pistol. "Where's Eleanor? Where's my woman?"

Was he so incensed by her absence, he didn't notice her sitting in full view upon the bed?

She bit her lips against a frazzled giggle—Reginald, with a pistol? The very thought was overly dramatic for a man who preferred inside entertainments to any manner of outside sport. Was she dreaming after all?

Nay. For her slumbering brain would never conjure such nightmarish attire for one so fastidious. Appeared as if he'd dressed himself blind, his every piece of vibrant hair askew, sticking out at odd angles from yet another fancy beaver, his waistcoat buttoned askew, neckcloth untied and—*gasp!*—an unbecoming stain on his jacket. The venison stew?

Another giggle threatened.

"'Ere now!" the burly innkeeper plowed inside behind Reginald. "Monied cove or not, you go' no call to go busting down me doors an' breakin' in me rooms."

When Reginald turned the wavering pistol on the innkeeper, any desire to laugh evaporated. "Says who?" Reginald asked with a newfound hardness to his voice. "I have a single shot in here that gives me the right to do whatever I damn well please."

The innkeeper attempted to overpower Reginald, and the man she'd previously known to be the unassuming opposite of violent—until recent months, that is—ducked toward his boot and popped back up wielding a knife.

When had Reginald started going around armed?

"I'll 'ave you arrested an' brought up on charges, I

will!" The innkeeper yelped, jumping back when Reginald aimed for his arm.

The pistol gestured wildly between the bed and the doorway as Reginald came farther into the room.

"Simply protecting my property, my good man. The piece on yon bed is mine," he said all proper-like. Then the façade crumbled and he cocked the gun, aimed the weapon at her and then back at the innkeeper. "I am taking back what I own. Now leave off or I will have *you* arrested—after I shoot a ball of lead in that tiny pea you call a brain."

To show he meant business, Reginald lunged forward and swiped at the man's face, the glint of metal flashing between them.

Heavy eyebrows flattened, the innkeeper backed down, backed into the hallway and bellowed from the back of his throat, "You're payin' for th' damages on anything else you break! An' I want you all outta 'ere in ten minutes or I'll 'ave you *all* brought up—"

Behind her, Nash growled. It was the first sound he'd made.

Already in the hallway, the innkeeper jumped at the gritty noise. "Make that five minutes and no bullet 'oles!" Cursing under his breath, he wrenched the sagging door shut and stomped off. "Bloomin' gentry!"

Sheathing his knife but keeping the pistol aimed at the bed, Reginald leaned against the closed door, took in the scene. His nose wrinkled, eyes narrowed. "Well. If it isn't Little Miss Innocent." His eyes took in the bloodstained water in the wash basin next to the bed. "But no longer, eh? Finally got a man to prig you like I couldn't?" His shoulders seemed to droop, then he forced his arm up, stiffening his posture. "Are you trying to ruin me with my brother? Now I won't know if you're carrying my brat or his!"

"Your *babe*? Is that what this is all about?" She'd lost a babe in her horrid dead-body-vomits vision. "You're *trying* to get me with child? Of all the preposterous notions!"

"Preposterous? What? Don't think I can do it, do you? Don't think I'm *man* enough?"

"Oh, Mr. Tate, all of this just to prove that you *can*? What has your brother done to you?" Ready to confront Reginald herself, take his blasted knife and carve some sense into his thick skull, Laney started to climb from the bed.

Nash's hand clamped down on her shoulder and he hauled her backward against his chest. Knees still reclining on the mattress, his stalwart presence granted a comfort that had been lacking only a second before.

Reginald stalked closer, pointing the gun with a steadier hand than she would have believed possible given the way he'd been drinking lately.

He aimed the weapon over her shoulder. "Take your sordid paws off her." The barrel lowered toward the center of her chest. "And you—don't 'Mr. Tate' me in that pitying voice. I *own* you, Eleanor, lest you forget. Now get away from him, get the hell off that bed and get yourself dressed. You're coming with me."

Nash tightened his fortifying hold and she responded, "Nay, I am not. Never again."

Nash's grip didn't waver. Nor did he speak.

"Aye, you will. We're leaving. Now." Reginald sighted in just over her head. "Let her go—or at this range, I daresay I shall blast your brains into the next room. *Eleanor*. Move *now*."

When had her life become a farce? She couldn't be sitting on a bed, in nothing but a sheet, with a red-haired beast in front of her flourishing a gun as if he knew how to use it and a mute beast behind her. One who *hadn't said a word*!

Only hours ago they'd checked into their new lodgings—from The Black *Bore* to The White Knight Inn—and she'd indulged in more than one implausible fantasy before knocking on his door last evening. *His* door—her knight in rusted armor, the man who was supposed to save her. But who wasn't doing a bloomin' thing—other than tightening those fingers in a potentially bruising grip.

She swung to face him, unintentionally dislodging his comforting hold. "Do you not care?" she shrieked, incensed. Irritated. Full of fire and ire at them both. At Reginald for garnering the courage to finally stand up for himself—but doing it *now*, against her and not his brother. At her new lover for his seeming disinterest, for his lack of any effort toward fighting *for* her. "Do you *want* me to go with him?"

Mr. Nash "Frustratingly Silent" Hammond only blinked, staring at her with glittering eyes.

She shoved at his chest, hoping to rile a reaction out of him, hoping to see that she somehow mattered. Other than rocking backward from the force of her action, still nothing. Nothing over and above another single, solitary blink.

"Eleanor!"

With the hand that wasn't holding up the sheet,

Laney reared back and brought her fist down against Nash's granite chest. Hoping to jar some sense into him, some reaction from him. "*Well?* Are you ever going to speak?"

"No."

"*No?* That's it? 'No' *what*, you beastly blackguard? *No*, you refuse to say more? *No*, you do not care, or *no*, you don't want me to go—" Fire erupted along the back of her head. "Ahhhhh!"

Reginald had grabbed a hank of her hair. To keep from losing part of her scalp, Laney scuttled sideways off the mattress.

That propelled Nash into action.

Finally. A wave of relief rolled over her.

Only to vanish when he snarled and jumped to all fours on the bed. He crouched, naked, ready to spring. His blazing eyes piercing the man who clutched her hair tighter by the second. "Lve—" Nash cleared his throat, shook his head with such force it sent every strand of his wayward hair flying. "Leave. Her."

So he'd taken to grunting again?

Reginald pulled harder on her scalp, dragging her toward the door. Stupid tears filled her eyes. She tripped and fell to her knees. Scrambling to get her feet under her, she clawed at his hold. "Lemme go!"

Mr. Hammond bounded off the bed.

Reginald jerked her to a stop. He aimed the pistol over her head. "Halt right there!" Reginald shouted. "Take one more step and you're a dead man."

Nash kept pacing forward, if slowly. "You. Think...so?"

"I mean it!" Reginald scrambled, hauled her up higher and pointed the gun to her temple.

A frigid tremor arced through her, chilling her blood. Freezing her breath.

Not so steady now, his hand was shaking all over the place. The frigid metal of the barrel tapped against her head. *Tat-tat-tat-tat-tat.* Oh Lord. Now she was shaking too. She left off fighting and hung there limply. "I mean it," Reginald threatened, his voice so hard and cold she believed every word. "I do! Take another bloody step and I shoot her."

"Will he?" Nash pondered out loud, never so uncertain in all his life.

How does a chap rescue a damsel in distress when he himself is *distressed*?

Befuddled from too little respite from The Change. Too much self-castigation.

Muddled from too little sleep and too much Laney. Too little sex, and then—if possible—too much, and again *too much Laney*.

Miracle of miracles, his daylights finally behold the most beautiful creature he's ever seen and he's just plowed her arse without a dram of care or finesse.

Not only that, the stunning female expects him to *buy* her and has positively appalling tastes in hats.

Then her soon-to-be *former* owner breaks in, crazed with jealousy...

How could Nash be expected to gather his wits sufficiently to save *her* when he smelled his own fear coming off his body in droves? When the recently tamed atoms of his being—the ones that had just begun settling back into the normal order of things after the most hellish night—started reverting back into disorder?

But the sight of her—kneeling at that bastard's feet with that prig pointing a gun to her head?

Now Nash was the one crazed with jealousy. With terror.

"Mr. 'ammond...change!" Laney begged, eyes swimming in pain. "Please! Be the cat!"

She didn't need to say his name. Didn't need to blink or plead with her shimmering gaze or beseech him with her startling words because he already knew.

She was counting on him to save her. And that's exactly what he'd do.

Attempts at clear-headed thinking hadn't gotten him anywhere this morning. Giving in and giving himself over, he abandoned his efforts at cogitation. Allowed pure animal instinct to reign as he did something he'd fought against with every cell of his being since turning twenty-five.

Nearly six years of being strong, of staying in control—of being *alone*—vanished, and despite all efforts to the contrary, Nash called on *Roho ya Simba*, the Spirit of the Lion, to come to him.

He opened his mind, his body and his heart and implored the universe as he'd never done before, prayed with everything in him that he'd be able to come back to her when it was over. Prayed he wasn't making the worst mistake of his life. Because while his form had wavered between human and feline in the midst of fornicating and fighting the annual Change, he'd never, *never* willingly relinquished his body and embraced the beast within.

How does one give themself over to that which they have spent their entire adult life combating?

"Surrender!" he called to the fribble—giving the man one last chance.

The gun tottered, but when Laney broke away, Dandy brought it up again, knocking her across the face. "Mine! Now get up before—"

Surrender.

With a roar that would have done his African ancestors proud, Nash gritted his teeth, tensed his legs and gave himself over, changing into the beast in order to save his beauty.

Laney fell back from the second blow Reginald tried to land, but his feisty woman turned to kick out at Reginald, who was gaping slack-jawed at Nash, the gun forgotten at his side.

It was happening. He knew it, sensed an invisible hand pressing down on his head, lowering his body to the floor. Idly, he wondered what the other man saw, but then Nash stopped thinking, stopped...processing. Because all he could do was feel.

Feel the searing burn along every sinew. Feel his skin pull tight, stretch and give way. Feel his nails thicken, sharpen, turn into talons. His mouth grew heavy and wide, pointy canine teeth elongating past his lips. Spine lengthening, curving, forcing him downward. Fur growing. Tail growing—what a strange sensation, that. Mane...fluffing around his neck as if to strangle him for taking so long.

His timing might have been off, but he was *on* now.

On point to save *his* woman—the only one who had ever seen through to the awful truth lurking within his soul. Seen it and hadn't run screaming from him.

Whiskers twitching, extended ears flicked forward, Nash swished his tail and pounced, placing himself between Laney and the red-haired molly boy who was even now pissing himself, leaving a puddle on the floor and the stink of his cowardice in the air.

Laney was crying. Her slug of an owner blubbering.

"*Wangu.*" *Mine.* "*Wangu!*" Nash howled, clueless whether either of them understood him.

Reginald stumbled back into the busted door. "You —you..." He fumbled behind him for the knob. "You can—have her...have her... George John...won't..."

Nash growled low in his throat, let saliva drip off his fangs. Tried to spit a wad for emphasis but wasn't sure how to control the absurdly long tongue in his mouth.

Laney grabbed hold of his flank. Frantic fingers flexed against his leg. Or hip. He wasn't sure what, but he felt her all the same and padded backward, solidly leaning into her, praying she knew he wouldn't hurt her. Relieved to realize he could still *think*.

Wasn't incensed with hunger and disgusting craving for human flesh—the deep-seated fear Blake had confessed once, when the two were well in their cups.

But the drool dripping over his jaw was discomfiting. Rather disgusting. Nash gave his head a fierce flick, flinging spittle toward Tate.

Blubber Boy flinched and kept groping for the door handle. "Aaaaayyyyyyyyyy!"

"Mr. Tate," Laney called.

Just as he wrestled the door open, Fribble spared a panicked glance over his shoulder.

"Don't go there—where you're heading." Her fingers stroked along Nash's spine toward his nape. A ripple of awareness vibrated up his coat. "To that house party where you thought to take me. You don't want to go there. You don't..."

Halfway across the threshold, the not-so-dandy-anymore dandy paused. "Eh? *You know?*"

From his left eye, Nash saw Laney nod. Oh, now that was bizarre. The broad bridge of his nose bisected his vision. Without conscious thought, his right eye focused on Tate. Watched his face drain of all remaining color—not that there was much left.

Realizing Nash wasn't advancing or tearing into his throat, he sputtered, "You have *seen* it? With one of your bedeviling apparitions? Pah." 'Twas apparent the man believed even as he derided. "As if I would put my faith—"

Her nails dug into his fur. "Trust me, you do not want to go there and do those things. 'Tis not you, none of it. Not the you I used to know."

How could she say that when the bastard had just hit her?

"I have to!" Fribble looked cornered. A rank coward. White livered and pale faced. "Have to...George John—"

"Find Neils. Leave London together. Move to India. America. Anywhere *away*. You'll be...happier."

"Happy?" he blubbered, so distraught the gun dropped from his lax fingers. He glanced down, as if surprised he no longer held it. "Happy? *Happy?* Forgot what that's like. Oh, look at my pantaloons!"

"Mr. Tate." Laney climbed to her knees and leaned forward. Nash turned sideways. No way was he permitting her within six feet of the bastard. Crying or not. "Did you mean it?" she asked eagerly. "You'll release me?"

One aghast look at Nash, who snarled for good measure and rose up on his hind legs, paws in the air, just to see if he could—he could—and her no longer dandified dandy nodded with so much enthusiasm his latest hat toppled to the floor. "I p-promise. You are f-free. Just d-don't let it near m-me."

"I won't. But neither will he do—"

This had gone on long enough. Nash padded forward three steps.

That was all it took.

"Sorrrrreeeeeeee," echoed down the hall as Molly Boy retreated. Leaving a puddle.

But more importantly, leaving Nash alone with his rescued damsel.

And one hell of a responsibility.

GOOD GOD ALMIGHTY. He was never drinking anything other than ale for the rest of his life. As long as he was making promises, Reginald decided he'd swear off venison stew while he was at it.

He'd heard excessive amounts of liquor had been known to induce top-shackled hallucinations, but this —*this...*

He'd had plenty of time yesterday and last night to think. Ever since his stomach began gurgling and things started coming out both ends... Ever since he began wondering whether each moment might be his last—and wishing more often than not it were—time had slowed to a crawl, allowed all manner of introspection to creep through his mind.

Perhaps he'd shit out some of his brains in the privy yesterday, but he could still tell time.

And it was past time to remove himself from George John's influence, past time to give up his contrived association with Eleanor and past time to get the bloody hell away from that...that...*thing* in her room. Its room. The thing's room. Broken-door room.

Reginald barreled into *his* room, evaluating his possessions with a glance.

No time to wait for the next stagecoach. His trunk would stay, but not all the contents.

The hairs on the back of his neck rose with every second he dallied. Though he feared his door might be unhinged any moment by the unhinged *thing* in the next room, he spared moments to scrounge. But with purpose...

Money. Eleanor's papers. His spare beaver—certainly not as fine, but it would have to do—and his prized snuff tin, the precious gift from Neils.

Neils.

Pocketing what he'd retrieved and all of the money he could carry, Reginald was back in the hallway and heading downstairs in under a minute.

Time to gallop back to London, locate Neils, beg his forgiveness and board the next ship across the channel.

And if George John didn't like it—when he received the letter Reginald would write and post only *after* the ship docked—then his brother could go ferk himself.

His chapped arse protested vehemently at the thought of more travel, but there was no help for it. He refused to remain around uncanny, all-knowing Eleanor and her snarling *pet* of a pussy one second longer.

Pausing at the foot of the stairs only long enough to secure a horse, pay his shot and shove Eleanor's bloody indenture papers at the frowning innkeeper, Reginald was out the door and on his way before the next shitty thought hit.

How did he expect to gallop to London when he and horses got along about as well as cats and rats?

***

"MR. HAMMOND!" So amazed, relieved, *ecstatic* she could hardly breathe, Laney rushed toward her rescuer, arms outstretched.

"*RRROOOOWWWWOOOOWWW!*" the feline unexpectedly roared, stopping the impulse to hug in its tracks.

Heart threatening to beat right out of her chest—with fear or joy, she wasn't sure which—she skidded to a halt, tripping on the sheet that had come loose during her tussle with Reginald.

Deep down, she knew she shouldn't fear him, but after that monstrously loud fang-baring display, she couldn't stop the frisson of...uncertainty...that whizzed down her spine, around her bum and then up again, exploding in her stomach.

"Oh my heavens. You are majestically terrifying when you do that." She glanced at the space between them, noticed her bare toes—all the way up to her bare breasts. "Merciful me, I'm still not dressed."

One furry front leg took a step toward her.

Without meaning to, she jumped back and Nash Hammond promptly rumbled another roar.

She squeaked and gave him a wide berth. "Aye, definitely scary. But thrilling too, I must confess."

Spotting her dress, she leaned down to pick it up and stood, holding it in front of her. Exactly how did one converse with a shaggy beast? A beast with the most soulful eyes...

Swallowing, she shook out her dress and attempted to pretend as if standing naked in front of a giant cat— who was really a man, one who she'd just been thoroughly intimate with!—was nothing more than a commonplace occurrence. "Impossible," she said out loud. "I could sooner stop the sun from rising."

Making a mew of curiosity, Mr. Hammond padded softly over to the busted door and plopped down in front of it like a barricade. A massive feline barricade.

"I shall be happy to talk more when you...uh, are human and not growling at me." He turned his furry head and wiped his jaw against one shoulder. "Or no longer drooling."

The words she'd just uttered echoed between them and an embarrassed laugh escaped. The situation defied explanation. Her gaze kept skittering from the window to the dress she was struggling into to Mr. Hammond.

The sight so filled her with amazement, she was making a complete hash of attiring herself, turning every which way in her muddled efforts. Avoiding the unpleasantly aromatic puddle, she accidentally bumped into Reginald's abandoned beaver which brought home the bewildering events of the morning. Another nervous giggle threatened and she swallowed it down. "Did you see how his hat fell off when his jaw started working like a hooked fish? The look on his face?"

Her long skirts finally swished into place, and nose wrinkling, she step-skipped away from the puddle. "I cannot believe he wet your floor. And *you're* the four-legged animal!"

Behind her, Nash made a strange noise, a cross between a snort and a growl.

"Oh, you smell it too?" The dung cart had just stopped beneath their window, the driver halting his donkey to inspect something on the ground.

Outside a fast-moving blur caught her attention and she turned to investigate. "Would you look at that?" she trilled once she realized what she was seeing, so lighthearted, 'twas a wonder she wasn't levitating. "Reginald's already outside—running away without even taking time to pack. And the sun's finally shining! What a glorious— Wait a minute." Laney stuck her head out the open window. "The stables! Oh, Mr. Hammond," she called over her shoulder, "I do believe he's...he is! Reginald's climbing on a horse. Scaling one, more like."

She pulled back inside the room, laughing so hard she gave herself the hiccups. But at least her dress was on, spencer tugged into place to conceal the buttons she couldn't quite reach.

"Pardon me," she said after another hiccup, staring at the golden-eyed lion barring the way, "but Reginald cannot ride. He's a complete hash when it comes to horses. He fell off one as a child, has remained intimidated ever since." Neither could she stop checking the view out the window. The one before her only made her tongue flap.

"Oh dear me. The driver of the dung cart just scooped up my hat, the candles too. I daresay he'll make his missus very happy indeed when he arrives home. And look—Reginald's holding on for dear life, bouncing all over the place! His horse is a bonesetter for sure. Fitting, do you not agree? There he goes, trotting away in a cloud of dust and curses. I suppose that means the ground's finally drying. *Poof*." She snapped her fingers. "He's gone, almost as quickly as you turned into a cat. Fascinating, that. I'm ever-so happy I finally witnessed your transformation."

She was jabbering again, but couldn't seem to stop herself. Not when she'd been provided with undeniable proof that her mystifying visions were true. Not when her entire body still quivered with the strange crazy-wonderful sensations Mr. Hammond caused to riot within her. Not when he wouldn't stop growling at her.

And most assuredly not when she'd just been granted her freedom.

She spied her slippers and slid them on. One

stocking was ripped to shreds—how had that happened? The other kept drooping at her ankle. "No matter. I'm free! Free! Did you hear him? I'm free!

"And you *are* the big cat I kept seeing. I knew it. Impossible but true. Your eyes, you know—they give you away. Wait till I tell Mary Delilah about this." Nash sidestepped when her skirts hit him in the face. "Oh! Forgive me. I simply cannot believe it. Can*not* believe it."

She did a little jig around the magnificent creature who was now on his feet and watching her warily—probably reluctant to get whacked by her dress again—still searching for the rest of her attire. "Gads, what a rum morning! I don't believe I have ever been in such exalted spirits!

"Do you realize..." She paused to take a breath and tugged on the gloves she'd just unearthed. "Over thirty-six months I was with him, pampered by him, and he treated me fine until recently."

Without conscious thought her hand went to her right arm, then she shrugged, too excited to stay still. "I want to pet you but, um, that will have to wait. To be perfectly honest, I'm not certain about those teeth. They're really...well, *long*. You do realize that I shall not be satisfied until you explain"—she waved her arm back and forth, encompassing his length—"this whole cat-change thing, don't you?"

Laney twirled in place. Where was her parasol? Had she brought it with her last night?

"But not quite yet. I need to walk off this agitation. I'm far too betwattled to sit still for explanations right this moment. Joyfully agitated, but still. I apologize, Mr.

Hammond, but I need to *move*. Oh, I do hope you understand." When a snarl rumbled from his throat the moment she started to stroke his shaggy head, she jerked back, bumping into the door. "Soon. I shall return soon and you can explain the marvel that is you, all right? Without, uh...grunting at me, do you not agree? You *can* understand everything I'm saying, can you not? Heavens. I have never been faced with anything like this before. You don't happen to see my parasol anywhere, do you? Just shake your head. Nay, the other direction. Hmm. Did that mean no? I shall assume so. Very well. I'm sure it will come to hand later. For now—for now, I'm free!"

So giddy her feet kept dancing as fast as her words kept trilling, she heaved on the door until it came loose enough for her to slip through, then paused. Glanced at him. "Uhm... Do you want to come with me now?"

Could she help it if her voice rose toward the end, imagining the stares, shrieks and swoons to be had should she escort him in his current form into the taproom?

He rumbled and shook that gorgeously shaggy head of his, full of mane and whiskers and—dare she hope, *man*—somewhere in there...

"Nay? Understood. I shall just"—she shoved and pushed—"prop this back in place. Done." He snorted from the other side. "There now, Mr. Hammond," she spoke into the keyhole. "Take care and I shall see *you* soon." *I hope.*

Flying down the hallway, she ran into the innkeeper who looked slightly mollified compared to earlier. "Ah, miss? Madam? Eh...ma'am?"

"Aye?" Still smiling, she halted, clueless how a *former* indentured servant should be addressed.

"Th' gent wot's jus' left told me to give you these." He handed her a piece of crumpled, torn paper. A bedraggled roll she recognized very well. Her relative hadn't cared sufficiently to use anything fancier, when they indentured her to Mrs. Michaels. And when the milliner relinquished Laney to Reginald for a handful of coin, that woman had simply signed her rights over to him, scratching out the old and inking in the new. Over the last few months, how she'd come to hate the tight scroll and all it represented. "An' 'e did pay for the damages to me door, so seeing as 'ow 'e appeared to be th' one causing all th' trouble..."

"He was," Laney confirmed, contemplating what she held and thinking about more than just the present. She was thinking about her future. "Most assuredly."

"Then as long's you an' your mister 'ave th' coins to pay for your room an' I don't 'ear any more of them strange noises coming from in there, you can stay. Everybody's plans got thrown off with these infernal rains an' ole Toby ain't gonna be th' one to strand you folks out in th' night."

Laney chose not to point out that it was *broad daylight*. Not much beyond early morn. "Thank you. I'm not positive yet exactly what plans...the, ah, mister and I have, but be assured I shall tell him of your kind offer."

The page weighed heavily in her hand. Her scrip to freedom.

Freedom or...her future? Which did she cherish

more? A life of independence or the outcome she'd glimpsed several times over since climbing into the stagecoach and encountering Mr. Hammond? An outcome that still raised as many questions as it answered, but foretold happiness indeed.

If she was willing to chance it...

Trusting in the cursed-blessed visions more than she ever had in her life, Laney held on to the promise of a future with the irascible, impossible man upstairs —Grandmama would be so proud—and released the document in her possession, handing the coil back to the innkeep. "When my good Mr. Hammond comes downstairs, be so kind as to give this over to his possession. After all the excitement earlier, he's, ah, *resting* and would rather not be disturbed right now."

"Very well, m'lady." Responding to Laney's tone and manner, he let the courteous, if erroneous, address fall from his lips.

She let it.

"I'll just retrieve my bonnet from Mr. Tate's room and go for a little stroll. Would you please send up one of the maids to attend my toilette?" *And do up my buttons!* "And if you could see your way to not let Mr. Tate's room until this evening? That would be sublime and allow my dear Mr. Hammond to gather my belongings. I'm afraid Mr. Tate attempted to commandeer some of my personal effects that did not rightfully belong to him"—wasn't that the truth?—"and Mr. Hammond is helping me secure them."

10

NEW HOPE AND NEW HATS

———◦———

LANEY HAD ASKED for a few minutes. Nash gave her twenty-nine.

Not because he was feeling generous or anything of the sort, but because he was still in the form of *a deuced wild cat!*

Panic brimmed. He squelched it—barely. And only because once he heard his name, he'd cocked an ear toward the stairwell and easily made out the remainder of the conversation she had with the innkeeper.

What was the man supposed to give him once he came downstairs? *Resting*, his furry arse.

Ah, but...

...My dear Mr. Hammond to gather my belongings.

My dear Mr. Hammond.

Confident she intended to return, for her personal clothing and hideous hats if nothing else, Nash waited.

First patiently.

Then impatiently.

Then with the fear of God running through him. Now that he'd succumbed to the curse, was he destined to stay like this forever?

Hadn't exactly thought that part out, did you? When you rushed in to save a whore?

"She's not a whore!" he shouted. Only it came out, "Rrr-Kaa-owwww!"

The loudness made him jump.

Good. Satisfying to note you agree.

Damnation, he had to make his way back to two feet instead of four paws. Get rid of the spittle puddling beneath his jaw. Banish the tail he'd stepped on twice. Fight his wayward cells to change back. For he had unfinished business with the pattering miss who'd just skipped outside.

Explanations?

Laney thought *he* owed *her* explanations?

If anything, he needed to regain his human form so he could inquire how in blazes she'd learned about his secret—why she hadn't jumped out the window in fear or expired on the spot.

How she'd known to encourage him to "Be the cat!", practically rendering him mute all over again.

———◦———

FORTY-SEVEN MINUTES NOW.

He'd tried every possible thing that came to mind...

Thinking himself human. It hadn't worked.

Wishing himself human. Hadn't worked.

Demanding himself human. Hadn't. Fucking. Worked.

Begging. Pleading. Nay and not one bit.

Spitting and growling and hissing hadn't helped a lick.

God-demming his grandfather and that maleficious African "healer"—the two Nash considered wholly responsible for the curse—had only brought a surge of pain firing up his legs. All demmed *four* of them.

Why wasn't she back yet? *Soon* did not extend beyond forty-prigging-seven minutes!

Had Dandy returned and claimed her now that she was wandering about unattended?

Had some other dissolute dastard done the unspeakable and snatched her up for his own?

A low growl vibrated past his pointy teeth and long tongue. *You finally decide you want responsibility for something—someone—and you go and lose her posthaste?*

Dem him all over again! He should *never* have let her leave.

One hard propulsion from his hind legs and he was at the window, his overly large, fluffy-maned head scooting the curtains aside, his broader-than-usual nose sniffing like mad while he cast surreptitious glances from both sides of his feline face. Surreptitious because the *last* thing he needed was for some mad-for-it fox hunter to catch sight of his newly formed muzzle and sight the open end of his hunting rifle between Nash's eyes.

He sniffed again.

The recent rains had washed the landscape clean. But he caught it—caught them both. The weakening odor of Dandy's dissipating fear—confirming that the bastard was long gone—and the sweetly alluring fragrance unique to Laney. His lusty lady.

Subtle but present, easily overpowering the other scents invading his nostrils because hers was the one he focused on. His eyes followed a dirt path out past the stables, one that set off through a field, edging alongside a thick grove of trees.

Wherever she'd wandered off to, it wasn't far, not since he identified her direction so readily, could still scent her presence.

God. *Laney*.

After bumping his head on the window ledge, Nash turned around and padded to the bed. He rested his heavy jaw on the mattress. Seeing out either side of his face with one hell of a broad nose in the center was taking some getting used to.

Mayhap it would just wear off. If he waited long enough, mayhap...

Mayhap?

Mayhap hadn't gotten him anywhere, now, had it?

***

Back in London

"WHAT ARE YOU *DOING*?" 'Twas a feminine hiss.

One Tyndale ignored, more intent on locating better paper and a knife or sharper pencil than reengaging the troublesome sprite. A few remnants of paper resided neatly on the desk, and a blunt pencil.

But for what he wanted, neither would work sufficiently.

He needed more than a tiny scrap, not to mention
the useless dull pencil. He'd rather a fine point—and
he'd left his blade at home, else he would make his
own. His broken blade, thanks to his latest and most
untidy of interests.

"Should you really be nosing about Lord Blakely's
things?"

Pulling open the third drawer, he ignored that too.
He scooted the single chair out of his way. Crouching to
ruffle his fingers over the sides and back of the deep
drawer, he took a perverse sort of pleasure in not
responding to Wylde's woman.

After a couple dozen more ribald comments—that
he should not have tolerated, but found irritating this
bit of muslin too fulfilling to halt—he'd ushered the
trio of his cousins and their friend on their way.

In truth, had he not been exceptionally busy,
fending off queries as to the identity of His Responsibility? From his persistent cousins, aye, but also from
the additional handful of Den patrons who exited in
the interim.

All while he'd protected the chit from blatant
discovery, keeping her locked behind him and away
from notice. Not that her squirming had helped that
endeavor.

Once the narrow street-side door clunked shut,
he'd allowed the fidgeting bundle to retreat back to the
opposite corner. No need to bother himself shielding
her when no one else was around.

The third drawer proved fruitless and, as his knees

met the floor, he opened his last hope, rifling its mostly barren interior. A slim object met his questing fingers. "Aha! Found you."

With a pleased grunt, he freed his prize and climbed to his feet.

With more gratification than it should warrant, he placed his bounty on the desk and interlaced his fingers. Stretching his fingers and palms first one direction and then the other, he heard the satisfying *crack* and *pop* of his knuckles releasing tension, preparing to dance over the single, sizable scrap of paper he'd found during his search.

"So. You...are..." He gazed across the room at her, attempting to decide how he wanted to proceed. "Wylde's ticket to Fortune?"

She frowned at him. The action brought to life one lone dimple beside her mouth, lit by one of the two lanterns in the room.

"I do not believe he sees me as such, nor I him. What would make you say such a thing?"

"Just making scintillating conversation." As he spoke, he unfolded the page, creased it differently and used the edge of the desk to tear off the portion he wanted. Finished, he took the pencil in hand and peered at her through the dim light. "Was that not your wish?"

A disparaging *pfft* left her lips. "Do you not mean *slumbering* conversation?"

The dimple had deepened.

The antechamber revealed its secrets only when the inner door was open. No matter that the environs of The Den were lit in such a way to encourage scintillating deeds, never mind conversation, that earlier glance had revealed significantly more than he could see right now, discounting her face.

That dimple of hers, along with the shadows surrounding the rest of her, gave him an idea.

Pure, unadulterated instinct guiding his actions, the pencil found its way into his loose grip and the graphite quickly bled onto the page.

WHAT WAS HE DRAWING? And with such rapt attention? Not to mention such swiftness.

How Tempest wished she could draw with such apparent ease—and joy, the first sincere smile she'd seen thus far curving his silent lips.

Though it galled, she refused to admit to jealousy, not over something so trivial. Even if her watercolor attempts prompted chuckles instead of compliments.

"Why must you and your"—she faked an exaggerated yawn—"sleep-inducing conversation turn to maligning my intended?" Though he wasn't, not in truth, defending Lord Wylde's honor only seemed right. "That is rather low, even for you, Lord Tyndale."

The first hesitation of his wrist and fingers coincided with a light shrug. Then after a single glance at her face, he returned his attention to the paper before him, all hint of a real smile wiped free. "All that furor surrounding his last engagement. Made me wonder if he was fortune hunting yet again."

To her knowledge, Lord Wylde had no need of anyone else's fortune, possessing his own, *"Yet again?*

For shame, Lord Tyndale. You speculate over and speak of that of which you have no knowledge."

"Mayhap." Said as though the topic—the one he had brought up—now bored him.

Several silent moments later, his face animated once again. His furious scribbling and the secretive smile burgeoning across his lips renewing her unease.

Thoroughly disconcerting, how diligently the reprobate applied himself now to his self-chosen task. Why, his demeanor made no hint that he was even aware of the definite scream and three squeals that came from behind him.

Not a scary frightened scream, she didn't think. More the sound she imagined coming from a wound-up-tight automaton—one turned too far, threatening its demise—once it's inner workings had been released.

Only hers were not—released, that was. Her inner workings feeling every bit as tight and tense as ever.

Where was Mr. Adam?

Had his escort of Francine gone smoothly? Or had Lord Blakely perhaps not been at home? Or—please, no!—had the recently secretive scoundrel been at home and yet chosen not to admit her cousin for whatever reason known only to himself?

More immediately, just *what* captured Lord Tyndale's attention so thoroughly she'd be convinced he quite forgot her presence—save for the rare, half-second he'd lift his head and spear her with that black gaze she found completely unreadable?

All at once, she knew.

"Wait." She rushed forth, determined to prove herself right. "Are you drawing me?"

'Twould be flattering if he'd striven to mask his irritation at being tasked her keeper. But completely inappropriate. Completely improper—

"Stay back!"

When she would have achieved the distance to see for herself, he skewered her progress with that harsh command and one pointed finger. "'Tis my efforts. I have not given you permission to view them."

His eyes fairly glittered. Her inner workings swooped again, but not with the exciting sizzle the squeals had brought forth, but with dread. "But you shall?" She hated how her voice sounded more pleading than confident. "In time?"

Mayhap 'twas nothing to be dismayed or worried over. Perhaps he simply liked her dress and wanted to sketch it for one of his sisters.

But he has no sisters.

A maiden aunt, then? Tempest was grasping and she knew it.

Worst still, *he* knew it.

For he finally lowered his pointing finger, the hand still holding that dratted pencil. "You may see when I deem it finished." He gave a grim smile, one that did not bode well. "For a price."

NINETY-TWO EVERLASTIN' minutes, he'd remained a blame cat. Ninety-two!

And if Nash had to go another ninety-two or smell Reginald's piss another second—*he* would jump out the window and likely get a bellyful of lead blasted through him, and that certainly wouldn't help his cause with Laney.

And what exactly do you want with her? that annoying, persistent part of him wanted to know. *It's not as if you* looo-oooove *her.*

Nash licked the side of his right paw and brought it to his ear, scratching his head just where he fancied she'd almost petted him. Nay, he couldn't claim to love her. 'Twas too soon for that.

But he did *like* her. A significant amount. Lusted after her. Significantly more. Wanted to be with her and learn about her. Was beyond hot to make her smile and secure her happiness and see where this...odd acquaintance between them might go.

You don't deserve her or a future with—

"RRrrrRRWWwauuow!" Translation: "I do! I do deserve her!"

At the very least, Laney deserved to hear the awful truth about him and what he did to Phineas—then *she* could make the decision.

And he'd tell her. Just as soon as he figured out how to speak English in such a way that it didn't sound as if he were murdering a boatload of badgers.

ANOTHER FORTY-THREE MINUTES ELAPSED...

Nash peered into the looking glass he'd just pilfered from the room next door. Tate certainly wouldn't have need of it again.

Demmed if he wasn't a new man!

All it took was having a dawning of universal

proportions and raiding Tate's trunk after speaking with the innkeep.

At least Nash was walking on two legs now, had shed his mane, his fur and his fear of fox hunters. His muzzle was gone too, nose returned to normal, he was pleased to note. And had he ever worn so many clothes? Certainly not such tight ones. He looked bang up to the mark, if he did say so himself. But that wasn't all he needed to say...

The only thing still bogging him down was uncertainty surrounding what Laney might make of his confessions. But confess he must.

Using the "cursed lion" excuse could only get him so far. Valid justification or not, for the first time in memory Nash *wanted* to rise above his beastly nature. Wanted to mature into the kind of man his brother had always been—one who not only accepted responsibility, but more than that, *embraced* it.

A challenge he finally felt ready to face.

If he could only gaze again on Laney's winsome face without roaring his head off and scaring the bugaboo out of her. Poor princess, she'd tried to cover it, but it'd been easy to discern—his fearsome fangs and vicious-sounding vocals had put her in a petrified pucker.

His tongue might no longer be lolling about past his jaw, but regaining human form hadn't magically turned Nash into a silver-tongued devil, especially not when he considered his reaction to seeing her features for the first time. Given how he'd expected to behold a veritable hag beneath the veil, 'twas no wonder he'd been struck dumb.

A more stunning female he couldn't fathom.

Thick, wavy hair framed an ivory complexion, the blush on her cheeks luring him to touch. But there hadn't been time.

Pink, pouty lips, swollen from kissing *his* cock, had beckoned with an inviting curve all to themselves. Even when pressed into a tight line and trembling with her tears, those sweetly tremulous lips tempted... He'd wanted to kiss her mouth, see those plump lips bloom in a smile. But he hadn't had a chance.

Her eyes, mirroring his own uncertainty, had gazed at him rife with confusion, even *after* he routed Tate, but dashed if he could recall their exact hue.

Grey? Green? *Striped?*

Dem. He had to see her once more. And again after that. And again, *ad infinitum.*

He'd found his very own virgin all right. All that he'd ever wanted...a simple, ordinary female, one who was just his.

But Laney was far from a simple peasant or mere servant. She was far from *ordinary.* Now that he had the opportunity, why was he still standing upstairs on his newly cleaned floor instead of outside tailing her scent?

Why? Why wasn't he racing out the door to find her?

Because you, Nash the Lionhearted, his conscience piped up, *unlike King Lear's Kent are most assuredly not qualified for that which ordinary men are fit for.*

Ordinary? Bah!

Nash stumbled backward and crashed against the

bed, sinking onto the mattress when his legs refused to support him.

Was that why he kept lingering, waiting for her to return? Deep down, did he truly think he deserved to have his penis pegged to a pine pier? Or piked with a pine pin?

No, he god-demmed didn't!

He deserved to have that ordinary life he craved. With the *extra*ordinary woman he'd just saved.

Now that he'd regained the ability to speak, nothing would hold him back. Nothing!

Except perhaps the blasted nervousness anchoring his feet in place, hobbling him more than chains ever could.

Acting the brave man took courage. And at the moment, Nash had never felt more like a cowardly lion, one who wanted nothing more than to tuck tail and *run*.

———•———

"WELL NOW, don't you look dapper?" Laney exhaled in pure relief.

Mr. Hammond had come for her!

The longer she'd walked, the more restless her limbs. The more boggled her mind. The greater the weight squishing her chest—and it wasn't the tight lacing on her stays the maid had offered to do either.

Laney had been too impatient to wait.

For it wasn't every day one woke to the wonder of sleeping with a man for the first time. Or explored that man's body with intimate precision. Or had their own body explored and *plummeted*...

Not every day one witnessed their lover transform into a monstrous feline. Or realize they had quite lost a piece of their heart—completely without meaning to.

From surly stranger to reluctant rescuer and then pouncing puss, the man who now possessed her indenture had become so much more. More intriguing, inviting, invigorating... More sexy, sensual and sublime.

But most of all, more *accepting* of Laney, of "Eleanor" even, than anyone had been since Grandmama, outside of Mary Delilah—who didn't know the whole of it, Laney always keeping her "blessings" to herself.

Why, she'd spoken freely with him from the moment they'd met, even abandoned her polish and decorum lessons in the heat of more moments than she liked to admit—oh, but those heated moments!

Was it any wonder that she lacked the fortitude to face him in such a confined space as the invaded inn room so soon after discovering she held rather tender feelings for the man?

Rather tender?

All right. Passionate feelings. Possessive feelings. *Personal* feelings that she suspected might soon turn to longings and a lifetime of...like. Aye, *like*.

After all you have done with the man in the last forty-eight hours, you still shy from thinking L-O-V-E?

Nay, she didn't. And that was part and parcel of her plaguing panic. For she had positively, absolutely no idea of what he might be feeling for her in return—other than irritation.

Ergo, 'twas easier to remain outside, alone with her disconcerting thoughts. Awaiting his arrival.

Never anticipating 'twould take so drastically long.

But he was here now. If a trifle reserved, contemplating the sky rather than looking at her when he inquired in a rusty voice quite unlike his own, "Permit me to walk with you?"

"Certainly." Subduing her own unease, Laney skipped ahead and curved her arm through the crook of Mr. Hammond's. "Do my eyes deceive me or are you actually wearing a hat?" She smiled up at him, but he avoided her gaze by ducking, giving her a clear view of the fancy headwear. "First one I have seen you don, if I'm not mistaken. Wait. Is that *Reginald's*?"

"Shouldn't pose a problem. Doubt he will think to return for it, and I won't be wearing it long." He guided them onto the path she'd been following back to the inn. Over two hours she'd waited and walked, waited and rested, waited and hoped. *Two hours*, speculating whether he was going to come after her or not.

"Oh?" Then because she couldn't wait any longer, "What kept you?"

Instead of answering, Mr. Hammond took a little-used detour off the main path, directing them straight through the copse of trees she'd skirted previously. Once in the shade, the dank earth compressed beneath her feet.

Three paces in, he stopped. "Your slippers..."

Laney tugged him forward, savoring the thought of being outside *alone* with him. "Given time, they shall dry."

"You were looking for this, I believe?" He shifted

and brought her parasol up between them, his eyes darting to hers and then away again.

"How very thoughtful." His gesture warming her heart, she took the parasol in her right hand, but kept her left firmly ensconced over his arm. "I won't need it here in the shadows, but will happily use it once we emerge. Thank you, kind sir."

Every bit the gentleman, he inclined his covered head. His long hair had been pushed to the side, trapped beneath the hat band. His attention wavered between guiding their steps and glancing toward her face, attempting to see beyond the everyday bonnet's protruding brim.

It was the plainest she'd packed. Her fingers had stumbled when selecting it after dressing, tempted to put one of her others on. In the end, despite how very vulnerable it made her feel, she'd tied the plain bonnet firmly beneath her chin and marched out of the inn, ready to face the day and her future. Whatever uncertainty either might hold.

Focused on snatching glimpses of her, he stumbled over a fallen branch. She allowed her feet to still and turned toward him.

With increasing intensity, his eyes roved over her naked face. She resisted the impulse to look away which became nigh on impossible with every second he stared. "Truly, Mr. Hammond, what *kept* you?"

The muscles in his forearm flexed beneath her gloved fingertips. "You said you would return, did you not?" he inquired without inflection.

She wanted to take her parasol and wallop him across his starched-up shirt points. *Was that Reginald's shirt as well?* "Aye, but I thought you'd *follow* after me. Eventually."

His nostrils flared as if catching scent of something. "It was expected of me, then, to come for you?"

"Well...yes. With your miraculous abilities, one would think—"

"Abilities?" erupted from him, and his arm turned to granite. "My form may change, but I assure you that does not translate into possessing a talent for knowing what notions lurk within the female mind." His voice had smoothed from its earlier rasp but was no less intense. "Even looking upon your face while we speak, seeing how your lips move, your eyes spark, you are still as much a mystery to me as when you were veiled."

A mystery? *Her?* No one had ever said such a thing.

He remained stiff, his uncharacteristic awkwardness somehow mitigating her own, enough so she could share, "I feared perhaps your journey north took precedence over our...um..."

"Our what?" he inquired in a somber tone.

"Ah...association?" she hazarded, uncertain how to term their relationship up to this point.

His eyelids closed heavily, then he blinked them open, piercing her with that glowing gaze of his. "*Never.*"

What did that mean? "Never?"

He took a deep breath, one that strained the fabric stretched taut over his broad chest, but didn't speak. Laney looked closer at his chest—if she wasn't mistaken, the burgundy tailcoat had belonged to Reginald too! As had the pinstriped waistcoat beneath it.

And his cravat was a work of art. "You look magnificent."

"For you," he said, impressing her all over again. "Returning to your earlier concern, at current, I cannot fathom anything that might claim precedence over our...association."

The sentiment behind his strained words calmed her further—if her rapid breathing and rioting stomach could be considered *calm*.

"You're bruising."

Flummoxed, she murmured, "What?"

"That bastard," he swore, bringing his fingers to her face and skimming over the area where Reginald's gun had left its mark against her temple. "If I ever see him again, I will—"

With a terse growl, he jerked away and heaved another breath.

"You'll what?" she whispered, face thrumming from his touch.

His eyes narrowed. "Kill him. A slow and painful death I shall take great joy inflicting."

Before she decided quite what she thought of that chivalrous yet bloodthirsty statement, he raised one arm and mashed the beaver lower on his forehead. Then he captured her hand, laced their fingers and started weaving his way unerringly deeper into the woods.

Long strides of his legs she rushed to keep pace with.

Other than the sounds of their shoes racing over the earth, they proceeded in silence. Silence that didn't extend to the furious pounding of her heart or the wind-ruffled leaves surrounding them or the jubilant chattering of the birds darting overhead in celebration of the clear day.

Did they too perhaps think Laney was heading toward a fortuitous future? One complete with gazebos, Mr. Hammond and...*children*?

When they came upon a small creek swollen from the recent rains, he slowed his furious pace. Taking advantage of his sudden stillness, she commented, "You do know that while I very much appreciate...how you..."

His grip tightened on her hand as he went first, assisting her across the slick stepping stones. Securing her hold on the parasol as much as his outstretched hand, she concentrated on placing her feet directly where his trod, not wanting to drench her slippers.

"Appreciate?" he prompted once he'd gained dry ground on the other side.

She paused and lifted her gaze from the rushing crystal waters to sweep over his fashionable attire. She'd never seen him equipt in such finery. "While the sight of you done up as the most proper of rum-togged swells is wholly attractive, Mr. Hammond, I find I rather miss the impertinent young man who goes about sans hat and steps on hems."

Seeing the twinkle enter his expression for the first time since joining her, she breathed easier, ready to celebrate along with the birds. His thumb slid over the back of her gloved hand and her entire palm tingled.

Palm? Who was she bamming? Her entire body reacted to his touch. The fluttering in her stomach increased from a riot to an all-out rebellion, her breathing went all tantwivy and her foot began a swift slide off the rock. "Aaaa!"

Rescuer extraordinaire, Mr. Nash Hammond hauled her against his chest before the water claimed so much as her little toe.

She grabbed his lapels.

Hands firm about her waist, he carried her farther from the creek, not placing her on the ground until reaching drier dirt. Not easing his hold until he'd leaned back against a thick tree trunk, and not until after allowing her body to glide along the entire length of his. "Ohhh..."

With one palm fastened on her posterior, he secured her in place—as if she had any intention of leaving. He touched the brim of her bonnet with his free hand. "And I find that I much prefer this to those veiled atrocities you wear like a suit of armor."

He gazed at every facet of her face while he spoke, the look in his gleaming eyes as much of a caress as the finger that stroked down her temple, feathering over the bruise.

"No more veils," Laney whispered the promise. "No more hiding."

"Very good. But don't throw the others out. I have use for them."

"A use for my hats?"

He nodded. "Along with this infernal contraption on my head."

She relinquished her hold on his jacket in order to touch his cheek, his jaw. Both smooth. Showing her what *he'd* been hiding since before they'd met. "And what use, pray tell, could you possibly have for my hats?"

"Target practice."

Laughter entered his eyes but failed to reach his lips. He spread his strong fingers over her bum and pulled her closer. "Don't move," he rasped.

"Wouldn't dream of it."

He lowered his head to hers, descending slower than a lake freezes in summer, as if giving her an opportunity to flee his improper embrace.

She didn't move.

Just before their lips connected, his hat brim bumped into her bonnet.

He swore and released her, jumping back as if she'd slapped him.

Which she most certainly hadn't!

They'd been about to *kiss*! Their first real lip-to-lip, tongue-to-tongue kiss. "Mr. Hammond?" Laney resisted the urge to wallop him in truth. "Why did you stop?"

NASH RIPPED the offensive hat off his head and hurled the expensive beaver through the air. When it landed in a soggy pile of underbrush, he stomped over to it, *on* top of it and back again, all the while shooting quick glances at a gaping, gawping Laney. Eleanor.

The serene beauty before him seemed more an *Eleanor* than the lusty wench he'd spent the better of the last two nights with. On one hand, 'twas difficult to reconcile the vastly different women—one street reared, courageous and mouthy; the other polished perfection, eloquent elocution, and just as courageous.

Hmm. Mayhap they weren't so different after all.

On the other paw, not only did she possess knowledge of his greatest secret—which he definitely needed to find out *how*—she'd experienced his great rudeness. Yet, astonishingly, she continued to appear every bit as interested in him now as she was before.

Even with all his terrible transgressions, God saw fit to deliver, practically in his lap, such a female? The embodiment of everything he'd always wanted—complete with everything he hadn't known he needed? Bravery and pluck. Determination.

That stunning form and face...

Grinding his heel into the hat once more, he suffered the unfamiliar knot of trepidation and finally raised his gaze. "Forgive me, Eleanor."

She gave her head a sharp shake. "Laney, please."

"Laney. I apologize for ever thinking you were a sow."

She blinked.

"I apologize for not agreeing to help you the first time you asked."

She raised her eyebrows.

He clenched his hands to keep from mauling her again. "I apologize for taking you in anger, for taking your *virginity*, for treating you like..." He swallowed, squeezed his fists. "Like a whore."

Her eyes widened, then *she* swallowed and licked her lips, but before she could say anything, Nash decided to hell with it and rushed forward. He grasped her wrists, ignoring how the handle of the parasol dug into his palm.

"Truly, I hold vast regret for every single blasted

thing I have done wrong with you. *To* you." He loosened his hold and slid his fingers down to hers and clasped them lightly. "Please, Miss Buckley, can you ever find the forgiveness in your heart that my abominable actions do not warrant but that *I* need, desperately so?"

Given how his formal skills were as ill-used as a pickpocket's, he nevertheless managed to perform a credible bow as a solitary butterfly danced upon the breeze between them. Straightening, he lifted her free hand to his lips and placed a kiss on the back of her knuckles through her glove, wishing he could dispense with the barrier as effectively as he had his hat.

Looking up at her through the cloak of his hair—she wasn't the only one who had a penchant for hiding—he pleaded, "Will you grant me the chance to rewrite our blighted past and make everything up to you? Please?"

Without waiting for her to respond—to deny him—he firmed his hold and dragged her off the path. "Follow me, if you would," he said, not giving her a choice. "Only a bit farther."

Through the thickly clustered trees, weaving around their tall, stately trunks and over surprisingly dry ground given the recent downpours, he forged a trail with nary a hitch to his step, tugging her behind him.

"While you were out walking," he explained, "and once I determined 'twas past time I come find you, I brought this down...and...I..."

Then the small clearing he'd found earlier was before them, the faded quilt from his room spread over drying grass, the sun streaming down from above, its bright light playing bo-peep with the leaves overhead, highlighting the crude basket full of breads and cheese he'd arranged, complete with an unopened bottle of wine and clean glasses. He'd paid dearly for the privilege of bringing everything outside, but found Mr. Innkeeper and his lady wife accommodating once gold crossed their palms. He also had Laney's indenture stashed inside to return later. Later, after he'd said his piece, assuming she remained for the telling.

Swallowing hard, he waited for her reaction.

Pushing her way past the last tree, she came up beside him and gasped. Tugging her hand free, she stepped around the quilt and faced him across it, head cocked, today's ordinary bonnet shadowing her face though he'd yet to learn her expressions. What was she thinking? "You said you wanted to make it up to me. Make what up, exactly? And in what manner?"

He wasn't so far gone that he didn't remember the carefree years before the curse took control, the years in which time was all he had, time to indulge to his heart's content and hone his lovemaking skills as only a young man without responsibilities could. He'd once prided himself on giving his partner pleasure first. He hadn't always been a ruthless *taker*.

Considering how he'd permitted The Change to occur and given how her exquisite body had brought him release such a short time ago, surely his animalistic urges would remain at bay for several hours. Surely, he prayed. Sufficient time to honor her as he'd neglected previously. Honor her body before his own. "Let me show you how it's supposed to be between a man and a woman. Let me love you as you deserve. Let me—"

"Love?" she whispered, her hand flexing upon the parasol, the other fisted beneath her mouth.

"Your body," he implored, not ready to think beyond making physical amends. "Let me love your body."

He didn't have the right to ask for more. Not yet. "I swear to you I won't become rough this time." Lord help him uphold that vow. "I shall demonstrate the patience of Job, I promise," he swore like a dolt. Who compared themselves to biblical figures during a bumbling seduction? "I promise I will not do anything you...do not...want from me..."

He fumbled to a stop when she began untying the ribbon beneath her chin. The one securing her bonnet.

"Go on." She removed the bonnet, revealing a mass of pinned-in-place glorious hair. Sauntering toward the quilt as if she had all the time in the world, she placed her hat and the parasol in the corner containing the victuals. Then she sat down precisely in the center of the patch-worked fabric. "You were saying?"

Nash stormed over to the nearest tree and gripped an overhead branch with both hands, digging his fingers into the bark. "I was saying..." He practically choked on the words, seeing Laney ease the pale blue shawl from her shoulders—more specifically, seeing the bare skin of her upper chest the maneuver revealed. Wait a min— "You changed dresses."

She smiled and dimples appeared on either side of her saucy mouth. "That I did, and you have an abominable habit of not completing your sentences."

"I promise you shall not be left aching this time."

"Left *aching?*" she queried with no small amount of surprise, confounding him all over again.

"I promise," he swore, clutching the limb so tight 'twas a wonder it didn't spontaneously compress into a pencil.

"But I wasn't left..." She waved a gloved hand in front of her face, as if waving away her protest, waving away his asinine claims that he could satisfy her. No wonder, given how he had treated her thus far. Nash felt the blockhead all over again.

"Ahh," she said airily. "Please forgive the interruption." By now she'd neatly folded the shawl and placed it beneath the bonnet. Her slippers quickly followed, and then she turned her attention to her stockings—they'd been replaced as well. Only now they were being *displaced* as she gradually revealed her legs to his lecherous gaze. At the strangled sound coming from his throat, she paused in her efforts and looked up. "Aye? Do continue. What other promises might you have to offer?" Her brow furrowed as she glanced around, beyond the small clearing. "Though should I not be concerned *we* might be interrupted? By anyone who could chance by?"

"No one will. That's one promise I can keep. If a being on two legs dare even think to leave the path and venture our direction, I will hear them in a trice."

"Hmm." Did she believe him? His breath gusted out when her posture relaxed. "*Promises*, dear sir..." Delicate fingers fluttered his direction before resuming their task. "Do go on. For I am enjoying your most edifying speech. It is much easier to decipher than roars and *merrroowws*, you see."

"Your body..." He pushed out through his clenched jaw—for at this moment a good *meow* seemed preferable to his bumble. "I promise to assuage the ache, to... satisfy..." Damn his muddled thoughts! Must he make such a confounded hash of everything? "I know you must be sore from what I—God, I'm sorry—but..."

One side of her mouth lifted in a tiny smile and the first stocking followed the shawl. Finally! Any slower and he'd likely combust.

"Sore? Of a certainty," she confided, running her covered fingertips up the length of her lower leg. When she neared the apex of her thighs, she promptly lowered her skirts, hiding the tantalizing view.

Was she intentionally trying to seduce him?

The equally tantalizing thought disappeared when she remarked, as if commenting on nothing more than the weather, "Truth be told, my bum's rather making itself felt."

At that admission, he forgot how to breathe.

"Were I to be completely forthright, I must also confess there are *several* places on my person that are more than a little tender."

Wood splintered beneath his fingers. Nash glanced up, realized he'd been scraping his nails into the limb and it was gouging him right back. His hands didn't care; nor did his eyes—they returned to the temptress on the quilt.

As if she undressed in front of a man every day of the week, she extended her second leg out past her dress and peeled back the remaining stocking one agonizing, mouthwatering inch at a time, exposing the creamy skin of her thigh and then her lightly muscled calf.

A piece of chipped bark dropped in front of his face. He blew it away, emptying his neglected lungs and watched, captivated, as she shifted on that *tender bum* of hers, raised the hem of her dress and stroked her palm over the bared flesh. "What about you, Mr. Hammond? Are you tender anywhere?"

Lightheaded now, Nash was startled when a twig snapped off in the vicinity of his little finger. He remembered to inhale, and then ground out, "Tender? Nay. Hard as stone. Hot as flame." *Horned for your honeypot.*

"Mmm. Poetic in your torment, are you not?" she laughed.

He growled low in his chest.

She shot him an innocently sultry look from beneath lowered lashes, which should have been impossible because innocents weren't sultry and, thanks to him, she was no longer innocent. But somehow this particular woman managed to be both. Provocative yet pure. Demure yet beckoning. How? Any other innocent exposed to his beastly side would be haring off as if he carried the Great Plague. But not Laney. Why?

"'Tis comforting to note, at least, from what I can see, that you are not growing fur or claws this time," she said, blasting his confusing musings straight to hell. Before he processed her statement, the vanishing stocking revealed perfectly formed toes and joined its mate. Laney rose to her knees and turned her back to him. She spoke over one shoulder. "Help me with my dress, would you, Mr. Hammond? And do please explain about your twitching whiskers and swishing tail. I am beside myself with curiosity, wondering how—"

"Cannot. Not now." Control broke, along with the branch. He lunged forward and dove to the quilt, swooping Laney up on his way down.

"Omph!"

They hit the ground and he rolled to his back, rotating the squirming woman above him until her body covered his. Her eyes sparkled at him.

Moss green.

They were green, the softest, loveliest shade. She brushed a hank of hair off his forehead. "I do believe your definition of patience and Job's aren't quite the same."

"Patience be damned. I want you naked." With fingers gone clumsy, he lifted his arms to her back and worked the buttons of her dress sight unseen. She held her upper body aloft and toyed with his ear.

One button slid free. A second, a third.

He couldn't stop gazing at her. "You are so very beautiful. You know that?"

"Thank you." A slight blush rose to her cheeks. "I confess to immodest relief upon hearing that you think so. For all you did earlier in your room was snarl."

"The cat possessed my tongue, but it's nimble enough now to pay you a thousand compliments. Shall I demonstrate? Eyes like velvety moss, hair the sheen of a raven's wing..." His fingers snagged but eventually the fourth button released. "How could I not be enamored with what I behold before me? Finely arched brows, beautifully rounded cheeks—"

"Rounded?" she giggled. "Like a pig's?"

Mangling that fifth buttonhole, he winced. "*I'm* the swine. You're an impish cherub. An angel."

She giggled and he made quick work of buttons six and seven by ripping the fabric.

"*Angel*, Mr. Hammond?" Those dimples appeared again. Positively enchanting. "I daresay no one has ever compared me to the heavenly realms before."

"No mister," he reminded, wrestling the eighth and remaining buttons free and tugging the neckline down. If he hadn't managed to open enough, the dress could dem well keep tearing. "I refuse to wait another minute to see these luscious beauties."

"My bosom?" she breathed, sitting upright and easing the dress past her shoulders. Kneeling over his torso, she held the dress to her dugs and batted her lashes playfully. "I rather thought it was my bum you fancied."

Nash found himself panting. What happened to taking his time? "I fancy all of you, I have discovered. The dress?" he ended on a growl.

Smiling indulgently in the face of his extreme discomfort—she hadn't once slid her body over the raging erection he'd been sporting since that first stocking had decamped—she straightened, pulled the dress over her head and flung it over her shoulder, leaving her every charm bared to his gaze. Several strands of her glorious hair had escaped and now trailed down over her upper chest, coiling enticingly near one nipple.

No shift. No stays. *Just skin.*

His cock twitched at the realization: she'd forgone undergarments.

Scandalous. Satisfying.

The breasts he so admired plumped together when she brought her hands to his waistcoat, the perky tips turning rosy and rigid once exposed to the air, pouting for his touch. His tongue?

"Lean forward," he commanded.

Instead of obeying, Laney stretched her arms over-head, causing those bounteous beauties to lift and sway. "I think not," she taunted, "not without more promises and more explanations."

"Eleanor." He needn't have tried to harden his voice. "Catherine." For every syllable edged gruff. "Buckley."

And all the minx did was grin.

11

FROM INDENTURED TO INDEPENDENT

"YOU REMEMBER MY FULL NAME." For some reason, that warmed Laney's heart.

The glow didn't dim when he continued, even though he practically hissed at her, "I want a taste. *Now.*"

Simply knowing he stared at her breasts, admired them, made her nipples pucker. But she wasn't about to give in to his growled demand so easily. He had over two hours to make up for. Two hours, two days before that, and a host of confusion.

Wearing nothing but her long gloves, she tightened her thighs along his torso and brought her arms down to begin working the most intricate design she'd seen yet in his cravat. "Very impressive," she complimented, smiling at him. "Which knot is it? The Mathematical? The Oriental?"

"Haste. And I'm out of promises," he said with real

regret, his broad hands coming to rest on the outside of her hips.

She kept at the linen, certain if she looked down or he looked up, they'd both see how wet and ready her woman's flesh had become for him. "The Haste? I have yet to hear of that one. From—"

"From me hurrying too dem fast to get to you," he admitted just as she pried the stubborn knot free. She pulled the several-inch swath of fabric from behind his head, ready to place it atop her clothing pile, but he stopped her. "Nay. I want you to tie it around your neck."

Perplexed by the request, she nevertheless did as bade, tensing her legs to balance herself while she drew the fabric around her nape. Although unused to dealing with the five feet of starched linen, it took but a moment to fashion the neckerchief into a lopsided bow, the ends trailing down over her— "Ah! You fiend."

Nash Hammond had taken the opportunity to bring both his hands to her breasts. "Simply showing my appreciation."

"You can appreciate me any time," she informed him when he began kneading the aching mounds. "Mmm, like that," she encouraged. "A little—*harder*." She gasped when he complied.

"Now that I find myself in this position," he mused, his fingertips tweaking her nipples, "I realize there *is* another promise I can make."

"Oh?" She pushed herself into his touch, yearning to ride his erection through his pantaloons, to slide her moist slit right over the nankeen fabric and abrade herself to heaven, but refraining. Refraining because more than anything, she wanted him to take her there. Wanted to know the bliss of Nash Hammond's promise to love her as a man loved a woman.

Had she ever thought to experience *that*?

His tweaking motions grew fiercer. Little pinches on her nipples that sent lightning streaking from her breasts to her belly—and parts south.

He left off pinching the tips and curved his hands beneath her breasts as if gauging their weight. "Hmm. While not quite as large as I imagined..."

Laney made a mew of dismay. Was he disappointed? Now that he saw all of her?

His palms returned to caressing the mounds, his fingers plying deep into her flesh. "I promise that your bosom boasts the most glorious pair I have ever had the pleasure to pleasure."

"Mr. Hammond! Mmmm, Nash, I—" She was biting her lips, twitching her hips, fighting to keep from lowering herself on his body. "I don't want to ruin your pantaloons, but I..."

"Certainly not," his low voice intoned. "They and my boots are about the only thing on my person that are *mine*. But I invite you to ruin anything else that strikes your fancy."

She whimpered a laugh, unwilling to soil such finery even if it did belong to her *former* owner. "Mr. Hammond!"

"Ah." He released her breasts and bracketed her waist, tilting her pelvis. "Ah yes, my eyes confirm what my nose already discerned. Glistening tidings await my cock between your thighs."

"For shame, to speak such things out loud. *Outside*," she admonished.

Glistening tidings indeed.

When he licked his lips, her entire muff responded. Shameful or not, so ready was she to do the slithery, she only wanted to hear more. "How naughty you are. Pray, continue."

His fingers tightened when she relaxed her legs and attempted to rub her inner workings over his waistcoat. "Not yet," he tut-tutted. "I do believe I have changed my mind, for did I not make a promise—"

"Several in fact." She squirmed, touching her needy breasts now that he'd abandoned them for her waist. "But I want...crave..." Knowing it and *saying* it were altogether different. "Please!"

"Ah, sweet princess." He lifted her up and off him. She acceded with a squeak of protest. "I know that you're aching now, but believe me when I tell you 'tis all for the best."

He guided her to her back, then came down between her splayed legs—and him still fully attired except for the linen neckcloth she now sported. Unfair!

He scooted down between her legs and braced his hands on her thighs, spreading them wide and opening her folds to his gaze and the naughty intentions she'd just accused him of. Or so she hoped.

His fingers tapped along her flushed skin, coming closer and closer to her center without ever touching. "Now tell me, Miss Buckley, what exactly would you have me do? I am completely and utterly at your service."

She arched forward, trying to grip his shoulders,

but he pushed her back down and grabbed her parasol. "Here. Open this," he ordered. "Twirl it overhead."

Beg pardon? Words failed her.

Placing a lingering but too-brief kiss upon her thigh, he demonstrated by opening the parasol and spinning it as he placed her numb fingers around the handle. "Very good. Aye, just like that. Keep your hands busy while I go about my business."

"Your business?" Her parasol had never weighed so much. "What happened to *at my service?*"

"The business of easing your ache. *After* I fan it higher."

"Oh. Oh!"

Her sensitive bits flinched, then fairly melted when he placed his strong fingers on either side and spread her weeping flesh wide for his heavy-lidded gaze, followed immediately by the encore of his tongue.

WITHOUT FURTHER ADO or added talk of promises or easing aches, Nash set himself upon the self-appointed task of driving one Miss Laney Catherine Buckley wild with lust and weak with desire. And, most importantly, replete with satisfaction.

Ignoring the iron poker still tucked away in his pantaloons—straining and complaining, but for once, his pizzle wasn't ruling the day—Nash breathed deep and leaned in, ready to lick and love Laney to her first well-deserved release.

But before he focused solely on *her* delight, a taste for his. A taste to satisfy the beast, not the lionesque beast yearning to get free, but the selfish beast that was

Nash Hammond, who had never dined on anything quite so sweet.

Placing his mouth at her quiver, he pushed his tongue deep, experienced her nectar again flowing over his lips and drank it down. Took her essence into his soul, imagined her honey gliding along his cock, then applied himself to rousing her higher.

He swallowed one last time and pulled back, just a fraction, the better to see. Her breathing was labored, her eyes closed, the parasol balanced precariously above them both spinning like a top.

With a gut-felt smile, he perched himself on one elbow and threaded his free hand through the riotous curls guarding her intimate secrets. He fisted a handful of the short black hairs and tugged sharply toward her abdomen, lifting her skin and exposing her creaming entrance. She let forth a whimper, the parasol spun faster and her body wept harder.

He inspected every nuance of the intriguing view. It wasn't often that he found himself outside in the light of day and certainly never with a willing wench. But *wench* didn't seem the appropriate term. Be that as it may—that he lay here between the open thighs of an extraordinary blustery yet dainty female, one without a stitch on—his eyes flicked overhead and he grinned. Well, without a stitch other than his neckcloth and her long, velvety-soft gloves.

The term *wench* might very well fit the situation, but it most assuredly did not fit the creature.

"Why'd you stop? Touch me again!" she ordered loudly, bucking within his hold.

But then again...

In awe of his good fortune, he leaned down and flicked her pearl with the tip of his tongue. The tiny knot flinched and then came back for more. Another two flicks, a tight circle, a long, slow sweep down her fragrant slit and he was gone.

"*'Tis torture, and not mercy: heaven is here...*'" For once, the original line seemed perfect. If only for a short while hence, his lips were about to greet heaven's gate. "How about another promise, Princess?"

She moaned and attempted to push more intimately against his mouth. Nash resisted.

"I can promise you without a speck of reserve," he said sincerely, probing her folds with inquisitive fingers from one hand while still tugging on her midnight curls with the other, "that even were I to give extensive thought to the matter, never could I conceive of another more fortuitous position...or puss."

He returned his mouth to the top of her cleft and slid two fingers straight inside her sex. Her body offered no resistance, only pure welcome. The muscles of her passage tightened, drawing his fingers deeper. He kissed at the hardened nub beneath his lips, bit gently around the taut nerves and pulled his fingers out, then shoved them right back in. Again and again.

A whisper of wind preceded the parasol's crash to the ground. Nash smiled against her core and kept licking.

With the parasol gone, her hands were free. Free to delve into his hair, free to latch on and pull. Ah, but slick fingers were a wonderful thing and her gloved hands slid right off. Nevertheless, Miss Laney was determined, and before Nash knew it, she took hold of his ears and ground her crotch into his face.

He wasn't one to complain. Loving her with his mouth, with his hands, he put everything he had into making his woman find her pinnacle. His eager erection could wait. Could wait to be sheathed snug inside her slick warmth. Could wait until he'd at least earned the semblance of honor he figured it took to allow his cock the privilege of stroking a woman like Laney to satisfaction.

To the blessed sound of her whimpers, the undulations of her hips and the loud thumping of his own heart, he licked and tapped and lashed every bit of her beautiful jewel.

He knew she was close. Knew it by the way her pelvis arched into his hands, by the way her treasure started to quiver beneath his lips. He stilled. Kept his tongue affixed to the apex of her cleft, felt that tiny pearl reaching for more and tried it again—intentionally called on *Roho ya Simba* to come to him—and there it was. His tongue grew more agile, the texture altered, became more abrasive as he held it in place.

Laney groaned, lunged against his mouth again, this time with more force. Her every muscle, every fiber, from the thighs beneath his hands, to the nub beneath his tongue, tensed, strained, then to the music of her screamed orgasm, *released*. Relaxed.

Vibrated, shook and quaked.

Just as he was doing with every facet of his being, to the majesty of her shouts and squeals. "Blast me! Bless me!"

. . .

HER SHOUTED "BLAST ME! BLESS ME!" echoed around their small clearing, caressed Laney's ears with the same intensity his tongue had caressed more delicate parts only seconds ago.

Blast me, bless me. It wasn't until the third, softer refrain penetrated her brainbox that she realized she'd been the brazen wench to squeal them.

Her entire body shook as if a herd of wild horses trotted across her heart. She tried to slow it down before it beat clear out of her chest. "Oh me, oh my. *That* certainly wasn't a very ladylike comment, now, was it?"

Nash Hammond looked up, his glorious face centered between her thighs. "Is that what you aspire to be?" he asked evenly. "A true lady? Because I cannot give you that."

Was he intimating there were other things he *could* give her? Other than what he'd just done? Oh my.

"A true *lady*? Heavens, no." *Her?* Little Eleanor Buckley having aspirations to marry a titled gent? 'Twould be laughable if those horses weren't still galloping over her lungs, stealing her breath—nearly as much as the glimmering eyes of the man gazing up at her.

After years making hats in the background while watching Mrs. Michaels grovel with the titled ladies who entered her shop, Laney knew that sort of "elevated" station came with its own burdens. Restrictions. Why, females of rank couldn't even leave their own homes without a maid or footman in tow. Couldn't even speak to others without a proper introduction and setting. How very stifling.

As to the men?

The interactions she'd had with Reginald's odious older brother, no matter that his title was lower in the hierarchy, and his equally off-putting cronies, only confirmed her belief that an ordinary type of man and life was all she sought.

Ordinary? You with your cursed blessings and this particular mister with his furry ones?

"Where 'ladies' are concerned, I only seek to emulate their qualities in deportment and manner. Yelling curses like a street urchin is no way to..." Her words fell off when he began climbing up her body, stopping once he reached her breasts, and then he left off staring at her in order to stare at them.

Seeing Mr. Hammond leaning over her naked bosom, feeling his clothed body between her legs, against her quivering sex, knowing she wanted his staff there next, made ladylike comparisons seem naught but ludicrous. "'Tis only..." She paused when he began licking the underside of one breast. "Only that ever since learning how a proper female behaves, I have made—" She bit back a gasp when he did it again. "Made it a priority to conduct myself..."

His mouth edged upward toward her areola, his eyes connecting with hers. "Even in the bedroom?" His incredibly raspy tongue came out and he licked her nipple once, twice, then around it, staring at her all the while. "You believe you are bound to behave like a lady in the bedroom?"

She wove her gloved fingers up the back of his head and pulled him down, asking without words for him to kiss her fully. "We're not in any bedroom that I can see."

His head resisted the pressure. "And for that impertinent comment, punishment is in order."

He swooped down and sucked her nipple into his mouth. He drew on it sharply and her stomach contracted, concaved, even as her chest pushed higher. "Bedchambers aside, I do believe being a lady is vastly overrated," she said on a moan.

After administering deep suction, he released her saliva-covered breast and blew on it. "To be honest, Princess, your definition of ladylike warrants severe modification."

At that, she attempted to pull his hair. Again the silky strands slid right through her fingers. So she resorted to pinching the strong muscles of his neck. "What—what do you mean? Since learning how, I aspire to be everything that is refined."

Mr. Hammond moved to her other breast but began plying the first one with attention from his warm palm. "Not that I claim extensive experience dealing with females from the upper tier, but it seems to me that ladies don't exactly approach strangers with the request to *buy* them."

"But there was reason enough—"

He pinched her nipple, causing her molars to clack together. "Ladies, my dear, don't pretend to be whores for hire and invite themselves into strangers' bedchambers."

He had her there.

"Never have I woken to find a *lady's* lips wrapped around my cock."

He *really* had her there.

"Ladies don't necessarily enjoy disrobing strange men in the daylight hours...while *outside*."

Only then did Laney realize she'd released his neck and was frantically tugging at his lapels, trying to remove his jacket. "If I respond that I no longer consider you a stranger—or even strange—will you please remove your attire and love me properly?"

His teeth suddenly found their way to her nipple. Biting down, he growled around her flesh, "Properly? Are you saying my tongue at your quiver wasn't good enough?"

Laney managed to wrest his jacket free and concentrated on working the wrist buttons loose on his shirt sleeves. Her breasts preened like golden idols this demon was paying homage to. Had she ever felt more decadent? More free?

"Your tongue was wondrous as you very well know, you wretched man for making me speak thus aloud. But as you are currently demonstrating and fulfilling promises, I want it all and I want it now."

His teeth were gone, replaced by his licking tongue. It scraped across her puckered nipple, causing a tremor to rack her frame. She began tugging his shirt over his head. He abandoned her bosom long enough to cooperate. When he emerged, there was a taunting glint in his eyes. "It? What exactly do you mean by 'it'? I think this wretched man needs *it* spelled out."

He knelt there, leaning over her, his muscular arms braced on either side of her torso, that delectably smooth, powerful chest appealing to her more than any pastry or sweet bread she'd ever lusted after.

But that was all.

He knelt there, unmoving, still wearing his pantaloons, his dark, straight hair half covering one eye, waiting.

Waiting for her to say it blatantly? Or just...indicate it?

"T-A-K-E-O-F-F-Y—"

"Laney." 'Twas a growled order.

"Take off your pantaloons, please, sir."

The glint deepened. "Whatever for?"

"Because I..." She scrambled to a sitting position. He allowed the move but leaned forward even more so that his very presence surrounded her, their faces but inches apart.

"Aye?"

The scoundrel! He was going to make her say it after all. "Because I want your cock in my quim!"

He smiled and ran a fingertip down her cheek. "Very good, my pretty princess. Now take off your gloves."

"Wh-why?"

Mr. Hammond leaned back—finally—and his hands went to the fastenings on his pantaloons. "An exchange forfeit, you see. Your gloves for my pantaloons."

She debated before agreeing. Was she not the one who had been on display all afternoon? 'Twas surely time he reciprocated. "Are you wearing anything else?"

He left his pantaloons partially undone and swiftly dispensed with his boots and stockings. "Nary a stitch."

The bow tied beneath her chin seemed to shout its presence. "But I'll still be wearing—"

"Leave it." He'd gone back to being churlish. Amusing, how it no longer bothered her. In truth, she thought his brusque mood close to charming. Especially since it obviously portended her gaining exactly what she'd asked for—him naked and his sugar stick inside her mound.

"Why yes, m'lawd," she said saucily, beginning to peel back her left glove with more haste than she'd shown undressing previously. The glove came off and she playfully batted it over his head. "Anythin' you say, m'lawd."

"Peppery wench," he complained, but didn't stop removing his pantaloons, standing for one brief moment while he ungracefully stepped out of the tight legs, then sinking back to the quilt as nude as she—except for the lopsided bow around her neck.

"The second glove," he prompted when her efforts ceased. Legs straight, arms curved behind his head, his corded stomach in between, he stretched out on their private blanket as if he had not a care in the world. "It's still on," he grumped, pointing with his toe. "Unacceptable."

Laney was too intrigued by the view the midday sun and his sprawled position afforded to take offense. "Gads. You look 'ellish fine," she said without thinking and then corrected herself. "I mean *splendid*. Mr. Hammond, you look splendid."

And he did. Magnificent muscles, hairy legs—but not overly so—sculpted shoulders, those sensual side-whiskers—

She abandoned her teasing stance and flopped down next to him. Leaned over and kissed beside his ear, encompassing the edge of one angled side-whisker and his surprisingly smooth cheek. "How is it that you are so silken now when earlier you were so very rough?"

He turned his head and stared into her eyes. "Rough? Share your definition of rough, if you would. If memory serves, I have been *rough* with you more than once. Which—"

She kissed his mouth, cutting off his words, then couldn't help licking his lips. The remnants of her own cream tantalized and she licked him again. Only when he brought his hand up to the back of her head to pull her closer did she finally answer. "Not rough —*whiskery*. Earlier. Your jaw."

Instead of explaining, he raised his head and captured her bottom lip, taking it into his mouth, sucking on it once, then releasing. "Simply speak your thoughts, Princess. Use whatever words come to those luscious lips and don't moderate them. Refined elocution or street cant. There's no need for you to ever guard yourself with me."

"Why?"

"Because I daresay I know you better than any man —your body certainly—and I want you to be authentically yourself around me henceforth. No more deceptions."

She curved her right palm over the hard, tensed muscle of his shoulder. "That is well done of you, but I was asking *why* must I keep answering you explicitly when we both know that *you* know exactly what I mean?"

Of its own accord, her gloved hand moved lower,

stroking leisurely down his chest, stopping over his thick pectoral, fingering his pebbled nipple. She wished she could feel it without the barrier of her glove but, as Mary Delilah would have said, *ainsi va la vie.* 'Tis how life goes. And based on the way things were progressing, her life promised to get more interesting by the second.

Laney continued drawing designs over his nipple with the utmost of attention. A little hiss came from his throat and she centered one fingernail right on top of the knot. "Hmm? I am certain you know what I mean. Do you deny it?"

Mr. Hammond captured her inquisitive finger, pressed her palm flat with his strong hand and guided her arm lower. "I don't deny that I crave your dainty fingers wrapped around my cock. I want to feel you gripping my shaft and pumping it like you did this morning, only I anticipate being *awake* the entire time."

His guiding hand moved at a drunken snail's pace, causing her palm and fingers to traverse the hard muscles of his stomach one agonizing second at a time. "I don't deny that after you touch me and explore me, come to know me, that it will be my turn to know you again. My cock will know the wonder of breaching your slit, of sliding deep inside your hot petticoat even as my nose now inhales the fragrance of your arousal, as my lips know your taste. I don't deny I want—"

"Stop!"

What he'd done earlier with his mouth had shot sparks through her and she'd loved it, but now, it was as if his teasing left her craving so much more. Left her *burning*. With every heated word he uttered, her need for everything he described grew beyond any desire she'd known before. "That is what you want?"

She wrenched her hand from beneath his firm grasp and grasped *him*, did exactly as he'd painted in her mind—anchored her hand at the base of his wide shaft and slid upward, along smooth solid muscle. "You want to *hear* it, do you not? Well, fine! I feel your sleek hardness beneath my fingertips and I crave to join with it. Crave to feel you inside me. My loins, so recently satisfied by your tongue, now protest their empty state and are weeping for more. For *this*—"

She began to climb over his reclining form, still stroking his erection, still pumping him with her gloved hand while her Netherlands swelled and creamed, readying for his invasion. When he persisted in remaining passive, she tried a different tack. "I desire yer cock in my cunt so dreadfully bad I fear I'll forever be a wanton whether you grant me wish or not." He raised one eyebrow, but still didn't touch. "You fiend! I need you to tup me!"

Laney was almost crying, tugging on his rod with abrupt, inelegant pulls, remembering how he'd jerked away the last time his cock entered her puss, remembering how alive and electrified he'd just made her feel with his mouth and dying to feel that way again.

On either side of his waist, her legs shook. His erection was tall and red, straining upward toward her cleft.

Just as she moved into position, angling her pelvis to sink down and take him inside, he braced his hands along her thighs and held her aloft, stopping her. He spoke through gritted teeth. "The other glove. *Off* now."

Beyond thought or argument, she held herself suspended above him, released his cock and ripped off her right glove, flinging it as far as she could manage. "There!" she cried. "Please don't make me wait a—"

"Touch your neck." When she hesitated, he snarled, "*Do it. Now.*"

Confused, Laney brought both hands up and encountered the bow she'd tied earlier.

"What are you wearing?"

"Nothing. I'm not wear—"

His fingers tightened on her thighs. The muscles above his collarbone strained, the thick ridges in his neck standing out. "*What* are you wearing?"

Her fingers grasped the long ends of fabric. "Your... your cravat?"

"*Whose?*"

"Yours." She finally realized what he was doing. It sickened her as much as elated her. Her legs went weak, but he continued holding her above him. "I'm wearing your leash."

He shook his head, brushed his thumbs over the edges of her slit. "Nay, 'tis not a leash, but it is mine. *Mine.* Say it."

"I'm...yours."

"I own you."

That sounded so final, but her body responded to the command, dripping desire over his hands. "Oh God. Nash. Mr. Hammond, I need—"

"Say it." Both of his thumbs entered her, the action causing her lower body to contract and convulse toward him. "Nash, please!"

"*Say it.*" He slid his thumbs inward, then back out,

spreading her essence over her cleft before centering his touch on the tight knot above. But he refused to move, to caress her further, no matter how she squirmed within his hold. "I own you. Let me hear you admit it."

She swallowed down the instinctive retort and let both her visions and her heart guide her. "I...am yours. You...own me. Now take me!"

"Not yet. Take it off." He spoke harshly. "Give it to me. Now, Laney. Heed me."

Delirious with desire, she tore at the knot, so wild for him she'd do whatever he wanted. Anything to end the hunger gnawing at her heart, in her quiver. Just...oh gracious. The bow had gotten tighter since she'd fashioned it. Her efforts were hampered by the steely look in his gaze. No glint. No glowing. Just pure, unadulterated possession.

The look intimidated her. Thrilled her.

The tiny knot of nerves throbbed beneath his stationary touch. She whimpered, her hands grappling feverishly with the linen, trying to gain purchase, a fingerhold—anything to get it off her neck and get him in her body.

Finally, *finally*, the knot gave way. Before she could hand the fabric over, he snatched it from behind her nape. He held the neckcloth in front of her face.

"Do you see this? Proof of my ownership." He balled it up and flung it away, his eyes never leaving hers. The possessive look was gone, replaced by an intensity she couldn't decipher. "You are free, Laney Buckley. *Free.* Do you hear me? No one should ever own another."

"But I gave—"

"It's of no consequence. You heard yourself—I owned you and now I have granted you your freedom."

"But—" Did this mean he no longer wanted her? One glance at his groin confirmed the inaccuracy of that thought. Now that she had what she'd always wanted—true, legal freedom—Laney wanted Nash to take it back. Mentally, she'd given herself to him the day they met, though she hadn't realized it at the time. Physically, she'd given herself to him last eve when he'd breached her maidenhead.

Just hours ago she gave herself to him again when she'd told the innkeeper to give Nash Hammond her indenture papers.

"Laney?" Her name was an impatient growl, his hands back at her thighs, pressing deep into her unsteady flesh.

"Aye?"

"I want you, but I won't *take* you, not like I have previously." His hands tightened. His arms trembled. "This time, I'm asking. Asking you to give yourself to me."

All that was left...

Emotionally. All that was left of her, he was demanding. No...*asking*.

"*Aye.*"

"Then roll over, woman."

Nash was humbled by how quickly she complied.

He gripped her arse with both hands and bent forward. Angling his head, he placed a kiss squarely on her mole. Her appealing, off-center and perfectly imperfect mole. He couldn't find a single fault with the rest of her body, so figured his affinity for the unique mark made sense.

He kissed the mole again, adding a little nip. When he straightened and slapped the spot his lips had just caressed, she squeaked her surprise. "Now roll back."

"Whatever do you mean?" She glanced over her shoulder while arching her lower body toward him. Invitation abounded. "Do you not want—"

Another slap. "Over, Princess. On your bum."

Though hesitantly, she did as bade.

Never fuck facing forw—

Consigning his conscience to the devil once and for all, Nash closed the distance between them until their lips were but a kiss away. "Face-to-face this time, Laney. Do *you* not remember? 'Tis my aim to demonstrate how a man loves a woman. A special woman."

Her eyes grew wide and that demure yet saucy tilt skewed her smile. He parted her knees and, shaking as if it were *his* first time, positioned his cock at her pink-flushed quiver, held himself steady with one hand and resisted the urge to sink in. But he did indulge in a little cock head exploration along her slit, agonizing though it was, and lowered his upper body until his lips were back at hers.

"Kiss me, Princess?"

And as her mouth lunged upward, he plunged downward. Into hope.

• • •

LANEY CRUSHED her lips against his, experiencing the forceful glide of his tongue into her mouth as his staff speared past her last defense, stretched tender flesh and lodged deep inside.

His chest came down, flattening her breasts, abrading her nipples. His hands wound in her hair and held her head steady for his slow assault.

Slow and tortuous. Both the paced motion of his tongue stroking along hers and the way his body entered hers. Held steady. And stayed.

Swollen, delicate muscles yielded to hard, firm circumference. Finally, after waiting for what seemed an eternity, her lover claimed what she freely offered. Now surrounded by clutching, hungry, *loving* parts that, ironically, given the care and gentleness he was showing her, wanted to be *pummeled*.

Instead of telling him—for his lips and tongue occupied her mouth most delightfully—she sought to show him, sucking his tongue deep inside, tangling hers against it, pushing the flexible muscle into her teeth, tasting remnants of what must be her own release. Even when he groaned, she didn't ease the pressure. Instead, growing bolder, she raked her nails down his back and dug them into his flanks.

Stubborn man, he refused to respond how she'd hoped. His caresses remained feather soft, fingertips to her cheek, her forehead, his tongue and lips lovingly exploring her mouth when she stopped sucking on his in order to breathe. His cock stayed seated deep, stroking languidly in and out of her grasping passage, touching her in places no other man ever could—or would.

Regardless of how treasured, how cherished or *special* his actions, she craved the fire that had branded their previous encounters. So she took matters into her own hands, scraping her nails over his buttocks. Ignoring his flinch and doing it again.

Her loins writhed beneath his heavy frame, desperately trying to buck against him, to get more friction, more of *something*, but his weight kept her pinned.

Pinned?

Pins? *Hat* pins.

Threaten to use her precious hats for target practice, would he?

Promise to treat her body to considerate sexual affection, but in doing so hold a huge part of himself back?

She bit down on his exploring tongue. Scored her nails down his bum one last time, then hauled off and slapped him. Reared back and did it again, popping his flanks and loving the sharp sounds that blasted through the silence.

Loving more how he jerked. Growled. Ground into her and received the message—without her ever having to say a word.

His tongue changed texture, setting off all manner of sparks along the roof of her mouth. His cock stiffened even more—if that were possible—and sped up, lurching into her faster and faster. Deeper and deeper.

She spanked him again, let her hands express all the frustration that came from years of flowing through life, letting circumstances and those in authority sway her to their wishes, expelling the aggravation of always stifling her true self.

The years of biting her tongue while she waited on ladies and did Mrs. Michaels' bidding, followed by even more pretending to be a perfectly proper "lady" while living the *lie* of the life of a mistress—more pretending. The clankers, the confusion, and aye, the fear—of being alone, of "seeing" the future and finding it very bleak indeed...

It all came pouring out of her every time the flat of her hand connected with his arse and it felt wondrous!

Her soul felt wondrous. Her cleft felt wondrous!

Harder and harder he plunged inside, rubbing against the flexing muscles that kept trying to pull him closer and then propel him out.

The unfamiliar weight of him pressing into her was heavy. Her chest hurt, squashed under his body. Her lips were tender, the bottom of her tongue sore from dueling with his, but still she kept driving him on, kept spanking his backside and rocking into his fierce thrusts, kept hearing the growls in his throat, noticed how his nails grew sharper, tickling along her scalp... felt his teeth *prick* her lip! And even as her loins cried out for his mouth and tongue again, even as her quiver hugged his shaft so tight 'twas a marvel he could keep sliding at all, Laney realized she wasn't slapping him anymore to rid herself of her past.

Her personal demons were gone.

She was slapping him for the present—to edge him on. Wilder. Fiercer. But alas, it seemed her efforts were no longer needed.

Mr. Hammond rolled to his back and brought her with him, still pumping inside. She was on top. She was in control, mayhap partially, but control nevertheless, riding him, her knees giving her the leverage that had been absent before.

He tore his mouth from hers and aligned their cheeks. His breathing was loud, his jaw raspy again. "Like this, Princess? Is this what you're after?"

His hand landed on her right flank. She flinched and nodded, swiveling atop his pubic hairs, and he did it again, wedging his other hand between their bodies, sliding over her slick flesh, stilling when she moaned— leaving his fingers there for her to dance around, rock over...

Another slap. Harder. Louder.

She rode his rod, pressed that sensitive spot over his fingers, luxuriated in his hot breath at her ear, and held on. Faster her hips flew, faster his palm came down. Faster her heart beat, her blood flowed.

Her breath caught. Toes curled.

Everything exploded at once.

The tiny knot he'd brought to life swelled, extended, retreated. Extended again, then celebrated.

Her channel clamped down and clutched.

Her bum smarted, burned and rejoiced.

Nash drove into her higher, slower, longer. His arms clamped round her back and he was hugging her, lunging into her and murmuring over and over and over, "Don't leave. Don't leave me. *Usiniuche!* Don't leave! *Usiondoke...*"

⟡

BACK IN LONDON

He watched. He waited.

How he hated.

Hated how the urge had taken hold tonight.

It wasn't in his plan, not tonight. Had not been inscribed in his journal, the beautiful date circled, starred, squared... Allowing his knowing eye to return to it over and over in the approaching weeks, to appreciate, to know, to savor...

Nay, that pleasure had been denied him. For the first time. And one of them would pay. Pay dearly for the loss.

He did not like being caught unawares. Rather, he preferred to be the "catcher". The one who stalked his prey.

As he was doing...right...now.

A grim, soothing smile lifted his cheeks. He pressed his back against the shadowed stone where he waited, invisible and silent.

The thrumming multiplied. Grew in intensity strengthening his flaming limbs.

Like his smile, the cool night air tried to soothe the blaze. But to no avail.

For the fires lit within, burned hot and hard, threatening to consume him ere he put them out the only way he knew.

Damn the clouds and minuscule moon tonight—he'd lost sight of the strutter. Damn her.

And the daggle-tail he'd considered more than once? The willowy clapper always jawing about something... 'Twould be divine to slice—er, *shut*—her up. That little bird-of-the-game bitch had snuck off amidst a group of her own. Twice now, she'd escaped him. His fists clenched, nails bit crescents into his palms. Damn her as well!

And the other two? One had been taken off, beyond his reach by the burly, ill-dressed escort she'd somehow claimed.

The other? He'd gotten a closer look earlier. She would do. Oh, aye... Would she do.

12

SKETCHES AND SECRETS COME TO LIGHT

<hr>

STILL BACK IN LONDON

"WHAT DO YOU MEAN, *FOR A PRICE*?"

Lord Tyndale's flattened eyebrow and tilted, naughty smile, made his probable meaning clear. If only Tempest were wearing her walking boots and not her slippers—the sturdy boots she lived in on the rare occasions she escaped with her stepfather to his country estate—she'd offer to introduce her foot to his backside.

"I might be willing to wager for it," he said as though daring her to accept the challenge.

"Pah. Wager over something as sedate as scribbled fruit in a basket? Flowers in a vase? Do not waste my time."

"Not even close." He lifted the sheet for half a second, flashed it toward her, then anchored it back on the desk. "A scintillating sketch," he promised in a boastful tone. "You did request something of the sort, did you not?"

"Pah." But her derision was quieter this time, as his words engendered no little amount of anxiety. Had he penciled *her* in an obscene—

"Shall I next draw what goes on beyond yon door?" he surmised as though considering that very thing, his pencil still making errant marks. "I can salve my conscience—by not *telling* you a whit—and quench your inquisitive nature, by *showing* you every detail. Brilliant plan. Do you not agree?"

She gasped. She choked. Her face went up in flames even as part of her screamed *Yes! I most assuredly want to see that!*

But her saner side prevailed. "Nay. You must not! For all I know you will draw *me* on that stage!"

"Hmmmm. Now why did I not think of that?" Keeping his left fist firmly on the edge of the first page, he drew forth another scrap. "Pity you shall never know, unless you agree to pay my price."

Exasperating idiot. Where were her boots when she needed them?

She'd often thought Lord Wylde would have made a smashing older brother, with his quiet demeanor yet strong, comforting presence; if so, then Lord Tyndale would be the plaguey, pigtail-pulling one.

"Alas, whatever you believe," Tempest said, voice dripping disdain, "I doubt your work is worth a farthing. I shall keep my money. Let you bask in your own inflated egotism."

Lord Tyndale chuckled. "Bask in this, sweetheart."

With one raised hand, he waved the single sheet of paper, as if inviting her perusal.

'Twas dark enough, she had to approach to see any detail at all. As she came closer, he raised it higher, toward the illumination cast from the lantern behind his shoulder.

Pure surprise held her in thrall. A second became an hour as the exquisite illustration met her eyes and greeted her senses.

She'd anticipated a hash of harsh lines, dark and unruly like the man who had made them. Expected to be repelled by whatever his vexatious brain had thought to form.

She hadn't anticipated true talent, to find the wretch actually had a "style", a delicate, nuanced way of bringing life to a blank page.

She certainly hadn't expected to feel both flattered and perhaps a trifle embarrassed by the wondrous rendition of her countenance. For 'twas most assuredly her face she beheld.

Though Lord Tyndale had indeed sketched her likeness, he'd completely changed her hair. Instead of straight and tamed in a coil atop her head, he'd drawn it loose and free, curling with abandon (something her hair would *never* do—the curly part; the abandon she had not a clue), edging her face with inviting, loose ringlets and caressing her shoulders with fragile coils.

How odd, looking at her phiz as though another might. With lips slightly plump—well-kissed she'd think, even if she hadn't *known* they had been earlier tonight. How, with naught but his hand and a smudge of graphite, did he make her cheeks look slightly flushed? Her ordinary blue eyes re-created in black upon the page fairly glisten and sparkle, as though they laughed with the beholder? Shared in some private, joyful secret with whoever met her gaze upon this page?

Though scandalous on its own—the very act of Lord Tyndale drawing such a detailed representation of her—none of that was what had her gasping, paling, reaching for the desk between them to steady herself. "You could not— You must not!"

"I most certainly could. And did." The dastard gloated, holding the beautiful, horrid drawing by its topmost corners, lifting each of his hands in an alternating fashion, making the picture dip and sway. Emphasizing the missing clothes beneath the glorious face and hair—the *nakedness*. The—egad—"bouncing" *bare* breasts he'd fashioned beneath the detailed depiction of her face.

Oh Lord in heaven. If anyone were to see this, to conclude that she'd encouraged such a thing... Why, she'd surely be cast into the very depths of London, if not straight to hell.

"Anyone who sees that will think you—you..." Her hands clenched upon the desk not sufficient to keep her stomach from toppling toward the floor. Her long-ago dinner from threatening to pitch the opposite direction.

As those nipple-tipped, perfectly formed breasts continued to bob before her dazed eyes—thanks to his gloating efforts—she finally found her voice. "People will assume that I—I sat for you. That you— you —"

"That I what?" His up-and-down motion finally

stilled as his grin blossomed even more. "Have an enviable gift for portraiture?"

"That—that—*that*—doesn't look like me at all!" Since when did she sound buffle-headed? *When you saw a nude picture of yourself with your flaws glaring you in the face?* No! It wasn't that. It wasn't. It was the thought of everyone seeing that and thinking she had—

"It looks exactly like you." He stated it with a calm assurance she desperately wished she could steal.

Without thinking it through, she pointed to her chest, her fingertips aimed toward her right breast. "Nay, it does not."

"Hmmm." Now he just looked composed—and thoughtful, dash him—his gaze going straight to her chest, focus veering horizontally in such a way she wished for a broom handle she could poke him in the stomach with. *Better make that his eye.* "Just what are you hiding under those prim stays and plain shift?"

"Nothing you shall ever see!" And what would make him think her shift was plain? Asinine imbecile! "I will be ruined. Utterly!" Tempest heard the shrill of her voice and shuddered, gluing her treasonous hand back to the desk. "Anyone who recognizes me," she stated in the calmest manner she could manage, "will conclude we have been together. Intimately!"

"Ah, but you and I both know that *you* have not had the pleasure."

"Oh! You scoundrel!" Forget her country boots. What she needed was a mallet—nay, a sledgehammer! —to beat some sense into him. "It matters not, you fiend! Just the mere hint of such a thing will ruin me! Completely and forever."

He laughed out loud. "*Now* you think about your reputation? After barging in here—*here* of all places? After hounding me to open this door and let you take another look?"

He laughed again, as though incredulous at the thought, raising the drawing over his head when she lunged for it. "And this—my little scratch here—you think *this* is enough to ruin you?"

Up till now, she hadn't given much thought to her reputation, mainly because she hadn't done anything to risk destroying it.

Oh no? What about tonight's kiss on the Stantons' terrace? Over before it barely began. No risk there.

Being here—at The Den? That was in support of Francine.

The risk of ruin hadn't occurred, nor had it mattered, but of a sudden, it did. Vastly so. It was one thing if she chose to be a little reckless, mayhap a little wild—after decades of subdued living and constant peacemaking, was she not due a little pleasure? But another—

Decades? Part of her chortled. *Just how old do you think you are?*

All right, so that was an exaggeration. But given the trials surrounding her childhood, the witless twit she'd been forced to portray in the years since—until recently—it often seemed as though Temperance had been playing the adult far longer than she'd ever been a child.

"Come now." Tyndale's tone mocked. "What does it

signify? 'Tis not as though Rowden possesses an exalted title or you a sufficiently large dowry that has you labeled a Diamond and sought after to such a degree that your every action is scrutinized so closely anything done tonight will make a difference."

That legitimately raised her ire. She may not have spent time with the man, after her mother ran off and married without permission, but she was the granddaughter of a duke! The niece of one as well. And her stepfather's title of Viscount was perfectly notable.

How dare the arrogant arsehole malign her family? *How dare you think such language?* The supercilious scoundrel dare disparage her? *Even if you have been beyond reckless tonight?* Even if!

Exasperated with him as much as herself, she nearly spat, "You, sir, have neither tip nor toe with regards to knowledge of my dowry, of my stepfather's funds or *anything* else about me!"

"Oh no? Shall I contradict your high-and-mightiness? First, 'tis *my lord* to you, not 'sir'. Second, I *know* you care naught for your reputation, else you would not have ventured to set one dainty, *improper* little foot in this establishment. Third, you care naught for your safety, else you would not have ventured through London without *proper* escort. Fourth, you care nothing for—"

"Stubble it." So irked with him that she wanted to scream, she slapped the desktop. "I shall not dignify those possibly just claims with a response. Instead, I shall tell you what I *do* care about, what my every action tonight—and even before—has been prompted by. Something, no doubt, you cannot begin to understand, *Lord* Tyndale: I care about *family*."

And she did, fervently so. She may not like her mother, nor her sister; yet had she not altered her own nature for years to please the two of them? To maintain peace, attempting to keep them pacified and free from the grumbles? Acted the twitterhead whenever they were around, appeasing each without ever defending her own interests should they contradict? Doing all she could to keep cousin Francine from their unwarranted jealousy—masquerading as ire, impatience downright disagreeableness—as well?

But she'd behaved thus willingly, for she adored her stepfather and loved Francine. As to risking ruin now? Any besmirchment upon her reputation might affect them and that was unacceptable. "I care about protecting and helping my generous and kind cousin. I care about *avoiding* blustery, unpalatable, sullen behavior"—she described her sister—"and instead believing in goodness and light and joy, concentrating on those to better improve the lives of those around me."

Thanks first to Lord Wylde, and then to Francine, Tempest had discarded the self-imposed shackles she'd assumed years ago to please her mother and sister. How ironic that a forced betrothal with Lord Wylde— who "won" her across the green from her irresponsible mother—would prove to be the person who gave her the confidence to start speaking aloud her thoughts instead of hiding every one, hoping to mollify her sister's frequent wrath?

Lord Tyndale, uncharacteristically, had not only fallen silent, he'd taken a half step back as her words grew in intensity, as though to avoid the heat she emitted his direction.

But more than that, he lowered his arm to his side, finally within reach—if she could just stretch over the desk before he moved. "In truth, you miserable fiend, *everything* I have done for years was to please the two most miserable people I have ever known—and now I shall lump you in with them for your untoward behavior and wicked drawing and rude assumptions and—"

Giving him no hint of her plan, she propelled herself onto the desk and ripped the page from his loose grasp. "There!"

She had it!

Finally had possession of the best and worst, most horridly gorgeous drawing she'd ever chanced across. Because the woman that he drew in the picture? While it might have been *her* face, to perfection, the bosom he'd depicted? The beautiful, symmetrical breasts he'd drawn with such utter, divine detail?

As mortifying as it was to admit—even to herself—that particular picture was considerably more striking than she herself would ever be, had she posed in truth.

A giant sigh heaved from her as she accepted the veracity of what was so easily ignored in laced stays. Stays that shifted, propped and plumped things that... in their natural state, were...wholly *lopsided* to her shame and chagrin, something she'd never told another soul.

Not her mother nor her cousin—definitely not her sister... Not even their shared lady's maid nor the occasional seamstress or dressmaker knew Tempest maintained a small wad of stuffing bunched under her right breast any time she left the privacy of her bedchamber. *Always* with stays in place, not only to enhance the fullness that was lacking but to direct its downward—and, heaven forbid, sideways—propensity into the proper form. The cotton wadding her closest ally at all times, unless she was sleeping (sometimes even then)—so that no one had ever been in a position to notice the discrepancy nor surmise the extent of the uneven mounds dotting her upper torso.

But even as her fingers crumpled tightly upon the page, his fist covered hers. "Oh no you don't, you blasted baggage."

With one arm trying to still her, his other hand worked to loosen her fingers.

Tempest squeezed her fingers against the page until they went numb. "Let me have it!"

His brute strength easily outmatching hers, he tugged her closer. She fought back with her free arm, pushing at his shoulders, yanking his cravat, anything to distract his hold over her hand.

"Never. I drew it. Which makes it *mine*." He hauled her upper body against his, causing her to slide across the desk, scattering whatever had been neatly arranged before and toppling things to the floor in a noisy cascade.

'Twould be a relatively simple thing, to prove she had not disrobed and sat for Terrible Tyndale and his outrageous sketch.

But even as the errant thought formed, she knew such a thing would never come to pass...

If she were to tell him *why* his drawing was so very erroneous, he would demand she prove it....

Show me the truth of your claim. All you have to do is remove your dress and pull down your shift.

As if she'd ever!

She tried to tug it from his grip. By now, they each clamped fingers over a portion. Her legs flailed, feet kicking air, as the fingers not clenching the page worked to loosen his.

For a price.

His earlier taunting words chimed in her mind. She couldn't win against his superior strength—no matter that she sensed he refrained from using the full force of it against her.

"For a price," she gasped, stilling even as she held on to the picture for as though her life depended on it —which in some ways it very well might.

"What?" Breathing hard, he paused in his efforts against her.

"You said I could see it for a price. What price do you require for me to *have* it?"

"A kiss. A good one."

As if she'd ever! But she could pretend. "Fine! You shall have it."

She scooted back, slid clumsily off the desk until her toes reached the floor, arm still tugging. "Let me have it."

"Nay. Kiss first. Possession after."

Miserable miscreant.

Holding her arm at an awkward angle, unwilling to loosen her grip a whit, she marched around the desk, ready to put the years she'd spent pretending to be a jolter-headed jingle-brain to use.

Just as she came within kissing distance, the door behind him eased open.

The guard Mr. Adam called Bay—the man he'd told to keep an eye on the club—poked his grizzled head in. "Someone said they heard a ruckus. Mr. Nicholson back yet?"

"Nicholson?" Lord Tyndale repeated blankly, releasing the paper and straightening his waistcoat. Patting his neckcloth. Raking one hand through his disheveled hair.

Salvation! The interruption proved hers, surely, as Tempest turned from the pair and rolled the paper with haste, tucking it between the breasts that had caused her no little amount of angst tonight. Pushing the small scroll deep into her stays and, just as quickly, retreating across the room.

She had it! The potential instrument of her ruin. Now to ensure she kept it...

LANEY AWOKE to the inelegant rumble from the vicinity of her stomach. How long had she dozed? A quick glance showed neither had her companion stirred—as well as one stirring view.

Dappled shade covered their nude bodies, but that was all. She still hadn't broken her fast for the day and was hungry indeed. After Reginald burst in on them, she'd been far too flurried to eat and, well...she'd been rather occupied since, had she not?

At another grumble from her neglected middle, Nash shifted. A moment later he rose on to one elbow and looked down at her, hair in his face. "'Pears I fell asleep."

She brushed it back. "We both did."

The track of the sun across the sky measured several hours by her estimation. Several hours since Nash Hammond had truly *loved* her, whether he realized it or not.

Suddenly shy, she reached across him for her dress.

Mr. Hammond caught her arm, brought it to his lips, then halted. His grip tightened as he angled her arm away from the shade and into the light.

"What happened here?" His voice was colder than she'd ever heard it. "What did that bastard do to you?"

She tried to tug free. "I knew I should have left my glove on."

Nash tensed his hold. "Laney?"

Wanting to see the scars as he saw them, she forced her gaze to her forearm even though she'd become adept at avoiding the sight. Two circular marks, not much larger than a silver twopence, one much deeper than the other. Jagged, uneven flesh, now a soft, shiny pink. Healing, but still an ugly reminder of the position her indenture had put her in. Though one of the scars was fainter, she doubted either would ever completely go away.

Instead of snarling a demand for explanations, he lifted her arm to his lips and kissed each spot. Then he did it again, the dry application of his lips more profoundly healing than any number of treatments from Dr. Hanson's Cure-All Cream.

The gesture also brought emotions welling to the surface. "Mercy, Mr. 'ammond," she sniffed, never more exposed and vulnerable. "You didn't make me act this way when you 'ad your 'ead between my legs, but kiss me arm and I'm weepin' like—like..."

Her lips felt all swollen and wobbly. Tongue trembly.

Nash tugged her into his embrace, tingling arm and all. "Shhh. Princesses don't cry." He pressed his lips to her head. "Have you not heard? It makes their crown fall off."

Which had her smiling through the tears because now her heart and her forehead were tingly too. "Aw, stop it. Me 'ead'll be too big for a crown, the way you go on."

"I want to know." His thumb smoothed over the scars. "Want to know everything about you. How this happened. How you landed in Tate's treacherous clutches...but"—here, his voice softened—"'tis your choice, just as everything else will be from here on. You don't have to tell—"

"Mr. Tate, 'e was good to me at first, 'e was," she interrupted, knowing she *did* have to tell him. But she needed to tell him as the adult Laney she'd grown into, not the little-girl-lost one she'd been, when she was sold into millinery slavery. While not horrible, being forced to leave every familiar place and person at only thirteen... Well, of a certainty, it *had* been horrible.

Mashing her lips together, she willed the excess of tears and emotion to dissipate. Four lungfuls of air later, a fraction of composure returned. Mr. Hammond hadn't loosened his hold a fraction either, which helped immeasurably. "Reginald treated me grandly, at least at first, but recently, well, things changed between us. I had always known he wanted me for his mistress. When I moved in with him and he didn't try to touch me when we were alone, contrary to how much attention he showered on my body in public, I thought he was waiting for me to gain a year or two. But the more I observed between men and women, I came to realize he never really wanted me as his mistress, he was just using me as a shield to keep his family from learning of his...male paramour."

Behind her, around her, he waited patiently, pure quiet strength supporting her while she composed herself to tell him the rest.

"A few months ago, he came to my bedchamber. I was...I'm ashamed to say, willing enough, but his body wasn't. After the first four attempts led nowhere except to his frustration and swearing, I thought he had given up." Laney also thought she detected more growling and gripped Mr. Hammond's hands tight, taking courage from his presence. She couldn't remember feeling so safe, not even when she'd locked herself in her room and seen Reginald leave the house. Never in fact.

Secure for once, both in body and mind, she whispered what she hadn't told another. "Then he tried it again with more...*force* and I ran. Only to have him bring me back. I really had nowhere to go. Mary Delilah had just moved from London and Reginald found me at the first place he looked—Bailey's Sweet Shop, just off Bond. I have a deplorable weakness for Bailey's, I must confess. Reginald apologized profusely and promised to leave me alone." She expelled a heart-felt sigh. "I almost believed him too."

Mr. Hammond relaxed his hold and shifted until her back rested against the quilt. Hovering over her, he traced one eyebrow, feathered his thumb down her cheek and held his hand there. "The rest?" His voice was tight. "Your arm? This journey? I know you weren't with him willingly. I smelled your fear."

He had? "Well, I smell something delicious in that basket and want a taste."

She attempted to roll away, but he caught her, held her firm against the quilt, flat on her back. "Finish your tale. Procrastinating will only make it loom larger."

As if it weren't already large enough. Focusing on the muscles of his chest, she concluded quickly. "By now, he'd stopped associating with his friend Neils and had begun drinking copious amounts of strong spirits. That and consorting with an entirely new caliber of *friends*. Men his brother introduced him to. Men who leered at me when they visited, as if they knew some-thing I did not. Men who appeared to be prodding Reginald toward his downfall. And mine as well. The last time I left the house without his permission—and this only to post a letter to my friend"—Laney held up her arm, then let it drop—"he *persuaded* me upon my return not to do so again.

"Truly, I don't think he's cruel, just confused."

"He's a mollified piece of horse dung, and if I ever cross paths with him again, I vow to you he won't be in a position to hurt another female as long as he lives." As hard as his words, his touch remained whisper soft, tracing over her jaw, her chin. "I swear it."

"Thank you. I appreciate the sentiment more than you know, but I don't believe that will be necessary. I trust he'll be heading abroad before the month is out. Shh," she continued, hearing the snarl begin in his throat. "Shh. He didn't harm me permanent—"

"He scarred you permanently."

"But not on the inside, not anymore."

Nash evaluated her arm. "Hmm. An imperfection in the perfect princess. Kind of you to point it out."

She laughed. "I'm far from perfect—look at me, hiding from the world as I was, attaching those preposterous veils to every one of my hats."

"Ah, so you realize that now, do you?"

"I do." She nodded, felt the quilt beneath her head and raised a hand to his warm chest. "But that doesn't give you leave to shoot my hats."

"We shall decide that at a later date—there *is* the matter of a single dueling pistol that was left in my room. There's a certain ironic satisfaction to be had, honing my skills on his hat."

"But not mine?"

"I am relieved to hear you're ready to set them aside."

That was no answer, but she was too content to argue. "If only I'd braved facing the truth sooner—about Reginald and myself, I wouldn't have landed in this predicament."

"I, for one, am grateful for *this predicament*." Nash sat up and tugged her into his lap—his hard, *naked* lap. "And don't belabor the point too finely—we all hide from something, do we not? Me? I have been hiding from myself for more years than I want to count."

She explored his kneecap...just as his palms gave every appearance of exploring down her hips and thighs. "Now that you have broached it, will you not please tell me about *yourself*—your body—why and how you're able to..." She left off fondling his leg to make a sweeping gesture that included his entire form behind her. "It isn't possible, what you do, but I have seen it, twice now—"

His hands stopped roving and he brought his jaw to the crook of her shoulder, the warm puffs of his breath a caress as he spoke. "Twice? Explain yourself, Princess. Then I shall return the favor."

She turned her head and eyed him. He'd demanded everything be stated plainly. Could she do any less? "To clarify, so that I'm not continuing—or explaining—under any misapprehensions, you'll tell me how you're able to become a cat?"

A space of silence...then, "I will."

As long as she was bringing things out into the open... "And have you ever before shared this tale with another?"

The gleam was back—along with his relaxed hands, which took up residence on the inside of her legs just above her knees. "My family knows. There are others who bear my curse as well, but"—his fingers splayed—"if you're asking in a roundabout way whether I have told another woman, then the answer is an unequivocal no. Do you feel suitably special now? Because you should. You are."

"I felt *special* earlier." Laney leaned back against his chest and let her legs relax open. Would he take the hint? "But this reinforces it. I suppose there's nothing for it, then."

"Your confession?"

She took a deep, uncomfortable breath. "Family curses. Interesting things, family curses."

When his fingers refused her invitation, she aimed a look over her shoulder, gauging his receptivity. Only interest shone in his eyes, no ridicule or doubt. No grandiose dose of lust, either. Well. What did she expect? Just because her rebellious insides were becoming all tingly and itchy again didn't mean his *outsides* were doing the same. Drat and darn.

"Curses?" he prompted.

"Grandmama always said it was a blessing being a visionary. Mum called it the work of the devil."

Nash abandoned her leg and took one of her hands to align their palms, his long fingers outdistanced hers significantly. "Perhaps because the 'blessing' skipped her generation?"

"Fair suspicion, but no. Papa was Grandmama's son. An accident in the fields took him when I was a babe. Grandmama told him not to go out that day, but Mum insisted he'd be given the sack otherwise. I think that's why she was always so bitter."

"It's difficult, I know, giving credence to things you don't understand." He brought their connected hands to the quilt, placed hers palm down and began tracing between each finger. "But you have yet to tell me—"

"About us. I know. I have a tendency to ramble when..." *I'm discombobulated. Not used to sharing. Not used to feeling...*

"Ramble on, Princess, for I have nowhere pressing

to be." His other hand combed through her hair as he demonstrated with his every action that the gentle lover she'd lain with after their first night hadn't been conjured by her secret desire for tenderness but was very real indeed. She sighed at her remarkable present, thankful all over again for the rain, Reginald's impatience and her fortuitous seat on that particular stage.

She stared out at their little slice of meadowy heaven. Surrounded by thick trees, tufts of grass, weeds and flowers, all beaten down by the recent storms, but now working to stand tall in the light of a new day.

She could do no less. Firming her resolve, she confided, "I told you how Mr. Tate changed in his actions and demeanor the last few months, but what brought my dire circumstances into immediate focus is that the other night...I witnessed my wake."

"Your *wake*?"

"In a vision, to be precise. I was...dead."

At saying dead out loud, a tremor charged through her. A second followed, shaking her from top to toe, as she couldn't help but recall the clarity with which she'd witnessed her body on the floor, cold and stiff. The tremors Nash absorbed with his embrace. "The way things were progressing, I knew 'twas only a matter of time before Reginald maimed me permanently or succeeded in raping me—by then I was no longer willing—but that particular vision added an element of panic to my already desperate situation. I realized if I stayed with Reginald, he'd eventually kill me."

His entire body drew taunt. "That walking-dunghill *bastard*."

"Mr. Hammond!"

A pent-up breath burst from his lips. "And now? Has that outcome been averted? What if your vision was wrong? Mayhap you were mistaken."

"When I showed signs of being a visionary, Grandmama explained how what we see only reflects the outcome should a current situation continue without change. My experiences have proven that as well. If I take action or advise someone and they alter the direction they're heading, I invariably see another, altogether different outcome."

"Dead? God, Laney." His arms tightened and he pressed a kiss to her shoulder.

"When Reginald woke me that morning and ordered me to gather my belongings, he refused to tell me our destination nor how long we'd stay, but I sensed it was my last chance. I had to escape. I didn't know what awaited us at the end of the journey, but the peril inherent in it dogged my every step."

"Why me? What in God's name made you approach me?"

"Oh heavens." She scrambled from his lap, twisted around and knelt on the quilt facing him, trying unsuccessfully to keep the embarrassment from her face.

"Aye?" At her obvious mortification, his features relaxed. "I gather that 'oh heavens' portends something scandalous the way you're blushing." His voice fairly sparkled. His eyes did too.

"If you must know…"

"Oh believe me, I must. Tit for cat and all that."

She laughed. Here she was, recounting the most horrifying experiences of her life and she laughed.

Yet…exactly how much did she share?

He watched her every move. She breathed slowly, weighing her words. "I saw us—you and me—mmm... shall we say, in an indelicate position, and I realized if it *were* a vision, then it meant that you came to my rescue.

"It seemed to me that the only way for that to occur —given how fiercely you scowled from your dark corner in the coach—was if I approached you and asked."

"Today?"

Flummoxed, she queried, "Today *what*?"

He glanced at the quilt, then the shadowed area hidden between her bent legs. "Today's indelicate position? What we have done here—is that what you saw?"

She shifted until her knees pressed together, reveled in how his gaze immediately rose to her breasts. "Noooo."

"This morning, then? Before Tate barged in?" Like a predator, Nash climbed to his knees and advanced, placing one hand on her thigh.

"Not this morning, either." She tensed beneath his touch and swayed toward him.

He brought his other hand to her waist. "Last night? The night before that?"

"Neither."

He drew closer. "Going to remain mysterious about this?"

"'Tis required, I'm afraid," she said with mock regret, coming to her knees so that their torsos meshed. She clasped her hands behind his neck. "*A true lady always seeks to cultivate secrets.* That's the only way to ensure a gentleman's interest beyond the moment."

He pressed her lips together and raised one eyebrow. "Where did that balderdash come from?"

No reason he had to know that *everything* she knew about ladylike behavior came from Mary Delilah. Let him think she was the brilliant one. Although *brilliance* and *balderdash* didn't exactly go hand in hand, now did they?

"Determined to retain a bit of mystery, are you?" he said, lifting her up and swinging around until he fell back against the quilt with her in the crook of his arm. One powerful, hairy leg snared hers, forestalling any retreat—not that Laney had plans for anything of the sort. "Even though this *gentleman* has already expressed his interest? In any infinite manner of *interesting* ways?"

"Does it bother you?" More because of curiosity over how he might answer, rather than because she really felt the need to, she asked, "May I not keep a part of me to myself?"

He sighed. "Were we both...*happy* in this indelicate vision of yours?"

"Exceedingly."

He grunted and she stifled a laugh.

"Was it...*after* the other vision you told me about? The one of your wake? Is that something you're at liberty to share, my lady of mystery?"

She thought back to how she'd looked in the gazebo, how her curves had matured. Their talk of children. "Oh yes. I can confidently set your mind at ease on that count."

13

TRULY CAUGHT IN HER
UNINTENTIONAL WEB

NASH MARVELED at the beauty in his arms, at the beauty inherent in this particular day. Had he ever known such peace? Doubtful.

So she wanted to claim the title Lady of Mystery? If he could always hold her thus, he might agree to anything.

"Very well." A gossamer thread descending from a branch overhead snagged his attention, the spider at its end coming closer as it spun the silken line. "You said if it *were* a vision, then it meant that I rescued you. A vision as opposed to what?"

"A daydream?" she squeaked, playing with the fine sheen of hair currently covering his chest.

Never ceased to amaze him, how the amount of hair on his chest and jaw changed depending on his moods, state of arousal and the seasons. At least he didn't grow hair on his palms! Something to be thankful for, whether he owed his appreciation to the sun gods, the African healer or plain old-fashioned luck—or mayhap just *Felis leo* because come to think on it, the wild cats didn't boast hair on their pads either.

The spider continued its downward trudge, heading toward a collision with Laney's naked bosom. Still too far to reach, unless he moved, which wasn't in his immediate plans.

To someone who rarely took the time to ask the name of a wench before he prigged her, much less spent any effort seeking to *know* anything about her beyond the juncture of her legs, he'd certainly evolved in the last few days. At least beyond the primitive state of brute he'd wallowed in for years.

The way Laney's delicate fingers delved through the fine hairs on his stomach, her nails and fingertips exploring his two-penny hide, well...the experience did something to him—made *him* daydream, night dream, spin windmills and air castles about the future.

A future in which he could always fuck *facing forward*—unless the mood struck him otherwise—and one in which *his* dreams were truly possible. The ones of family, a ladylike wife—when in public, that is. In private, she could be as bawdy as...as...the delightful contradiction lodged in his arms whose hand had reached his groin.

"Daydream, eh?" he forestalled further exploration by anchoring her hand with his, keeping track of the spider. So she'd been thinking of sex with him from the onset? His nostrils flared, recalling the scent of her arousal. Knowing now it had been for him and not Tate only made his prick flare as well. Strokes to his ego abounded, so did the spider—bounding lower and lower. "Just what naughty, indelicate position did that innocent mind of yours conjure?"

Weaving spiders, come not here... When it got within arm's reach, he'd—

But Laney beat him to it, casually lifting her free hand, pinching the silken thread he wasn't even aware *she'd* been aware of and depositing the little eight-legged bugger in the grass. Calm as she pleased. Batting the spider away with less care than she'd bat a silk fan.

The action raised all manner of questions. "Thought you detested spiders."

"Mmm?"

"That first night when you crashed into me at The Black Boar, you said bugs are loathsome creatures."

"I did, did I?"

Prevaricating again, that much was obvious, but for what purpose? "I thought we agreed no more hiding."

She rolled over and propped her arms on his chest. Nash bit back the *oompf* the sharp points of her elbows brought to his lips and waited.

"Another dark, disturbing vision, I fear. I had reached the conclusion that if you wouldn't assist me, then there was no help for it—I must escape on my own. I started devising a plan and *boom!* God, the universe, maybe Cornish pixies...I know not which, but some deity to whom I'm forever indebted thought otherwise and showed me the error of my ways. Quite disturbingly, I might add." She toyed with the hollow in his throat, avoiding his gaze, but then her lips curved into a smile and she lifted her eyes. "So I chose not to run. I came to you instead and here we are."

Here we are indeed. He contemplated inquiring as to the content of this "dark, disturbing vision" but something in her relaxed demeanor held him back. Why spoil such a lovely moment? Lovely, disregarding the dagger-status of those elbows. Unless...

"So were I to leave right now, you would remain safe from Tate? From whatever threats he presents? Can you assure me of that?" *Assure yourself?*

Her fingers froze over the column of his throat. "I believe so, yes. Is that..." *What you want?*

He sensed what she didn't voice. Hell no, it wasn't what he wanted, but neither was he confident after *everything* was confided between them, that *she* would want to stay. "Ah, but if I left, then our 'exceedingly happy' future would not come to pass, correct?"

"In all likelihood, it would not."

"'*My brain more busy than the labouring spider...*'" Nash made a pondering noise, one that was meant to alleviate the tension in her fingers, as well as the lump in his throat. "I cannot recall ever being *exceedingly* happy. Not since I was very young."

"Oh? And...?"

He smiled into her gravely serious features. "Believe I'd like very much to give it a try."

Relief washed over her expression and her hands went around his neck, fingers delving into his hair, her thumbs into the bottom of his throat, when sudden curiosity filled her gaze. "Why do you do that—mutter such eloquent phrases at times?"

"When I journey, there is ample time to read. The plays by William Shakespeare are among my favorites."

"I have never seen one of his plays—"

"Never?" He couldn't imagine the lack, one of the few things he enjoyed doing everywhere he landed being to check the playbills for any upcoming performances. "That fiend parades you about for his own selfish gain but never takes you to see *any* of The Bard's finest?"

"Think naught of it." With a flick of her fingers, she brushed off his concern. "But to know so very much, to recite his lines with such ease, you must read frequently."

And now she had him by the tail—and tonsils. "I am alone frequently."

"Not anymore, I do hope. Though I do like your recitations, excessively so." The minx smiled, her innocent appreciation warming everything in him. "You sound magnificent when you do that but...is it not *your* turn to offer explanations, Mr. Hammond? I recall the intriguing matter of curses and *cats*."

"Ah yes." Not quite innocent. Or feeble-brained either—no forgetting here. He sighed against the pressure of her fingers. "Very well."

"Before you tell me, may I avail myself of one of those sweet breads from inside the basket?"

As the woven lid was still securely closed, he couldn't help but prod, "How do you know what's inside? Did you *envision* yourself eating it?"

"No, you wretch. The tempting scents of gingerbread cakes and black butter has bombarded and besieged my senses ever since I woke, and if you don't share..." She leaned over him, aiming for the basket. Nash beat her to it, holding it out of reach while she climbed up his chest, arm outstretched. "Mr. Hammond!"

"You shall what? Forcefully apply your palm to my flesh and spank me again?"

Face flaming, she scrambled off and sat on the opposite corner of the quilt. Discomfited or not, her grin wouldn't be repressed. "Invitation, my good man?" Pursing her lips, she tried again—unsuccessfully—to wipe the smile from her face. "If you do not feed me posthaste, I vow I will eat every square of cake and every dollop of black butter, leaving you with nary a crumb."

He rolled to a sitting position and placed the basket on the quilt as a peace offering between them. "You must threaten another punishment, Princess, for I would be most pleased to make do with the wine and cheese. Tut, tut," he told her when she reached over the basket for her dress. "Remain you as you are."

"But I'm naked!"

"As am I." If he kept her nude, she wouldn't run. At least not without giving him a chance to complete his explanations. He'd never hated the thought of baring his soul more. "Do you not appreciate the freedom inherent in being alone together *like this* especially after being cooped up in that damp stage for days? Do you not want to celebrate *your* freedom?" He waved to the secluded clearing they occupied. "What better way?"

"There is that, you wicked man." With a small huff, she abandoned her clothing search and assumed a sensually languorous pose at his feet, stretching out on her stomach and kicking one foot playfully in the air while propping her upper body on her elbows.

He whistled his appreciation and placed one gingerbread cake at her fingertips. She flashed him a splendid smile through her thick hair—all but one section still haphazardly pinned near her nape now cascaded over her shoulders and pooled on the quilt. "You also give me the freedom to be indulgent, slightly wicked myself, which I never thought to enjoy so very much. That warrants celebration, do you not think?"

Oh he did.

"But I'm still not certain how I feel being attired or *not* attired out here, where just anyone might traipse by."

He wanted to tangle his fingers in the glossy mass. He wanted to love her all over again.

"Mr. Hammond?"

He cleared a throat gone dry. "Trust me when I tell you my hearing is such that were a single foot to trod beyond yon path, I would know and have us both shielded before anyone ever reached the creek." More likely, he'd scent them before that, but was so focused on the sprite before him, savoring and memorizing her every fragrant nuance, that it was easier to depend on his ears rather than distract his sniffer.

Grabbing a hunk of cheese and the wine bottle, Nash scooted the basket off the quilt and joined her, lying on his stomach after a quick twitch of his hips—rearranging his cock. He reached for that luscious curtain of black hair, brushing it behind one ear. "You have yet to take a bite. What are you waiting for?"

"You."

That dern spark—the one centered in his chest—flared to life again and he determinedly put it out. He had no cause getting all feverish or *sparkish* over her, not when she likely wouldn't retain her seductive, receptive demeanor much longer. He'd be lucky if he made it through the time it took her to enjoy her first two cakes.

"Eat away." Saluting her with a piece of blue Stilton, he turned his attention to the view. The trees? Bah. The stubby grass? Bah. The brilliant blue sky overhead dotted with the occasional cloud? Double bah. *Laney's arse?* Nash swore he heard Handel's *Hallelujah* chorus praise each divinely inspired inch of her creamy, rounded derrière.

While she devoured her cake and asked for another, the cheese crumbled to dust in his mouth. Even cheese as good as this—reminiscent of the Gorgonzola he'd developed a taste for in Italy—paled in comparison to what he *could* be savoring...

Long, shapely legs—those tempting toes still pointed and waving in the air—snared his attention. He admired the feminine display, then swallowed hard when he realized how unfashionably long her hair was. How the coal-black strands crisscrossed over her shoulders and down her back, the tips stopping just at the point where those delicious dimples heralded the rounded cheeks of her bottom...just inches above that mole.

"Do you not want to share?" She offered him the last bite of honey cake.

He swallowed again, wiped his lips and continued evaluating her arse. "Not yet. I prefer to eat one thing at a time before moving on to the next."

"That's...odd."

"Odd?" After everything else he had to confess, she'd think his eating habits were more typical than taking afternoon tea with the king.

"Come now, Mr. Hammond. You have been quiet long enough." She rose to her knees and leaned forward to search the basket until pulling forth the dish of black butter. "Though I grant you 'tis beyond liberating to be dining stript to the skin as we are, and I'm sure it might easily lead to any number of delightful conversations and intimate actions"—her voice had gone all smoky as she sent him a look from beneath her lashes—"will you not please tell me about *your* family blessing?"

"Blessing, eh?" The smell of spiced, sauced apples filled the air when she began dipping the honey cake into the spread. His cheese all but forgotten, he applied himself to de-corking the wine. "Is that what you now call it?"

Her tongue came out and swiped the smear of black butter covering her bottom lip. His eyes went from the container of mashed apples to her arse, his gut clenching, hands flexing around the neck of the wine bottle.

"Certainly. For the word *curse* has such a gloomy connotation, do you not think? And as exceed—"

"As exceedingly happy people, we may no longer be gloomy?" Miraculous, was it not, how normal his voice sounded when he was strangling on renewed desire?

"Precisely."

The cork popped and he caught it with one hand. "You, Princess, are a prime piece."

"And you, my dear prince, are dawdling."

"Precisely."

"Hmm." Evidently willing to allow him time, she took another bite, savored it going down, then licked those damnably luscious lips and asked, "Do you not want to try a honey cake? The gingerbread was good, but I vow these must be the best I ever tasted."

"Mayhap later, once I'm done with the cheese." *And you.* After downing several gulps of wine in the guise of seeking courage, he offered her the bottle.

She swallowed her last bite. "Do we not have glasses?"

"Who needs 'em?"

"INDEED." Laney reached for the bottle and took a sip, spilling more down her chin and on the quilt than landed in her mouth. "Drat me, I fear I'm not in the best position to drink."

When she attempted to sit, Mr. Hammond planted one hand between her shoulder blades. Heeding his unspoken wish, she relaxed back onto their pallet. When he didn't say—or do—anything else, the earlier fear tumbled from her. "You *are* aware that you took an extraordinarily long time to come after me this morning, leading me to think you had decided not to."

He claimed the bottle and climbed over her, straddling her thighs. "Dare I confess why?"

Her bum twitched. "Though I may regret asking, do expound upon it, if you please. A girl likes to know the true reason when a gentleman keeps her waiting."

"So now I'm a *gentleman*, am I?" Cold liquid drizzled down her spine.

Laney tightened every muscle to keep from flying off the quilt. "Only for the purposes of this particular conversa-*tion!*" She squeaked when he leaned forward and his tongue lapped at the wine. "Afterward, it too may be up for discussion. *It* being your status as a gentleman."

He spoke against her shoulder, his warm tongue teasing her between the words. "Well, Miss Buckley, this gentleman failed to arrive in a timely manner because he was all amort."

"All-a-what?"

"Struck dumb by your beauty. '*What, sweeting, all amort?*'" he intoned, sounding amazingly somber for one who was drinking wine off her back.

"Oh-mmm, what a rapper!"

"What? You doubt I could be betwattled by the sheer wonder of gazing upon your countenance? 'Tis true." She looked over her shoulder and watched as he winked at her and then tipped the bottle into his mouth, gulping down several swallows.

Tossing her head as if tossing off his Spanish coin, she couldn't deny how his compliments warmed her all over. A second later, she sizzled when he brought his lips to her spine and released the heated liquid over her skin. Before it drizzled down her sides, he laved it away, saying amidst wet kisses, "That confounded me more than once this morning, I'll have you know, coming to terms with the prize in my bed. But the principal reason this gentleman failed to greet you sooner is because he was unable to exit his room."

"Seems an odd affliction to have." She couldn't stop her bum from arching toward him, her skin meeting his hair-roughened thighs. "One must merely turn the handle and step through the doorway."

"Difficult to do, Princess, when one is *still a cat*."

Laney wiggled fingers over her head like a stage show magician waving his cane. "Why did you not just change back?"

He growled and the cool trickle of more wine dripped down her back, lower this time. "Because I didn't know *how* to accomplish that seemingly simple feat."

"But I saw—" She broke off when he lowered his entire body, easing his chest along her backside and continuing to lap at the wine, licking just above her quivering buttocks.

In between licks and kisses, he murmured, "Continue. Exactly what *have* you seen?"

As her inner muscles danced a quadrille, she couldn't help but tilt her hips until her mound met the quilt. "Hmm...in order to cultivate that alluring mystery we agreed I may retain, I am not sure precisely how much I want to share... *Mmm*."

"Busy cultivating, are you?"

"Interruptions will get me nowhere."

"Forgive me," he said with mock contriteness,

belied by the way his hands crept under her stomach and edged toward her breasts. "Do go on."

Laney spread her legs, ignoring the twinges of soreness, hoping for more friction. Hoping he'd *do* more. "I have seen you in the future *as a cat* and you didn't appear to have any difficulty altering yourself from one to the other. Though I'm thinking *cat* may not be the correct word." She felt his nose—at least she thought it was his nose, seeing as how both his outstretched arms had just reached her breasts—sniffing along the seam of her bum. "It's, ah, a different species altogether, isn't it? I saw pictures once. A cheetah, if I'm not mistaken?"

"Cheetah?" Offended to his very soul, Nash nipped her butt. "So the lady considers me a *cheetah*?"

"Calm yourself, Mr. Hammond. I never accused you of being a cheater. A wretch, a scoundrel, a knave perhaps, but never—"

He nipped again. "The sun-loving, lazy scoundrel above you is certainly no cheetah. And lest you might wonder, I never cheat at cards, either."

He tightened his hands around her breasts, gloried in the points of her nipples poking into his palms. The scents buried between the cheeks of her arse turned him to stone. "Care to try again?"

On a groan, "Lynx?"

"You're getting farther off the mark. At least cheetahs are from the same continent." Giving her nipples one serious tweak, he slid his hands from beneath her torso and grabbed the dish of black butter, placing it within reach. "Has your learned friend not taught you any better?"

Given how her entire body started quaking and the sound of her muted laughter was clear, she appeared to be enjoying her own private amusement. "I would be outright lyin' if I said I didn't remember."

How could she giggle at a time such as this? Especially given the position of his hands—which had just gripped her buttocks and spread them wide—and his face, which was centered above the most beautiful pink nock...when it dawned. "Lyin'. *Lion?* And you have the ballocks to call *me* wretched?"

"You're supposed to be telling me of your family bless— Ah! Why do you seek to distract me with...mmm..."

"My tongue?"

"Mr. 'ammond!"

Her earlier cream had combined with his release and dripped down between her legs. From his position, he had easy access to it all. In between licking forays, he told her, "If you cannot bring yourself to call me by a name other than *mister*, I shall have to think up one myself."

"'Tis only because I"—her breath caught when he slid his mouth to the side and sunk his teeth into one creamy globe—"hold you in such high esteem."

"High esteem, eh?" Did he have her bamboozled. "I question how worthy I am of your regard, but—"

"Stop talking," she groaned, raising her arse to his lips.

"As the lady wishes..." Without further ado, Nash dipped his fingers in the black butter and swiped them down the inviting crevice between her cheeks. He took a gulp of wine and leaned in, licking straight down, devouring the sharp tang of fermented fruit, buttery spiced apples and the unique tastes and textures of Laney's equally delectable arse.

He brought his arms up and anchored them over her lower back to keep her in place—not that she was fighting him—so he could lavish his tongue into every crevice it could find...the little depression at the very top of her crack, around the puckered, flexing ring, *inside* her hole.

Her whimpered squeaks mixed with his heartfelt moans as his cock frigged between her closed legs. Fingers splayed wide, he grasped for purchase, dug his hands into her sides while his tongue licked and lapped at her arching, rocking derrière. Had he ever tasted fruit so fine?

Nostrils flaring, he pressed his face to her butt and inhaled. He was boosey over her, as cup-shot as if he'd swilled three entire bottles of wine. No, make that six. Drunk on the most intriguing baggage to ever cross his blighted path.

His cock flailed between her legs—legs she suddenly widened, changing her angle, grinding her center into the quilt. One of her hands snaked under her torso and he moved to assist, releasing his hold on her waist and sliding his arm under her pelvis, finding her fingers, nudging them out of the way and pressing his hand to her nub.

The tiny pearl protruded, eagerly greeting his touch. She rose and fell beneath him, thrashing over his fingers. A low thrumming started at the base of his erection, spread outward, encompassing his ballocks, his entire abdomen… His hips pumped faster, dragging his cock along the quilt, his tongue delved deeper and Laney groaned, stiffened and then released in a torrent that gushed past his fingers, soaking his hand and the quilt.

He withdrew his tongue, bit the side of her arse, kissed it, and then straightened onto his knees and straddled her legs. Stroking his rigid shaft with one hand, he flipped her to her back with the other. She rolled over with a lethargic whimper.

Eyes closed, face flushed, she licked her bottom lip and smiled, settling back into the quilt.

He needed to see her when she came, needed to watch the expressions on her face. Needed to imprint the experience in his mind in case it didn't occur again. He grappled for the wine bottle, curved his fingers around the neck and placed the side of the slick glass between her legs against her sparkling, just-pleasured flesh. Her eyes flew open, the verdant depths flaring with interest. "Still thirsty, are we?"

Shaking from his need to spend, he rasped out, "I want you to come again. While I do naught but watch."

Kneeling over her, he fisted his formidable erection. "Go on, now. Take it and pleasure yourself."

Beneath the focus of his steady gaze, first with hesitation, then with growing delight, she assumed control of the bottle and rubbed the glass over her slippery folds.

The blush returned to her breasts almost instantly. Her previously mellowed breathing accelerated to panted gasps before he'd gotten a good ten strokes in.

He gloated over how bright red, swollen and *wet* her juicy seam was. Tasted her arse on his tongue and he blasted off like a cannon, spraying semen as if it were shot over her upper thighs and midnight curls. Everywhere that bottle wasn't, his seed laid claim.

His cock relaxed marginally, still stiff and straining to be *inside*, but he'd sworn to himself to give her body a chance to recover. To give her a chance to deny him—once and for all—after she learned what else he needed to expunge from his soul.

As if his own release triggered hers, she tensed her thighs and lifted her arse off the quilt, rubbing the bottle in a frenzy against her folds. Her lower body undulated like waves in a storm, riding the glass...those puffy, pouting lips spread on either side. When some of her cream trickled from the bottom edge, Nash licked his lips as his cock lurched in his hand. He tightened his fingers at the base and grabbed his ballocks with his other hand and squeezed himself as if strangling the very life out.

Laney sent a moan toward the heavens and released again, her juices dripping off the bottle and between her legs. Unable to stop himself, Nash abandoned his shaft and dove forward. Wrenching the bottle out of the way, he licked every bit of her slick skin, swallowing down her desire. Taking her inside himself and only just then noticing how the feline atoms of his being had been absent from their entire encounter. That realization started him to shaking all over again. How was it, with this one particular female, he could enjoy the ability to simply be a *man*? A man loving a woman...

One you don't have the right to love.

Her slowly contracting flesh slid along his face and Nash kissed it all, the roaring in his ears finally abating enough for him to hear her whispered, "I was so very wrong before."

His entire body humming from his release—from hers—he willed his heart and breathing to slow. With one last swallow, another slow, luxuriant lick of his tongue, he pulled away and her bottom sank to the quilt, flinching at the wet fabric. Grabbing her and rolling them both to a dry portion, he secured his arms around her back, he forced himself to hold her gaze. "Wrong about what?"

Perched atop him as she was, he felt her inner trembling. It mirrored his own.

Tracing one finger over the twin scars on his lips, she said, "I'm ashamed to admit I always thought it wouldn't matter who I took into my body, that one man wasn't any better or worse than another, as long as they fed me and gave me a safe place to sleep every night."

Safe? "Did you feel safe with Tate?"

Her eyes flicked to his. "For the most part. Until recently. But I'm not talking about him, you fiend, I'm talking about this."

"This?" Being more naked and exposed and vulnerable than he ever had in his life? Did she feel it too? "Define 'this', if you please."

"That regardless of who owned me, and by extension my allegiance and...and..." She looked away and finished in a rush. "Owned my body, I could not have done this with anyone else. You have shown me that, no matter the similarities in, um, coupling parts, the actual procedure and outcome can vary significantly and I'm ever-so grateful it was you."

"Me? Procedure?" *Coupling parts?* Despite his hammering heart, he stifled a laugh. Only Laney! "Just *what* are you attempting to say?"

She caught his gaze again. "I just said it."

"My dear, if I understand you correctly, you have all but reduced intimate love play to the mundaneness of having a rotten tooth extracted."

"Do you not see?" She sounded so earnest, her words and expression at odds with how her body still quivered in the aftermath, how his did as well, that he tried to remain equally solemn. "I'm expressing my joy and appreciation that you were the one to introduce me to such...personal delights and—"

"Personal delights?" Solemn proved impossible and Nash did laugh at that.

"Now you're just being contrary on purpose." Her eyes narrowed at his continued humor; he sought to compose himself. "Truly, Mr. Hammond, I cannot fathom the void that would have been left in my life had I not known of this. I'm so grateful my initial convictions were wrong."

"I must admit your words are all a rumfoozle to me. Exactly *what* are you declaring a wrongness about?"

She stiffened, left off toying with his mouth and dug one toenail into his shin. "That I was so very wrong about it simply being something anyone could do. That it—"

"*It?*"

"Tiffing, tupping, prigging, you rotten beast! You

know I'm talking about us rubbing bellies and I shall extract *your* teeth if you don't quit mocking me."

He took pity on her—and his abused shin. "Forgive me. Do go on, please. I wish to hear the rest."

Her foot relaxed. "You have shown me that it *does* so intensely matter who I give my body to. Not just legal keeping, mind, but into your *care*."

While he still didn't grasp every morsel of what she'd just proclaimed, the basic fundamental was clear enough. Having such sentiment directed toward his sorry hide warmed him straight through the years of loneliness and isolation. Burnt them away as if they'd happened in another lifetime entirely. And the more he thought on it, they had.

The lifetime before Laney.

BACK IN LONDON

STINKING BLISTER!

Patience lifted her slipper, fingered the hole worn through the sole and blamed Temperance. Stinking sister!

Actually, *everything* tonight was all Franny's fault. Stinking cousin!

Could Patience help it if her slippers were made for dancing, not traipsing? If she were made for dancing, not paying off rude hackney drivers who wouldn't keep their insulting comments to themselves, their leering glances, their gap-toothed dirty smiles—their horse-dirty hands from her pristine person?

Could Patience help it if she had suffered excessively in her young life? First a strict father, who preached to his congregation from the pulpit, and to his family with the rod?

Then a self-absorbed mother, who cared more about wagering and winning than she did taking her dear daughters to the dressmaker? Leaving poor Patience to fend for herself?

Her unpalatable duty to hide her mother's activities from not only the help, but also from her new husband? Had not Patience even been willing to give Lord Rowden a chance to be a proper stepfather? But nay, he would rather escape off to the country than stay in town with them, leaving Mother easy prey for unscrupulous pigeon hunters.

Thank heavens for Lord Hansen. He had seen through all the trials Patience had to endure. Seen through her exasperating mother, excessively silly sister and exceedingly uppish cousin to the real gem within their midst—Patience herself.

"Blast." Poking at the blister didn't bring relief. It was going to pop and ooze grossly over her kid slippers. Just one more thing she could blame on Temperance.

Leading her astray tonight—into this wickedly dark part of London.

Where was she? Weren't there supposed to be people afoot this time of night? Granted, it was closer to sunrise than sundown...

And why hadn't she thought to find a footman before she left to follow?

Oh, because they had to make do with a dearth of servants, since Mother couldn't be troubled to budget.

Being out here, huddled against the stone façade of some multi-storied building, fervently wishing she had—instead of slapping the hackney driver—paid his outrageous price and ordered him to take her back home.

Well now, she huffed, the pain in her foot pricking her pride. *Well now, stupid blister, stupid sister. I'm smarter than you both.*

It took four tries, and a few more curse words, but she ripped the sleeve off her dress—had no intention of wearing it again this season anyway—and folded it up before shoving it inside her slipper, to cushion her foot. "There now."

Shoulders back. Chin up. Eyes narrowed in concentration. There! When the clouds scudded across the moon, she saw another hackney.

"Driver!" she called, trading the security of the stone wall at her back for the promise of deliverance. "Driver! I want to hire you."

Limping across the humidity-dampened stone roadway, scurrying after the rolling hack, she screeched, "Driver! Stop this instant!"

But the imbecile failed to slow.

Footsteps sounded behind her. Her heart stopped. Then thumped hard and fast. Chest ached. Blister popped.

The steps approached, swiftly.

She turned, stiffening, ready to defend herself—

Only to hear a carriage rolling at a fast clip from the opposite direction.

Torn, she wavered. Had the driver changed his

mind? The wheels sounded louder and the footsteps fell silent.

Decision made, she met the approaching carriage in the middle of the road, more majestic than an old hackney. Only to come up short at the crest on the side. "Thank heavens. 'Tis you!"

Rescue had arrived.

14

THE CONFESSION AND THE CROWN

<hr>

"THANK YOU FOR THAT. I hope I prove worthy of your esteem," Mr. Hammond spoke without a hint of amusement, after her fumbling declaration. Then surprised a relieved sigh out of her when he captured her lips in a bruising kiss.

Made a mull of it, expressing wonder at all he'd shown her, but there it was. Who knew she could be so wicked when it came to matters of the flesh? Her mum would have expired on the spot. Grandmama would have cheered.

She followed his lead and kissed him back with all the desperation he was showing her, that perplexing *Don't leave* and *Usiniache* he'd uttered not long ago still echoing through her mind.

Where did he think she was going?

Nowhere, *ever*, if she had any say.

He shifted until they were on their sides. His

tongue surged within her mouth, as if searching out her secrets, exposing them and making them his own. Clasping his strong shoulders, she gave him everything she had, praying it was enough.

After a minute, his lips gentled, his tongue calming until he ended their connection with little pecks along her lips. Little pecks that kept crisscrossing her mouth...never stopping...

He was avoiding her again. Stalling. After admitting she knew he impossibly turned into a cat, what could be left? Better to blow with the wind, to her way of thinking, and bring everything out now rather than worry, wait and wonder, likely building things up bigger than a gollumpus.

Pulling back, she brought her hands to the sides of his face. Her fingernails anchored into his side-whiskers, leaving her thumbs free to edge toward his lips.

His lips were wet and slightly swollen—like hers felt. Only he looked *guilty* as though he'd tripped an old lady and laughed as she fell. "What is it, Mr. Hammond? What has you in such a sad trim?"

He held her gaze, his full of shadows. When she touched his mouth, he mashed his beautiful lips together, obliterating the two slashes she'd traced with her tongue only seconds before. A quick shake of his head was his only response.

She relaxed one hand and brushed it through his hair, petting him. After what they'd just done—what she'd let him lick!—there was no way he was getting away without telling her *something*.

Secrets aside, Laney wanted his love. For that, she first needed to gain his trust.

Her fingers returned to his lips, caressing over them until they unclenched. The old scars stood out in stark relief. "When we met, you appeared absolutely abysmal." Much as he did now. "Self-loathing filled your haunted gaze. Why was that?"

Retreating, he flopped on his back and stared up through the leaves until he hid his face under one arm. The other lodged beneath her waist—and could bloody well stay there. She had no intention of moving a muscle. Not anytime soon.

"Mr. Hammond?"

"And herein lies the first test of our sharing tales." Bitterness coated his words.

"And tails." She trailed a finger down his exposed hip until encountering his bare flank. "Do tell."

That brought a quirk to his mouth and a slight shift until he was gazing at her with one eye. "Exceedingly happy indeed if I can smile when I'm about to confess my second-darkest secret."

"Second darkest? Oh my. If you assign them numbers, they must weigh heavily." She propped herself up, crooking one arm under her head and placing the other directly over his pounding heart. "I shall endeavor to wait patiently, then, until you're ready to tell me, though inside I am a seething cauldron of impatience."

The arm under her waist curved until his fingertips touched her bum. "I'd like to know the inside of your seething cauldron again, but—"

Breaking off, he wrenched his arm out from under

her. Full of that impatience she'd claimed, he sat up, anchoring one bent leg in front of him. His arm curved around it and she watched his fist clench and unclench.

Peering down at her through the fall of hair that buffeted his expression, he finally said, "Why did I look like a sad hound the day we met? Because I did the most heinous thing just hours before. Not that it excuses anything, but the curse that alters my form is strongest when the sun is in Leo."

"In Leo?" She followed suit, sitting up, careful to keep from crowding him, as if giving a wild animal room to run. An illusion only. "Forgive me but I know nothing about astrology."

"Or astronomy either, it appears." His head angled toward the sun, partially blocked by the branches overhead. "The crux of my family curse is this—for a few weeks every year, all the males battle outside forces. Inside forces, perhaps. I'm uncertain which—mayhap it is both. But annually, once we reach twenty-five, we are cursed while the sun passes through the constellation of Leo, the lion."

He left off scrutinizing the sky and reached for his pantaloons. "The exact days change from year to year, but typically from early August until the middle of September I battle a monster. I *am* a monster."

Her heart twisted at that. "Nay. You are not."

"I am, damn it." Aggravation evident in every motion, he tugged the narrow pant legs over his feet and past his muscular calves, still avoiding her gaze. "Which only partially explains my state the day we met."

Silently, she snatched Mr. Hammond's shirt and pulled it over her head.

"My grandfather had a renowned penchant for hunting big game. By the mid 1700s, he'd gone on hunting expeditions in Africa so many times, 'twas a wonder he still called England home." He located his stockings and slung them both over his shoulder. Too overwrought to slide them on properly?

Rather than interrupt, as he'd just begun explaining how his grandfather had killed two lions while they were mating and had been attacked by a third, she listened and watched—and plotted her next move.

"He nearly bled to death from the wounds until a local tribesman, a doctor of sorts, was summoned and healed him. But only after a ceremony in which the old codger was clueless," he added, abandoning the search for his shirt and drawing his waistcoat on directly over bare skin.

By now, she had seized his boots as well, stuffing her feet into each.

She watched as he haphazardly did up the buttons on his striped waistcoat, apparently not realizing how improper—or attractive—the exposed muscles in his arms looked or how inviting his bare chest looked beneath the misaligned waistcoat. "Either insensible from loss of blood or uncaring because it was a different culture, my demmed grandfather was pitch-kettled by what was going on, had no idea he traded our souls for his life. It was decades before our family learned *Simba* spirit medicine was used to heal his body, and in return, part of *our* bodies are controlled by it every year."

"Controlled by...lion spirit?"

"*Roho wa Simba*, aye." On his knees now, Mr. Hammond razed the pile that previously contained her neatly folded stockings, dress and shawl, scattering everything in a humble-jumble due to his unchecked efforts. "Which is how I finally resumed human form this morning. Though I had begun to despair ever eating again without fangs or excessive drool, it finally occurred to call on lion spirit to return me to my prior shape, just as I had called on it to change and save you."

Oh, she would have to save this image of him—standing there in his bare feet, hopping from the damp spot caused by her release and the wine, muscles bulging from the exposed sections of his waistcoat, hair windblown from running his hands through it...and still stoically explaining away, without ever once glancing in her direction. "Did you not say that you never *changed* before?"

"I have not—not voluntarily, that is. Today was the first, Princess. Several firsts, in fact, and I...I... Where in the bloody hell are my boots?"

"Over here."

He finally looked at her. His eyebrows shot skyward. "You are wearing my boots?" He stepped forward. "My *shirt*?"

Still sitting on one side of the quilt, she shrugged. "I could not chance you running away."

"Who said anything about leaving?"

"You refused to look at me and you kept pulling on all your clothes. What else was I to think?"

"'Tis deuced difficult, telling you this. You could have me consigned to Bedlam or transported to New South Wales or—"

"Do you forget that I already knew?"

Mr. Hammond crouched beside her and picked up her hand, idly caressing the back. "That is the only reason I share this much."

"Then why did you start dressing?"

He brought her hand to his lips. "Because I'm a clod. I make you remain nude and elucidate, but I don't have the pluck to do the same."

"You are the bravest man I know," she told him truthfully, curving her fingers toward his a second too late—as he'd just stood. Distancing himself? "To learn that you sacrificed like that for me, succumbed to your...blessed curse to save me from Reginald...well, I am honored by your efforts, truly honored. You have rescued me in so many ways and I—"

"Save your appreciation, Laney, for you may decide it should rightly be condemnation instead." He stalked across the clearing and bent low, speaking over his shoulder. "For it was my brother's wife I attacked just hours before we met, which explains why I was in no mood for convivial conversation."

Attacked? "Hours?" she said in as neutral a voice as she could muster. Then, "His *wife*?"

"Might as well be." He stood, moved to his left in the grass and crouched again, keeping his back to her. What was he doing? "They're affianced, banns all but done, only Blake had kept the feline part of himself a secret from her. When the feral instincts to Change became too great, rather than take a wench to calm them or confess to Francine, he suffered. Suffered like I have never seen."

"I have." But the words were said too softly for him to hear. She spoke again, louder. "You suffered last eve, all through the night."

"Did I?" He discounted his own anguished hours as if they were nothing more than he deserved, standing, walking a few steps, then kneeling again. "Blake's self-denial affected more than his body, did he but know it. We're connected during this time of year and my cells also responded to the beastly urge riding him, altering to such a degree that no matter how much I..."

At this, he glanced her way, but he'd stopped too far away for her to read his expression. "Regardless of how often I...*you know*...peace eluded me. When I arrived in London, Blake was behaving like an old soaker—totally disheveled. Hadn't donned new clothes in days, from what I could tell. Completely opposite of his customary grooming. Even had me chain him to the bed to keep from going after her, from destroying his home. A short while later, Francine appeared and I—I..."

He stood abruptly. A veritable bower of ragged, weedy flowers protruded from his clenched fists. Arms stiff at his sides, he walked toward her. "Not to belabor it, let me simply say I behaved like a despicable brute."

Vexing to note, was it not, that *now* was the first time Mr. Hammond exhibited any difficulty expressing himself? And it had to do with *another* female. One Laney wished she'd never heard of. "What does 'you know' and 'taking a wench' have to do with stifling your curse?" *And just exactly how did you attack Francine?*

"Sex, Laney," he said as though cursing—and still evading her gaze. "Nightly sex is the only way we have found to stay fully and functioning *human* during Leo. Lion spirit. Lion sex. They both equal lion offspring. And the *Roho ya Simba* lives on."

SPIRIT OF THE LION.

Merciful heavens.

Laney concentrated on breathing, the usually ignored act taking on new significance as she consciously lifted her chest and drew air into her lungs, then pushed it out. Again. And again.

Absorbing everything he'd said and inferring everything he hadn't...

'Twas a moment before the absolute stillness reached her. The silence.

Not the kind where birds twitter in the background or leaves rustle. Not the kind where one expects a response or prays for forgiveness, but the kind of soundless finality when one knows the unpardonable has been done and nothing can ever make it right.

The stark silence following his confession chilled her soul—because she sensed how it affected him. His remorse and self-castigation. His desperate need for absolution.

In one fluid motion she rose to her feet, reaching for him. "Mr.—"

"That's not the worst of it, either," he said swiftly,

stepping away. "As if what I did to Francine isn't enough, I caused another to lose her life."

Her hands shot out and she gripped his nearest wrist, refusing to allow his complete withdrawal, tolerate his attempted escape. He dropped the scraggly weeds and froze, not fighting to jerk away but neither responding to her touch.

"Another?" she questioned. Even as the air in her lungs pinched and burned.

"Another woman, and her in addition to Phineas. He's gone too and the blame rests firmly on me."

The breath she'd worked so hard to acquire whooshed from her lips. "And I thought I had secrets?" Tugging on his arm, she pulled him down until they both landed on the quilt. Cautiously, she encouraged, "Share the rest with me?"

He nodded once, but said nothing.

"Starting with Phineas," she prodded. He'd mentioned the name during the long night. "Who is he?"

"Our cousin, he's older than Blake by a year, older than me by six. He's been missing. Eleven long years this month." Extracting his wrist, he set his fingers to stripping leaves away from the lank stems. "As the eldest three boys of this generation of cursed Hammonds"—his words became more bitter—"we'd heard a whisper or two, near-silent murmurings during family gatherings about The Change, but we thought it nothing more than a lark, something told to adventuresome boys to keep them from straying too far.

"My brother inherited when he was nineteen, but even at that young age, he took his responsibilities seriously, acting as head of the family, looking out for everyone. Some months after our father's body was returned to us, after a presumed—but questionable—hunting accident, our mother left. Supposedly seeking answers.

"Instead, only leaving Blake and me with more questions. Because she disappeared. But not, to our disbelieving astonishment, before revealing The Curse to Blake, in all its ugly glory, by way of my father's journals. Letters he'd penned to us both, Blake and—"

"Wait. Your mother is missing? Like Phineas?"

"Nay. Not like him at all. By *her choice*." Did he but know it, the grief resounding through his stoic recital made her bite her lips against the tears that wanted to fall for the pain she sensed emanating from him. "Whether true or not, I consoled myself, thinking she missed Father such a vast degree that she ended up at the coast. Somewhere they had traveled together early in their marriage and spoke of fondly. Walked out into the ocean and...into...oblivion—"

"Oh, Nash." She reached for his furiously busy hands, tried to still their frantic efforts. "Mr. Hammond..."

He wrenched from her comforting touch. Not ready to accept any solace for his assumed part in the tragedies he now shared? "Phin and I? We still thought the entire thing a royal jest. Ridiculed Blake anytime he broached it, wanting to discuss the deep, dark Family Secret, willing to entertain the *possibility*. We laughed at him, more fools us, accused him of being overly interested in spreading Banbury tales."

"What about your cousin's father? Did he not

impress upon Phineas the truth?" Laney tugged the long sleeves of his cuffs down and closed her fists around the fabric, hugging her middle, absorbing his presence that lingered on the linen because, ironically, though he'd sat just inches away, Nash Hammond now seemed farther from her than he ever had in the stagecoach.

"Phineas inherited the curse from his mother. She was our eldest aunt, had married a country baron who convinced both her and Phin the curse was pure nonsense. By then Grandfather had passed on and our other uncles had either settled sedately in the northern shires with their own brides or traveled abroad. Every summer, Blake lives in fear that bastard Hammonds will appear and wreak havoc in high society London."

The spindly weeds stripped as naked as his emotions—whenever he chanced to look at her—he started plaiting them together. "So Phineas was set to get married. 'Twas an important alliance, joining two powerful families and all that. He'd been betrothed to her forever it seemed, loved her too, I gather, but the wedding was scheduled during the time of Leo the year Phin turned twenty-five. The *day* he turned twenty-five. Blake pleaded with him to cry off or to change the date at the very least, but Phineas wouldn't have it. And me, buffle-headed me . . ."

His fingers mangled three of the stems. He tossed them aside and started afresh.

"What about you?" she queried softly, hugging herself harder when he remained silent so long she thought he'd decided not to finish.

"Me? Hell, Princess"—his self-loathing and rough

voice startled her anew—"I deserve to be stuck in the pillory and pelted to death because over one too many bottles of brandy, I encouraged the insanity. 'Marry her,' I said, full of drunk wisdom—Blake had just gifted both Phineas and me with adjoining estates. Nothing grand, mind you, but he'd found two country abodes, manor houses really, for sale just a short ride from each other and bought them for us. Said he wanted to make sure his closest male relatives were provided for. Phin didn't need it, was marrying into one of the richest families in England, was set to inherit himself once his father passed on, but that's the kind of man my brother is. Always watching over others. Whether they warrant his care or not."

Once he finished plaiting every green stem, his fingers and words paused. In the silence broken only by his harsh breathing, he traced over the leggy stalks. She unwound one arm and tapped the back of his wrist. "Did your cousin postpone his wedding?"

He flipped his hand and grasped hers, finally lifting his gaze. Expression anguished, he shook his head. "What should have been a celebration turned into a bloodbath. 'Marry her,' I'd laughingly encouraged. 'You shall have the fortune of prigging a virgin on your wedding night to commemorate the day of your birth and the curse will be avenged!' More fool I."

"Oh, Mr. Hammond..."

"We had a great laugh over it, too full of ourselves to realize we were simply not two young drunks comparing the virtues of a particular wench. We were trifling with people's *lives*." His fingers tightened, squeezing the feeling from hers. "The day after the wedding, when by suppertime neither of them had emerged or taken in the food trays left by the maid, the bride's mother entered the bedchamber. She found chaos. Blood everywhere, her grown daughter incomprehensible and incoherent. Phineas was gone. Vanished as if he'd never been there. Except for all the blood—and the fur."

"His...wife?"

"Wouldn't speak, from what I gather. Parents hauled her off to London to consult with physicians. They were looking into dissolving the marriage when she...she took her own life."

"And your cousin?"

He released her numb fingers and turned to face her, more guilt than any man should ever bear drowning the depths of his eyes. "I know not. Dead, most likely. We have not had word from him since the wedding. No one has." Warily, he wiped a hand down his face. "So you see why I cannot call my curse a blessing. No god would condone these tragedies. Regardless of how I might wish otherwise, I don't deserve to be exceedingly happy. I killed two people, attacked another and—"

"Stop it right now!" She rose to her knees and gripped his upper arms. "Cease your prattle!"

"My prattle? That is what you call my heartfelt confessions, madam?"

She dug in her fingernails and shook him with all her might. "When they are wrong, *aye*! I shall not deny that goading Phineas into marriage was a mistake and what happened as a consequence is tragic, and I hurt for the pain you heap on yourself because of it, but you were barely more than a child yourself. At seventeen, even eighteen, I thought Reginald the most dashing, generous man in the world. Would you hold that against me?"

His arms tensed beneath her assault but he didn't move. "Despite the age difference, Phin and I were always close. It was my fault. If instead, I had attempted to dissuade him..."

He looked away. She seized his jaw in one hand and urged him to face her. After only token resistance, he swiveled his head, scowling. "*What?*"

"You said he loved her."

"He did."

"They *wanted* to marry. I sincerely doubt anything you or anyone said to the contrary would 'ave changed their minds."

She may have commanded his attention, but a single shrug of his shoulders was the only indication she was reaching him at all. It wasn't enough. She cupped both sides of his frowning face, ready to rip it off his neck if he didn't listen. "You must forgive yourself and release these demons you're 'olding on to. They're destroying you inside."

From the way he swayed toward her, searched her gaze with his, he wanted to believe her...wanted to accept her understanding and forgiveness and make them his own. But then he jerked back, tried to escape her relentless hold. She wouldn't have it.

"And Francine?" he asked harshly. "How do I atone for that? I cannot claim age as an excuse. Not that what I did is excusable. Ever."

She gentled her fingers before she bruised his

cheeks and heaved a deep sigh. "Nash Whose-Middle-Name-Should-Be-Stubborn Hammond, you said that much of last night is a blur. Why is that?"

"The Change. It alters us. While we fight it—"

"Do you not see, you willful, stubborn man?" She pulled on his hair when he tried to retreat, yanked him right back in place. Eyes narrowing, he stayed. "The same thing happened before with *that other woman.*"

"Other woman?"

"*Francine,*" she practically spat, insanely jealous of the unknown female solely because Nash *cared* about her.

"Nay, I do not."

"Don't what? Believe me? Because—" And then his hands were bracketing *her* face, halting her tirade.

"I don't care about Francine, not beyond as a sister-to-be. What gave you such a chuckleheaded notion?"

She'd said that out loud? Of all the things to *tell* him!

She remained silent and he slid one broad hand to her nape, curved the other around her back and brought her into intimate contact with his body. Ludicrous though their joint attire, all she could focus on was the intensity he directed at her. "Blake loves her to destruction—his own, if he's not careful, but she must be special to have tamed my duty-driven brother. Though I'm ashamed to admit it, I hated her for what she was doing to him and ultimately me. Through no fault of her own, my pain had increased so that by the time she finally appeared, I treated her abominably."

"But, Mr. Hammond. Nash...you held me last night —through your own suffering and I *do* remember. All of our time together, I remember. The grunts, the growls. When you get *rough*." She held his gaze—even through that last part—never more proud of herself. She really wasn't hiding anymore. "And I confess I like it when you get rough."

"Do you, now?"

She nodded against the pressure of his fingers. "Whenever you are altered by the lion spirit, I think your mind distorts things. I believe, when you return to London and face her and Blake, you will find they don't condemn you even a fraction as much as you condemn yourself."

"And you will come with me?"

"Me? Return to London?" She tried to put some distance between them. Her efforts were futile. "Heavens, no. I'm never going back. Reginald may say I'm free, but I'm not certain how legal it is to dissolve an indenture or what the proper process involves. For all I know his brother may start looking for me the moment he realizes I left. If I so much as set foot in town, he may have me brought up on charges for running away or stealing or any manner of things the miserable cur could claim if he took a mind— Mr. Hammond! *What are you doing?*"

He'd pushed her bum to the quilt, risen to his knees, and had his hands at her head. "Measuring your brainbox."

"Have you lost your mind?" Of a certainty, she had...sitting there, crumpled atop the crumpled quilt among a pile of exceedingly crumpled weeds while long, sinuous fingers created patterns over her head. Patterns that caused her entire attic to purr with pleasure.

He only murmured, "Do believe I have enough."

"Enough of what?" she demanded, peeling his fingers off her scalp and holding tight. "Surely not wits, for I declare all of yours have gone begging!"

"Likely, they have." He leaned down and pressed a kiss to her forehead. "If I can be standing outside in nothing save my waistcoat and pantaloons, exposing my soul...with neither of us running for the nearest ship." A wobbly smile curved his lips, and to her utter relief, he lowered himself and sat beside her. "Amazing, that."

"But we're in the middle of England!"

He picked up several hanks of plaited weeds and started weaving them together. "That we are and your faith has convinced me that no matter how great my guilt or how small our country, I shall never be easy with myself until making amends directly to Blake and Francine. Even over Phin's dedicated gravestone, if I must. And I want you to come—"

"But I cannot go back!" She sounded like a screaming shrew, one with no ladylike training at all. "Pardon me. I choose not to return." *Choose it with all my might.* "I do not want to ever cross paths with George John or his cohorts again. As he's a dedicated Londoner, I'd as soon steer clear."

"Life brings surprises every day. I never thought I would meet a woman who looks better in my boots than I do."

Unwilling to argue, she nodded toward his handiwork. "What are you doing?"

"Paying homage." After that cryptic remark, he wound the woven stems around and over several times and tied them off. Then he plopped the circlet on her head. "Every princess needs a crown, don't you think?"

And while she was still absorbing the warm, tantalizing haze his words—and her new hat—gave her, he caught her gaze, his most serious once again. "Blake will take care of it, you know."

"Take care of what?"

"You. The indenture. He will make sure you remain free from this older Tate, legally and any other way that concerns you."

"Why would he bother himself to do that? What even makes you think he can?"

"He shall do it because I ask him to. And he can because he's a marquis."

Zoodikers.

BACK IN LONDON

"COME ON, Magnum. Fly, boy. Fly like the wind." Adam muttered the encouragement, knowing his trusty steed would take him swiftly through the dark streets of London, encouragement or not.

Both of them were breathing hard, the cool after-midnight air not enough to dampen the sweat of stress, the adrenaline of anxiety.

How fortunate he'd been, finding a horse so in tune with him, the big black beast rescued shortly after Adam had appeared here and proving the third-closest friend he'd found, next to his borrowed cat and E.

Erasmus. Lord Blakely—to the *ton.* The man who

gave his trust just as sparingly, who expected Adam to capably handle things in his absence. "If expectations were wishes..."

And if he only had a magical genie to rub and three wishes of his own.

Yeah, jackass—if you only had three? *Just what would you wish for? Something for yourself?* To find Elise—who may not be here at all? To instantly be back at The Den, with all of tonight's crazy erased? To have that bottle of Budweiser you wished for not ninety minutes ago to appear in your hand?

Yeah, that.

Or something for those you care about? That Elise find the happiness that had eluded her back in Texas? In her own time? That the curse not burden E? That the murderer you both seek would slip in his own blood, crack his head upon the cobbles and die a nasty, painful death?

Yeah, that too.

But what, then, of the effervescent English miss?

Hell, made her sound like a fizzing antacid.

Does the thought of dealing with her not give you heartburn?

Not...exactly.

If you wished her gone, then you might not be racing toward her now, heart lifted in a curious fashion unlike anything you've experienced since—

Magnum whinnied and reared, both front hooves coming off the pavement a good four feet, knocking some sense back into his wandering thoughts. "Eyes on the prize, idiot."

But just what *was* the prize these days? A peaceful

night's slumber?

For Lucy Mae—one of E's "working girls" to stop flirting with him? To stop flashing twinkling eyes and gorgeous tits his direction, trying to entice him to toss his good sense aside and toss her skirts?

He gripped the reins, leaned over Magnum's mane and slapped his palm and fingers twice over the flexing, galloping muscles in the hard pet Magnum liked. "Come on, boy."

The big horse unerringly knew his way back, where oats and his stall waited. Poor guy had no idea that wasn't their immediate destination.

Knowing that he still needed to escort the adorable, bubbly English miss home—after the horrible goings-on of late—made apprehension ride hard on Adam's shoulders. Neither of them should be out, alone, like this. Thank God E had been at home, had welcomed Francine inside, so at least that responsibility—delivering her safely—could be checked off his list.

But the rest of it? Seeing her cousin home safe? And then himself? Making sure things at the club had run smoothly during his absence... Getting everyone out, the girls settled in their rooms upstairs, and the place locked up tight for the night?

The club. Where he normally enjoyed spending his evening hours, after sleeping in during his days. But tonight? This summer? He turned his head to spit the nasty taste from his mouth.

Too many murders. And the last one—that they knew about—one of E's girls. Adam shuddered as the grisly sight he'd seen up close twice now eroded the barriers he tried to erect and the scenes, in all their stench-filled, red-dripped gore fought to take hold.

When normally, he'd make himself picture something syrupy sweet and laughingly trivial to override the wretched memories—unicorn kittens or buttercream cupcakes with rainbow sprinkles, or how Lucy Mae liked to catch his eye when she was going down on another man—

Tonight, none of that saved his sanity.

Because what rose, harder than his dick and faster than a winning field goal, was not the way it had felt to hold the little miss, how she'd fit his bigger frame perfectly and smelled both wholesome and arousing, nor how swiftly he'd responded to the press of her against lonely muscles that hadn't cuddled with anything other than his sister's cat for years—and that only when Marsh was in the mood—

No, what raced in to replace gruesome, grisly memories was her flashing eyes. Her bright smile. Her surprising boldness given her youth. How she'd stood up to him, standing strong for her cousin. How she'd rushed to correct him: *"Oh, I am not a real lady, just a simple unadorned miss."*

Yeah, well, with a titled stepfather and her cousin the daughter of a duke—which meant his Swiss Miss was most likely related to one as well—he wasn't just barking up the wrong tree, thinking about her, he was living in the wrong century. Which he was. Which just made everything so messed up.

Swiss Miss? What happened to English?

How could he be wondering—even now, what

other surprising remark might peep out of her smiling mouth next?

Well, shit snacks and double damn. She might not have been the prettiest woman he'd seen since miraculously finding himself in England, but she was the first he wanted to see again. Wanted to talk to, see if the instant attraction was mutual, might lead anywhere—

And that's what you'd wish for, you dumbshit? A chance with the English lady? One so far above his current peon status that he might as well wish he could fly to the moon—or for a time capsule...

Because men like him, the working, lower class of "Regency" England didn't have a shot in Hades with someone like her, not in this day and time. Not given who he wasn't. What he wasn't. Not titled. Not unencumbered. Not free to dream or make plans. Not while he waited for Elise.

"You've no business thinking or wishing about anyone else. Least of all a heartburn-inducing miss with more courage than sense. Moron." Magnum snorted his agreement just as Adam kicked the big horse in the sides, pushing him past the mews where he stayed and slept, and straight up the block to the front of The Den.

Dropping the reins, knowing his horse would stay put, Adam jumped to the ground, trying to ignore the excitement—the anticipation—that filled his chest as he sped to the door.

TWO MINUTES EARLIER...

THE MOMENT TYNDALE finished reassuring Baywick and the guard went back to minding the regular club customers, leaving Tyndale and his Responsibility alone, he dropped to the floor, higgledy-piggledy piling everything back on to the desk. Everything the Bothersome Annoyance had scattered. He was half surprised she hadn't begged Baywick to save her from the mean artist's clutches.

"There." He slapped both palms on the desk and pushed to standing. "At least that's one jumble taken care of for—"

But he was speaking to air. Where did she go?

He glanced around the room which took all of one second. Even, stupidly, looked behind the desk.

That little baggage. Used the distraction of the regular guard sticking his head in to flounce away? To steal off with his drawing?

Audacious little piece. Wylde could have her.

He'd give her to the count of *fifty*—a minute or so— to get her aggravating arse back inside or he'd go after her. Meanwhile—smiling grimly, he picked the pencil once again—he'd draft out his next masterpiece: the drawing she'd all but dared him to complete.

A count of fifty became one hundred fifty as he became lost in the welcome respite that the act of drawing provided.

Something he'd all but forgotten, in the recent months of worry. The ease he felt, becoming immersed within the world he created. His mind floating, no longer agonized with guilt or responsibilities, no longer burdening him with his failures. Just a few seconds of oblivion. So very needed and welcome.

Only...a moment...more.

He worked on lining in the background proportions after rough sketching the trio, making sure the woman's face—if not her other *scintillating* parts—looked directly at the audience, the viewer of his sketch. Perverse satisfaction thrummed through him. For the female's face, though small, was recognizable. But the horizontal line behind the stage was off, needed—

"Where is she?" The narrow street door groaned at the abuse as the mustached American barreled in. "Where the devil is she?" the man bellowed.

Tyndale spared half a glance, not wanting to take his attention off the nearly finished draft.

"What did you do with her?" The blustery ruffian advanced as though greeting an opponent in the boxing ring. "Why is the desk all—"

"You know..." With a snap, Tyndale flattened the pencil against the desk and straightened. "I think I may have a word with Blakely about your attitude toward your betters."

He eyed the other man, expecting some deference. Some respect.

"Pray, *my lord*, forgive me." Respect was nothing but pure sarcasm. "I am quite on edge, you see. Where, please tell me"—the other man's throat gave some sort of snarl—"*where* has Lady..."

After turning the drawing face downward, Tyndale tugged at the sleeves of his waistcoat and circled the desk. Damn, his muscles had gotten tighter than he'd realized. He raised his arms in a good stretch—not above stretching out his answer, just to irritate Blakely's man. He really did need to learn how to treat peers.

Tyndale lowered his arms and gave a fake yawn. He'd probably pushed his luck—and the other man— far enough. So he deigned to answer. "Oh, you mean Wylde's little piece?" He flicked his fingers toward the street door. "Scurried out of here when—"

"You let her *leave*? You motherfucker!" The man roared forth, hands twisting Tyndale's neckcloth, twining the fabric tight against his throat as the wall slammed into his head, dazing his senses. "Do you not know what's been happening around here? There's a killer on the loose, for God's sake. Baywick!"

A killer?

Motherfucker? Not a term he'd heard before, but the pestilence with which it had been spewed in his face made the meaning clear as crystal.

What wasn't clear was his bewildered brain, as white orbs peppered his vision. He clawed against the grip on his cravat, striving to loosen the fabric and gain a breath. The slightly shorter man was strong as an ox. Wide as one too. But Tyndale wasn't exactly a mully-puff either.

He fought against the restrictive hold, brought his knee up between the other man's legs just as the American released him with a shove to the side and yelled for the guard again.

Baywick entered as Tyndale gulped air and shook his head, working to erase the vicious spheres spiraling before his eyes.

"The other one—" The huffing American

measured the height of Wylde's woman against his chest. "She's gone? Left?"

"No, sir," the guard replied. "She was here not three minutes ago."

As Tyndale's lungs filled, so did his regret.

He pushed off the floor, jerking back when the American thrust a finger in his face. "We're getting out there and finding her!" the man yelled. Unnecessary as they were barely six inches apart. "And if we don't—if something's happened? *You'll* be next."

At the door, the man pointed, indicating Tyndale should scour left while he ran the opposite direction. Also unnecessary. For Tyndale himself had bungled things horridly—letting her leave without giving chase straight away.

He took another breath, heading out into the dark, his sore neck turning back and forth as his long legs ate up the distance between the club and his guilty conscience.

15

OF VICTUALS, VISIONS AND VOWS...ER, BOWS

NEARLY A SENNIGHT LATER
STILL AT THE WHITE KNIGHT INN

NASH WATCHED Laney dab at her lips with an embroidered handkerchief, displacing the last remaining crumb hugging the side of her mouth—the light repast they'd partaken of at the inn's tavern vanished betwixt the two of them in a flash.

"For basic fare," she said on a soft smile, folding the handkerchief and tucking it neatly back into her reticule, "the food here rivals anything that has come before." She slid a glance toward the open doorway leading into the kitchen. "Do you think I could persuade the innkeeper's wife to tell me what she does to get these biscuits so delightfully crunchy on the exterior yet tender in the middle?"

"Why? Are you taking up kitchen duties next?"

She dimpled, leaned over the table to whisper, "Only if I weary of bedroom duties."

"What-ho! Minx."

Neither had spoken much of the future—too content savoring the present? Granted, he'd mentioned moving from their current location on a time or two and she'd either shaken her head or neglected to respond. Could he blame her? The inn was clean, the owners friendly. If only he didn't have a looming task elsewhere, one he'd prefer to ignore but that niggled uncomfortably nevertheless, he could foresee being happy here indefinitely.

What about those responsibilities you keep considering?

Not now.

Then when?

Shaking off the worrisome thoughts—how dare they try to mar their day?—he slid his booted foot further beneath the table, to nudge one of her slippers, exceedingly pleased to feel the responding caress of her other slipper against his shin, before she retreated and he imagined her placing both feet back on the floor, primly pressed together. His wanton lady. She never ceased to amaze nor delight.

The large, clean room was sparsely occupied, only two or three tables beyond their own with travelers currently partaking. By now, thanks to his keen hearing, they knew exactly when the noisy stage lumbered in or rolled out, and avoided dining downstairs during the resulting crush.

"Another biscuit or three?" The innkeeper's daughter, a plump smiling gel several years older than Nash, bustled over to ask. "More ale?"

"I am done for now. Would you care for more?" He nodded at Laney. Watching her indulge her love of anything sugar laden only deepened his joy. Curious feeling, that. One, until the last handful of days, he would not have thought of in the same sentence as himself: joy.

But she was already shaking her head. "Thank you, but no, not today." The woman left to check on her other customers and Laney said to him, "Else, I vow I shall turn into a piece of candied ginger."

The biscuits had been mighty delectable, hearty and sprinkled with dried fruits and spices. But after his first one, he'd gladly given her his other.

"What troubles you, Mr. Hammond?"

He gasped. Quickly turned the blunder into a cough. Dem. She'd noticed? "Goodness." He pounded his chest. "Must have choked on a raisin."

Her arms crossed over her chest and she tilted her head. Beneath the sensible bonnet, her eyes pierced straight through his inept bamboozle. "Mayhap I would believe that—had you eaten a raisin." She indicated his plate, where the remnants of several pieces of dried fruit glared up at him, blatant proof of his clanker. "Now is not the only time I have discerned such. So tell me, Mr. Hammond, please and without prevarication, if you will, what has given you the mulligrubs?"

"What is troubling me?" Uncanny, that—how in tune with his moods and thoughts she often was. "That you persist in calling me *mister*."

"*A true lady always exhibits the utmost respect, even with those closest to her.*"

"Ballocks." Quoting her little friend again. "When you were together, did you always refer to Mary Delilah as Miss— What was it?"

"Middleton. And no, I did not."

He had made his point. "Well, 'tis 'Nash' to you."

She arched one brow and stuck out her chin, giving him quite the defiant look. "Mr. Hammond."

He growled, couldn't help it. Jerked his head to the side until the comforting slide of hair crossed his vision.

"You think to defer? To distract? To hide? Tut tut, dear sir. Tell me what drags down your spirit and, mayhap, 'Mr. Hammond' shall be replaced."

One could only hope.

"Nothing brings me down, not today." Did he sound convincing? Grinning through the attempted deceit, he gestured out the window, in the direction of town, a mere ten minutes' walk, where they were headed after their leisurely meal. "Is not the sun shining? The food sublime? The company equally so. The—"

"Mis-ter Ham-mond." The reproof in those simple four syllables was absolute. "Come now. Despite the pleasure in the day, perhaps with the company, and definitely with the meal, I continue to perceive a slight haunting of your soul that lingers. Will you not share?"

By now, after days' worth of quality conversation with the biscuit-loving delight across the table, Nash knew more than ever that he owed his brother some information. For Laney had mentioned a name or two about her life in London that his mind persisted on fixing upon, giving him potentially even more insight into that mysterious Suspects list in Blake's possession.

It continued to bother him, how his selfish need to escape kept him from sharing what he'd known then, after chancing across it. Only compounded by what he knew now—or suspected he might, assuming the people in question were one and the same. Was he ready to share that with her?

And ruin the most perfect, idyllian span in memory?

Nay. He was not. He shifted in the hard chair. "You have annoyingly astute senses."

"Thank you." She leaned forward and brushed his long hair back behind one ear. "You really should let me trim this. Now do explain."

His demmed ear tingled. "Explain? As I was saying, Princess, the day is sublime. The—"

"Nash Hammond." That same arm that had caressed him not six seconds prior reached forth and gave a good yank. "Troubled soul?"

Ugh. Keeping up with this woman would lead him a merry chase. *Good, then, is it not, that you don't mind running?*

Dem. Now the skin behind his ear smarted, where she'd attempted to pull his scalp clean off. Pity, that tingled too. "Truth is, a prior act of selfishness plagues me. One I hope to rectify." When, he wasn't sure; how, he had decided. He could post a letter to Blake. Tell him that way.

Cowards die many times before their deaths, the valiant never taste of death but once.

Double ugh. All right. So in person needs must. Between that and what else he needed to atone for—

All these you may avoid but the Lie Direct; and you may avoid even more if you think about it long enough...

Aha! Another idea occurred—thank you, Shakes! Why had he not thought of it sooner?

Laney. With her unique ability, might she be able to help? Could her blessed curse be what his brother needed to solve the murders and mysteries plaguing him? Ones Blake's garbled ramblings only hinted at, his stalwart sibling reluctant to burden Nash when he showed up, battling The Change just as fervently. Reluctant to ever trouble anyone beyond himself.

But now... "Laney, were I to ask you a question, about a situation or someone else..." He flicked his head back, clearing the rebellious strands that persisted in hanging across one eye, so he could see her clearly. Mayhap he should let her cut it. *Mayhap you should tell her the ugly truth.* "Would you 'see' anything about that? Have a vision?"

"I know not. Never have I attempted to seek them out. Rarely has a vision been as satisfyingly pleasurable"—she glanced away, pressed her lips together, then caught his gaze, her cheeks highly flushed—"as the ones I have had of us. Too often they are harbingers of dismay, dreadful situations that I attempt to avoid or trouble that has befallen others and, through my knowledge, I am able to provide some manner of assistance. Why do you ask? Have you something specific in mind? Planning your next horserace wager, are you?"

"That is one vice I have yet to pursue. Nay, nothing so trivial. What do you mean by others' troubles? What others, precisely?"

She sat back, possibly surprised by the intensity with which he'd asked. She began tugging on the gloves she'd removed to eat, her gaze indicating the window. "Let us begin our stroll, shall we? I will share more as we walk."

It had taken every modicum of fortitude Laney possessed to confront Nash Hammond with the perplexing worry she'd sensed emanating from him in quiet moments.

For when he was active, when they were together laughing and talking, kissing and groping, he seemed at peace, exceedingly happy even. She was, of a certainty. Had no desire to change anything about their current situation.

That might be remiss of her, but so be it. Neither of them had spoken of the future, the future she had seen with such clarity. Neither had she experienced any further visions confounding her with tragic outcomes, which assured her acceptance and serenity around their current situation.

Though Mr. Hammond was the exemplification of every girlhood dream, every womanly anticipation she ever had about a man of her own—before Reginald and his brother had dashed those dreams to shreds—knowing he still suffered kept her from complete contentment.

Well, that and her one other concern. Trifling, really. So very childish. One she was determined to discount. Only every time they got naked and slid against each other, hot and sleek, only afterward, did the doubts return. But here, fully clothed, confident in her own allure? Her doubts seemed silly indeed. So she shoved them firmly from her mind.

He held the tavern door open and gestured for her to precede him into the glorious day. Glorious, if he would but confess his secrets. *What of yours?*

Shoved aside.

A few feet beyond the tavern, she paused to open her parasol—this one a simple style they had chosen together, along with the sedate bonnet she now wore to appease his curious hat-hating sensibilities. A secret smile threatened because Laney knew it was only a matter of time before she returned to wearing her spectacular head wear —

But no—for most of it was left, abandoned, in the London townhouse she'd shared with Reginald. Never to return.

No matter. No matter at all.

What was the loss of a few favored hats in exchange for the potential of a splendidious future?

He came abreast and took her arm. They walked silently out of the courtyard and onto the side road that led into the quaint nearby town. "My visions. You ask of 'other' people I have had them about?" That was easy enough to answer. She was not the one still keeping secrets. "While the majority of visions have concerned myself and *my*...future—"

She stuttered to a halt, gripping her parasol and staring into his fathomless eyes for courage. "Why oh why did I not have any about Reginald *before* now? Before I went to live with him? I could have avoided the entire...frightful..." Unbidden, tears brimmed and she blinked them angrily away.

Nash halted the furious parasol spinning she hadn't been aware of and gently dabbed one knuckle beneath her eye, which only made her lips tremble as she fought back any further signs of fear. "Come now, my sweet. Had you not still been with him, our paths may not have crossed."

My sweet. Now she was blinking again, but with happiness. He had not called her that until now. Touching, it was, to have a pet name. One so insanely appropriate.

Shouldering off the distress, she gave a light laugh —a real one. "You are correct. As to others, I have only ever had them about those close to me. People I knew and was able to help in some way." A swift sweep of her gloved fingertips erased any remaining moisture and she went on to give several examples of past visions, their feet walking slowly in a matching cadence—until his sped up, and she could practically see his mind cavorting with possibilities. "What is it?"

"Can you see what you want—"

A fierce shake of her head halted that, so he queried instead, "Could I perhaps ask a question, prompt your curse—er, blessing?"

"I do not know. I have never attempted it thus. Have not discussed them with anyone save my grandmother." She tugged him to a halt, allowing another couple to pass before continuing in a softer voice. "Do you not realize how *peculiar* we both are? You—*a lion*. Me— seeing the future. Why, the wrong person privy to that knowledge would be enough to see either of us dangling by a rope. *But together?* Nash, it defies comprehension."

"Dem, woman. Took you sufficiently long."

"What?"

"To call me 'Nash'."

She gave him a light shove, positive she had already called him that a time or two before.

"Your secrets—all of them," he said sincerely, "are safe with me."

"As are yours."

A single, deliberate blink told her he accepted her promise as well. "So. Back to *your* blessed secret. You have not sought answers before with intention?"

"Nay, only waited, watched when a vision came, and done my best to understand. To make changes, alter my course when I needed to. To warn others if that was indicated."

"I was...considering a particular topic that troubles my brother."

"You rarely speak of him."

"*Of rich and exquisite form; their values great; And I? Am only something curiously strange...* I misquote, to give him due. Blake is... The very best of men and at present I gather he seeks the very worst."

"High praise, Mr. Hammond. And though you may be curiously strange, I also admire your exquisite form."

He snorted. "Back to 'mister'?"

"Until you learn to value yourself as you do your brother, aye, I believe so."

A snarl purred from his throat, and for once, she could not tell if he were perturbed or being playful. "If I can assist, I shall willingly do so. At present, I feel so very inept. Why have a curse if one cannot call on it?" She gestured up and down his form. "As you did."

"Ah, but lest you forget, that was after years of pained resistance. You are well ahead of me in that regard, given your acceptance of your blessings."

"How shall I try? Have you given thought to that as well? Because, though I now cast my mind wide thinking of your brother *the marquis*"—which still caused no little amount of amazed betwattlement —"nothing comes to me but remnants of those delicious biscuits, the ginger still branding a spicy fire within my mouth."

At that, his eyes heated. "Spicy fire in your mouth indeed. But that is for later. Now is for truth." With a quick glance at their surroundings, he took the parasol from her loose grasp and escorted her off the main path and behind a large tree trunk, its leafy branches providing dense shade on the ground below, cooling the air around them.

Or was that her trepidation, making itself felt? The thought of disappointing this man weighing heavy.

"Close your eyes." At once, she did so. "Pull in few calm breaths. Do not try to focus or concentrate. Simply tell me whether anything comes to mind or a scene flashes in your garret..."

She gave a light shiver. "I vow, the weight in your tone is sufficient to make me anxious indeed."

"None of that now... I know 'tis unfair of me to cause you distress over topics that have nothing to do with you—"

"Stop that. If it concerns you, I care. I care about disappointing you."

"Do not worry over the outcome, hmm? Just allow yourself to answer. I shall prompt a time or two and then we will see."

She opened one eye to peer at him and tilted her chin downward. "The longer you take to begin, the larger the task looms."

"Aye, madam." She blinked it shut. Took another breath and took comfort when he tightened his fingers around hers. "Then we shall begin at once. Missing women in London. Have you any knowledge of that?"

Her eyes flew wide. "Missing *women*? Zoodikers! How many? When? Where in London?"

"Shhhh." He stroked his thumb over the back of her hand, her fingers still held snugly within his grasp. "Do you see anything?"

Several seconds passed. Eyes closed. Eyes open, staring vacantly as she looked beyond sight, the scenery before her a blur as she sought knowledge that refused to come. "Nay," she told him, focusing in on his hopeful gaze. "Nothing. I am so very sorry—"

"None of that now." He gave her arm a light shake. "You already told me your blessing has only affected yourself or those in close proximity to you. It was a wild chance."

"Let me try again. Ask me something else. About someone else. Any—"

"Joanna Jane Withenby."

Refusing to allow even a spec of jealousy or curiosity to mar what he now requested, Laney breathed in. Out. In. Kept her eyes firmly closed. Felt her lids fluttering. The breeze kissing her cheek. Sought to blank her mind. Open her senses. *Joanna...* A plait? *Jane...* Yes! A long dark braid. Hints of grey within the—

Thunk! She startled as the door shut firmly in her face, a hard snap that made her wince.

Her eyes blinked open to see Nash Hammond watching her closely. "Anything?"

"I believe so. But it was over so swiftly. My visions usually abound in details and this was nothing but a long braid. Dark hair shot through with—"

"Dem. Nay. She never wore it in a plait. 'Twas either off her neck or completely down the way Papa preferred betwixt the two of them, late at night."

"Joanna is your mother." And now she felt doubly wretched for not bringing him some sort of accurate answer. "Are you sure she never wears it—"

"I am sure. Wait." He released her hand to dig in a pocket, retrieving a sovereign. "Here. This is one of the coins Blake gave me." He curved her palm upward and dropped the coin in it. "What about that?"

She closed her fingers over it, immediately noticing the heat. "It's warm from being near you but naught else."

He leaned down and kissed her cheek. "Then I shall trust that we are not near any danger, nor is anyone or anything nefarious close to you. For now, I will be content with that."

And for the moment, she would be content with his response, hopeful their exchange had banished whatever lingering haunts dogged his being.

THE NEXT DAY...

"STOP FIDGETING! I vow, you're worse than a little boy with leeches in his breeches."

Nash slid his hand higher on her thigh, moving mounds of lacy petticoats out of his way in the process.

"Mr. 'ammond," she squeaked, "I can guarantee you makin' *me* fidget won't 'elp your cause at all!"

He loved the way she did that—became all flustered when he groped her. Forgot to be a lady. He found the treasure he sought and eased his fingers near but didn't do more than touch her curls. Her humid heat was almost his undoing, but he clenched his opposite hand around the arm of the chair he'd been plastered to since agreeing. If he stopped distracting her, perhaps she'd stop torturing him.

Or so Laney had said on more than one occasion since he'd complied with her wishes earlier that morning.

After all, hadn't he finally come around to her way of thinking? It had only taken a mere week of her daily admonitions, detailing what a bang-up fellow he was before he finally started to believe the persistent baggage.

Now she had him pondering of all manner of things from a fresh perspective, such as apologies and family and making things right with his. It was time to stop running, time to release the guilt he'd harbored over his past mistakes so that he had room to concentrate on his present and future.

Time to stop hiding. As she had.

So here he sat, allowing her to cut his hair. Once he

no longer thought of himself as a beast, Nash admitted he needn't look like one either. Oh, but how she brought out his beastly instincts.

She wiggled around the chair, moving in front of him, her alluring scent knocking him in the face.

Bloody hell. Being still would only get him so far. He let his fingers probe higher.

"Mr. 'ammond!" Her arm flinched and the scissors *snapped* shut.

Pain seared his ear. "Damnation, woman!"

His fingers flexed in her alcove but didn't retreat.

"An' what did I tell you? 'Ow am I supposed to trim your hair when you go an' do a foolish thing like that?"

His middle finger dove deep. "Like what?"

"Touch me 'ungry bits, you ornery cat!"

"Are you not finished by now? How long does it take to snip off a little hair and a lot of ear?"

"Oh!" Her foot stomped. The action only served to give his finger some delightful friction. Evidently, she must have agreed because a soft moaned "Mmm" met his abused ear. Then, "Nay, I am *not* finished."

"Finished torturing me?" Nash loosened his death grip from the chair and flexed his fingers—all of them.

"With your hair, you knave!" The scissors hit the table with a clack. She tried to step away, but he whipped his free arm across the back of her thighs and held tight. Her legs squeezed around his wrist, trapping him. Oh hell, what a place to be trapped.

"You call what *I'm* doing torture?" Her words were nothing but breathy air. "What about your fingers?"

"What about them?" Since she was now standing before him with nary a protest, he ran his free hand up and under her dress and searched along the crack of her arse. Finding what he sought, he smeared her cream from arbor to anus. "Just making sure you stay well oiled, Princess."

She clutched his shoulders. "You make me sound like a rusty hinge."

"Not at all. Like a well-loved woman."

"And there you go again, spreading that word around." She groaned and thrust against his invading fingers. "Although that's not all you're spreading."

Love. He'd all but told her. All but... Time to push for what had been hounding him since their trip to town yesterday. The conviction that it was time. "Come to London with me."

"Now why would I want to go and do such a clumpish thing? When I'm exceedingly happy right here?"

As she tended to do if he so much as broached leaving their romantic retreat, she deferred, but this time he was staring right at her and finally figured out why. Though not as transparent as when she'd avoided him or blatantly changed the subject, the action was significantly more telling for all its subtleness.

He stilled his caresses. "You just blinked and kept your eyes shut when you answered me."

Those shielding lids flew open.

"You're still hiding!" He didn't mean for the words to come out as an accusation but they did. He sought to soften their blow, anchoring his fingers high in her treasure and pulling her, shapely bum and all, as close as he could. He kissed her stomach through the fancy dress. "Granted, not under an ugly hat or behind a veil, but you are still afraid to return to London. Even with me. Afraid to face something, something more than the legalities of your indenture, I do believe. What, I wonder, might it be?

"And this, after *you* professed there were no more secrets between us."

She looked wounded, but at least she was gazing at him now. Those green eyes mirroring uncertainty, she blinked and opened her mouth to speak but remained silent. Closing it primly, she gave a delicate shrug.

Yesterday, she'd forced him to bare his troubled soul. 'Twas only right he returned the favor. Thinking hard, he allowed his hands to fall away from beneath her skirts but kept her securely in front of him by raising his arms to toy with the pins in her hair. "Would you say no if I suggested a trip to...Italy? Or to Scotland?"

"Scotland? *Italy?* Together?"

"Of course together, you silly peagoose. How else would it be?"

She stepped from his slack hold and walked backward until she flopped on the bed, her skirts fluffing up around her legs. She began nervously fingering the ribbon on her dress, glancing at him through the fall of ebony hair he'd disheveled just moments earlier.

"Don't. Leave. Me," she said without inflection. "Every time we're intimate, you say 'Don't leave' or sometimes *usiniache* and *usiondoke* leaving me confounded. Mr. Hammond, you say *don't leave*, but not once have you asked me to stay."

Nash bolted from the chair and knelt before her,

attempting to catch her gaze. "Oh, my sweet princess. I thought you knew."

Knew all that was in his heart. Knew how he loved her ladylike ways, loved her raunchy dockside demeanor, loved too how only he could make her forget every "lady" lesson she'd ever had.

But she refused to look at him. Instead, stared at her hands. Her fingers were mangling the pretty ribbon they'd picked out together on one of their walks into town. "Tell me true. Are you talking in your heart to Francine?"

"Francine? What on earth gave you that impression?"

"Are you saying 'tis untrue?"

"Completely!" Hard floor greeted his kneecaps when he leaned forward.

"But the way you keep wanting to return to London. Did you not tell me at the beginning of our acquaintance that you cared nothing about your destination? That you only wanted to *escape* your past? Why are you now so determined to go back? Does it have to do with who your brother seeks? What we talked about yesterday? Or is it because of *her*?"

With jerky motions, Laney slid that long length of blue satin through her fingers. He curved his palms over her thighs. "Because now I have a reason to return. Because I finally admitted to myself that I *do* care, about any number of things. You, Miss Buckley, are at the very top of that list and, other than knowing I owe her an apology, Francine barely rates the last rung."

A small smile curved her lips and she left off

destroying the ribbon to bring her hands to his shoulders. "Truly?"

"With absolute certainty. And I'm also certain your hair-trimming skills warrant a return trip to Bailey's." He mentioned the bakehouse she raved about. "I need to thank you properly for turning this shaggy beast into a civilized one."

"You're not a beast." Her fingers tickled his nape but he refused to flinch away.

"Neither have I frequented a sweet shop in decades. Would you not like to introduce me to your favorite one? The somber truth is I feel compelled to return in time to make peace before my brother's wedding. And because of you I realize that no matter how uncomfortable the notion, I shall do better facing him and Francine now rather than allowing things to fester to the point I don't feel I can ever go back. Since meeting you, now that I'm no longer intent on running, I have learned a funny thing—guilt grows the longer it remains unaddressed."

Her fingers began caressing his shoulders, her eyes once again beaming with their customary sparkle. "You really aren't thinking about her when we're tupping?"

"Most assuredly not." Nash prayed that honesty shone from his own eyes. His throat had gone tight, making swallowing difficult despite the slight touch of her fingers stroking beneath his chin. "Not once, not since telling you of my shame have I thought of her. But I think about *you* every minute. Why else would I still be holed away in this inn instead of outside on the road?"

"So it's *me* you ask not to leave?"

"It is, though 'tis more than a little daunting to learn I have been expressing that sentiment out loud. It has been so very long since I allowed myself to care about someone, that the thought of you—who I care about beyond expression—*leaving* only leaves *me* feeling adrift. Something I never hope to be again. How very humiliating, that I was verbalizing that— Wait." He gripped her fingers and swallowed again. "Have you just tied your blue sash around my neck?"

"I have."

"Now my embarrassment is complete." But for her smile, it was a small price to pay. "No self-respecting man not of the dandy class would be caught wearing frills and furbelows, much less wearing a bow around his neck."

"But it becomes you so." She freed one of her hands to arrange the loops of the bow.

"Ah, Princess. If you have developed a penchant for tying things, I'm quite positive there exist any number of body parts we can practice with that would be infinitely more—"

"Do hush. I'm illustrating a point here."

"And that would be?" Apparently satisfied with her handiwork, she rested her palms on his shoulders. His legs shifted, protesting the unforgiving floor beneath his knees.

"Do you recall the day Reginald left? Do stop growling, Mr. Hammond."

As most of it had been for show, 'twas easy enough to comply. "Yes, Princess," he said as contritely as he could manage—not horribly difficult with a satin ribbon bumping into his jaw. "Do go on."

"You had my indenture in the basket and—"

"I intended to give it to you but was distracted when we..." He raised and lowered his eyebrows. "Several times in fact."

"I know precisely what we did, you wretch. But you only had the indenture because I *instructed* the innkeep to give it to you."

"You told him? You wanted *me* to have such valuable an item?" Ah, so that was the conversation he'd overheard. What a surprise indeed. For upon their return to the inn, Nash had placed the document squarely on the trunk he'd requisitioned from Tate's room and they hadn't spoken of it since.

"I did, as a symbol of giving myself over to your care. Now tell me what is around your neck."

"A frilly-arse bow."

"Whose?"

"Yours." He suspected he knew where she was heading, but chose to make it as difficult for her as she had for him. After all, she'd just subjected him to wearing blue *satin*. Although, it did feel rather...silky. Hmmm. All manner of possibilities began careening around in his brain. His body followed.

"And I believe that makes you...?" Her feet snuck out from below her hem and hooked around his back.

"Mayhap...yours?" he stalled, allowing her legs to pull him forward.

"Again with more fervor."

Laughing, he slid up between her legs and pushed her down on the mattress. "Laney Buckley, you own my hope." He came down on top of her. "I might as well give you leave to own my heart."

"Aw, Mr. Hammond, I do believe you're every bit as gallant as Mr. Shakespeare." She started tugging on his shirt, trying to free it from his pantaloons.

Leaving the demmed bow around his neck for the time being, he shifted until he could grab a thick handful of material. Hauling the fabric up her legs, he muttered, "Woman, you wear more petticoats than—" He wasn't jolterheaded enough to finish his original thought: *any woman I have undressed.* With a muttered cough, he finished, "Any blasted female needs."

"This last layer, the one you're having such difficulty navigating," she said in her remarkably credible lady imitation, given how she was grappling to eliminate the barrier of his shirt and rubbing her heated crotch against his fumbling fingers. "Is my newest petticoat. Mary Delilah and I bought matching ones just before she moved. We, *mmm*, both loved the embroidery and"—she gasped a heated little moan that fired him up—"handmade vandyked edging. 'Tis my absolute favorite, I'll have you know."

His shirt untucked, her nails latched on to the skin of his back. Nash scooted her legs apart and freed his prick faster than he could say *black butter.*

"Well, this is *my* favorite part." To emphasize, he slid the tip of his cock straight along her slit, dragging it up and down, coating himself and his fingers with her thick honey. "And it's Nash. By God, woman, I have my cock at your cunny, the least you can do is call me by my name."

"Mr. Nash Hammond."

"*Nash,*" he snarled, situating his booted feet more firmly under him so he didn't fall on his arse. Viscous fluid trickled freely between the swollen lips of her center. He painted his shaft with her slick juices, groaning at how very responsive she was. "Ready, are we?"

"For you, *Nash*? Always." Her nails scraped beneath his unfastened pantaloons, digging into the flanks of his arse.

He lurched forward, but refused to allow his cock entrance. "*"Tis torture, and not mercy: heaven is here..."*"

"Mmm, you're so eloquent, *dear Nash*, but I do believe I have already heard that one," she moaned, rocking against him.

"I shall commit new ones to memory on the morrow." Arm and legs trembling, he anchored his knees against the bed, his staff at her portal.

"Will you, now?" Laney threaded her fingers through his remaining hair and pulled sharply. Her lower body undulated against his cock head. "That will not be necessary, I'll consent to accept repeats, *Nash*."

"Gracious of you," he said on a fast breath, quickly losing his.

"Did you notice how I said it three whole times without laughing?" she asked on a giggle, ruining her claim.

"I noticed," he said, smiling down at her, continuing to tease her heated flesh—and himself—by prolonging the sweet, sweet torture. Anticipating the bliss of their joining.

Feet around his thighs, she squirmed toward the edge of the bed as her nails dug deeper. "Why do you persist in waiting?"

He shook with the effort to keep from spearing into

her. The dem bow was strangling him. That or maybe L-O-V-E. "Thought I'd see if I could get you to draw blood agai— Ow!"

Those nails of hers pierced his skin and Nash split her crease, his self-control in shreds. His cock spread her woman's flesh, pushed past her body's token resistance and lodged to the hilt. She surged up to meet him, ground her nails in. "God, Princess, you're perfect."

"I'll not allow *you* to claim perfection for you're not touching me 'ard enough, Mr. 'ammond!"

Perfect except for her fascination with his deuced last name. Her quiff rippled along his shaft, clamped down when he retreated, but only to plunge back in. Staring at her flushed, precious face, Nash marveled at the peculiarities of life and lionhood and his lovely, unladylike Laney. If he'd searched every continent across the globe, he couldn't have found another female more suited to be his mate.

As though privy to his thoughts, she whipped her hands from his flanks and slapped him through his pantaloons, a look of intense arousal narrowing her eyes. "Touch me bum, you rogue! You know I like it best when you don't 'old back!"

Grinning, he dove his hand past her damnable embroidered, vandyked (whatever the hell that was) petticoat, tearing a seam in his haste, and found her crack.

"Finally!" she cried, evidently not holding another ruined article of clothing against him, favored or not.

Sliding his fingertips along the heated seam, he nudged her anus with his middle finger. Her bits gripped his cock and held tight, pulling him in and squeezing him harder even as his finger teased the puckered hole open.

He leaned forward and merged their lips. She sucked his tongue inside and bit down once he was embedded in her mouth. Nash's heart smiled. His lips followed and he eased his thickest finger past the tight sphincter and into the hot cavern. Her spicy little nock sucked him inside and welcomed him home.

She groaned and clenched tight—on his tongue, his cock and his finger—until she was riding all three, the sultry, grasping passages of her body all taking him so deep, so far... His control was slipping, he knew. Knew he was about to pound into her without a dram of restraint. More than that, knew that she craved it, *loved* it.

Loved him.

Knowing because she wrenched her mouth to the side and screamed it as she came, strong and wet with muscle contractions caressing his cock and finger and murmurs of "Love you forever, Nash 'ammond!" blessing his eardrums.

He gripped her arse, wondered if he was about to lose a finger—he'd already lost his heart—and felt his cock rejoice at pure, undiluted acceptance.

Kissing her lips, her jaw, her neck, then raking his teeth over all three, he stroked inside her, savored how her loins quivered all around him. His cock responded, shooting jets of semen toward her womb as her body drank him down. He poured out all he had, for thoughts of retreating or escaping, thoughts of being undeserving, had all evaporated beneath the joy that was Laney.

Knowing he owned her heart—by her admission, by her *choice*—gave him leave to own her body as he never had another's. Gave him the freedom he'd been lacking.

The freedom to fulfill his future...facing forward. Whatever that future might hold.

The powerful orgasm wiped him dry. Constricted his ballocks, knotted his gut and his throat—oh wait. That was her bow.

By the devil, it felt great.

So did his cock. And his finger. And his near-to-bursting heart.

Sinking into the mattress with a sigh, she blinked up at him. "Good—you finally realized it."

Who could ascertain anything when their mind—and ballocks—had just blown sky high? "Realized what?"

"That I'm not going anywhere. For the first time, you didn't ask me not to leave."

"Oh. Well. Grand, that." Grandest orgasm on record. His ears backtracked. "What did you just say?"

"I'm not going anywhere," she assured. "I promise you that."

Calm settled over him unlike any he'd ever experienced. Not since learning his father had been killed. Not since accepting his mother wasn't coming home. 'Twas a soul-deep sort of calm, one that not only reached his heart, but the lonely lion who resided even deeper.

Laney's eyes flashed. From lush forest to glittering

fire. "Especially not since knowing you father my children."

Calm turned to chaos.

Despite the waning release and flouncy bow, he managed to strangle out, "Ch-*children?*"

Bravely facing the future was one thing; being told what it held, quite another.

She nodded and tapped him on the nose, an incongruous action given how they were both still shaking. "Several, in fact. *Cubs*, I believe you might call them."

Dismay descended heavily, squashing out his peace. Dismay and apprehension, followed by amazement. That and his newfound friend—hope.

Nash lowered his lips to hers. "Interesting, would you not say, how that notion *doesn't* send me racing for the nearest exit?"

16

THE WHITE KNIGHT RIDES—AND ON HIS OWN HORSE!

THE FOLLOWING DAY...

AFTER A SINGLE KNOCK, the door to their room opened, swinging smoothly on its new upper hinge as it had the past week since being repaired. "Your trunk is downstairs," Nash Hammond told her, leaning against the doorframe, hands behind his back. "Innkeep says the coach will be by in minutes, so make haste."

"Haste? Ha. You were gone significantly longer than I expected, Mr. Hammond." Laney glanced back to the small desk, where she'd been polishing her letter to Mary Delilah. "I shan't have any trouble readying this before the mail coach stops for fresh horses. You, sir, left me with time to write a veritable tome."

"Then it was all for the best that my, *ahem*, tasks were not accomplished as quickly as I had anticipated."

With a flourish worth any lady, Laney signed her

name and waved the sheet to dry it. "What tasks might those be?"

"This for one." He brought one arm around and held up a small parcel. "Since I know you developed a fondness for it, I persuaded the cook to wrap up some of her honey cake and black butter to take with us."

She did a poor job of muffling her squeal of delight. "*Very* worth waiting for indeed!" Pitching her voice lower, she drawled, "Though I wouldn't say I'm the only one who's developed a fondness for that particular treat."

"Mmm-hmm."

"You said *tasks*, plural." She folded the page into a tight square, turned it over to write Mary Delilah's direction, noticing out of the corner of her eye that he hadn't yet come into their room, was still leaning against the door frame, watching her actions and looking as recklessly handsome as ever, despite his efforts at polish.

He dipped his head in a credible bow. Still from the doorway. Still with one arm behind his back.

"What else?"

Seeing her appreciating his pose—or perhaps the haircut she'd finally finished this morning—he all but preened. The hand holding the treat patted his breast pocket twice. "I have the recipe for her ginger raisin biscuits."

Ladylike behavior be damned, she squeaked freely. "You marvelous man!

"I do so like your new hat," she told him. Putting down her quill, she capped the ink bottle. Instead of putting a bullet through it, he'd let her remake one of

Reginald's beavers—one without either bird or horse droppings. Nothing overtly ostentatious, it now sat at a rakish angle atop his head. "You look mighty dashing this morning, Mr. Hammond."

Closing the door, he finally came forward. "One of these days, Princess, I'm going to cure you of that nasty *mister* habit you have developed."

She tilted the candle to seal the letter shut. "'Tis a sign of respect."

"'Tis a sign of distance, if you ask me. If I put my mind to it, I'm certain I could come up with something infinitely more suitable." He dropped a well-worn copy of *The Times* next to her sealed letter. "I found this for us to read on the trip. Days old, but fairly clean."

"Thoughtful of you." He could peruse the newspaper; she would concentrate on the recipe he procured. "At this moment, though, I'm more interested in hearing what appellation you deem more appropriate than 'mister'. My dearest? My handsome, energetic, feral lover? Oh! I have it—my *prince*?"

"Tut, tut." He reached her side and ran his hand over her carefully arranged hair. A new style that had taken her most of the morning to perfect. Now that she had someone to show off for, someone who really cared about her and not just her outward trappings, she found herself surprisingly particular about her appearance.

His fingers tightened and he tilted her head. "In lieu of mister or prince, let's try *king*, shall we? It's more stately."

Pursing her lips at his high-handed tone, she eased

her head from his grasp and blew the candle out on a light giggle. "My king? That will be the— Oh heavens."

When her words ground to a halt, the teasing glint in his expression hardened. "What is it?"

"Nothing but a brief memory," she said evasively, standing and smoothing her dress. "All is well."

His features eased, but he gave a commanding nod. "Then try it."

Sputtering on a laugh, she complied. "My k-king."

"Very well done of you. Now tell me what you remembered." He reached down to retrieve her traveling valise and his bag, one dark eyebrow raised in inquiry.

She conceded. It was always more fun when she taunted him with her visions, teased just enough to keep him wondering. Though disappointed she had not been able to help him yesterday, she remained thrilled that she hadn't seen any more about herself, for it meant the direction of her life was right on course for those afternoon lovemaking sessions she'd glimpsed in the gazebo. "A reminder of the first vision I saw of us."

He stopped moving. "Do share, Princess."

Gathering the letter and newspaper from the table, she allowed a secretive smile to flirt with her lips. "Let me only say you shall eventually receive your wish minus my mirth, my majestic, stately king," she added, rolling her eyes. The action caused her gaze to snag on the paper. She raised the corner and scanned one section. "Um, have you read this?"

"Not yet. Why?"

"I thought you said the wedding isn't until November."

"What wed— *My brother's?*"

Nodding, she studied a certain heading. "Mmmm. Blake and Francine's."

"It isn't."

"I beg to differ." Laney emptied her hands and scrambled to open the paper over the table. "Look! Right 'ere it says—"

"Well, I'll be damned." Nash skimmed the announcement, muttering the passage... "'*The brooding Marquis of Blakely, Erasmus William Charles Hammond, founder of an infamous assemblage we shall refrain from naming in the interest of not offending moral readers*' so on and so forth...'*wed the mysteriously talented Lady Francine Montfort.*

"'*For any with deplorably short memories, Lady Francine is the daughter and sole progeny of the Heartsick Duke, who those of us with excessively brief recall remember him fondly and still mourn the loss of. Yet surely he would celebrate along with us knowing that his talented daughter has now found herself in our hearts as well. One must assume her talent is extraordinary to capture the heart and ring of the equally mysterious Blakely.*

"'*The ceremony was held yesterday morning...*'" Her stately king tightened his fingers on the page and gave a low whistle, still muttering to himself. "Married, by Jove. My brother is married."

He looked up, speared her with his intent gaze. "This doesn't change anything, you realize. I still need to go back. Still want to."

"I know."

"And I want you to come with me." In the act of folding the paper, he shot a quick glance downward. "Cannot imagine— *Bloody hell!* Did you see *this*?"

He pointed to an article at the bottom of the page, one highlighted by a cartoon sketch of a large, shaggy cat. A cat with an exaggerated target drawn on its side.

Laney lifted his arm and saw the caption beneath: LINCOLNSHIRE'S VERY OWN LION?

She gasped, and quickly read... "'*Residents of rural Lincolnshire terrorized by the thought of an escaped circus animal in their midst. Or is it simply a wild cat whose exploits have been exaggerated?* Felis leo, Felis sylvestris or Felis we-do-not-knowis, *local hunters gather the last weekend of August in Horncastle to run the animal to ground.*'"

The paper crumpled in his grip. "The devil they say!"

"Phineas?" she breathed, loosening her hand from the steel-hardened muscles holding the page aloft.

"The properties Blake bought us aren't far from there." Nash dropped the paper and gripped her arms as the sound of the stage clanging in the courtyard reached their room from the open window. "Do you know what this means? He may still be alive!"

"Have you not already checked there?"

"Blake hired a caretaker once Phineas went missing, stationed the couple on the grounds, assigned them to watch over Phin's estate just in case he ever appeared. They never sent word."

"But the organized hunt." Terror gripped her insides, a swift scarring boil where happy bubbles danced only moments before. "What if they shoot—"

"They *cannot*. Will not," he said, closing his eyes against the possibility. "Life would be vastly too cruel for him to have survived this many years only to perish now."

"Wait. What town did you say that—"

"Horncastle."

She loosed herself from his grasp to retrieve the folded, addressed square. She held up the letter she was about to post, and he read the direction. "Mary Delilah Middleton, Bedford Estate, North of Ho—" Eyebrows raised, he broke off. "Your friend lives near *Horncastle*?"

"Not far from! Moved there several months ago when she was hired away from the school as a governess and— Oh my!" Laney rummaged through her reticule and pulled out the last letter she'd received from her friend. Tattered from being stuffed in her bag, from the weeks of frequent handling, she nevertheless ran her thumb over the familiar writing and easily found what she sought. "Listen— *'And dearest Laney, you shall never believe the story I share next. It appears the nearby woods are haunted! But not by an ordinary ghost, nothing so droll. Nay, you see, the Lincolnshire Wolds are inhabited by a phantom feline. One that appears and then vanishes! I would love to confess 'tis nothing more than a prank, but, dearest, I cannot. For I have seen him!'"*

Nash was pacing and mumbling. Fast, furious steps that clomped through the room balanced by the methodical utterance of any number of things. She did her best to follow his nonsensical ramblings. "London. Stage. Marriage. Phineas. Bloody Lincolnshire. Wring his bloody neck, I will, for being alive all this time and not telling me!"

Across the room he stormed, his boots clunking on the wooden floor as if so much nervous energy had built in his feet they were ready to take off. "Horses. Stage. Princess. *Phineas.*"

THE STAGE WAS OUT. The northbound one came through already; no time to wait for the next.

Prodded on by such exhilarated excitement, by such fulsome fear, the two opposing forces clashing through his body and cells 'twas a wonder he didn't combust into a winged griffin and soar through the roof, fangs bared and roars heralding his anguish and possible exhilaration at the thought Phin might still be with them.

Why hadn't Phineas contacted them?

What if it isn't him?

No time for that worry. God-dem Scheduled Hunt.

Nash forced himself to stop his furious pacing.

He spun to face Laney. "Do you ride?"

He'd never thought to ask before as they both thrived on long country walks, and when they weren't snugged securely in their room—in bed—they were outside, finding other meadows to *explore.* Before she even opened her mouth, the crestfallen look on her face answered for her.

"I fear not. The opportunity to mount a horse never occurred."

He snapped his fingers. "Right. Tate hated the beasts. Then it cannot be separate horses. Dem it."

Several, more profane words spewed forth as his mind raced to find another option. At her third apology, he rushed forward to assure her, "No matter. I should have enough blunt to buy a pair and a curricle."

"*Buy?* Nash? What are you thinking?"

He stared down at her, his hands automatically finding home on her precious waist. "London's out. The best wedding present in the world I can give Blake would be to locate our cousin. I'm for Lincolnshire—with your company, if you're agreeable. Might I assume you are?"

"Do you even know how to drive a pair?"

"Aye. Our father taught us, me and Blake—Phin too —one summer."

"But why *buy* horses? Isn't there a stage—"

"No time. The next one that direction isn't until tomorrow. We cannot wait that long. The hunt is set to begin this coming weekend." His fingers flexed above her hips, causing her petticoats and dress to sway along his legs. "Laney, there's no time to lose. Perhaps this is simply the impetus I needed; I have thought 'twas high time I started my stables. From what I hear, I already have more than a fair start on my nursery."

She dimpled and he picked her up and swung her around. "No time like today! What do you say, Princess? Do you not think it's time I took you home?"

Laney gripped his shoulders and her cry of delight filled the room. "*Home?*"

"To my manor." His grin spread wide and he lowered her feet to the floor. "Sounds rather grand when I put it that way, does it not? *My manor*, so very hoity-toity, when we both know I'm anything but. It's only a few hundred acres, mind, grows barley and sugar beets from what Blake told me."

"From what he told you?" Incredulity lit her eyes. "Meaning you do not actually know?"

His face heated beneath his hat. "Never had reason to. I have not seen it."

"Oh, you wretched man! You own several hundred acres you never cared enough to visit?"

"I care now. Thanks to you."

"*All ready!*" The call came from the open window.

Nash walked over and poked his head out. "Unload the trunk, would you, my good man? The missus and I will not be going that direction, after all."

He straightened and faced her, crossing his arms in front of his chest, waiting. It took but a moment.

"Missus? *Mrs.?*" Even her shrieks made him smile.

He unhooked his arms and pulled a note from his pocket, made a great show of tossing it on the floor, just in front of her slippered feet. "Here. I believe you dropped this one."

"If that isn't an absolute hummer!" She bent to pick it up, shooting him a suspicious glance before turning her attention to the note. "What are you about...? Oh my." The loudest squeak he'd heard yet made its way past her lips. Followed by another. "I... I..."

"Seem to be having difficulty expressing yourself, Princess." Her eyes eagerly scanned the card while he waited, heart in his throat. "I confess, I do love you, you know, 'tis simply that I'm not used—"

"Mr. Hammond!" And then she jumped into his arms—almost knocking them both out the window— the remainder of his words swallowed by her kisses.

The piece of fancy parchment he'd paid dearly for was left face up on the table but only until Laney packed it safely away in her reticule, directly before boarding their new curricle two hours later.

"Did you notice? It's Nash," he confessed after a number of very thorough kisses.

Lips wet and shining, Laney cocked an eyebrow. "What's Nash?"

"My *middle* name. Augustus is my given. Henry my third."

Her eyes lit up. "Augustus Nash Henry Hammond. Very stately indeed. My father was Peter. Peter Philip Buckley. What say we name our first son after both of you? Augustus Peter."

Nash nearly choked. "What say we don't."

"But—"

"Philip Nash. And that is the best you shall get from me."

"Philip Nash," she repeated in an awed tone. "'Tis a wonderful name."

"He shall be cursed. You realize that, do you not?"

"No. He shall be *blessed*. We will see to it."

And so they did.

Laney, my Lady,
Blessed am I by Your Love.
I grant You mine in Return.
Will you Consent to be my Wife and bear my ~~Cubs~~
Children?
Infinities of Love,
Augustus Nash 'enry 'ammond

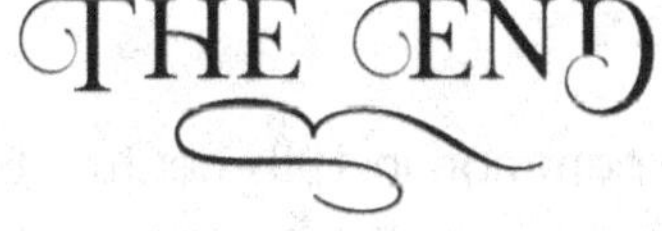

Author's Note

Thank you for reading *Deceived by Desire*. I love inhabiting the world of my Regency shifters and hope you do too. If you enjoyed the story, *please* leave a review at your favorite retailer, telling others. Reviews really help authors!

Phin's tale is up next. Read on for the blurb. But first, a bit of historical lore…

Indentures were common in 19th-century England, as were orphans. By some estimates almost ten percent of children had lost both parents by the time they turned fifteen; over thirty percent had lost one. Leading up to the Regency, average life expectancy barely reached the upper-twenties for the rural working class, according to some of my resource materials. It could be lower in large cities.

The typical term for an indenture, also known as an apprenticeship, was seven years. Those in the middle class often chose to become indentured in order to learn a specific trade—milliners, cooks and even soap makers were among the occupations stipulated by a 16th-century law that required one to study as an apprentice before practicing independently.

For the poor, especially a poor child or orphan, things were bleaker. A child could be apprenticed at age nine for twelve years, only gaining freedom once reaching twenty-one. The person who owned the indenture was considered the "master" and they were legally allowed to beat their apprentice.

Laney was fortunate in that hers was the more palatable seven-year indenture, and while she developed a distaste first for hat making and then for Reginald, she was well fed and cared for. I did take some liberties when it came to Mrs. Michaels transferring Laney's indenture to Reginald as my research failed to yield information of that sort, but given the economy of the time and the tardiness with which the upper class often paid their bills—a year's wait for shopkeepers wasn't unusual—I cannot imagine Mrs. Michaels not jumping at the chance to transfer Laney's indenture for the right price.

Black butter, which we witnessed Nash developing a fondness for, was the Regency equivalent of what we call apple butter today.

I also had some fun with the article and announcement posted in *The Times*. When this story takes place, the weekday editions of the paper were only four pages in length, marriage announcements were blunt and to the point—boring—and the only drawing or cartoon to be found anywhere was at the masthead—ironically, a lion! Well, to be precise, the masthead featured a full-maned lion on one side and some bearded, billy goat-unicorn-looking thing on the other.

>^..^< Larissa

BLURB: TAMED BY TEMPTATION

BOOK 3 - ROARING ROGUES REGENCY SHIFTERS

Wanted—Dead or Skinned:
Unbeknownst to Phineas, discovery looms ever closer with an organized hunt and *his* furry head as the prize.

His memories in shambles and self-exiled for a crime he cannot remember, a Regency lord spends his time existing as the animal he is. Avoiding others for their protection, if not his own. Until he chances across a governess and her charges who keep needing rescued...

Governess by day. Seductress by night.

With her every breath, country governess Mary Delilah Middleton denies that she's anything like her mother—high-class whore to London's rich and titled. When the mythical apparition who haunts the nearby woods takes an interest in her, Lilah's dedication to "ladylike" behavior falters beneath her fascination with the forbidden.

Doomed to live as a lion, he longs to be a man.

Once he beholds the lovely Lilah, listens to her entertaining lessons and saves her from an attack and her boisterous charges from one calamity after another, Phineas S. Lyton wishes to be a man once again, to experience passion in all its rousing glory. But the sun is in Leo and Phin's out of time—a price is on his head and hunters are tracking the injured wild cat in their midst...

Tamed by Temptation

Learn more by visiting
https://larissalyons.com/books/tamed-by-temptation/

ABOUT LARISSA
HUMOR. HEARTFELT EMOTION. & HUNKS.

A lifelong Texan, Larissa writes sexy contemporaries and steamy regencies, blending heartfelt emotion with doses of laugh-out-loud humor. Her heroes are strong men with a weakness for the right woman.

Avoiding housework one word at a time (thanks in part to her super-helpful herd of cats >^..^<), Larissa adores brownies, James Bond, and her husband. She's been a clown, a tax analyst, and a pig castrator(!) but nothing satisfies quite like seeing the entertaining voices in her head come to life on the page.

Writing around some health challenges and computer limitations, it's a while between releases, but stick with her...she's working on the next one.

Cat pics and other goodies at LarissaLyons.com.

MORE BANG-UP REGENCIES

Regency Christmas Kisses

Warm and witty winter stories. HEA and smiles guaranteed.

A Snowlit Christmas Kiss

When a mischievous feline keeps nudging two lonely souls together on a wretched, snowy night, a few Christmas kisses might be all they need. But he's engaged, and she's decided to never marry, so in the morning they go their separate ways, leaving pieces of their hearts behind...until a Twelfth Night Ball brings misunderstandings to light and merry tidings to one and all.

A Frosty Christmas Kiss
(formerly *Miss Isabella Thaws a Frosty Lord*)

Blind from a young age, a Regency heroine risks her overbearing father's displeasure by attending a house party, never dreaming she'll meet a formidable lord who will discover all her secrets and still want her for his own.

Top Pick! "This entertaining read conjured up the atmosphere and exquisitely formal dance of manners so beloved in Jane Austen's books...I am enchanted by the grace and artful wordplay that accompanies this tale." *ELF, Night Owl Reviews*

"I love the way that the book reads as if it were written in Regency times. I'm a fan of Carla Kelly Regency romances and I was in the mood for another story of that caliber. I definitely got that with *Miss Isabella Thaws a Frosty Lord*." *EKDuncan*

Mistress in the Making Trilogy

A fun, emotionally satisfying, steamy tale told in three parts: Seductive Silence, Lusty Letters, *and* Daring Declarations.

Seductive Silence, Part 1
FREE at all retailers

Lord Tremayne has a problem. He stammers like a fool
—at least that's what he learned from his father's
constant criticism and punishing hand. Daniel now
hides his troubles by barley saying anything. But then
he goes looking for a new mistress and finds a
delightful young woman who makes him, of all people,
want to spout poetry. He thought he had a problem
before? Avoiding meaningless dinner prattle is nothing
compared to the challenge of winning the heart of his
new lady lust.

Lusty Letters, Part 2

Thea's fascinating new protector has secrets—several.
Hesitant to destroy her newfound circumstances, she
stifles her longing to know everything about the power-
fully built—and frustratingly quiet—Marquis. But
then his naughty notes start to appear, full of humor
and wit, and Thea realizes she's about to break the
cardinal rule of mistressing—that of falling for her new
protector. *Egad.*

Daring Declarations, Part 3

An evening at the opera could prove Lord Tremayne's
undoing when he and his lovely new paramour cross
paths with his sister and brother-in-law. Introducing
one's socially unacceptable strumpet to his stunned
family is *never* done. But Daniel does it anyway. And it

might just be the best decision he's ever made, for Thea's quickly become much more than a mistress—and it's time he told her so.

Lady Scandal

Sparks—and stockings—fly when an interview for a husband turns into a game of forfeits—played with articles of clothing—a scandalous lady and one handsome rogue learn how very right for each other they are.

Lady Scandal **awarded the Golden Nib!** "I can't praise this book enough. Regency fans, if you like gorgeous wit in with your devilishly superb, well written, sexy reading matter, Lady Scandal should be on your 'Must Read' list." *Natalie, Miz Love & Crew Love's Books*

Top Pick from ARe Café: "[Lady Scandal] is the most flirtatious, sensual, and delectable treat." *Lady Rhyleigh, ARe Café* ~ Selected as a **Recommended Read**!

COMPLETE BOOKLIST

Historicals by Larissa Lyons

ROARING ROGUES REGENCY SHIFTERS

Ensnared by Innocence

Deceived by Desire

Tamed by Temptation (forthcoming)

REGENCY CHRISTMAS KISSES

A Snowlit Christmas Kiss

*A Frosty Christmas Kiss**

A Moonlit Christmas Kiss (forthcoming)

*(formerly *Miss Isabella Thaws a Frosty Lord*)

MISTRESS IN THE MAKING series (Complete)

Seductive Silence

Lusty Letters

Daring Declarations

Mistress in the Making - Bundle

FUN & SEXY REGENCY ROMANCE

Lady Scandal

Contemporaries by Larissa Lynx

SEXY CONTEMPORARY ROMANCE

Renegade Kisses

Starlight Seduction

SHORT 'N' SUPER STEAMY

A Heart for Adam...& Rick!

Braving Donovan's

No Guts, No 'Gasms

POWER PLAYERS HOCKEY series

*My Two-Stud Stand**

*Her Three Studs**

The Stud Takes a Stand (forthcoming)

**Her Hockey Studs - print version*